BEACON *on the* HILL

a novel

Linda Kenney Miller

HarperHouse
Publishers

Beacon on the Hill is crafted as historical fiction. While much of it is based on actual history and events, its substance is infused with creative storytelling. Some names and dates have been changed to protect the anonymity of descendants living in this century. Much of the dialogue is based on material found in the minutes and journals of the National Medical Association and in John Kenney's personal papers dating back to 1897. The use of the words "colored" and "Negro" as opposed to black or African American reflect the usage by the race in the twentieth century. Photographs provided by The Tuskegee University Archives and the National Medical Association Archives.

Harper House Publishers makes books available for purchase for educational, business, marketing or sales promotional use. For more information please contact:

Harper House Publishers, P.O. Box 682286, Marietta, Georgia, 30068-0039

ISBN 13: 978-0-9799802-3-7

ISBN 10: 0-9799802-3-2

FIRST EDITION

Library of Congress Cataloging-in-Publication Data

Miller, Linda Kenney
   Beacon on the Hill / Linda Kenney Miller – 1st Edition

1. Beacon on the Hill. – Historical Fiction. 2. The Negro in medicine – Historical Fiction

2007907410

Book interior design by www.KareenRoss.com

Testimonials

"Beacon on the Hill is a story of great historical significance whose poignant message is as timely now as it was in the 1930's. From his perspective as Booker T. Washington's personal physician, John A. Kenney, M.D. documented never before published anecdotes and events as they happened as he accompanied Dr. Washington on his Goodwill Tours throughout the South. The "Requiem" chapter reveals details of Dr. Washington's death that even his family did not know. This book is a must for anyone who wants to understand Negro history in the twentieth century."

—Margaret Washington Clifford,
Granddaughter of Booker T. Washington

"John A. Kenney, MD, was a seminal historic figure in transforming the health care and dignity of African Americans. At a time when both were ignored or trampled upon with impunity, Dr. Kenney forged an approach that made a huge difference in the first half of 20th century America. A friend and colleague of Booker T. Washington and Robert R. Moton, the first two presidents of Tuskegee Institute (now Tuskegee University), like them, he knew the power that resulted from building and focusing networks of institutions effectively on the amelioration of both social and personal traumas.

So, with this vintage BTW approach, as well as his support and guidance, Kenney spearheaded the development of two (2) hospitals—John A. Andrews at the Institute, where he was medical director for 22 years; and the Kenney Memorial Hospital in Newark, NJ, which he subsequently awarded to the community.

But, he did not just build hospitals; he directed them and their staffs in research-based programs of community outreach as well as informed individual health care. His medical programs in community health and hygiene eradicated small pox and typhoid epidemics in Tuskegee and much of Macon County, AL. He established the nurse training program at Tuskegee, inaugurated the John A. Andrew Memorial Clinics, and founded the Journal of the National Medical Association—serving as its editor for 32 years.

Dr. Kenney was also a strong advocate of human dignity and social justice. He was a vocal supporter of President Moton in the struggle to assure professional and leadership opportunities for African Americans in the new Black Veterans' Hospital that was built by the federal government on land donated by Tuskegee Institute (now Tuskegee University). The many threats on his life and against his family forced him to flee the South in 1923. But, his impact on the health system for Blacks remained behind and was re-energized upon his return in 1939. George Washington Carver, a friend and colleague as well as one of his many patients, saw a Divine Providence at work in Dr. Kenney's sojourns.

In short, Dr. John A. Kenney was an indefatigable, courageous and enlightened health care hero of America. On behalf of the entire University and its far-flung alumni, I express our admiration and gratitude for his life and contributions. We also offer our deep thanks to his granddaughter, Linda Kenney Miller, for having written this gripping and informative book about him."

 —Benjamin F. Payton, Ph.D.
 President, Tuskegee University

"This is an excellent tribute to a wonderful man who paved the way for so many African American medical doctors. *Beacon on the Hill* should be read by all future doctors for it truly provides key examples of how dedication to the field of medicine results in a successful practice. In his lifetime, Dr. John A. Kenney made numerous accomplishments and *this book* outlines most of them. I am pleased that Hampton University played a major role in shaping his career. Thank you Linda Kenney Miller for sharing your grandfather's life with us; I am sure he would be proud."

 —William R. Harvey
 President, Hampton University

"Beacon on the Hill by Linda Kenney Miller, a Fisk alumna, is a great read for a number of reasons. Many would view the rich tapestry of the life of a compassionate physician, public health expert and scholar as a story of a black man - indeed an extraordinary

black man. This book is more. It is a must read for those of us who understand that history illuminates the present and provides for the reader an insight into today's challenges of leadership and commitment to profession and family. Linda is a remarkable story teller. The voice of her grandfather, John Kenney, M.D., resonates with honesty, wisdom and grace. I recommend *Beacon on the Hill* to those who seek a role model to instruct our actions as we face the myriad challenges of the 21st century."

> **—The Honorable Hazel R. O'Leary,**
> **President of Fisk University**
> **Former U.S. Secretary of Energy**

"It is an honor for me to applaud the work of one of our most distinguished citizen's grand daughter, Linda Kenney Miller, who has written a story about her grandfather that speaks to the dedication and determination he had to serve his community and empower our City. The collection and preservation of the evidence of Dr. Kenney's remarkable achievements will give hope and inspiration to a new generation of African Americans and all Americans. The hospital he founded was critical to our City's endurance and strength. This book will bring to life this remarkable humanitarian, a true Newark hero."

> **—Mayor Corey A. Booker**
> **Newark, New Jersey**

"Beacon on the Hill by Linda Kenney Miller is vibrantly stimulating and invokes an earth-shattering look at how two people united in purpose and commitment rose above the many hurdles that made up life's experiences in early African-American history. Many times the true unsung heroes in this Nation's history are hidden in the multiple threads woven together that make up the fabric of American life as we know it. The book's portrayal of John Kenney's triumphs over adversity and his tremendous accomplishments in improving healthcare, promoting social justice and general philanthropy is a must read for everyone who wants to be inspired toward greatness."

> **—Winston Price, MD, FAAP**
> **Past President, National Medical Association**

"The basis of *Beacon on the Hill* took 75 years for Dr. John A. Kenney to live and another 50 years to bring forth his story for public consumption, enjoyment, and motivation. Linda Kenney Miller has done the public a great service by sharing much of what her grandfather, Dr. John Kenney, left in memoirs, correspondence, writings in the *Journal of the National Medical Association,* photographs, and other assorted documents that the family possessed in their personal collection for the last 50 years."

    —Robert M. White, M.D., FACP
    Internist and Oncologist, NMA Member

"Praise to Linda Kenney Miller for bringing to life one of the most powerful stories in history. In Beacon on the Hill, the story of John A. Kenney, M.D. motivates and inspires us - and leaves us thinking how we can bring his outstanding example into our life today."

    —Dr. Jill Kahn Author of The Gift of Taking,
    Honor Yourself First…All Else Will Follow

"Linda Kenney Miller has skillfully brought to life her visionary grandfather and a significant piece of American history in this compelling first novel. John A. Kenney, son of ex-slaves, in a determined life well-lived from 1874-1950, found solutions to the same problems that afflict us today: being disenfranchised, threatened by terrorism, fearful of plagues. It is a classic story of character and courage in the face of adversity, love, sacrifice and duty to race and country – inspiring no matter what your race, age, gender, religion, or politics – and an urgent reminder of where our thoughts and priorities should lie in this time of Presidential elections."

    —Mardeene B. Mitchell, Author, Literary Manager

Dedication

To Lisa, Shelby, Phala, Myla,

Teddy, T.J., Randy, and Gavin…

THE TORCH IS YOURS.

Authors Note

I was compelled to write this book. I had in my hands a significant historical account of black history and medicine in the twentieth century, and I realized that this story, springing from my own family, might never be told. Although I only vaguely remember my grandfather, Dr. John Kenney, who died in 1950, from the moment I opened an old box containing his memoirs, I was irrevocably changed.

His papers had been passed around among various Kenney families since his death. We all had scanned some of this historical material, saying that we really should do something with it. When I moved to Georgia in 2000 and took all of the boxes with me, I too said that I was going to do something with it, although at the time, I wasn't sure why. Maybe it was because people in Tuskegee always told me that I looked like him with my reddish hair, light eyes and freckles. Maybe it's because I have a streak of the stubbornness he had or because I enjoy having the last word. For whatever reason, I have always felt close to my grandfather.

One day, while browsing through one of his boxes, I discovered a paper he had written titled "How I Did It." Something deep stirred within me, something that began to move me more than I would have ever imagined.

In this paper, he was stressing the importance of doing what was right, just, and good. He said things like, "It is not he who lives the longest, but he who loves the most and serves the best that impresses himself upon his day and generation." I was intrigued. This was certainly in line with my current spiritual quest to discover "Why am I here?" and "What is my purpose in life?" I was passionately seeking answers to these philosophical questions. I kept reading.

He continued, "If I have succeeded in making the world a little bit better, in elevating my race a little bit higher, in making somebody a little bit happier, then I am content."

I was hooked.

As I delved further into the myriad assorted files, correspondence, newspaper articles and journals, a kind of fear came with the realization of just how important a piece of black history this was turning out to be. This story needed to be known, and it looked like no one else was going to tell it. It was up to me.

There, in the boxes, was his unpublished poetry from 1897, his private correspondence with the giants in Negro medicine, and his personal documentation of historical events, as well as photographs and numerous artifacts that were museum-worthy. I came to realize that my life's purpose would revolve around telling this story, because the more I read, the more I realized it was so relevant for us in these times. I felt there was a sense of urgency in getting it out as soon as possible. Not only the black race, but all Americans, all peoples, need role models for integrity, people who stand for unity against the forces that would divide and conquer.

This story speaks to the indomitable human spirit and the will to live. It speaks to personal responsibility and duty, to the importance of service to our fellow humans. This is how we find purpose in our existence. My grandfather wrote, "Service has been my guiding principle, and I feel that despite all obstacles and criticisms and all enmities, I have been richly repaid. Is it not far better to wear out in productive service than to rust out in useless ennui?" He stressed that it is not enough to be born, to live, and to die. You must leave the world a better place than when you came into it. That is why we are here.

Growing up in Tuskegee, Alabama, in the 1950s, I was only vaguely aware of some of my family's history. I knew that my father's father, this dear grandfather, John Andrew Kenney, M.D., had been the medical director of the John A. Andrew Hospital at the Tuskegee Institute, just as my father Howard Washington Kenney, M.D., was at the present time. I used to wonder how we ended up in this rural "'bama" town! I hadn't yet begun to fathom just how important Tuskegee was to the development of the black people in this country, that it had been a seedbed for some of the greatest African American leaders in the USA! I knew that at some point my grandfather had relocated to New Jersey and built a hospital in Newark named the Kenney Memorial Hospital. I remember my father driving us past that building in Newark on a trip "up North" when I was fourteen years old. We Kenney children were only barely impressed, and much more interested in getting to wherever it was that we were going.

As I got into the writing of this book, I began to wonder why we were not taught more about our family's history. I realized that in the fifties and sixties we were totally focused on becoming model citizens in our segregated town and in the segregated South. We, meaning the colored children, were told that we had to "work harder," "do better," and "be better" than our white counterparts if we wanted to be accepted by mainstream American society. We spent our childhood trying to prove that we were worthy – when reality was telling us that we weren't.

And then came the fight for integration. The resultant upheaval in the South during the civil rights era was violent and dangerous. I was always apprehensive when we traveled out of the safety of the Tuskegee city limits into rural Alabama territory. I didn't breathe freely until we were back home – or, if we were on a trip, until we were above the Mason-Dixon Line. We would drive all night to reach Washington, D.C. There was no place to safely stop. There we would have a celebratory breakfast on the banks of the Potomac River.

My parents made a decision to send my siblings and me up North to boarding schools after elementary school. This would get us out of our segregated environment and, they hoped, provide us with a good education unfettered by prejudice and racism. I was sent to a small, integrated, and totally progressive Quaker school in Poughkeepsie, New York called Oakwood. This was an experience that changed my life dramatically.

From rural Alabama to upstate New York was an education unto itself. For the first time in my life I was going to school with white people. I was terrified. There were approximately twenty black students with an enrollment of two hundred white students. It took a few months before I realized that the black students were treated just like the white students treated each other – in fact, in some instances, even better.

These people went out of their way to show us acceptance and even love. They knew the circumstances that many of us from the deep South had endured and it was clear that racism was not tolerated in this environment. For the first time in my life I felt accepted and appreciated for who and what I was; race didn't matter.

After many challenges and changes, I graduated in 1963 and enrolled in a historic black college, Fisk University, in Nashville, Tennessee. My mother had gone to Fisk, and my sister Diane had transferred there from Wellesley College in Massachusetts, where she had had enough of being the "token" black student. I was back in the segregated South in a segregated school, although Fisk was segregated by circumstances. Whites could enroll there; they just chose not to.

The fight for integration was in its heyday. Freedom fighters, protest marches, and sit-ins were the norm. I was targeted to be arrested by a Nashville policeman during a march after I was mistakenly identified as an "exchange student". I managed to slip out of line and make my way back to the Fisk Campus. As students, we were both studying history and making it simultaneously. By the time I graduated in 1967, Nashville had been successfully integrated to the extent that we could eat in restaurants and shop in the department stores.

The next thirty years in Washington, D.C., encompassed teaching junior high school, marriage, motherhood, and a new career in medical office management. I worked for my father, who had moved to the area and opened an internal medicine practice. After he retired and returned to Tuskegee, I worked for a number of black physicians in the area with a goal to establish standards of excellence in black medical practice, standards that I had learned from my father. In all of these practices, I had access to the *Journal of the National Medical Association*, which came on a monthly basis. As children we had spent most summers going to the NMA's yearly conventions, and I always scoured the *Journal* to find out what city these would be held in and to see if I knew who the current president and officers were.

I had no idea until years later the importance this publication would have in my life. In 1995, while reading the centennial issue of the *Journal*, I was surprised to see an article on excellence in medicine, featuring John A. Kenney, M.D. It was a reprint of a report on the Hookworm Commission that he had read before the NMA Annual Meeting in 1910. Although the Kenney family was very proud of my grandfather's recognition, at that time I still had no clue. After remarrying and moving to Georgia in 2000, however, I decided to go through the boxes I had brought with me from Washington, D.C. I was amazed and excited about what I discovered.

I learned that the John A. Andrew Hospital on the campus of Tuskegee Institute, where I had had my first summer job and where my father had been medical director, was partially funded through my grandfather's efforts, along with those of Booker T. Washington. We had also lived for several years on the grounds of the Veteran's Administration Hospital, which precipitated the inflammatory crisis that forced my grandfather, fearing for his life, to flee from the Ku Klux Klan in the 1920's.

I also found a pamphlet that told me my paternal grandmother, Freida Armstrong Kenney, had been the first black woman to graduate from the Sargent School in Boston, a school that later became part of Boston University. And recently my mother informed me that Freida (her mother-in-law) had taught her mother (Phala), my maternal grandmother, when she was a student at Tuskegee. The school, Children's House, is the same elementary school that my sisters and brother and I attended! Further mysteries were solved and connections with these early years uncovered, which will appear in the Epilogue – including the most shocking discovery for me personally.

In time, I came to believe that I was being guided on a spiritual level. When I was looking for an idea to express a certain sentiment, I would pick up a random file and the answer would be right there on the first page. Oftentimes I would go to bed late at night after not being able to put my hands on something I was looking for. In the morning the elusive article would be right on top of my work. During my conferences with my literary developer, Mardeene Mitchell, she would often ask me, "Are those your thoughts or his?" When I read the passage, I couldn't always tell. It seemed as if our words and thoughts were one voice. I felt as if, at times, my grandfather was speaking through me.

The more I learned about his life, the more I realized that events in my own had prepared me to appreciate what he meant to the black race in medicine as well as in history. The "coincidences" in my life became chillingly clear. I was brought to tears for several reasons. I felt grief because I was just now discovering what a legacy I was heir too, humility in knowing that I was the progeny of such an outstanding American, and gratitude that his story would now be told.

I thank Booker T. Washington for his wish to "lift the veil" of ignorance from the black race. In hindsight one might wonder where the race would be today if we had followed his tenets more closely. And I thank my grandfather for his voluminous journals and papers which helped "lift the veil" of ignorance from me so that I could appreciate not only my rich family history, but the history of my race of people who historically chose to survive and succeed with dignity. It is my hope that this book will continue to lift the veil and that the African-American race will stand tall and proud in unity; a duty we owe to our ancestors.

Linda Kenney Miller

It is not that I have accomplished so much –
but that which I have was wrought with so little, that
it may be of some inspiration and encouragement
to my children and some others who follow me to face the
vicissitudes of life without fear, but with determination to
meet and overcome all obstacles in their path.
I hope that a knowledge of my struggle to justify
my existence will help minimize their own obstacles,
and give them inspiration to take the torch where
I drop it and, like the runners of old, carry it on
to the next station so that it may burn brighter
and brighter from generation to generation."

—John A. Kenney, M.D. 1946

Chapter 1

The Klan Is Coming!

The night seemed to taunt him. An incandescent moon darted in and out of opaque hiding places, diminishing his view of the driveway leading up to the house. The wind, howling under the eaves, interrupted his concentration each time it reached a crescendo. Frustrated, John took another glance out the window and closed his manuscript. He got up from the desk and walked to the kitchen, so deep in thought that for a moment he forgot why he was there. Shaking his head, he felt the pot to see if the coffee was still hot, and then poured himself a cup.

The events of the day replayed themselves in his mind – again. He had told the truth, and had made his position emphatically clear. He wondered if that would be his death knell. Yet, doing anything less would have made him a traitor and a liar, and would have blighted everything that he stood for. It had taken years of laborious work to become a physician and, now, medical director at Tuskegee Institute; and even though the current crisis might divide the entire country, John Kenney was determined to stand for what he thought was right. He had not gone looking for trouble; trouble was brought to his door. But it was also the door of his wife and children.

John set his coffee on the desk, and pulled the lamp closer to his work. Slumping into the chair, he told himself that this kind of thinking was counterproductive. He needed to get back to his work editing the medical journal. The article, "Multiple Stab Wounds to the Abdomen," did little to relieve his anxiety.

The ringing of the telephone startled him, and he was momentarily annoyed at the intrusion. Everyone in the house was asleep, and he certainly didn't need the children to be awakened to further distract him.

"Who could be calling at this hour?" he muttered. Yet, deep inside, he knew; and a tight knot of fear constricted his solar plexus. Praying that this was simply a call to drive out into the back woods of Macon County to deliver a baby or perform a surgery, he hesitated, not wanting to pick up the phone and confirm his worst fears. It rang again.

"Hello?" he growled into the receiver.

"John, it's Warren. I got an urgent call from Charles Hare warning that you've got to leave town now! Get your family, and get out of Tuskegee. The Klan is coming to torch your home. After that speech you gave in town today, they plan to make an example out of you. If you don't go now, I am afraid there will be no more Kenneys. I've got to go now…someone's…"

The telephone went dead. John stood in stunned silence. A cold sweat broke out on his brow, and his heart began to pound audibly. As the hair stood up on the back of his neck, his breath quickened, and in a moment of shock and confusion he couldn't think what to do first. Then his body began to move, even though his brain wasn't yet functioning. He instinctively grabbed his rifle, checked the doors and windows, and ran into the bedroom to wake Freida.

"Get up and get dressed now," he urged her. "Hurry! We have to go! That was Warren on the phone. The Klan's coming. Throw what you need into a bag, and we'll head for Cheehaw and get the last train through here."

Freida was fully awake now. While her frightened eyes acknowledged the danger, she immediately sprang into action with deliberateness and precision as if she had half expected it to come to this. She woke up John, Jr., and told him to wake up Howard and Oscar. She decided to let little Elizabeth sleep, and just pick her up and take her as she was. The boys hurried about, throwing an extra set of clothes into a bag, while

Freida wrapped some foodstuffs in canvas for the train. She knew there might not be a dining car for coloreds, and not knowing where they were going or how long it would take, they would need food.

John went from window to window, making sure he didn't see any movement or hear any sounds that would suggest they had company. The night was jet black, the woods looked more forlorn and menacing than usual, and the train station seemed miles away. This place was no longer as he remembered it. *Why do we live so far from town?* The question flashed through his mind, heightening his fear and escalating his adrenaline-induced state of alertness. Just the other day, he had been reassured and calmed by the solitude of their house in the woods, giving them privacy and refuge from the business of Tuskegee. Now...? He questioned his decision. After all, this was 1923, this was the deep South, and this was Alabama.

John was locking the shutter on the bedroom window when he heard the usual squeak from the front door as it creaked open – only this time the sound was slow and steady, almost as if the door weren't opening. He ran into the front room, gun aimed and cocked, only to see little Elizabeth peering out into the blackness, excited but not understanding what all of this commotion was about in the middle of the night. He scooped her up and slammed the door shut. The others came running.

"We are ready," Freida said calmly. She had not asked any questions, just trusting her husband's instincts and motives. She knew the seriousness of the situation, but she remained calm. Her demeanor tempered John's apprehension and anxiety, and gave him some relief. She was his rock.

"Daddy, what's happening?" asked John, Jr.

"I'll explain later - just do as I say. Help your mother with that bag, and keep as quiet as you can."

They extinguished the lights and waited in the darkness of the house, making no sound, to be sure that they were still alone. After a few minutes, they made their way to the car and quietly loaded the bags into the trunk. The children and dog huddled in the back seat, while Freida and John, with the rifle between them in the front seat, watched the road for anything out of the ordinary. They drove slowly to minimize the noise.

"Where will we go, John?" Freida finally asked.

"You and the children will go to your folks in Boston. I will come when I can."

"No! I won't leave without you!"

"Freida, this is bigger than just you and me. There is too much at stake. We must protect our children first and foremost, and I can't leave the hospital and put all of my work and Dr. Washington's in jeopardy. Don't worry, I'll be fine, as long as I know you and the children have reached Boston safely."

"D," Freida said softly. Only she and the children knew that "D" was her pet name for John. When she used it, he knew it was a verbal confirmation of the unconditional love that bound them together.

Turning off the headlights, John turned onto a side road short of the station. "Here we are. I'll park a ways away, and we'll hide the car where the trees are thick. Leave the dog in the car, and he'll bark if anyone comes."

The family huddled together in the dark, crouching in a clump of pine trees, and trying to stay out of the light of the moon sneaking out occasionally from between ominous clouds. This desolate, cleared-out tract of land in the woods served as Tuskegee's train station; and the one-room log cabin with its separate entrances looked lonely and too far away. The air was cold and crisp, and twigs snapped beneath Elizabeth's shoes as she moved nearer to her father.

"Quiet," John whispered. "Shhh."

A car drove slowly along the graveled road. John signaled to his family not to make a sound. He could see the headlights coming closer, and he pointed his rifle in their direction. The car turned to the right and circled the train station slowly. The family could hear the train whistle in the distance, and John knew they would have to make a run for it if the train arrived in the next few minutes.

The car parked next to the station house and two white men got out, talking softly. As one man pulled out his pocket watch, John could see the shiny butt of a holstered gun glistening in the moonlight.

In the distance, the light on the locomotive moved slowly toward the station. As the train approached Cheehaw, the engineer blew the horn and peered out of the window to see if he had any passengers. The two men moved closer to the tracks. The conductor waved from one of the cars as the train slowed to a stop. The familiar screeching of brakes and the hissing of steam from the engine valves were sounds that John had heard many times in anticipation of a trip "up North," but tonight he knew this train was taking his family away.

The conductor stepped off the train and engaged in conversation with the two men. Then he began to slide a long black crate off the train. John motioned for his family to follow him to the last car, and they entered it quietly on the other side of the train. John, Jr., Howard and Oscar – their faces stoic – climbed aboard. John motioned for them to stay down and out of sight. Freida hugged her husband tightly as little Elizabeth clung to her father's pant leg, whimpering. John picked her up and handed her to her mother as the train resumed its steaming and hissing – like a giant black serpent waiting to slither off into the darkness. The uncertainty ahead was less than the danger behind. John had no choice but to let them go...and pray.

"All aboard!" the conductor called into the darkness. John settled his family down and kissed Freida, as the train whistle signaled for departure. With one last look at his wife and children, he jumped off the train and ran into a clump of trees on the opposite side of the station, his movements muffled by the train's departure. He watched the two men carry the crate to their car, lower it to the ground, and pry it open.

"They sent about two dozen of them and plenty of ammunition. We've got something that will settle this matter once and for all. You can't outrun a bullet now, can you?" The men laughed, loaded the crate into the trunk of their car, and drove off into the night.

Darting from shadow to shadow, John reached his car, relieved that his family was out of harm's way. He thought about his friend who had informed him of the Klan's intention, and to whom he would forever be indebted for the warning. He understood the danger that lay ahead of him, and he knew he would find the resolve to face it. There was no turning back now.

On the horizon, the glow from a burning cross illuminated the smoke that billowed upwards and merged with menacing clouds in an eerie alliance. Every atom of his being reverberated with indeterminate emotions that he could neither define nor identify. It was almost as if he had lived this before – in another nightmare. The fright, resolve, pain, and determination were new and unsettling, yet their familiarity in his spirit was historical, ancestral, cellular.

His family was fleeing under the cover of darkness, his home had been torched, and he was driving into an abyss from which he might never return. The fright in his family's eyes had been almost more than he could stand, and knowing that he was the cause of it gave him great remorse. He loved them more than life itself, and could not bear it if anything happened to them, much less the thought that he might be responsible. He knew that he was right in principle, but was it worth his and Freida's lives and the lives of their children?

Pulling the rifle closer, John drove with only glimpses of moonlight defining the road. He decided that it would be prudent to drive to the hospital. The Klan wouldn't have the nerve yet to come onto the campus of Tuskegee Institute. He hoped he would be safe there for a while. Sensing the danger, his hound took to the front seat with ears alert, a trusty companion letting John know that he was not alone.

John drove through the night, thinking back to how it all began, to his life as a child on the Kenney farm. His father's words echoed in a memory from a lifetime ago: *"There will be a time when duty calls that you must take a stand for what you truly believe in as a man – no matter what the cost!"* This was surely the ultimate price, and this was surely the time. Now, tonight, he was reliving what his parents must have felt, time after time, when they were bought and sold as slaves in the state of Virginia.

Chapter 2

Barefoot Virginia Farm Boy, Son of Ex-Slaves

The mule plodded laboriously along the dusty road, pulling the heavy wagon slowly to the Kenney family's new land. The fifty-mile trip would have been quicker had they been given a horse, but Master Wingfield had said he had only a mule to spare. Even though they had been emancipated for ten years John and Caroline lived with a wariness that often tempered the euphoria of their liberty. The powers that be couldn't be trusted; they'd lied before. Any day now "they" might change their mind and snatch "the Negra's" back into bondage; just as quick as they had handed them their freedom.

Caroline sang songs to the children in the back of the wagon to keep them occupied, containing her own excitement, while her husband kept his eye on the road. "Wade in de wata, wade in the wata, chil'ren, wade in de wata, God's gonna trouble de wata." Their children, John, Jr., Andrew, and Margaret sang along and clapped their hands enthusiastically, already intrigued by this new place they were heading to.

"Ma, are we almost dere?" John asked impatiently. "I wanna see it!" He was her firstborn, her "big boy," always asking questions and seeking answers, more inquisitive than many seven-year-olds.

"Not yet, John, just be still. We movin' fast as we can."

"I'm hungry, Ma," shouted Andrew, the younger boy, attempting to take the attention from his older brother. "I'm hun-gry, hun-gry, hun-gry!" he teased.

"Not so loud, Andrew," Caroline chided. "I hear ya." She reached down into a crocus sack and pulled out a few pieces of beef jerky, giving each one a piece.

"I cain't chew this," whined Margaret, the youngest. "Too hard."

Caroline took back Margaret's jerky, replacing it with a small piece of corn pone.

"I want dat! I want dat," Andrew pleaded incessantly, seeing his sister get something else.

"Hush up!" Caroline said to the children. "Dere's mens on de road up dere!"

John looked up to see five or six men on horseback in the distance, white men. He sensed the seriousness in his mother's voice, and tried to climb onto the seat between his mother and father.

"Stay in de back!" his father said sternly, pushing him away. Then John saw his father reach down and pull the rifle from between his legs. They got closer and closer, and John froze when he saw the glowering, unfriendly looks on the faces of the group on horseback. As the wagon approached, one man held up a rifle and commanded his father to stop.

"Let me see your papers!" the rifleman ordered, cocking his gun and pointing it in their direction.

Not saying a word, John's father reached into his shirt pocket and produced the permit his former owner had given him. The paper authorized him to hold and occupy the land he had bought and to which they were heading, this land that represented the start of a new life. Slave patrols still operated illegally in certain parts of the South, and even though coloreds were freed men, they knew it was better to comply than to resist. If you didn't, the possibility of your disappearance from the face of the earth was highly probable. And there was no one who would right the wrong, anyway.

John could see sweat glistening on his father's face. His pa didn't seem to be looking directly at the men, but somewhere between their horses. Caroline was sitting stark still in the front seat, her eyes averted and, instinctively, John knew not to speak, or move.

"He's a free Nigra," the rifleman said to the others. "Let him pass."

A moment ticked by as the men exchanged looks before they parted down the middle, on each side of the wagon, and then motioned for it to proceed. As the Kenneys passed through the phalanx of hateful-looking strangers holding guns, John heard his father slowly exhale. His parents were strangely quiet, and he had the uncomfortable feeling that something had just happened – but he didn't quite know what.

The journey that brought the Kenneys to this point had been long and harrowing. Born slaves, they had recently attained their freedom. Now they were caught between those who had a grudging acceptance of the abolition of slavery, and those who asserted an outright refusal to accept what was now law. This erosion of the traditional underpinnings of established Southern tradition provoked extreme reactions. There were even people whose violent tendencies were unmasked by the new paradigm of emancipation, and they posed the most danger. They were the ones you didn't want to run into on a lonely road.

To protect their family's interests as much as they could, John and Caroline Kenney had taken up a contract of marriage shortly after they were freed. This was one of the first institutions previously denied to slaves that they could now enjoy, to be husband and wife under the law. This also meant that the three children born to John and Caroline would be free, and protected by law from being sold or kidnapped - another practice that was against the law - but that still occurred from time to time.

The next obstacle was to own their own land. The couple stayed close to the Wingfield plantation initially, working as freed slaves for their former owners. When the law changed and the Freedmen's Bureau entitled every freedman to forty acres of land and a mule, John Kenney informed the Wingfields that he wanted to start his own farm and buy some land from one of their neighbors, Mr. William Simms. Wingfield assured John that he could come back and work for them when his farm failed; for, however much they respected their former slave's willingness to work hard, they knew that neither he nor his new wife Caroline could read or write. The near certainty of the Kenneys' failure meant that the Wingfields would soon be able to buy John's farm from him for less than he had bought it from William Simms.

"How are you even going to read the deed?" Wingfield had asked. "How are you going to sell your crops when you can't even count them?"

He might as well have been talking to a deaf man. Ex-slave John Kenney had waited a lifetime for the opportunity to own his own farm, and failure was not a consideration. Freedom had given him the chance to be purposeful and he had to hurry to make up for lost time.

The wagon finally rounded a bend, and passed a rickety wooden fence that had the name "Wingfield" and a land number crudely carved into it. John saw his father take out a map and study it.

"This it," he announced.

The boys stopped tussling in the back of the wagon, and all of the children stood up to see what this new land looked like.

"You hold on," Caroline warned her children. "We has to git up dis hill."

John's father brought the wagon to a stop at the top of the hill. He helped Caroline down as they surveyed their new property. John watched as they walked hand in hand down the hill. Andrew jumped down and ran past his parents, falling and rolling in the grass. John took Margaret's hand and followed.

"The Kenney farm," Caroline announced proudly to her family. She clasped her hands and knelt down in prayer thanking God for delivering her and her family from the beast that had preyed on the nation's soul. Slavery had tested her faith - and she had triumphed.

The land that made up the farm adjoined twenty miles of county highway near Redmonds, Virginia, between Charlottesville and Scottsville townships in Albemarle County. The land sloped down a hill, through a meadow, and up the other side to the Green Mountains. Three more acres were subsequently purchased, thus carrying the property line across the peak of a mountain to old Captain Hancock's line, a full distance of a mile or more. On the other side, their land bordered the Hardware River. From the hillside, they could see the Charles Bridge and, where the fall line of the river crested, the Indian Mounds circling the pastureland. The mountains would protect the farm's crops from nature's elements on the low side, and the river would provide irrigation on the other. The mountains also gave the land a natural border on the west, and the fence that they would build on the eastern edge would clearly mark the boundaries of the Kenney farm, leaving nothing to dispute.

From the hillside, Caroline watched her children playing barefoot in the lush field. She thanked God every day that they would not have to endure the hardships she and her husband had survived. She trusted her husband's unerring knowledge of men and affairs, unconditionally and unequivocally. His can-do philosophy constantly encouraged her, and she intuitively believed that the two of them had paid their dues. Now their long-awaited reward of freedom was inalienable, and this farm was part of that.

John watched as his father shielded his eyes from the sun, surveying his new land. The ridges surrounding the mountains sparkled with mica, slate, and granite flecks, providing a surreal backdrop in the distance.

"What is dat sparklin', Pa?" asked John. "It's twinklin' like de stars."

"Dat's nature, son," said John's father who took great pleasure in sharing his innate wisdom,"De minerals in de earth collide an' turn shiny. Dat ground is pretty ta look at, but it ain't no good for farmin'. Let's git de camp set up an' git settled so we kin work in de mornin'."

After dinner, Caroline and John bedded their children down for the night. They stood outside of the wagon surveying their land with wonder, not quite able to grasp that it would still be theirs in the morning. Exhausted from the exhilaration, they went to sleep beneath the twinkling stars.

Caroline heard her husband's usual morning greeting to the family coming from somewhere out in the woods. "Rise an' shine!" he yelled. She looked over to see her children stirring in the back of the wagon. John, Jr. raised his head, searching the woods in the direction of his father's voice.

"Dere he is!" he shouted excitedly, seeing his father emerge from the woods, holding his rifle over his shoulder and the corpse of a rabbit by the ears. John jumped out of the wagon, running to greet him. "Le' me hold it, Pa," he said. Taking the prey from his father, he held it out for his brother and sister to admire. The children ran to show Caroline, who gathered kindling to start the fire for breakfast.

After a repast of grits and fried rabbit, it was time to go to work. Caroline called for the children, who were washing in a nearby stream. All three came running, and their father laid out the plan for the day. When he was finished, he stood up and gave the orders. John and Andrew jumped up, little soldiers ready to go to work for their commander.

"John, Jr., go an' git de hand rake," he ordered, watching his son obediently run to the wagon and return with the tool. "Dis is how we'll work today. I'll cut de oats wit de cradle and scythe. Andrew and Margaret will come behind me and git de cuttings into bundles. Mother will tie de bundles wit hemp, and John, Jr. will rake up de loose straws. Now let's git goin'!"

The boys filed in behind their father, mimicking his stride. Caroline took Margaret's hand and followed her "men" to the field.

As the children took their positions, their father began indulging in one of his favorite pastimes, relating what he had learned growing up as a slave. Although he had been considered human property, compelled by servitude to ignorance and lifelong manual labor, he reminded them almost daily that they were members of a race of people who historically *chose* to survive, whose lessons and strength had come from the rigors of fighting for life itself. Now, for his children, the time spent in the fields was their "school." While the subject was agrarian, the lesson was always the relationship between man, nature, and God.

John, Jr., swatting the "sweat bees" that made him wish he were somewhere else, watched his father lean down to smell some honeysuckle. Remarking at how much more fragrant it was compared to last year, he said, "Ya learn from life, 'specially nature. Nature is free and cain't no man control it. It's always de same, and it's always different. Fall will always come before winter. Summer will always follow 'hind the spring. Always de same, but no season jes like the one before it. Life is kin to nature, and all of God's glory is dere. Ya jes nourish it, feed it, an' then ya can reap de bounty of the harvest. This here is your spiritual lesson."

"Yes, Pa," John said. He was listening with one ear and trying to keep up with the cutting pace that his father was setting. Some of the loose straws were getting away from him.

His father continued, not really paying attention to his workers. "Look at this farm, son. Rich land as far as ya can see. But ya have to give it what it needs; dere's an order to it. Ya cain't rush it or change it. It's regular, on time, an' sure. Nature takes ta give. The crops take from de sun, de rain, and de food from de rich soil before we are fed. Learn from dat. It's a lesson that will 'peat itself time an' time again. Be like Mother Nature and you will jes have the answer to life itself!"

"Yes, Pa," John repeated to show that he was still listening.

His father stopped cutting and looked up at his family, dutifully working. Margaret was gathering oats with one hand and holding herself with the other. "Do you need to pee, girl?" he called.

"Yes, Pa," she answered weakly, tightening her hold.

"Mother, take the child behind the wagon 'fore she ruins her clothes. She needs to learn ta take care of her needs 'fore she starts work, 'fore she be holding us up."

Caroline took Margaret by the hand and led her toward the wagon. The boys put down their tools to rest, but their father continued right on with their "lesson." "Take for yourself from what this life gives you," he started. "Aim high…shoot at the moon, 'cause if ya fail ta hit it, ya might surely strike a star. Take freedom an' make somethin' of yourselves. Then share what ya learnt with others as the good Lord shares with us. Dat's your duty. Dere is a purpose ta life and ya must learn it, den teach it ta others, but ya have ta live it, and *be* it." And always…*always*, honor ya word. Dats de mark of a real man, a God-fearing man. De good book says, 'Thou shall not lie.'"

Their father was always working and preaching, preaching and working, as if time were running out or as if it might come to a stop altogether. John and Andrew listened attentively until Caroline and Margaret returned to take their former places. The family worked until the sun crested the mountain, and the breeze from the river gave them relief from the heat. Then they loaded their bundles into the wagon and headed back toward their campsite.

Over the next several years, the family was able to build a house and harvest several profitable oat and corn crops. This was a feat that astounded the Wingfields, who could not understand how their former slaves had had such "luck." The Kenneys also met a number of their neighbors who were freedmen like themselves, determined to be self-sufficient whatever the cost. These families banded together to establish their own "society", and salvage the remnants of long-lost cultural traditions that had been all but obliterated. Those freedmen who could read taught the others who could not. Those who had knowledge of farming helped plant the crops of those who had never been in the field. Church services became transformational: this was the first time that ex-slaves were taught that slavery was not ordained by God, a revelation that made freedom even sweeter.

In time, John's father used some of his savings to build and operate a small country store that not only sold supplies to the nearby farm families, but also served as the day school for local youth. In addition, it was used on Sundays as a church. Performing as a deacon in the church and superintendent of the Sunday school, John's father refused to see his lack of formal education as a handicap to what he wanted to accomplish. In later years John described his father as "unlettered, but not uneducated."

On Sundays after the main church service, all of the families would gather around a "pot luck" lunch, and sustain each other by sharing the trials and tribulations of this new existence. No one was allowed to do any kind of work on Sunday, a Christian privilege they had often been denied as slaves on the plantation. This communal fellowship encouraged the families to come together and support each other. Families from all over the region began to be like pieces on Caroline's patchwork quilt: bound together by a cause and a purpose; each section supporting and adjoining the next one; in its entirety, a defense from the hostile world around them. There was no time for any excuses, self-pity, laggards, or laziness. To a man, all seemed to know intuitively that what they did – or didn't do – would be their destiny, or their defeat. The families sensed that they were laying the foundation for generations to come. Armed with a strong moral and purposeful justification, they had the job of instilling certain virtues in their children, who - in turn - would be better off and have greater opportunities because of it.

After the fellowship hour, the afternoon church service and the Sunday school for the children would begin. Either Caroline or one of the other mothers would conduct the lesson for the youngsters, still lively from playing outside during the "grown folks" hour. As the children sang "Jesus Loves Me" and "In the Garden," they formed a circle and held hands, swaying to the right and then to the left in unison, a tactic used to corral any leftover idle energy. After that, the children were engaged in earnest study of the Ten Commandments, with the promise of a test on the next Sunday to see who had learned their lesson.

John took his mother very seriously when she read from the Bible that if you "honor your father and mother, the land that has been given to you to live on will be yours for a very long time." He did his best to abide by that commandment, so that his father's land would always belong to his family. Every day as they worked for hours in the field, John's father would say, under his breath and to no one in particular, "An' dey said we would never work hard 'less we was made to. Ha! We'll show 'em."

The Kenney farm became a model of self-sufficiency for the community. The Kenneys raised their own crops, grew their own food, purchased more property, and gave back to those who needed a hand. John's father taught him the importance of living by certain principles; duty, honor and respect would be his salvation. His father was a living example; the esteem in which he was held encouraged others to want to emulate him. This almost proved to be John's undoing.

One day, his father and mother had to take the crops to town for sale. Caroline also wanted to stop at the country store for some supplies. This would leave the children home alone for a time, and John, almost twelve at that time, felt he was "grown up" enough to handle the responsibility. They were admonished to stay near the house until their parents returned.

John, feeling himself the man of the house now that his father was away, decided to parade his manhood. He called his brother and sister to the side of the house where the weeds were high.

"Watch me," he said. "I am Pa now. I am going to cut the 'oats'." He picked up the cradler, which had a long, sharp blade. The instrument had several equally long wooden prongs on it called "fingers" that were used to catch the plants as they fell. An accomplished "cradler" would use both hands to make the cutting sweep and, while holding the cradle with his right hand and arm, scoop out the grain with his left and throw it on a pile on the ground. Then he'd take a step forward and repeat the process.

John, Jr., straining to remember the moves he had seen his father make, took an awkward sweep at the weeds. After making the cutting stroke, however, he had to pull the cradle down with both hands to remove the patch of weeds. Suddenly the blade slipped, and he looked down at a terrifying laceration in the palm of his left hand that almost severed his thumb at the web. The pain was so great that his knees buckled, and he hit the ground. Kneeling in the dirt, he realized that his thumb was almost completely severed, and the blood was gushing out just like when his father took the goat to slaughter.

"Help me! Help me!" John screamed to his brother and sister. Margaret clamped her hand to her mouth in horror, and Andrew ran around to the other side of the house. Margaret fell to her knees in tears, and John, Jr. pressed his hand on top of the cut trying to stop the blood, which continued to come. Margaret was still wailing when Andrew appeared from the house holding a blanket from her doll carriage. He gave it to John, Jr. to wrap around his hand.

"Nooo," Margaret cried. "That blankey belongs to my dolly."

"What are we going to do?" Andrew asked fearfully.

John was beginning to feel dizzy. The blanket was turning crimson, and he struggled to make it tighter. His first thought was fear, and how he would hide this from his parents. He quickly realized that the bloody wad he was holding would make that impossible, especially since he was probably going to die before his parents returned home.

"Oh, my God," he uttered feeling even more sinful for using the Lord's name in vain, something his father told him never to do. "Help me, please!"

In that moment, John remembered their neighbor about a quarter mile to the north on the big plantation. He was an Irish bachelor named O'Keefe, who hid his bald head beneath a wig. He was known in the region as the "doctor" for minor ills and was even known to help the Negroes in emergencies.

"Let's go!" John hollered to his siblings. "Over to Mr. O'Keefe's!"

John and Andrew began to run, with Margaret trailing behind. "Wait for me," she cried as she tried to keep up. "Wait…."

John was running and praying, and it seemed like an eternity before they reached the O'Keefe property. O'Keefe was in the yard chopping wood, and stopped in wonder to see the Kenney boys running onto his place with the wailing Margaret trailing behind.

"Whoa!" he commanded. "What's going on here?"

"I cut my thumb off!" cried John. "I am going to bleed to death!"

"Let me see that, son," O'Keefe said seriously. He unwrapped the blanket and quickly rewrapped the bloodied material back on more tightly. "Come onto the front porch," he ordered. He went into the house and came back with a cambric needle, a spool of white cotton thread, some liquid antiseptic, and some bandages. He cleaned off the wound and threaded the needle.

"Since you are man enough to use a cradler, you will have to be man enough to stand me stitching up your hand," he told John, Jr. He began to stitch the wound as tears of pain slid down John's face, but John did not make a sound. When O'Keefe was finished and the hand was bandaged, he delivered an announcement that was more painful than the stitching.

"Now let's go and see your father."

The pain in John's hand paled in comparison to the fear in his heart. He knew his father hated to be indebted to anyone for anything – especially to a white man.

O'Keefe hitched up his horses and ordered the children to sit still in the back of the wagon. No one moved an inch. They reached the Kenney farm just in time to see John and Caroline returning from town.

"I have your children here," O'Keefe announced to the stunned John and Caroline. "Your boy tried to mimic his Pa with the cradler and damn near cut his thumb off."

"Oh, no!" cried Caroline as she ran to the wagon. "Is he all right?"

"He'll be fine, and I think he has learned his lesson. I had to stitch his hand, and he was mighty brave. I don't think he'll do that again."

"Thank you for your assistance, Mr. O'Keefe," the elder John said without emotion. "How much do we owe you?"

"You don't owe me nothing, John. That's what a neighbor is for. Who knows when I might need you one day? It is good to have credit in that bank! Bring the boy over in about a week to ten days, and let me look at the hand. We might can take the stitches out then." With this, O'Keefe turned his wagon around and drove off.

John could not bring his eyes up to look at his father who just shook his head in disbelief. Caroline put her arm around her son and led him into the house, followed by the rest of the family. She sat him at the kitchen table and wiped his face with a damp cloth. He felt his father's hand on his shoulder.

"Son, there is an order to all things. Ya can't rush the seasons, ya can't rush the time, ya can't hold the lesson without the learning of the mind. Now figure out what ya learned from this here lesson, and use that to help ya make a better choice next time. Like it say in the Good Book, there is a purpose for everything."

John couldn't believe that he wasn't getting a flogging and that his father seemed almost sympathetic. With his lapse in judgment made public for all to see, John began to really feel the pain in his hand. Caroline saw the discomfort on his face and reached for the medicine box on the shelf over the stove. She boiled some water and added a spoonful of tincture for pain that she kept for such emergencies. She mixed in a thimbleful of her husband's Kentucky sour mash and gave it to the boy to drink straight down. In a few minutes she watched his eyelids grow heavy and his movements slow. She led him to a pallet in the dining room and, after he lay down, she stroked his head until he fell asleep.

Years later, Caroline would recall that it was this incident that interested John in the healing arts. She also noted that ever since that fateful day, John had assiduously studied his father's habits in all the complexities of running the farm – knowledge that young John would need sooner than anyone realized.

His lessons after that incident consisted of successive steps in regular order. Season after season he raked the oats, practiced riding and driving the horses, and helped with the farm animals. He particularly liked learning how to use the drawing knife and cradler, and was soon as adept as his father. Over and over he repeated these chores, until he developed the skills to handle any of the duties of farm life.

On top of one of the mountains was a rich, cleared area that John was taught to cultivate. This was also the place where the family got its wood supply, even though the locale made harvesting and hauling difficult. In going to and from the mountain, John and his father would seldom follow the road, preferring to walk through the fields and woods. John stayed close by his father's side. Initially he was afraid that he might get lost; but the more they detoured from the road, the more confident he became in instinctively finding his way home. Their walks would often yield something special for dinner. His father would locate a sitting rabbit, squirrel, or woodchuck and mentally mark it, walking on as if he had not seen it; and leaving the poor animal frozen in place, hoping not to have been seen. Less than a mile from the farm, he would put his hands trumpet-like to his mouth and call.

"Whoo-oo-wee! Bring me de gun!"

Someone would seize the old "muzzle-loader"; which for many years was an old army musket, and guided by the father's voice, locate and hand him the gun. The children would trail their father in admiration and anticipation, hoping to be as accomplished one day. He would walk back within shooting distance of the quarry, raise the piece, aim and fire. It was always a sure shot, and whoever was still at home knew it too. At the crack of the gun, there was a chorus from the kids yelling "my head." Why each one wanted to claim the head was unclear, but whoever was first "won" the prize of the day. Caroline would roast the quarry and prepare some homegrown produce. The family would then celebrate the hunter – and enjoy the hunted.

Cash money was scarce in their environs, and John got his first lesson in finance when he was twelve years old. His father believed in working for himself, paying himself first, saving a portion, and then satisfying all of his outstanding obligations. As a means of working for himself like his father, John decided to take the hide of a recent dinner quarry, tan it and sell it for cash. He began the tedious process of rubbing the skin down with wood ashes and salt until the texture was right. The hide was then nailed to the gable of the stable to dry, or cure. After a period of days, it was ready for sale; and his father took it on one of his trips to Charlottesville, and sold it for fourteen cents. Like his father, John paid himself a portion; saved a portion; offered his father a few cents for brokering the sale; and then treated his brother and sister to some sweets at the community store, since he was now a businessman with savings.

Besides working with his father on the farm, John also assisted in the store and attended the county school during the fall and winter seasons. When he was fourteen years old, his father let him take the crops to market for sale on his own. John knew that if his father gave him this responsibility, he must consider him a man now, and John did everything exactly as his father had done it in the past. Before he got to town, he put one pebble in a small sack for every tied bundle of oats he had. He would subtract one for every bundle that was sold.

When he got to town, John tried to be unobtrusive, stepping off the sidewalk to let the whites pass by the way his father had taught him. He went to the same merchant who had given his father a fair price the last time, and obtained the same deal. He put his money under a slat in the wagon floor before heading back to the farm in case he was stopped, and he put his musket under his seat to be ready if he needed it. Proud to have successfully completed his mission, he turned his wagon toward home.

As John, Jr. crested the hill overlooking the farm, he could see a wagon in front of the house. As he got closer, he saw that it belonged to O'Keefe from the adjoining farm. As John approached the door, he could hear his mother crying as O'Keefe was talking.

"I'm sorry, Caroline," he said. "There was nothing I could do. I think it was something that got into his blood that took him so fast. Even though it was just a little scratch, if it was not tended to when it happened, it could be poisonous."

John, Jr. opened the door all the way. Andrew and Margaret were huddled in the corner whimpering, and Caroline was sitting in a chair by the bed. The elder John was in the bed, appearing to be asleep; but as John, Jr. got closer, he realized that his father was too still.

"Ma, what's wrong with Pa?" he asked as fear began to envelop him. Nothing could be wrong; his father was fine yesterday. John's heart began to pound in his chest, and he held his breath, wanting the moment to stand still.

Caroline reached out and took John, Jr. in her arms. "He's gone, John. He just lay down and passed out. I couldn't wake him, so I sent Andrew to Mr. O'Keefe's. When they got back here, it was too late." Her sobs filled the small cabin but John heard them from some far-away place. He was dizzy with emotion, teetering between the threshold of hope and the brink of despair. John steadied himself and turned confidently toward the bed, fully expecting his father to wake up.

He instinctively reached out to touch his father, drawing his hand back quickly when he realized his father was cold and stiff. "No, no, no," he moaned. "He can't be gone. I need him! I did everything he told me to do. I sold the crop. I made a deal; I was just gone one day." In his youthful naiveté John had never considered death something that would be relevant to his life, not for a very long time anyway.

He began to cry uncontrollably. O'Keefe took him by the shoulders and put an arm around him. "Come with me, son," he said kindly.

He led John to the stable and said, "Here, take this handkerchief. I am sorry for your loss, son. You are the man of the house now. We have got to bury your father, and then you have to take care of your mother and your siblings. There will be plenty of time for grieving, but right now your father is counting on you. Do you understand me?"

John couldn't believe this was happening. He wanted to go back to the pride and excitement he had felt when he was heading home. It was just a few hours ago that he had imagined his father patting him on the back and saying, "Job well done, son." This was not supposed to happen; this couldn't be happening. How could God have taken his pa when his work was not yet finished?

Pain and sorrow began to wash over John in waves. There was an ache in his heart that he had never felt before, and it completely immobilized him. He didn't want to be a man anymore; he just wanted to go back to yesterday. Long after O'Keefe had gone, John sat in the stable with the horses. He finally had to accept that his father was not coming to comfort him. Not now, not ever.

John splashed his face with water from the trough and walked back to the house. Andrew and Margaret were asleep in one bed, and Caroline had lain on the bed next to her husband. John sat by the bed in the chair she had been sitting in, and they stayed that way until the fire went out and the night turned to morning.

By the time the neighboring farmers came to help make funeral arrangements, John seemed to have matured overnight. His father was eulogized at the "church" he had built, and was buried on a plot that overlooked the mountain and most of the Kenney farm. It took a long time for John to forgive God for taking his father away. It would be even longer before he realized how this event affected Caroline, and changed his destiny forever.

A Family's Loss, A New Beginning

Caroline sat in her rocking chair on the front porch of the farm, watching her children doing their chores in the yard. John was showing Andrew how to chop the wood, and Elizabeth was flitting in and out of the hen house, grabbing freshly laid eggs for her basket. More often than not, there were as many cracked eggs in the basket as there were whole ones. Caroline didn't care. She was still numb, trying to figure out how she was going to take care of a farm and three children by herself.

Right now she was angry at her husband. How could he leave her like this? He had taken all of his knowledge, his skill, and his experience of how to live, and had just gone away. Without a word, he'd just left her. That wasn't their bargain. They had promised each other that if they ever became free, they would marry and have a family and grow old together. So much for his promises!

Caroline held on tight to her anger, letting it hide the fear that gripped her. She couldn't read, she couldn't write, she couldn't cipher, and she certainly didn't know how to make a farm profitable. Most days she just wanted to die and leave her problems behind, just like her husband had. "God help me," she prayed, over and over, day after day. The children were all that kept her going.

"John, come here," she called with concern in her voice.

John looked momentarily annoyed at having his work interrupted, but he walked over to see what his mother wanted.

"What, Ma?" he asked out of breath.

"What about the crops, son? When do we need to get new seeds for the corn?"

"Ma," John said with an exasperated sigh, "I told you not to worry 'cause I'll take care of everything. Besides, the corn's growing now. Next season we need to work the soil and grow oats again. The corn will strip the soil of nourishment now, and next season you has to plant somethin' else to put the nourishment back in. Like Pa said, things got to be rotated to grow right."

Rotating crops – who in the world knew anything about that, but men? At least, Caroline told herself, she still had John. He was a smart boy, and her husband had taught their son most everything he knew, maybe sensing something he hadn't shared with his wife. Once again, as she did several times every day, Caroline thought, "At least I have John."

Over the months since her husband's death, she had watched with pride as her son picked up the reins and assumed the role of head of the household. John had been trained well, and he eased into the responsibility with little difficulty. Because of the community bond his father had forged, assistance from neighbors helped ease the family's loss, and many other "fathers" stepped up to help John take his rightful place as man of the house.

Caroline knew that the family depended on the crops to pay the mortgage to the Wingfields each month, and she also knew that her husband had used money from the next season's crops to take a loan if he needed it. They might need to borrow money to buy supplies before the winter came, but she had no idea how to do that. She hated that slavery had defined her life and robbed her of the most basic understanding of how to succeed. Still, she did have John's help, and she was determined to show him her gratitude to make up for the adolescence that had been cut short.

John pulled off his sweaty shirt and wiped his forehead. "I'll be glad, Ma, when the crops are in and the winter season is here. I miss school and seeing my friends."

"It's comin' sooner than ya know, son. And I'm glad ya take to learnin'. When I was growin', it was said that coloreds didn't need to read and write. The massa said he would take care of us. We thought they was doin' us a favor till we saw that they made their chil'ren stay in school a whole year to learn readin' and writin'. And on top of that, they spent all their time readin' and writin' to each other. It smelled kinda fishy after a while."

John Kenney as a young man on the Kenney farm

"Well, Pa said school was important. He said goin' to school and ownin' land would keep us free. An' he also said don't go showin' off your learnin' or your land 'cause it makes people think you don't know your place."

"He should still be here to teach you things I don't know nothin' about, John. He should still be right here," said Caroline, her voice tinged with anger.

John felt that same anger rising inside him, but he pushed it back. "Got to get back to choppin', Ma," he said, walking away.

After a hard week of work, Caroline and the children went into town to sell the harvested crops and buy needed supplies. Caroline let John do the bartering, for she knew his father had shown him how to do business, "fair business." She preferred to look at the pictures in the store windows, especially the ones depicting life in the big city. She loved the pictures of Richmond, Virginia, showing scenes of tall buildings and cobblestone streets. The beauty of Monroe Park with its magnificent fountain and manicured gardens captivated her imagination, and she longed to see a real city for herself. Something about the congestion of a city gave her the feeling that if she were there, she would not feel so alone.

Sunday was the one day that Caroline could put aside her feeling of isolation, and let joyful singing and praying lift her spirits. The church was a universal gathering place, and it was one institution where the Negroes felt in control of their lives. Here they could dress up, show off, and commune in an atmosphere not compromised by the "peculiarities" of white Southern society. The church service provided physical as well as spiritual relief, and the "lesson" the minister chose to deliver set the standard of behavior for the upcoming week. On one particular Sunday the minister introduced the new teachers for the local school, a Mr. and Mrs. William Jackson, who had just moved to the community. The minister urged all of the parishioners who wanted to enroll their children in school to introduce themselves to the Jacksons.

Caroline was one of those near the head of the line. John, Andrew, and Margaret stood politely behind her.

"Hullo, Mr. and Mrs. Jackson," she said properly, "I's Caroline Kenney, and these is my kids that I wish to go to school."

Mr. Jackson smiled warmly and extended his hand, ignoring Caroline's grammatical errors. "I'm delighted to meet you, Mrs. Kenney. And who do we have here?" he asked.

"This here is John, Andrew, and Margaret," Caroline said with a broad smile, pointing out each one.

"It's nice to meet you, children," Mrs. Jackson said.

"Thank ya', ma'am," John said. He nudged Andrew and Margaret.

"Thank ya', ma'am," mumbled Andrew and Margaret after the fact.

"We are taking a list next Sunday of all of the eligible pupils. If you will come back then, we can see about schooling for the winter," Mr. Jackson offered, patting Margaret on the head.

"Thanks. We'll be back then," Caroline assured him.

As promised, she took the children back to church the next Sunday and signed them up for the winter session. John and Andrew would be in Mr. Jackson's class, and Margaret would be with the youngest children in Mrs. Jackson's class.

Before John knew it, he had finished the harvesting season and it was time for school to begin. Time had taken on a new meaning for John since his father passed away; now it let him know what type of work he needed to do, and on what date he needed to do it. Gone were the days of swimming in the pond, or hiking in the mountains, or playing soldier in the mountains with Andrew. He was the man now, and the boy inside of him had departed with his father.

Once school began, Mr. and Mrs. Jackson quickly spotted the students who were willing to work hard in academics. They exhorted these youngsters to learn enough to get beyond the educational opportunities offered locally, and to imagine a world of opportunities. Because Mr. Jackson thought that John was a serious young man whose determination would take him a long way, he often gave the boy perplexing problems to solve to stimulate his curiosity and test his creativity.

"John, I have a puzzle for you to solve," Mr. Jackson said one day after class.

"I like puzzles, sir," John said. "What I do?"

"Okay, here it is. You can think on it and bring me the answer tomorrow. You are standing behind Andrew, and he is standing behind you at the same time. How is that possible?"

John smiled, but as he pondered the answer, his smile soon turned into a frown. "That's hard; it ain't possible," he said. He was sure this was some kind of trick to fool him; or make him look like one.

"Sometimes you need to use simple thinking instead of looking for the hard answer, John. You think on it and tell me tomorrow."

The riddle nagged at John all day long. During recess, he took his brother outside and tried all kinds of manipulations. He drew pictures and diagrams in the dirt with a stick, and refused to give up. As he was leaving for the day, he was still working on the answer.

Mr. Jackson looked on with humor and admiration. *This boy is competitive and determined*, he thought, *both good attributes. Now, if he'll just stick with it.* He was closing the window in the classroom to leave for the day, when he saw John running back down the road to the school with Andrew in tow.

"I got it! I got it!" John shouted as he ran toward the school.

Smiling, Mr. Jackson closed the window and went outside to meet his pupils.

"Okay, how is that possible?" Mr. Jackson asked.

"Like this…," John said. He drew a straight line in the dirt and told Andrew to stand on one side of it, facing away from the line. He then positioned himself on the other side of the line and turned his back to his brother so that their shoulders were touching. John was gleeful in his victory. He was clearly not a fool!

Mr. Jackson clapped his hands, laughed, and congratulated his pupil, pleased with his persistence. A plan began to formulate in his mind.

"Good boy! We'll do that in class tomorrow, and see who else can come up with the answer. You're a smart boy John and that will stand you in good stead."

Before long, Caroline was receiving glowing reports of her son's accomplishments from Mr. Jackson. She was encouraged, but not surprised. She had always known that John was special. He had proved he could run the farm, and now he was excelling in school. He also worked at the saw mill for twenty-five cents a day during the "lay by" periods, and because he had such a good reputation for being a productive and expert farmer, he was even sought out to work at adjacent farms for similar pay. Then, with the crop out and the winter wood cut, John turned his attention to his schooling.

As the year with the new teacher neared its end, many of the local youth made plans to go to the coal mines in West Virginia during the summer. Caroline knew that work in the mines paid well, but mining was a dangerous job. She didn't want her boys to go, but they insisted that the money was too good to pass up. Andrew would go first, leaving John to tend the farm. Then the plan was for them to switch roles after a specified time.

The thought of John working in the mines kept Caroline awake at night. While both she and her husband had been ambitious for their children's future, oddly enough she was the one who, after her husband's death, had envisioned a future away from the farm – and even away from Redmonds, Virginia and its limited opportunities. Now she was beginning to feel more confident about acting on her ideas and opinions; and leaving the farm and the coal mines for a life in the city was never far from her mind.

That's why, when Mr. Jackson came to the farm to offer Caroline another option for John, she was more than ready to listen. She was baking an apple pie when he arrived, and the aroma wafted out the front door, titillating his taste buds and reminding him that he hadn't eaten lunch.

"Something smells mighty good in there," he said loudly after knocking.

Caroline put her teapot down and went to the door. "Hullo, suh. It's a surprise to see ya," she said, opening the door. "Take a seat please."

"Thank you, Mrs. Kenney. It was a long ride," Jackson said, noticing how clean and immaculate Caroline kept her modest house, a testament to the example she was setting for her children. What he saw made him feel confident that getting Caroline to consider his suggestion would not be difficult. "How are you?" he said, making small talk while he twirled his hat absent-mindedly.

"Mighty fine, suh," Caroline said, wondering why he was visiting and feeling somewhat uncomfortable. She was often insecure around highly educated Negroes. She couldn't help feeling inadequate and irrelevant in their presence, and was sure she had nothing in common with them to talk about – at least nothing that wouldn't elicit their sympathy, and she didn't need that. Her English was improving with the lessons she was taking at the church, but she wasn't ready to experiment with it just yet.

"I came about John," the teacher said seriously, looking directly at her.

"What he do?" Caroline asked, her posture now ramrod straight and her eyes wide with alarm.

"Oh no, Mrs. Kenney," the teacher said, reassuring her, "nothing's wrong. I came to offer John a summer job."

Jackson paused, waiting for Caroline to relax back into her chair. "Every summer I go to the White Sulphur Springs resort in West Virginia to work as a waiter," he explained. "The money is good and the experience is useful. They have space for one more waiter, and I wanted to know if John could go with me. He is a hard worker, and he would do well. And you wouldn't have to worry about him being in any danger, which is the problem with working in the coal mine."

"I know. I prays over Andrew all day. I likes your offer, suh. I will tell John when he comes back from the field. Would ya like to wait for him? The pie will be ready soon, and I can offer ya some."

"That will be fine, Mrs. Kenney," Jackson said, unloosening his tie. "The smell is really making me hungry."

When John returned home, he was surprised to see his teacher eating pie in the kitchen, but as soon as he heard what had brought Jackson to the farm, he was eager to learn all about this new experience. He liked Mr. Jackson, and the thought of making good money for the family appealed to him. Jackson, however, tried to prepare him for the experience of White Sulphur Springs.

"To survive," he warned John, "you will have to have the patience of Job, the strength of Goliath, and the humility and selflessness of Jesus.

Your job is to listen and learn, and to take all of the knowledge that you get and use it to accomplish your purpose in life. You will be exposed to an education there that, in other circumstances, would take you a lifetime to acquire. You just need to stay by me and follow my lead."

"Yes, sir," John said, wondering what in the dickens his teacher was talking about.

He would learn soon enough. The beautiful White Sulphur Springs resort would give John firsthand knowledge of both good and evil, with God and the Devil alternately testing his character.

White Sulphur Springs' White Society

T he moment John stepped off the train in the mountains of West Virginia, he felt as if he had arrived in another country. A short walk brought him to the main drive of White Sulphur Springs, a sprawling resort set among lush foothills dotted with cultivated trees, pruned to enhance the effect. Willows lined the drive, and the surrounding gardens smelled of magnolia and honeysuckle. Forsythia and iris, hydrangeas and azaleas, and a myriad of other brilliantly colored flowers filling the air with fragrance, were planted together like an exquisite mosaic created by God.

This was the scene that drew guests from all over the United States. From dawn to dusk, visitors could see servants tending the grounds with picks and shears, removing any wilted flowers and replacing them with fresh ones from the greenhouse. Rainwater, collected and stored for use in watering, ensured that the foliage would benefit from the minerals already present in nature's overflow. Such magnificence, spread before John's eyes, brought to mind his father's words – nature takes first; only then do we benefit by its beauty.

By day, the guests chose from a variety of activities: horseback riding, tennis, and water rafting for the hardy; and croquet, garden parties, billiards, and card games for the less physically active. The health conscious bathed in the warm mineral springs, and hiked in the picturesque mountains enjoying the clean mountain air and spectacular views. In the evenings, five-course meals preceded gambling and dancing in the parlors. After midnight, the gentlemen retreated to the drawing rooms for whiskey and cigars, and many a political deal was cut in the haze of smoke and inebriation; only to be debated and argued the next day and renegotiated again the next night. This cycle repeated itself day after day, night after night, and the consequences were often lost fortunes and political scandal. Some quarrels were even settled by duel – the ultimate lesson.

For John, the lessons he learned in the horticulture of the resort would quickly pale in comparison to the lessons in humanity. This was his first real foray into a world of racial prejudice and bigotry. Fortunately, his teacher was there to guide him and direct him through the quagmire of poisonous emotions. If not for this preparation and support, the indignities and the constant affronts to John's humanity likely would have destroyed him, and he would never have learned what he did.

For, although John lived in the segregated South, his isolation on a rural farm had sheltered him from much of the harsh reality of racial hatred. The only time he ever experienced the sting of being a Negro was when he went to town with his father to pick up supplies. The store owner always made them go around to the back to pick up their goods, but John hadn't really understood the significance of that insult. Since his father just shrugged it off, easily donning the cloak of obsequiousness and the mask of deference so he would be successful in his business dealings, John too accepted the situation. In this way, even though John and his father were shown to the "colored entrance" and offered the lowest crop prices, they managed to profit as much as they could at the time.

Ironically, it was John's training in gardening and farming that set him up for his first lesson in racial prejudice. Assigned to tend the flowers that decorated the entrance to the main hotel, he was pruning the rose bushes on his first day of work when a family of four, a man and his wife and two daughters, arrived with more luggage and paraphernalia than their carriage could hold. As the buggy came to a stop, several articles fell out onto the ground. John looked up at the commotion, and his gaze caught the eye of the gentleman driving the wagon, a burly man whose intense stare quickly turned angry. Confused, John returned to his pruning.

"Boy, get off your knees and get over here!" the man shouted. "Pick up this stuff! I shouldn't have to ask you – when you see white people in need, you come running to help. Who are you anyway? Are you new? I haven't seen you here before."

John hurried over to help with the fallen parcels. "Yes, suh," he replied. "I'm new here. My name is John."

"Shut up, boy! Just get this buggy unloaded and take our stuff up to our quarters. We've been traveling for most of two days, and we're tired and hungry, so hurry it up!"

By now several guests were observing the situation, and John kept his eyes focused on the ground, feeling even more confused and uncomfortable by the venomous anger being spewed at him.

"I'll git the porter for ya, sir. I's jus the gardner." John turned to walk away.

At this response, the man turned a shade that matched the roses John had been pruning, and his cheeks seemed to inflate like the hot air balloon that guests enjoyed in good weather. He threw his hat on the ground and hollered, " Wait a goddamn minute. Didn't you hear me, boy? I gave you an order, and I gave it to you and only you." John stopped in his tracks.

By now even more guests had gathered to survey the scene. John realized he had to choose between leaving his post in the garden and incurring the wrath of the overseer, or continuing to antagonize this bull of a man whose face was getting redder and puffier by the moment.

Sweat began to show on John's face and his breaths started coming too fast. Fighting off the dizziness that threatened to overtake him he walked toward the wagon. Never having been humiliated in public before, John wasn't sure what he had done to deserve this treatment. He just wanted the situation to be over. Instinctively, he knew that the huffing, spewing man before him posed the greater threat at the moment. He chose to worry about the overseer later. Preferring a private punishment to a public one, he struggled to unload the luggage.

"I guess you think you're special because you're a light-skinned colored boy and have that funny-looking red hair. Well, you're no different than other niggers to me. House nigger or field nigger – there ain't no difference to me, so don't think you're special. This is a good place for you to learn that." The man spat a wad of tobacco in John's direction and, followed by his family, stomped up the steps into the hotel.

It took several trips to get the luggage into the hotel, and John was fortunate not to encounter the angry giant again. That same day, however, the overseer docked his pay for leaving his gardening duties and, as punishment, assigned him to kitchen duty instead of the gardening that he loved.

John assumed his new role as a waiter in the dining room, determined to do a good job. Remembering his mother's words, "Do what you have to do to get where you need to", as well as Mr. Jackson's maxim, "Patience is a bitter plant, but it has sweet fruit," he approached his work with an eye toward future rewards. His first day on the job assured him that this would be a long and ugly summer.

John's first assignment was to wait on a table of four men. He later learned that they were politicians from Richmond on a junket paid for by their constituents. To them, he was "Boy" or "Kenney," and they didn't seem to care which they used.

"Boy! Bring me some hot coffee. This is as cold as a witch's titty." The simile earned a laugh from the men at the table. "And don't make me remind you how to do your job."

"Yes, sir," John said and hurried to the kitchen. Juggling dishes of food or drinks on a tray was a new experience for him and didn't come easy. As he loaded the tray with sugar and cream, a set of coffee cups, and a silver serving pot full of coffee, he noticed Mr. Jackson inspecting his work. Jackson's raised eyebrow caused John to pause.

"Get some of those clean napkins and some silver spoons. Serve the guests from the right side," he advised, "and smile."

John headed back to the dining room with his load, conscious only of the pot of hot coffee rocking and jiggling with each step. Smiling tentatively and holding the tray on his left arm, he began to serve the coffee with his right hand. The moment he grasped the silver coffeepot, he realized he should have picked it up with one of the napkins. The hot handle seared into the palm of his hand. His face grimaced with pain. Instinctively, he stepped away from the table as the pot slipped from his grasp, spilling coffee on the floor and scalding his own feet and legs. He had managed to spare the guests, but they showed no concern for his injury, which made the burns even more painful.

"Damn you, nigger!" cursed one of the men. He jumped up from the table and pointed a finger at John. "You could have burned us to death! What the hell do you think you're doing? Get out of here and get someone to clean up this mess. You've ruined a perfectly beautiful morning. I'll see to it that you get reported for this."

"I'm v-very sorry, gentlemen," John muttered, backing away. "I'll get someone right away." He felt light-headed amid the glaring stares of the dining room guests, and the excruciating pain of his burns. The last thing he remembered before he hit the floor was a touch on his shoulder, and Mr. Jackson's face.

When he regained consciousness, John was in his bunk with his legs wrapped in gauze dampened with a foul smelling potion. Mr. Jackson was sponging cold water on top of the gauze, which only made the smell worse. John grimaced in pain.

"You're lucky, young man," Mr. Jackson said examining John's leg. "You have a few blisters, but your skin didn't peel. It's gonna hurt for a few days, but if you can stand to work, the overseer will let you stay. He said if you can't work, you've got to go. What do you think?"

John was ready to leave this God-forsaken place. He wanted to be back on the farm where he could enjoy the natural relationship between man and nature, of species coexisting in mutual respect. Then he thought about his family, and how much they needed the money he had expected to make during the summer. He remembered his father and his lifetime of sacrifice.

"I can do it, Mr. Jackson. I have to." John sat up gingerly feeling new pain shoot through his legs.

"Well, let me wrap you with a poultice and dry rags. That should hold you until you finish your shift. We'll dress it again later. I'll switch jobs with you. You polish the silver, and I'll wait the tables. That way you can sit down."

"Thank you, Mr. Jackson."

Mr. Jackson was pleased with John's decision and fortitude. He knew that the boy would need all of that and more to last the summer. He also knew he needed to keep John out of the way of the guests he had offended at breakfast. They had demanded that John be dismissed, but because the resort was short-staffed, the overseer had relented, although with a strong warning that there could be no more mistakes.

John went back to his duties, determined to learn everything about how the dining room and the kitchen worked. He washed dishes, scrubbed floors, and watched the experienced waiters as they balanced trays unwieldy with food and dishes. He studied food preparation, and became the resident expert in picking out the best fruits and vegetables for the menu. And whenever he needed to move items around the kitchen, he carried them on trays.

After he was sure that the guests who had witnessed his coffee disaster had left the resort, John ventured out into the dining room again. This time he had practiced, and he could carry coffeepots, coffee cups, and breakfasts on the same tray with no wavering. He got used to the fact that people rarely said "please" or "thank you", or even acknowledged his existence, except when they wanted something. He got used to conversations that bemoaned the death of the Confederacy and debated the loss of so much human "property," discussions that were carried on as if he weren't there. No one could tell by his outward countenance, demeanor, or composure that his blood was boiling, and his very being railing against these affronts.

For all of its physical beauty, White Sulphur Springs was diminished in the eyes of the Negroes there by its sheer abomination for a race of people upon whose very existence the elite clientele depended. The colored servants cultivated the land, tended the gardens, harvested the crops, cleaned the quarters, served the meals, maintained the property, waited on the guests twenty-four hours a day, and were considered no more valuable than the animals that were slaughtered and butchered on a daily basis. They were invisible, which perpetuated the commonly held belief that they were happy in servitude and were doing what they were capable of – for, as many whites asked, now that they were free Negroes, why would they do this work if it wasn't their lot in life? Surely they had no higher aspirations, since a race with any intelligence would not be so accommodating and satisfied.

John, however, quietly pursued a quite different goal. During those summers at the resort, and sometimes at another nearby resort called Warm Springs in Bath County, Virginia, he listened well and learned how wealthy people thought and acted with regard to their wealth. At both locations what he saw and heard described an attitude toward wealth, and a constant conversation around how to get it, keep it, and grow it. As he waited on tables and serviced the recreation areas, he absorbed as much of the visitors' dialogue as he could understand, because he knew that he would probably never have an opportunity to hear this valuable information firsthand again. When he got back to the servants' quarters at the end of the day, Mr. Jackson was always waiting, ready to assume the role of tutor.

"So, what did you learn today, John?" he asked, sitting at the foot of John's cot and raising one bushy eyebrow.

"I heard Mr. Livingston say to his son, Master Julian – and he used us as an example – that us coloreds here at this place is hard workers, and thrifty, but we ain't never gonna get ahead 'cause we don't understand the 'culture of money.'"

"What do you think he meant by that?"

"I really dunno, sir." John lowered his eyes and fidgeted with his bed covering. He had no idea what Mr. Livingston had meant.

"It's 'don't know,' John, not dunno."

"Sorry, sir. Don't know," John repeated as clearly as he could. "But Mr. Livingston also said that as long as you work for another person and not yourself," he continued, "you never, ever get rich. He said that, year after year the coloreds is here to work, but they spend their money to live on while they're here and the rest when they get back home. 'Cause they do this over and over, they ain't never gonna have nothing."

Mr. Jackson relaxed his expression impressed with John's almost verbatim recall.

"He said we don't know nothing 'bout investment and how money grows. I didn't know you could grow money. He says if you ain't born to money, you need to make something that somebody else wants to buy, and then you turn your cash into assets and your assets back into more cash. I don't know what assets is, but they must be wurf something!"

"It's worth…worth, not 'wurf,' John. That is a word you need to know."

"W-o-r-t-h," John spelled out loud, proving that he could.

"Excellent!" Mr. Jackson replied. "You've done well. Now let me try to explain the most important thing you need to know about that information, much of it being preconceived." John's eyes widened as he tried to find the meaning in Mr. Jackson's words.

"An asset is something of value, something that is useful. The answer in all situations is work – but work for yourself. Use your own money to make more money. Be as independent as you can in the way you work, because we need to change the way we have been taught to think about money. Remember the old proverb: 'The example of wise men is good philosophy.' Your philosophy is being formed right now. It's also wise to learn to speak proper English", Mr. Jackson added. "Try to practice putting your words together the way you hear them in conversations between the hotel guests. Some of those people are highly educated."

John opened his trunk and took out a paper to write down what his teacher was telling him. He would start practicing proper English tomorrow.

"You must also not fear risk or failure. There is a lesson in each. Taking a risk is part of being successful. If you fail at something, that teaches you what not to do. Are you listening, John?"

"Yes, sir," John replied, looking somewhat wistful. He was think-ing about his father, who instinctively knew many of these truths without a formal education. He had used his savings to buy himself a farm; he had worked for himself and become independent because he lived on what he produced; and he used his savings to buy more land and make a profit. Yes…unlettered, but certainly not uneducated.

The next day, John was helping another waiter carry a large freezer of ice cream up a flight of stairs to the pantry. When the freezer finally landed at the top of the steps, John gave a loud grunt of relief.

From inside the pantry came a gruff female voice. "Who is that grunting out there? I told somebody just the other day what a bunch of babies this group of waiters is. Makes me wonder when their nurses are coming."

John peered into the room and saw a stewardess seated at a table. Embarrassed, he felt that her evaluation had been a pretty mean blow, but he swallowed it, wrestled the freezer into position, and returned to his work. Back in the kitchen, he learned from one of the staff that the middle-aged white woman who spoke was Miss Glover, who, along with her sister, was the resort's proprietor-partner and was an invalid confined to a chair. "She's a gruff one," the co-worker warned, "both her and her sister. You watch out for them two."

It was not long before Miss Glover called John to the dining room.

"Young man," she said, peering over her bifocals and scrutinizing him from head to toe, "when you're through in the dining room this morning, I want you to give me some help in the pantry."

John's heart gave a little jump. The kitchen worker's warning was fresh in his mind, but he decided to take a chance, hoping this would be a lesson about good risk and not about failure. "Sure enough, ma'am," he said. "I'll help you."

The pantry was Miss Glover's daily station and the headquarters for salads and desserts. As acting stewardess, she directed all of the culinary activities. Although a reputation for being cross and cruel made nearly everyone fear her, John wondered if her physical circumstances might be part of the reason for her gruff manner. This made him inclined to be patient, and he soon became indispensable. Miss Glover quickly took to calling him "Kenney," even though she called all the other workers by their first names. Before long, John was making more money from her extras than from his regular wages.

In spite of her eccentricities, Miss Glover turned out to be one of the best women John had ever known, and she could not have treated him better if he had been her own son. To John, she was pure gold. She paid him well, and if she got a hint by any means that he wished for something, she'd see to it that it was provided. On one occasion, she heard that John liked lettuce.

"Aunt Betsy," she told one of the cooks, "see that a plate of the nicest lettuce is put into the refrigerator every day for Kenney's dinner." The same was true of Miss Glover's finest desserts, and there were none better to be found anywhere.

This woman, whom John had been told to fear, someone he had even judged as a prejudiced and demeaning person, had actually become his advocate. By facing his fear, he had learned that not every white person was the enemy, nor as full of hatred and venom as they seemed. Not only did Miss Glover become his benefactor; but, with her generous tips, John was eventually able to buy his mother a decent house. The resort had taught him about investing his money in something that would make more money, but he also learned something far more important. He learned to trust his gut – to follow his instincts.

He never knew why Miss Glover befriended and looked after him, but he did know that everyone had told him to watch out for her motives. Yet, he sensed a genuine desire on her part to help someone in whose shoes she could easily have been born. In spite of the warnings that he continued to hear most of that first summer, he chose to follow his own head and heart, and not be swayed by others. He accepted Miss Glover's help whenever it was offered, and he repaid her with hard work and loyalty. Some of his cohorts ostracized him for this obvious favoritism, but he chalked it up to jealousy and the "green-eyed monster" envy.

It was during these years, when John spent the summer working at the resort, that Caroline and Mr. Jackson made another decision - one that would ultimately determine the direction of his life.

Chapter 5

A Tough Education

Caroline was up before dawn, beginning the preparations for breakfast. She had not slept well the night before and was going through the motions, not consciously focusing on what she was doing. She swore silently as she realized she had forgotten to put baking powder in the batter for the hotcakes. Throwing everything out, she started over.

Lately, she had been restless during the night, her dreams turning into wakeful abstractions fueled by exhaustion. This morning, she had recalled flashes of images from the night before. She remembered dreaming that she was a big city gal strolling through the square with a huge pink parasol, followed by numerous handsome suitors trailing behind her and seeking her favor. In another dream, she had been a little girl again, crying and lost in the woods, wailing for her "mommy." Most disturbing of all was the vision of herself on the farm as a decrepit old woman, sitting on the front porch in her rocking chair. John, Andrew, and Margaret all played in the yard around her, but in the dream they were still young children and had not aged at all. That vision woke her, making her sit bolt upright in bed. Unable to go back to sleep, she got up to face another day that she expected to be no different from any other.

As she cooked, she stared, mesmerized, at the bubbles forming one by one on the batter she spooned onto the hot griddle. Her inattention almost caused her to burn the first batch of hotcakes, and she quickly grabbed for her spatula, flipping the hotcakes and then reaching into the churn to spoon some fresh butter off the cream. She heard John stirring in the bedroom, and smiled with satisfaction. She never had to wake him to do the chores. He was as reliable as day and night; you never had to worry that one would follow the other. His father would have been proud – young John was just like him.

"What's for breakfast, Ma?" John asked, pulling on his undershirt as he came into the kitchen. He peeked over her shoulder to see what was cooking. The aroma made his stomach growl and gurgle. The day before, he had come in late from the field and fallen asleep where he'd lain down, promising himself that he would rest – just for a minute – and then he had slept right through supper. To ease his morning hunger pangs, he poured himself a cup of steaming coffee and sat down at the kitchen table. The dark liquid felt good going down his throat and, in just minutes, his mind perked up and he felt that he could concentrate on his daily responsibilities. He needed a change; the sameness of life was beginning to dull him. He found himself thinking about the school season with anticipation, even though it was months away.

"What 'ya got doin' today, son?" Caroline asked, trying to make intelligent conversation. She handed John a plate of buttered hotcakes.

"Same thing I tell you every day, Ma. Nothing's different. Same old chores, harvest and hoe, harvest and hoe. Where's the syrup?" John took his knife and fork and cut his hotcakes into little square pieces, a habit he'd had since he was a little boy.

"Here 'tis," said Caroline, taking a tin of sweet maple syrup off the shelf. She opened the tin and passed it to John, watching as he poured the thick syrup generously over the checkerboard pieces on his plate, and began to cram the little squares into his mouth. She held her tongue, not asking him why he always cut up his hot cakes like that, something she usually did to remind him of how childish this ritual was. She had sensed a mood of restlessness about him lately, and she didn't want to inflame it.

"School's comin' here soon son, an' you'll have somethin' else to do. Things won't bore 'ya so round here then."

John ate the hotcakes as if they were a prisoner's last meal. He asked Caroline for more, and meticulously cut the new stack into little pieces. Finishing the last bite, he put down his fork, jumped up from the table, and was half out the door when he called back, "I'm gone, Ma!"

"Gotta git the crops to town when you gits back," she yelled, hoping that he had heard her. As she closed the door behind her son, she frowned at the overcast sky. She hoped they wouldn't be hauling crops in the rain; it would make the roads a muddy mess. She didn't need that headache today.

She picked up John's plate to put it in the wash basin, but instead, sat down absentmindedly at the table. Her mind was exploring possibilities and questions: Is this all there is to my life? How long can I go on like this? How long before John's spirit is broken? Is this what I want for me and my children? What would happen if I left here? Where would we go?

"I'm hungry, Ma!" came Andrew's sleepy call from the bedroom. "Is breakfast ready?"

"Yes, Andrew," Caroline answered with a sigh, "like always..."

Caroline cooked breakfast for Andrew and Margaret, and then watched them set about their chores. She wanted to get all of the crops sold before it was time for John to go away to the resort for his summer job. Each summer, when he returned from the resort to the monotony of home, she realized how much he had gained by leaving the farm. She knew that this added to his sense of restlessness, but without his experiences at the resort, he would not have matured as rapidly into the responsible young man that impressed her now. Encouraged, she continued to plant seeds in her garden of possibilities. The weather improved and the sun came out, and John and Andrew loaded the crops into the wagon for the trip to Redmonds.

"John," Caroline said casually as the wagon headed toward town, "Mr. Jackson says that you is a hard worker and you learns quick. I am proud of you, son. What's it like working at that resort? I hear rich white people go there and spin money like it grows on trees. Can you 'magine that? What it be like to have money like that?"

John, who was focused on the road ahead, took a moment before answering his mother.

"I learned that I should save my money, Ma, and get something called assets – something of value that's worth something. Pa knew that, and that's why we have this farm. As long as we own it free and clear, we have something of worth, and this is our asset."

"And this farm is yours an' Andrews 'an Margarets. But you're the oldest an' most smartest, an' I trust you to decide what we should do with our… 'asset.' Do you think you wants to stay here an' run this farm?"

John thought about answering this question truthfully, but he didn't want to disappoint his mother. The man of the house had already left her once, and he loved her too much to see her hurt again. He decided to tell her what he thought she wanted to hear.

"I don't know, Ma," he said with a casual tone that almost fooled Caroline. "At one time, I fancied that I could learn to be like Mr. O'Keefe. Remember when he sewed up my hand? I wanted to learn from him, and maybe make some money taking care of sick people when they are in need. And I could still work the farm too," John added, intending to placate and reassure his mother.

"So, you wants to be a healer like our neighbor?" Caroline's calm tone belied her astonishment at John's admission. She began to smile.

"Yes, I think I'd like that a lot, Ma," John answered, certain that this dream would never become a reality. He still liked to think about it though, and his imagination was his escape these days. It was all that he had to keep life interesting.

With that admission, John unknowingly planted a new seed in his mother's mind. Yet, to nurture that seed, Caroline realized that she would have to find ways to expose John to even more of the world outside of Redmonds, Virginia. The rural world they lived in would not allow him to think and grow further than the boundaries on the county map. She was certain that the world offered far more than she could see on the farm, and she wanted John to be in an atmosphere of learning that would open doors to that wider world.

With her mind full of possibilities, Caroline stepped down from the wagon and walked to the general store in town, while John drove off to sell the crops. She loved to browse among the newest stacks of patterns and bolts of fabric that had come from the city. Every now and then, she would treat herself to a small bottle of cologne or a new shade of lipstick if John managed to sell all of their crops. This day, she wanted to buy some fabric to spruce up her dowdy kitchen, although she hadn't always thought of it that way. Only lately had the room depressed her, and new kitchen curtains would give a lift to the room where she spent so much of her time.

She purchased new red and white checked gingham for a tablecloth and curtains and then, as usual, lingered at the magazine stand to look longingly at pictures of the big city. She decided that she would buy a newspaper, her first one, and let John or Mr. Jackson read it to her. When John returned with the day's bounty, they paid for their purchases and headed toward home. When they got back to the farm, Caroline couldn't wait for John to read the words under the pictures in the paper.

"This is the *Charlottesville Chronicle* newspaper, Ma," John said, reading what he could of the captions. "These are pictures of the city. The other pictures are of homes of two former presidents. It is talking about where President Jefferson and President Monroe lived. Do you want me to read it to you?"

Caroline's need to have her son read to her suddenly reminded her of her shortcomings, and she shook her head. "Nah," she said, not wanting to acknowledge her illiteracy, at least not right now. She just liked the pictures of the city, and for now that was enough. "I have my reasons," she said finally, putting the paper in a drawer.

Mr. Jackson came by the farm a few days later to finalize details for the trip to White Sulphur Springs. Caroline indicated that she wanted to speak with him privately, and when he had finished with John, Mr. Jackson turned his attention to her.

"Now, what can I do for you, Caroline?" he asked. He had long admired this woman, who managed to carry on by herself with only her teenaged sons for assistance. She emanated a quiet strength and resolve that he knew John had inherited.

Caroline went over to the bureau and took out the newspaper. She sat down and handed the paper to Mr. Jackson whose raised eyebrow asked the question.

"John says these pictures are of Charlottesville, Virginia, not too far from here." Caroline wrung her hands together for courage and continued on. "It's been in my mind that maybe I'd like that city life. I think I would like it for my chil'ren too." Caroline waited for a moment to gauge his reaction and then added, "What 'ya think?"

Mr. Jackson thought for a moment and said seriously, "I think it's a good idea, Caroline." Caroline's face shone with relief. "It's hard to work a farm alone, and your boys are going to want more for their lives as they get older. A move to the city may be a very good thing." Mr. Jackson knew that if the family stayed out on this distant farm in Redmonds, it would probably be the only life they would ever know. It was a full-time job to work a farm, and he sensed that John, and maybe even Andrew, who was more hot-headed and impetuous, would profit by exposure to city life. He was pleased with Caroline's foresight.

"What's Charlottesville like?" questioned Caroline as she opened the newspaper. "I likes the pictures." Her trepidation had evaporated in the face of Mr. Jackson's approval and her questions poured out unabated.

"It's a real big city, Caroline – big buildings and stores, lots of schools and universities, and beautiful parks and rivers. There is opportunity for coloreds there too. I know a lot of people, and our community there is constantly growing. I think you'd like it," Mr. Jackson said, appreciating the wistful look on Caroline's face.

"Would you help me if I decides to go to Charlottesville, Mr. Jackson?" Caroline asked, tracing the newspaper picture with her finger. She could already see herself standing on the city sidewalk, watching the hustle and bustle of city life swirling around her. "Can I count on you to help me with my plan?"

"If you decide that's what you want, I'll do everything I can to help you," he replied earnestly, putting his hand on her shoulder. His mind was already working on a plan that would benefit his protege.

No one who ever ventured across the threshold of change embraced it like Caroline. She became a different woman overnight, filling old empty spaces with solid plans for the future. Excitement and enthusiasm replaced her usual lethargy and fatigue. She readily made the decision to sell the Kenney farm and move to Charlottesville, a city that she hoped would heal her loneliness. Mr. Jackson got her a job as a housekeeper in the home of a professor at the University of Virginia, and he arranged for John to work as a chore boy and a porter in a grocery store that some friends of his owned.

Caroline waited for John to get home from the fields to announce the news. He walked in the door, dirty and dusty with wheat shards, as he headed for the steaming soup pot that Caroline had on the stove, taking off the top and smelling it.

"T'aint ready yet son," drawled Caroline, "Slow your horses' down, I got good news." John looked at his mother out of the corner of his eye, trying to gauge her disposition. He was still cautious of the change in her lately, remembering the conversations of some of the church elders speaking of the irregularities of women's moods.

John sat down at the kitchen table. "I need some good news right about now."

Caroline put her hands triumphantly on her hips and gave John a broad smile. "We's moving to the city, and I has a job an' one for you too! We gonna leave this place and start over!" Caroline proudly opened a box and showed John the newspaper clippings of Charlottesville that she had saved. "Mr. Jackson goanna' help us."

John was stunned. The thought of leaving the farm elicited ambivalent feelings. On one hand, he definitely welcomed the possibility of change from the drudgery of farm work; but on the other hand he felt an allegiance to what his father had started, and of the expectations his father had had of him, even though he was long gone.

John looked out of the kitchen window at the acres of wheat to be harvested. He quickly decided that he needed to think of his mother, and appreciate how much she needed a life. She was still a young woman, and there was nothing for her in Redmonds but sad memories.

"What 'ya say to that son?" Caroline looked at John with hopeful eyes, reading his silence as disapproval.

"I like it Ma," John said turning to her with a slow smile, "and I think Pa would too."

Caroline and John sat down and made plans to sell the crops and find a buyer for the farm as soon as Mr. Jackson found a job for Andrew and a school for Margaret. She proudly told Andrew the plan when he came home from the mines.

Andrew, however, decided that he didn't want to move. He wanted to stay in Redmonds, and work in the coal mines with his friends. Mr. Jackson offered to look out for him, and Caroline acquiesced, hoping he would soon change his mind. Margaret would attend the colored school in Charlottesville, which was more advanced than the little school in Redmonds. Mr. Jackson warned that she might have to be kept back a year to keep up with the more advanced curriculum in the city. Caroline considered this a necessary evil, and while Margaret initially rebelled, she embraced the move after just one day of difficult classroom work in her new school.

Caroline, too, took pleasure in the possibilities provided by their new home. She had always heard that if you were ever to hear the voice of God, it would be in a garden. Now, having planted her seeds, she was content to sit back and watch them grow.

John went to work for Mr. and Mrs. George Inge, graduates of Hampton Institute, one of the first colleges established for the higher education of the Negro. Mr. Inge was a college professor, and Mrs. Inge taught at the grade school Margaret attended in the city. Mr. Inge had a kind and patient temperament like Mr. Jackson's, and John liked his new boss right away. He was serious and hard working, and there was something about him that reminded John of his father, and John sought to please him.

On the first day of work, John showed up in his best church clothes – twill pants, a clean white shirt, and spit-shined black shoes – which earned him a smile from Mr. Inge. The store was smaller than John had imagined, about the size of the front room in the Kenneys' old farm-house. One large window at the front of the store held displays visible from the outside, and another small window in the storeroom looked out on the alley at the back. John could tell from the heat, as he stepped inside, that it was going to be a long, hot day.

"Good morning, John," Mr. Inge said with a grin. "I see you are all dressed up. I guess Mr. Jackson didn't tell you what you're going to be doing, so why don't you come with me?"

Mr. Inge led John to the back of the small store, where several large boxes of fresh fruits and vegetables were stacked on top of each other. "Today I need you to shuck the corn, shell the peas, and slice the watermelon; and then arrange it on the stands outside for sale. Not too glamorous, eh?"

"Oh," John said with a sheepish expression, "I didn't know. I'll get started right now, sir." He looked down at his good clothes, wondering how he was going to keep them clean.

"There's an old apron on the hook over there, son", Mr. Inge pointed to the storeroom door. "Cover yourself up as best you can. I'll be back after my third period class is over to see how you're doing. I've got to hurry or I'll be late." Mr. Inge quickly put on his hat and left for work, leaving John alone in the store.

Not quite sure where to begin, John put on the apron and began to shuck the corn, which had more field worms and partially eaten brownish cobs than he had ever seen. This wasn't the fresh corn he was used to growing on his farm. After cleaning about a dozen ears, he began to perspire, and the sweat dripping down his back made his shirt wet and sticky. He decided that since the store wasn't open yet, he would take off his shirt, which he hung on the hook. He put the apron back on and finished the corn, neatly arranging it on a vegetable stand. He tackled the watermelon next, cutting into the fluid green melons and arranging the bright red slices on cardboard fruit trays. The amount of watermelon juice dripping from his hands and arms made him glad that he had removed his shirt. Then he looked down at his shoes, which were wet with the pink liquid, and decided to remove his socks and shoes too. He set them aside and picked up the box of fresh green peas.

There was a large wooden bowl on a shelf above him, and he struggled to get it down, his feet slipping on the wet floor. He placed the bowl on top of the empty boxes and began to shell the peas, putting them into the bowl and discarding the pods onto the floor. Finishing his last task and breathing a sigh of relief, he decided to go outside to get some fresh air before he cleaned up the mess. As he stretched to put the bowl of peas back on the shelf, he lost his footing among the wormy corn husks, sticky watermelon juice and discarded pea pods. The bowl of peas went flying, and as he fell, John knocked down the vegetable stand and the fruit trays in one fell swoop. Lying prone and dazed on the floor, he could feel pain in his wrist and his hip. Then he heard the door open and a female voice call his name.

"John, are you in here?"

Before he could reply, Mrs. Inge strode into the store and stopped suddenly, almost tripping over the new chore boy half-naked and prostrate on the floor; and grimacing in pain amid the watery rubbish.

"Oh dear!" she exclaimed with alarm, realizing what must have just happened. "Are you all right? Let me help you up, dear." She grabbed John's wet arm but it slipped out of her hand.

"I'm okay," he mumbled apologetically. "I can do it." He got to his feet, almost falling down again in the slippery muck.

John was mortified and ashamed, but Mrs. Inge was gracious and understanding. "Didn't my husband show you what to do?" she asked knowingly.

"No, ma'am," John said getting up off the floor. "He just told me what to do."

"There's an old proverb I like, John," she said, getting a broom and helping him clean up the mess. "It says: 'Give a man a fish, and you feed him for a day. Teach a man to fish, and you feed him for a lifetime.' Did the *teacher* say when he'd be back?" she asked facetiously.

"He said he'd return after his third class," John answered, more embarrassed and chagrined with each passing moment.

"Then we don't have much time. Let's get this place cleaned up." Mrs. Inge helped John discard the ruined produce and set up the stands. She showed him where to get more boxes of produce from the storeroom and where the shed was out back, a shed where the tools were kept to help shuck the corn, shell the peas, and slice the watermelon. After everything was in order, she said to him, "No need to mention this to my husband. I will make sure that you get proper instruction from now on."

"Yes, ma'am," John said, more ashamed and humiliated than relieved. He was grateful to have such an understanding confidante, and it was a secret they acknowledged with knowing smiles and looks, every now and then.

Soon after that incident, John proved that, with the proper instruction, he was responsible enough to be left in charge of the store when the owners went to work. Mr. Inge was a smart businessman, and it was under his tutelage that John's financial philosophy was born. John's grocery store salary was eight dollars a month, and with his earnings he was able to open his first bank account at the First National Bank of Virginia. Mr. Inge congratulated John on his savings, and gave him financial advice on how to handle his money.

"Live below your means when you have to, son," he would tell John. "Create a surplus. Buy what you need and defer what you want until you can afford it. Eventually, you will save enough to be able to invest in the stock market."

Not wanting to embarrass himself and show his lack of knowledge, John just looked at Mr. Inge and said "okay" as if he understood. He had found that in some situations taciturnity masqueraded as an assumption of understanding, and he used the disguise more often than he was proud of.

Mr. Inge, knowing that John was timid when it came to subjects he didn't comprehend, said, "John, you must ask questions if you want to get the answers to things you don't know. Information is what makes you smart. Do you know what the stock market is?"

"No, sir," John replied, embarrassed that his ignorance had been so obvious. He hung his head to avoid looking directly at Mr. Inge.

"Listen, son, and I'll explain. The stock market is a center where the chief commodities of barter are the stocks and bonds of large corporations, such as public utilities, industries, manufacturing, transportation, building, and other commercial activities. Stocks are sold to acquire money the companies use to do business. Do you understand that?"

"I think so. Is the stock worth the same as money?" asked John.

"Yes, the stock represents money invested. Without this market and without the money of both big and little investors, the big businesses would not only have to suspend business, they would not even be in business," Mr. Inge explained.

"So, if I take my money and buy some stock, how does that make me more money?" John asked, interested now that he was getting some new information. He also wanted Mr. Inge to notice that he was asking questions.

"Stocks represent a certain amount of money loaned. Interest or dividends are paid on the stocks or bonds at fixed intervals, and with bonds, at the end of a stated time your money will be returned to you."

"Is that like gambling, Mr. Inge? The church says gambling is a bad thing." John had a sly smile on his face, thinking he had caught his mentor in the wrong.

"In a sense it is like gambling, but it is legal in the financial world. If you invest your money wisely, you can make more money over the long term – not money that will be gone today because you spend it, but money that will be invested."

John wrote down in his logbook everything that Mr. Inge taught him. The log was quickly becoming his bible, and he consulted it several times a day. Every day he saw the university students pass by the store loaded down with books on the way to class, and he liked to pretend he was one of them. Having his own book of lessons made him feel like a student too.

So did the "tests" administered by his employers. Daily, when Mr. and Mrs. Inge returned to the store from their jobs, they evaluated how John had handled the store that day. John liked to pretend that this was his school examination, and their suggestions were his homework for the next day. In turn, Mr. Inge was beginning to see John as the son he had never had, and he treated his employee like a member of the family, even taking him to church on Sundays.

During the hours John spent at the store, he also came to know some of the university students who frequently shopped there. They were sophisticated and intelligent, and he imitated their mannerisms and attitude whenever he got the chance. He wore his Sunday clothes on the busiest days, attempting to appear more like a serious businessman, and he was totally engrossed in the academic atmosphere of Charlottesville. After a few months, he took out his old logbook and wrote in it: "Someday I am going to be a doctor, just like the ole Irishman."

Before long, the small grocery store began to generate a significant profit, and John's work responsibilities increased in kind. Mr. Inge, impressed with his employee's hard work and reliability, made John the store manager and hired another youth as the chore boy. Then, having watched John grow into a promising maturity, Mr. Inge decided to see if he was ready to take the next step. He invited John to his home one day to find out what the young man thought about the future.

"I've been watching you for some time, son," he said with paternal pride, "and I wonder, have you thought about what you'd like to do to make a living one day?"

"Yes, sir, I've thought about it a little," John said, choosing to be noncommittal in case Mr. Inge wanted him to be a store proprietor. John thought that might be the job he was being groomed for, and he didn't want to disappoint his benefactor.

"Well, what sort of vocation do you aspire to?" asked Mr. Inge.

John looked puzzled, and Mr. Inge knowingly rephrased the question. "What do you want to become in life son?"

"I thought about being a businessman, and I thought about being a teacher. I also thought about being a doctor like the ole Irishman back home. But I don't know. I'm not sure I could do any of those jobs," John said, feeling insecure in the presence of someone as well educated as Mr. Inge. The idea of ever being as knowledgeable and educated as Mr. Inge seemed an impossible goal.

"You can do whatever you choose, John," Mr. Inge said with earnestness. "Usually we limit our own power by thinking that we can't do something. In other words, it is our own fear that holds back our success. But you must always try."

"Yes, sir," John said with a sheepish grin, feeling even more insecure about his earlier ambivalent response.

"I want you to consider enrolling at Hampton Institute, my alma mater. Whatever it is you choose to do in life, John, you must have a good education. I have some friends on the faculty there, and I am going to explore the possibilities if you think that it is something that you would consider doing. What do you think about that, John?"

"I think I'd like that a lot," John said, imagining himself as a university student. "I think I would really like that."

True to his word, Mr. Inge succeeded in finding John a spot at Hampton Institute. Although he had faith in John's innate ability, he was worried about John's tendency to want to please others while ignoring his own needs, something Mr. Inge considered a noble, but foolish, tenet. He also wondered if John's professional hopes and aspirations, plus the reality of the rigors of acquiring a higher education, would be a challenge that the young man could conquer. It would not be long before this question would be definitively answered.

A Monument of Love

John left the employ of Mr. Inge, and entered Hampton Institute in the fall of 1893. He had saved enough money in his bank account to pay his tuition, and he was proud to have earned it himself.

What a day it was for him to find himself at Hampton! At last, the whole wide world had opened up. He was in awe when he was ushered into the stone building on the school's campus, where he would take his first classes. He looked around at the other young men and women who would be his classmates, and felt privileged to be among them. Some of them seemed to be well dressed and sophisticated, while others were more like him, dressed in simple but clean clothes and a little unsure of themselves. Nevertheless, he decided at that moment that he would study hard and do well, having worked too hard already to get to this place.

New students were given a tour of the campus to orient them to the environment of this beautiful school surrounded by water. As John followed his guide, he was comforted by the waterscapes he saw from almost every vantage point, but on this particular day, the channel was troubled and pounding the banks. Looking out toward the water that lay some distance away, John remarked to the student guide, "I ain't never seen so many ducks in my life."

The guide looked snidely at this rural farm boy from Virginia and remarked, "Those aren't ducks...those are 'white caps.' It's just a mirage."

As the other students snickered, John fell silent. He didn't know what a mirage was, but he knew that he had made himself look stupid. His education had already begun.

White caps notwithstanding, John took to his classes like a duck out of water. While he was considered a bright student back home, he found it difficult to keep up with his classmates in so many new subjects. Everyone took classes in hygiene, brickmaking and bricklaying, the preparation of sulfuric acid for painting projects, and agricultural science. The latter was John's best subject, given his farm training, and he was happy to have something in which he could shine.

Mother English, however, was another story altogether. It was obvious by his language that he was a little "country," but since he was now a college student, he had renewed confidence – unfounded though it may have been – and he took every opportunity to show off his developing skills.

One afternoon, he saw a guide showing two visitors around the campus. Hoping to be noticed by parading his new language skills for the benefit of the visitors, he called across the yard to a schoolmate, "What have he got?"

His friend frowned and shook his head, a warning John failed to heed. Trying to ask who was with the guide, and determined to impress the visitors with his grandiloquent mastery of the mother tongue, John repeated the call: "What have he got?"

The reprimanding look John got from the guests and the guide, and the raucous laughter of his schoolmate, made John "go way back yonder, take a seat, and sit down." He crawled back into his shell and didn't venture out for quite a while.

With "accomplishments" like these, John barely succeeded in gaining entrance into the lowest class in the day school – the B prime class. These students, as part of their training, were required to complete work assignments around the campus, which helped to pay their tuition. The Commandant was a serious man named Major Moton, whose policy was education of the head, the heart, and the hand. John presented himself at the Commandant's office for instruction and assignment.

"Good morning, sir," John said politely. "I am here for my work duties."

"Yes, yes," the Major said, "go right down to the barn to Mr. Howe and Mr. Davis and present this note."

"Yes, sir," John said, taking the note.

When he got to the barn, he was directed to go to the Bone Farm near the Whittier school to seek out Mr. Davis, a colored man who, on that day, could just as well have been a white overseer. The sun was spiteful, and the humidity off the creek made the air feel like Hades. Already beginning to sweat, John presented Major Moton's note to Mr. Davis.

"Pitch in there loading that corn," Mr. Davis said without any attempt at politeness or greeting. The student workers were taking in the corn for ensilage. John pitched in for hours, and then helped to load the corn for transport to the silo, thankful for his experience with manual farm work. Mr. Davis was barely impressed with his work.

The next workday, which alternated with a day of school, the weather was bad, and John was ordered to work in the "vat." He had no idea what that meant, but he presented himself for work duty. The vat turned out to be the area where the night carts were emptied of bodily waste. This mammoth sewer also included waste from the animals, along with various forms of rotting and putrid garbage, with no buffer between John and the stench except some rubber boots and a shovel. He worked all day in the vat, refusing to shirk his responsibility, but in shock much of the time. When he was finally relieved, he trudged out of the vat in a stupor of exhaustion and revulsion. As soon as he got back to his dormitory, his roommate Joshua noticed his lethargy.

"What's wrong, John? You look like you've been scared by a ghoul."

John heard his roommate talking, but couldn't take in what he was saying. With his eyes refusing to focus and the stench of the vat still filling his nose, John dropped onto his bed and covered his head with a pillow.

"Well, since you're not in a sociable mood, I'm going to the dining hall. You better hurry up before the bell rings or you'll miss supper. We're having stew – again!"

At the mention of the word stew, John covered his mouth and threw up what was left of his breakfast all over his bed.

"I'm getting out of here 'fore I catch something!" Joshua said, running for the door.

John managed to pull himself up and clean off his bed, but now he had the stench from the vat and the smell of the vomit sharing space with every breath he took. When he was finally able to lie down again, he drifted off to sleep, only to be awakened by a wetness he could not identify in the dark. He lit the lamp and saw that he had had a terrible nosebleed, a rebellion of his olfactory nerves. From that day on, John never again took modern-day toilet facilities and other new improvements for granted.

The next morning, John rose feeling somewhat better, although he wished he could have stayed just a little longer in bed. He knew, however, that his teachers expected students to come to class unless they were dying. The school's founder and principal, General Samuel Armstrong, had set a fine example of strength and courage. His spirit pervaded the atmosphere, imbuing everyone, students and teachers alike, with his philosophy. He believed in perfection. He was a no-nonsense, no-excuses man of his word who believed that your word was your honor, and if you said it, you lived up to it.

All of the teachers were white missionaries. Like General Armstrong, they were men and women who forsook their native homes and all that this implied to devote their lives to the missionary teaching of a "backward race." In spirit, they adopted the colored boys and girls and made them "theirs", and they found pleasure in developing their young students. Most of these teachers, like Miss Hyde, Miss Davis, Miss Sherman, and Miss Freeman, as their names implied, had never married. They lived, they worked, and they died in the missionary cause, and God blessed them – for their spirits, whether living or dead, were at peace. They had met the requirements of the Master, and their students were the products of their collective efforts.

Nevertheless, these teachers were exacting taskmasters. No one dared show up late or unprepared for class. The students called Miss Sherman, their teacher of language, "The Queen of English." She ran her class like a parliament, expecting everyone to follow the rules, have respect for authority, and acknowledge that the ultimate decision maker was the queen herself. When she put her OK on a paper, it meant that every 't' was crossed, every 'i' dotted, and every punctuation mark properly placed. John learned this lesson the hard way.

The day that he had been assigned to work in the vat, he had also had a paper to write for Miss Sherman. Because his day's work left him unable to proofread the paper that night, now he had to hand it in without checking his work. Much to his dismay, Miss Sherman called on him at the beginning of class the next morning. "John, please stand and read your paper to the class."

Slowly, John rose and began to read the paper about his experiences working at the summer resort. His words were labored and slow, but he got his point across about the importance of saving money. When he had finished, Miss Sherman asked to see the paper. John handed it to her reluctantly, knowing it sounded better than it looked.

"John," she said, in front of the class, "your subject matter is good, your delivery needs work, but is passable, and the format is correct. I commend you, since all that was the point of the assignment."

John began to smile before she finished, thinking he had pulled one over on her.

"So all in all, I will have to give your paper an 'A' for content, but an overall 'F' for fail," she continued. The smile disappeared from John's face as quickly as it had appeared.

"But, Miss Sherman, you said...," he stammered.

"There is a comma misplaced, son. You know the rules about punctuation. You always have a comma after the day of the month when you're dating your paper. A misplaced punctuation mark merits a failing grade. This paper will get an 'F'. I will see you after class for additional instruction."

John sat down, humiliated. He couldn't help wondering if it would have been better to take some demerits for staying in bed, rather than have to wear this scarlet letter for all the world to see.

On another occasion, Miss Sherman took some of her male students on a field trip. They launched one of the school's sailboats on the water in the Hampton Roads, and were enjoying their sail, until the weather grew a bit rough. In a gust of wind, the boat tilted with such suddenness and to such an extent that Miss Sherman lost her balance, and was in danger of being tossed overboard. Several willing hands reached out to rescue her and, in great dismay, one of the boys yelled, "Kotcha, Miss Sherman. Don't worry, I kotcha."

"Let me drown, let me drown," she snapped, "but for heavens' sake use good English. It's 'I've *got* you'!" This retort impressed upon all of her students the seriousness of being correct in using the "King's English."

It was about this time that John noticed a young woman in his class, who impressed him with her dignity and grace. Her name was Alice Talbot, and she had come to Hampton on the Norfolk and Western Railroad from a little hamlet called Forest Depot, ten miles from Lynchburg, Virginia. She was smart but not boastful, pretty but not seemingly vain, confident and yet vulnerable. She had the most beautiful hair that cascaded down her back to emphasize her small waist, and her eyes played with John's each time they passed in the hall.

This was John's first encounter with a woman who stirred his emotions, and he was confused, although pleasantly so. He looked forward to his class with her, and he began going out of his way to steal a glance at her whenever he could during the day. He finally got up enough nerve to talk to her after chapel one Sunday evening. As she came out of the building, he was waiting.

"Hello," he offered without much inspiration. He silently scolded himself for sounding so tentative.

"Hello," she replied and kept walking. He scurried to catch up with her.

"My name is John. Oh, I guess you know that; we are in the same English class. May I walk with you?" He couldn't believe he was sounding so stupid.

"If you like," she said, without slowing her pace. She looked at him out of the corner of her eye and smiled to herself. She walked a little faster.

John fell in step beside her increasing his pace. He didn't know what to talk about, so he started whistling. As they walked along the shore, he couldn't help but notice how fresh she smelled, like gardenias perhaps. Now and then he stopped to pick up a few small rocks and throw them into the water, making ripples in the moon's reflection. She slowed to appreciate the view.

"Nice night," he said softly.

"Yes, quite," Alice agreed. "Did you enjoy Bishop Arnett's sermon in chapel tonight?"

"Yes, I liked it a lot. He was funny, and he had some good jokes. I liked it when he said 'Don't put politics in your religion, but put as much religion in your politics as you wish.' That was a good one and good advice too," John said, laughing.

"I liked the one about the little girl who, looking at herself and then at her auntie in the mirror, asked her auntie if she didn't think the Lord did better work nowadays," Alice said, joining John in laughter. "Humor is appropriate sometimes."

They strolled along a path to the campus, while John regaled Alice with the few lame jokes he knew. She giggled politely, and he noticed how she tilted her head when she laughed, how her body moved when she walked. Her small steps were so dainty and quick that she seemed an ethereal apparition in the moonlight. Before John knew it, they were approaching her dormitory.

"I hope we can talk again soon," John said, wishing he had more time to spend with Alice tonight before curfew began.

"Thank you for walking me home," she said, holding out her hand to shake his. "I'll see you in English class." She turned and was gone before he could reply.

The sensation of her hand in his sustained John for the night. It was a small hand, and soft. What, he wondered, was the rest of her like? He shivered, remembering the scent of her, the tilt of her head. If this feeling was anything like what people called love, then he only wanted more of it.

The next day, John waited for Alice before class and took the desk next to hers. When he had difficulty with the reading for the day, she slipped him a note saying that she would help him after class. Later, in the library, Alice patiently explained exactly what Miss Sherman had discussed. John stared intently into her eyes as she talked, nodding his head as if in comprehension, but understanding only how beautiful she was. He was smitten. And if he didn't learn any more than he already knew, he reasoned, then he would continue to need this lovely tutor. But savvy Alice soon recognized John's ploy, and convinced him that if he didn't show improvement, she would have to ask Miss Sherman to work with him.

After that ultimatum, John began to apply himself. He received monthly promotions until, by Christmas, the principal, Miss Elizabeth Hyde, called him to her office to commend him.

"Kenney, your teachers think you are ready for the a promotion to the honors class."

Proud and excited, John promised his teachers, and also Alice, that he would do his best to keep up with his class. He hoped, however, that his efforts would convince Alice that he still needed her as his tutor. Even when he was sure of his work, he sought her out for approval.

Alice was flattered that John needed her and, this in turn, convinced John that he could share his thoughts and dreams with her. He told her about his desire to be a doctor and, like his father, to devote his life to the service of others. Alice never doubted that John could accomplish his ambition, and told him so on numerous occasions. The only other woman who had cared so much about him was his mother, and John was determined not to disappoint either one of them.

At the end of the school year, John was promoted to the A middle class, making him an A junior classman. He had earned three promotions in addition to skipping one level, all of which he had accomplished during the first half of the scholastic year. And he continued to excel. By his third year at Hampton, he had been elevated from private to first sergeant in the battalion of cadets – quite a jump – and was also made junior custodian of his dormitory. To continue to earn money for his education, he took a job as a waiter in the home of one of his teachers, and worked there until he was an A senior classman.

At each summer break and during vacations, John returned to his job as a waiter at White Sulphur Springs – and to a kaleidoscope of situations and experiences. Each season brought a new crop of waiters, but in the summer of John's senior year, he was happy to see among the workers a few of the friends who had been with him for several summers. Seniority had its privileges, and John and his friends, Isaiah and Samuel, were called upon to wait for all of the parties and extravaganzas. When they were cleaning up after one particularly raucous party on the last night of the summer season, the three waiters got hold of some half-empty bottles of left-over spirits. The temptation to experience what they had witnessed summer after summer overcame their usual rationality, and they decided to have a celebration of their own. They finished their duties and agreed to meet behind the greenhouse after the guests went to sleep. Samuel gathered up the liquor bottles, Isaiah swiped the half-smoked cigar butts, and John supplied a whole pan of freshly baked peach cobbler that Miss Glover had set aside for him.

The moon sneaking in and out of the clouds gave the waiters perfect cover as they slipped into the greenhouse unnoticed. They hid behind the fertilizer crates, deeming this the best vantage point both for hiding and looking out, although the aroma was not conducive to a first foray into white people's indulgencies. Caught up in their own adventure, the young men shared their loot while they laughed and mimicked the clientele they had waited on all summer. After a few swigs from the bottles, combined with the smoke from the cigars, they no longer noticed the smell of the crates or the noise they were making. Feeling smug because the whole pan of cobbler was theirs, they delved into the delicious peach pastry with soupspoons from the kitchen, piling their plates high. Isaiah and John laughed as Samuel gobbled up his first plate, peach juice dripping down his chin. As he held out his plate for more, he let out a huge belch, which provoked even more hilarity.

John was in the middle of an imitation of the "hot air balloon man", when the door to the greenhouse flew open. He stopped in the middle of his gyrations, gripped by fear. Everyone looked up to see Mr. Jackson coming toward them, with a look of disbelief and disapproval on his face.

"Well, boys," he said, the famous eyebrow raised in acknowledgement, "I see you are having your own party. Don't let me interrupt you; just pretend I'm not here. Go ahead and finish your cigars, and make sure that you don't leave anything in those bottles. Pass me some of that peach cobbler, and then you all eat the rest of it, and I mean all of it. Don't waste one little morsel of Miss Glover's finest!" He made himself comfortable sitting on one of the crates.

John handed Mr. Jackson the pan of peach cobbler, and he helped himself to a generous portion. The pan was still half full when he passed it back to John. "Here, boys, eat up!" he said downing a spoonful and having great fun at the boys' expense.

As for the revelers, now that the atmosphere had changed, they didn't think their adventure was funny anymore. The combination of cigar smoke, alcohol, and sugary dessert was taking its toll.

"We're full, Mr. Jackson," Isaiah moaned holding his stomach. "I'll be sick if I eat another bite…sir."

"We don't waste good food, son," interjected Mr. Jackson. "Our people never had such delicacies as you are privileged to eat, and you must not take that for granted. Split what's left into thirds and share it with your buddies."

The boys did as they were told, looking more uncomfortable with each spoonful of cobbler. They eyed each other, hoping someone would come up with a solution to get them out of this mess. When the dessert pan was empty, Mr. Jackson urged them on.

"I see some liquor left in those bottles. Drink up, and finish those cigars too. There's nothing like a good cigar and some Kentucky bourbon to top off the evening. That's what real men enjoy."

John felt ready to throw up, but he swallowed hard and kept the contents down. Not wanting to appear unmanly, he lit a cigar butt and poured himself another drink. The other boys followed suit. The expressions on their faces made their true condition all too clear, but Mr. Jackson would not let up. He took out his own full-length cigar and lit it, blowing more smoke in the boys' direction.

"Look at this cigar, boys! One of the hotel guests gave it to me. It is an authentic, handmade, hand-rolled Cuban cigar. Do you know how much these things cost? Why, you would probably pay a week's wages for one of these. Want a draw on this one?"

The boys looked aghast at the offer. Dazed, dizzy, and nauseated, they certainly didn't want to hear about the origins of the cigar. They just wanted to get out of the greenhouse and go back to their cabins.

"Yes, the cigar was invented around the fifteenth century, I think," Mr. Jackson continued. He took another draw and, blowing the thick smoke in their direction, rambled on. "Sir Walter Raleigh was one of the early tobacco pioneers, and we can thank him for his role in the production of tobacco. The American Indians too played their part. Anyone want a cigarette? I have some of those too."

Samuel put his hand over his mouth, but the cause was lost. He jumped up and, not being able to make it to the door, vomited onto the dirt floor. Mr. Jackson remained nonplussed, still smoking his stogie and preaching to the boys. "And you know what Shakespeare wrote about his love of tobacco." Mr. Jackson stood and assumed the position of the esteemed bard and, doffing his hat and lifting his cigar in the air in reverence, recited, "'Thou weed, who art so lovely fair and smell'st so sweet!'" With this imitation, he took a long draw and exhaled the plume of smoke once more into the boys' faces. They moaned audibly.

"Okay, let's go. We still have work to do." With a wave of his cigar, Mr. Jackson directed the boys to clean up and follow him to their cabin. On the way, he continued to talk about tobacco and its success in America, pausing only to give each boy time to regurgitate along the path. When they got back to the cabins, Mr. Jackson had more instructions.

"After you boys clean up, meet me at my cabin, and bring a pencil and some paper."

The boys rolled their eyes and limped off to wash up before arriving at their teacher's cabin. Looking disheveled and physically ill, they sat down on the floor and awaited his instructions.

"Tonight, I hope you have learned a valuable lesson, and I want you to write me a paper on that lesson." The incredulous looks on the boys' faces almost made Mr. Jackson burst out laughing. Turning his back to keep his composure, he put his serious face back on. "Your papers will be titled 'Is the Cost Worth the Price?' In other words, was the cost of that little party you held in the greenhouse worth the price you are paying right now? Is the cost of your pleasure worth the pain of the punishment? Think about it."

"Mr. Jackson," John said with desperation in his voice, "we are very sorry. I can assure you that it will not happen again." He was hoping that contrition would satisfy Mr. Jackson, and render the essay unnecessary.

"That's good, John," the teacher said with a forgiving smile. "Your apology is accepted, but you still have to write the paper. You always have to weigh the consequences before you choose to do something that you know might be wrong. Write that paper, and when you have given me a paper that is perfect, you can excuse yourself and go to bed. I am going to lie down and close my eyes for a while. Wake me in an hour, and I will look at those papers and see who is excused."

With that admonition Mr. Jackson got undressed and into his bed. He was snoring in no time flat.

The boys looked in disbelief at their teacher sleeping peacefully. They still felt sick from the party and its aftermath, and having to write while feeling hung-over wasn't helping their concentration. Nevertheless, they began, and in one hour they woke Mr. Jackson as he had instructed. After one cursory look at the papers, he said that every one was unacceptable grammatically and had to be done over. "Wake me in another hour," he instructed. This process continued until near dawn, when the boys were finally dismissed, and told to get ready to open the kitchen for the day.

Such a sobering lesson was one that none of the boys would ever have to repeat, especially John. Physically feeling the consequences of his action, he found it hard to believe he had ever thought the party would be fun. He couldn't believe that he had been so stupid. As he and the others worked in the kitchen that next day, John shared his feelings.

"I feel horrible," he admitted, "and not just my head and stomach. I was thinking of how my mother would feel if she found out about this stunt. She would whack me good! My ma and pa sacrificed so much for me to get what I have in life, and I almost lost it all. Suppose the overseer had found us instead of Mr. Jackson?"

"Yeah," Isaiah said, putting a cold cloth on his head. "We would have been on the train by now."

"I hope you have learned your lesson, boys," Mr. Jackson commented. "Opportunity doesn't always knock twice."

"I also thought about Mr. Inge, and how disappointed he would be in me," John added, with a look of despair. "He is like my father, and I have never known anyone so moral, clean, chaste or straightforward as he is. I've never seen him commit a dirty or dishonest trick or ever had cause to suspect him of one, either in his business or social relations. He has never used tobacco or strong drink, or told a smutty joke or used a profane or obscene epithet. It was not only a privilege, but an honor, to be under the influence of such a fine Christian gentleman. The thought of disappointing him makes me sick all over again."

"You boys only have to look at some of the guests' behavior here to know what not to do," Mr. Jackson said with a look of disgust.

"You're right," John agreed shaking his head. "I have seen them stagger up the stairs after a night of drinking and then end up sick and with headaches, just like we did. Why didn't we see that?"

"We don't want stupid decisions to derail our progress, boys. You have to take risks in life, but you always have to be accountable and responsible for your own actions. This is just common sense, and the sooner you learn it the better. You all could have lost your opportunity here for the price of a drunken party."

"The cost was definitely not worth the price!" John agreed.

"You boys know that today is our last day here, and we should celebrate that we all made it safely through the summer. I want all of you to remember last night, and not have to learn that lesson again. Now, when we finish here, it's time to go and pack our things and leave the cabins clean like we found them. I hope to see you all back here next year." As Mr. Jackson shook hands with each boy, he smiled, pleased to have shared an important lesson he'd had to learn in his own tempestuous youth.

The end of the summer marked the beginning of John's senior term at Hampton. While happy to be nearly finished, he regretted that this would mean leaving Hampton and, especially, Alice. After spending so much time studying together, they had become quite attached. John had even found a way to increase his time with Alice. When he purchased his ticket on the Southern Railway to return home to Redmonds, he would arrange to detour through Lynchburg, Virginia, so he could stop in Forest Depot and visit with Alice and her family. Her parents, impressed with John's ambition, encouraged the relationship. And with their blessing, John repeated his transportation plan on the way back to school so that he could make the ride to Hampton with Alice beside him.

As John and Alice took the train back to Hampton for the last time, they held hands the entire way. They were lucky to have gotten two seats together in the middle of the crowded coach. As the train lumbered through the Virginia countryside, the monotony of the scenery lulled Alice to sleep, and soon her head was resting on John's shoulder. Every so often, he gave the top of her head a light kiss, oblivious of the other passengers in the coach who smiled at his tenderness. When Alice woke, John was still holding her hand.

"I can't believe school will soon be over, Alice. It seems like just yesterday that we were in English class together." John squeezed her hand to emphasize his point.

"Life is so strange sometimes," she replied. "When I was younger, it seemed as if I had an eternity to do all that I wanted to do in life. Now, as the reality of another phase is coming to an end, I am much more conscious of the rush of time."

"I don't know what the future holds, but I do know that whatever time we have, I just hope that we can spend it together." John looked directly into Alice's widening eyes to gauge her response.

She smiled and boldly returned his gaze. "I hope so too, John," she said. Then she broke into a smile and put her hands on her hips, saying, "God willing and the creek don't rise!" They both broke into laughter at her attempt at humor, imitating an old-time mammy back on the plantation.

Their ride back to school was over too quickly. John accompanied Alice to her dormitory, and then reported to the administration building to pick up his class schedule. At Hampton, all senior students were required to teach for a year in order to complete their senior studies. As he reviewed his schedule, he discovered that he hadn't gotten the teaching assignment he'd applied for. This would mean that he would not graduate on time with his class. The only other option to avoid the loss of credits and time would be to take some additional courses at another school. That would mean time away from Alice, which he abhorred, but it would also mean he would graduate with his class.

John applied to Shaw University in Raleigh, North Carolina, and was soon enrolled. While there, he took additional college preparatory classes, and when he rejoined his classmates who had spent the year "practice teaching" in the Hampton area, John discovered that his additional course work had put him ahead academically. He was able to graduate as the class valedictorian in the class of 1897.

Surrounded by his teachers when it was announced that he was at the top of his class, he basked in their congratulations and well wishes, and they admonished him to continue his good work. John was elated.

"Now, John, your hard work has really paid off. Your success will inspire others of your race, thus perpetuating the importance of learning and achieving," Miss Sherman said to her prize student. "We taught you well."

"I can't say that Hampton taught me how to work hard, Miss Sherman. That honor goes to my mother and father. But Hampton shaped me as a man, and taught me the dignity of learning. I owe you that," he admitted. "I am going to talk about that in my valedictory speech."

"I'll help you with that," Miss Sherman and Miss Hyde said at the same time. Everyone laughed, realizing that John had not asked for help and that, more to the point, Hampton teachers never gave up, not even when their job was done.

John's teachers did indeed help him with his speech, although they stressed that he should emphasize what he thought was the most important message: what he had learned that could benefit others. John met with his teachers in the old English classroom to prepare for the speech.

"I want to talk about the importance of knowing our Negro history and the importance of recognizing our accomplishments from the beginning of time," John said, opening his log book. "Our race can trace our influence back to the earliest civilizations. We built the pyramids, told time by the sun and moon. We influenced philosophy and politics and all aspects of culture. We weathered the boat ride and the auction block, the overseer's whip and the hangman's noose."

"Yes, that's true. And whatever you say, John, stress the importance of stability for the future of your race, and the responsibility of the race to see that that is accomplished. Here are some ideas for you," Miss Hyde offered.

"Let's start with an outline of ideas, John," Miss Sherman said, taking John's book and making a few notes.

The trio worked on the speech for several hours, and John went back to his dormitory to practice his delivery. He thought about how proud his mother would be to see her son giving the valedictory speech, and he clearly realized that Caroline's decision to leave the Kenney farm had set all of this in motion.

Graduation day was magical for the students and faculty. The moment they had all been working toward was finally really here. The decision to hold the commencement ceremony outdoors always depended on the mood of Mother Nature, and on this day she was ebullient. The sun was high in the sky but not hot, and the Hampton waters were still and calm. The campus was lush and green, mowed to perfection for the occasion, and the fresh saltwater smell subliminally signaled the upcoming vacation.

Rows of velvet chairs decorated in the school colors lined the embankment, and fresh spring flowers, also in the school colors, adorned the speaker's podium. As regally dressed students and teachers alike took their places on the promenade, the excitement in the air was tangible. After an introduction of the dignitaries and honor students, it was time for John's speech.

"Commandant Moton, Hampton Institute faculty and honored guests, and my graduating classmates and fellow students, it is my pleasure to speak to you today. Our task is clear. We must create stability for the future of the race." John looked over at Miss Hyde as he uttered these words, and she winked at him.

"Inside our cells are the memories of our race's struggle, from the earliest times up to now, and it is this knowledge that compels us to purpose. We must never forget it. It is because of our ancestors that we find solace and the strength to be honorable men. We have to build the ladder that those coming behind us must climb. This is how we will justify our existence."

Caroline, Mr. Jackson, and Mr. Inge sat in the audience listening to the young man they had all raised in one way or another. Alice and her parents were also in attendance, satisfied with their daughter's choice of a companion. Caroline wiped teary eyes as she looked up to the heavens, knowing that her husband was smiling down on his son with loving pride. It was all worth it, no matter what the sacrifices had been.

After the degrees were conferred, the graduating class formed a chain and held hands. It was announced that they would recite their class poem, written by classmate Wilbur A. Drake. It was titled "A Monument of Love," and it became the graduates' mantra:

Shall we not bravely meet our tasks – and for the right 'ere stand,
Until our influence shall be felt – throughout the southern land…
And to the friends who labor here, let every life prove true,
Not by the words we say to them, but by the work we do.

These dear old scenes where youthful hours, from autumn
    until May,

Were filled with earnest work and toil – we'll from them
    pass away,
But in the mind of everyone a memory shall dwell,
Though with full hearts we say today, to Hampton fare-the well.

John was thrilled to have graduated from Hampton Institute with
honors, but saddened to know that it would be some time before he saw
Alice again. Yet for now, another journey was about to begin. It was time
to go to work.

John Kenney, seated left, and Hampton Graduates. Class of 1897.

Doctor of Medicine

John applied to Leonard Medical School – part of Shaw University – and was accepted. The prophecy written in his log book years earlier had become a reality. Humbled yet proud, John walked onto the campus respectfully, aware of the historical significance of his new school. Leonard Medical School was the first four-year medical school in the country to train Negro doctors and pharmacists. It had been established in 1882 to educate freed men after the Civil War. He stopped in front of Leonard Hall, where he would take his classes. It was regal and imposing, with its Romanesque architecture. The brick building had high arched windows, with decorative stone carvings. Twin turrets on each side of the entrance reminded him of the medieval Christian churches that he had studied in religion class at Hampton. It was the most beautiful building he had seen, and he caught his breath, fully realizing that he had made it to this place.

As he entered the great hall, he was shown by a proctor to the amphitheater, and told where to sit. The seniors occupied the lowest seats closest to the professor. The juniors were one row behind the seniors, and the sophomores were one row higher. The freshmen, or "crabs," had to sit at the very top of the amphitheater in what was called the "Roost."

A senior proctor handed out the curriculum for the semester, as the professor told the students what to expect. All levels of students were taught together, tutorial style, with the more seasoned students assisting the freshmen during their matriculation. The professors at the University were white men, practicing physicians who were impressive in their dedication to making the Negro a capable and intelligent practitioner. These men were the only examples of what a physician should be like, and of what the financial and philanthropic rewards might be. They were big hearted, broad minded, and sympathetic – men who implored the students to study and work hard. They reminded them that their race would come to depend on them for medical care that was almost non-existent in much of the country. This responsibility was not lost on those who had been lucky enough to be accepted into the program, and the academic atmosphere was serious – most of the time.

On the first day of anatomy class, the teacher strode in, dressed in a fine suit and silk tie. This was unlike the white-coated professors that most of the other teachers exemplified. The students were impressed with his dashing personage, and he immediately commanded attention.

He pinned his anatomical charts on the board and turned to face his audience. He looked around the amphitheater and spotted the "crab" sitting next to John.

"Mr. Tatum," he asked, "What is the sternum?"

"Um…," Mr. Tatum mumbled, wiggling in his seat. Twisting and turning, and with all eyes on him, he replied, "It is one of the bones of the lower region that involves sitting." He indicated by manual gesture which part of the lower body he meant.

Amid the raucous laughter, the professor turned to the red-faced Mr. Tatum and admonished, "If you are still sitting on your sternum at the end of this course, the roost will be thusly attached."

John's desire never to be singled out unprepared in this way caused him to make his studies a priority. Although Shaw was one of the first co-educational medical schools, John had no time for socializing. There were a few attractive women in his class, but his loyalty to Alice was stronger than his desire for another female to distract him. Although they were only able to see each other during certain school breaks, and between his summer job and the beginning of the new school year, Alice wrote John almost daily and he wrote back when he could. He lived for her perfumed letters written on fancy pink parchment.

He would sit on the campus under the oak trees with his text books beside him, smelling the letter for some time before opening it, a prelude to the loving sentiments inside:

April 4, 1900

My dearest John,

Only my heart knows how much I miss you. It seems as if time is passing so slowly, although it is already spring. It is beautiful here this time of year, with the dogwoods blooming and the cardinals singing of their beauty. All around me nature is teeming with its glory, reminding me that yet another season is upon us. I wait impatiently for the day when I see you getting off the train. Do you think that we will have more time this year when school is adjourned? Last year, you had to report to the resort earlier than usual, and our time together was so brief. I'm sending you a package by return mail tomorrow with some surprises in it. A few things to eat and a few things to look at, will hopefully keep you thinking of me.

Write when you can,

Lovingly,

Alice

Alice's letters always stimulated John to continue to keep his focus on his purpose for being in medical school. His efforts won him a gold medal in chemistry at the end of his first year, and a candidacy for a physiology prize at the end of his second year. Although his quiz partner nosed him out by one point, he easily won the prize by the end of his third year.

The mutual longing John and Alice had for each other made the times when they were together intense, charged with excitement and passion. At the end of his third year, she came to Leonard Medical School to visit him before he went to his job at the resort. They boated on a lake near the school and took picnics in the campus gazebo, time alone condoned by Alice's parents who had come to know and love John.

He was respectful of this responsibility as he lay holding Alice closely in the tall grass, and it took all of his willpower not to betray it.

At the end of John's fourth year, on March 14, 1901, he received his diploma as a medical graduate from the hands of Governor Aycock, of North Carolina. He had graduated with honors in chemistry and physiology. He remembered that, only eight years earlier, he had been struggling with the King's English. Now he was John Kenney, M.D., Doctor of Medicine.

John (standing third from right), 1901 Leonard Medical School graduates

John went home to spend the longest season with his mother and Margaret that he had enjoyed in many years. Caroline was thrilled that her lifelong hard work and sacrifices had borne fruit, and that she now had a doctor to look after her as she was "slowing down." John was proud that he had been able to provide her with a home of her own, and pleased that he was a son of whom his mother could be proud.

While John studied for his exams and prepared to meet the Virginia State Board of Medical Examiners at Staunton, Virginia, he spent evenings in the cherry grove by their house, enjoying the trees' beauty and fragrance. Watching the development of the cherries added to the pleasure of those days with his family. When the cherries were ripe, he would make an evening meal of them, while he sat among the trees and remembered the poet Wordsworth's commanding words, "Come forth into the light of things/Let Nature be your teacher." John's eyes began to tear as unexpected wistful emotions washed over him; he was reminded of his father's version of Wordsworth's philosophy. John was still the student, increasingly impressed with the process and order of things; and with the knowledge that people will thrive and develop, like nature, if we take what we need from the opportunities of life. Then, we will be able to share our blessings with others. After all, that was the example set by his noble physician teachers who were doing just that.

Finally, the eventful day came. John said goodbye to his family, and left to meet the challenge presented by the Board of Medical Examiners. He was not nervous, just somewhat tense. The ride to Staunton gave him the opportunity to remind himself that he had as much chance of passing his boards as anyone else. He had studied and prepared, and he had confidence in himself, and faith in God. He closed his eyes and actually visualized himself receiving his passing score in the mail.

When he got off the train, he asked directions to the town hall where the examination was to be given. As he neared the building, he saw a number of white candidates outside milling around chatting. No one paid him any attention until he entered the auditorium where the test would take place. A couple of white men stopped talking, and watched him as he looked for a seat. He willed himself not to be fazed. A few others whispered to each other, and John noticed three other Negroes seated in the rear of the room. One was from Howard University, and the other two he recognized from Shaw. John nodded to them politely and strode confidently to the front of the room, taking a seat. Talk had spread about a number of colored applicants who had recently been thrown out of an exam in a Southern state because of "cribbing." John resolved that no such business would happen here.

The auditorium was large, and the seats filled quickly. John took off his coat, and sat facing the examiners, waiting for their orders. He received looks of indignation and curiosity, but aside from the chief examiner raising a questioning eyebrow in his direction, the examination began without incident. The colored applicants were not appreciative of John's boldness – which seemingly branded them as intimidated – and they did not fraternize with him. He had learned at White Sulphur Springs not to depend on comrades-in-arms for acceptance, which would best come from his own belief in himself.

John finished his examinations in the allotted two days, caught the first train westward, and went to his job as a waiter at Warm Springs Resort in the mountains of Virginia. This particular summer, one of his table guests was a Lawyer Mansfield of New Haven, Connecticut. He was impressed with John's ambition, and on the day he was leaving, he called John to his room.

"John, sit down. I want to talk to you." he said as he sat at a desk.

John hesitated, but took a seat at a chair in front of the desk. He felt somewhat awkward, not knowing what Mr. Mansfield wanted, but he was polite.

"I have been watching you since I've been here, John. I am sincerely impressed with you young man. You have the knowledge and understanding of what it will take to be successful in this life. You have graduated from medical school, and yet you are not too proud to be here working as a waiter. I would like to do what I can to help you on your way."

"Why, thank you, Mr. Mansfield. But you don't have to …"

"Nonsense, young man. Be smart enough to accept help when it is given freely to you. I am writing you a check for fifty dollars to help you in whatever way you see fit. If you need more, just write to me at this address."

He handed John the check, and a piece of paper with his address. "Thank you for the confidence," John said, as he helped the lawyer take his luggage downstairs.

The next year and the following year, John received checks from Lawyer Mansfield. He deposited these monies into his bank account, knowing that this capital would support his future efforts. He was happy to accept the help that was offered.

While John was waiting tables at Warm Springs that summer, his license to practice medicine in the state of Virginia was sent to him. When the envelope came, he held it for a few moments, preparing for the news that might be inside. Did he pass or did he fail? John tore off the end of the envelope and pulled the paper out. It read, in beautiful bold calligraphy, John Andrew Kenney, M.D., Doctor of Medicine.

John Andrew Kenney, M.D.

John stared at the license for a long time, elated but suddenly overwhelmed by a feeling of sadness. Tears welled in his eyes and blurred the writing. It was deja vu, he was a little boy who wished his father were alive to be proud of him. John's fellow waiters celebrated his success, changing his mood and praising his accomplishment. He put his license in his trunk, and continued with his waiter's job until the season closed. He returned home to Charlottesville, and prepared to set up his practice there; but it was not too long before he realized that, while his didactic training at Shaw was fine, his clinical work had been practically nil. He realized that he would need practical "hands on" training to round out his education. He applied to Freedmen's Hospital in Washington, D.C. for an internship. The answer was "no"!

John had worked long and hard, had sacrificed and saved, and had been disciplined and determined. He couldn't believe that he had failed to get into the program. He had not failed before. The defeat hit him hard. It was left to Caroline to remind him that people could triumph, even though a dream had to be deferred. "Do what you have to do, until you can do what you want to do," she reminded him. "And don't get impatient. Each day, work toward your goal. And understand this: timing in life is not up to you. Everything happens in its own time and at the right time. Your job is to persevere – no matter what!" This compelled John to look at failure in a new light. Maybe there was something to be learned from this experience. Humility? Resiliency? Adaptability? Patience? Perhaps the door that would open to him in the future would offer more than if the door had opened for him now. He convinced himself that he would continue to move forward toward his goal, no matter what. He decided to go to Washington, D.C. anyway. That would put him near Freedmen's Hospital and Howard University. Somehow, he would find his own opportunities.

John packed his bags, went to Washington, and got a job as a waiter, which provided his board. Classes at Howard University were taught at night: hence, the name "Sun-Downers" given to the Howard graduate doctors of the era. Several of them held government jobs, and practiced medicine only after government hours. John believed that he needed to be where the opportunity was, but since there was still no internship vacancy, he decided to enroll with the senior class of medical students and take an additional year of classes. This would give him some clinical experience. After six weeks of classes with the seniors, an intern dropped out of the program at Freedmen's Hospital, and he was asked to apply. His "failure" had become his opportunity. He was reminded of the time when he had almost cut off his thumb, and his father had taught him that, if he was smart enough to learn from his mistakes, the lesson in failure could be your next opportunity.

Near the end of his internship, John received a letter from his cousin, Dr. H.T. Gamble, of Charleston, West Virginia. He had graduated some time before from Yale Medical School, and he invited John to come and join him in his practice. He felt that, between the two of them, they could control the surgery of the Kanawha Valley; and this was a great temptation, since he was already in established practice. John was seriously considering this when a letter came to him from the Tuskegee Institute, inviting him to take the position of resident physician there.

Tuskegee Institute was a school in Alabama founded by Dr. Booker T. Washington. It was one of the first schools of its kind, dedicated to educating the rural youth and helping them become useful citizens. Now he had something to think about. Should he go with what would be a sure proposition – an already established practice? Or should he take a risk and go with the unknown? This was an opportunity to forge a new trail, but one whose path was a gamble – maybe a step in the right direction…or maybe not. He agonized over his decision, and finally sought the advice of Dr. E.A. Balloch, who was the dean of the medical school. He was also an accomplished surgeon, whom John had worked under for several months, and who had given him some special advantages. He analyzed the situation and gave John his opinion.

"If your cousin really wants you to join his practice, you can do that anytime – the opportunity will remain open. If you want to go to your home and open up a practice locally, you can do that anytime. Tuskegee is the opportunity that is a now-or-never decision. If you don't like it, you can leave. But this is the opportunity that will probably not come around again. If you don't take it, someone else will. You can stay a couple of years, and with a few thousand dollars in your pocket, you can be an independent man and do whatever you like." Independence, that elusive ideal that his father had constantly pursued but never quite grasped, was the temptation John couldn't resist. They both knew that without it, you were never really free.

That settled it. John accepted the call, finished his course at Freedmen's, went home to visit his mother, and registered his license in Charlottesville. Margaret had married a local boy and had begun a life of her own. Andrew also had a family, and still worked the coal mines in West Virginia. John was thankful that everyone was fine, and he knew that it was time for him to make his own life.

Alice had been on his mind a great deal lately. She reminded him of his mother – steadfast loyalty and commitment was their shared badge of courage, and they wore it proudly. He needed to see her. Impulsively he decided that, before he left for Alabama, he would make a side trip to Forest Depot.

When he arrived at the train depot, Alice was waiting for him. It had been too long since they had spent time together. They had corresponded by letter during his time in Washington, and he had forgotten how lovely she was. She came toward him with open arms. Her body was warm and soft as his arms embraced her, and he pulled her closer and tighter. He held her and kissed her deeply, oblivious to the stares and smiles of passers-by.

"It's so good to see you, John," Alice whispered lovingly. "I hope you can stay for a while."

"I've got a lot to tell you," John said earnestly. "Let's talk on the way to your house." As they walked to her wagon, John began to whistle, his unique sign of nervousness.

John put his valise into the back of the wagon, and took the reins to drive. They rode through the majestic countryside sitting close, Alice's arm linked through his. This place reminded John of home. The town was bordered by the Blue Ridge Mountains on the North, with the two Peaks of Otter jutting into the sky at attention. The rains from the mountain peaks snaked down, feeding the local creeks, streams, and springs, which ensured that the lush fields and gardens were constantly in bloom. The Southern side of town had breathtaking views of Smith Mountain Lake. It seemed like paradise. Why hadn't he noticed before?

"I've been offered a job at Tuskegee Institute," he finally said, slowing the wagon down. He talked at her, not to her, looking off into the distance.

"In Alabama?" she asked, already knowing the answer. Alabama was like a foreign country to her. Virginia was as far south as she had ever been.

"Yes. They want me to come and be the resident physician. It may be just for a couple of years. I'll see how I like it." He waited for a response from her, but she didn't react.

"Oh," she said, not looking at him directly, disappointment coursing through her veins as she envisioned more time away from each other.

"I've pretty much decided to take the job. It could be the opportunity I've been waiting for. What do you think?" John asked, looking directly at her.

"After all of your hard work and study, I think that you need to do what will make you happy, John, and only you can know that," Alice answered looking directly at John, trying not to influence him. "This has to be your decision."

"What would make me happy is for you to be my wife, Alice, and come with me. I know that you love your teaching job here, but I am sure that you can do the same thing in Tuskegee." He realized that his proposition sounded awkward, and not how he had meant it to come out. John stopped the wagon and put down the reins. His heart was in his throat.

"I'm asking you if you will be my wife?"

The tears began to well in Alice's eyes, and she took his hand in hers. A tear slid down her cheek as she looked at him, and he pulled her close. "Yes...," she said softly, "yes, I will be your wife, and I will go where you need me to go John. I would go anywhere to be with you." John held her for a long time, stroking her hair as she rested her head on his shoulder. He kissed her lightly, and grabbed the reins.

"Let's go and tell your parents," John said excitedly, as he urged the horse forward. "I want everyone to know how happy I am!"

The family celebrated the engagement that night with a small party. John apologized for not having a ring, but he assured Alice that the next time he saw her she would have it. He decided that he would go to Tuskegee first, and send for her when he was settled.

The next day, he boarded the train for Tuskegee. He walked to the rear platform of the train to get some fresh air. As he watched the Virginia landscape roll by, he realized that a new era in his life was dawning, and he was excited by the challenge. On August 1, 1902, he arrived at Tuskegee Institute, where his real life's work would begin.

Chapter 8

"Tuskegee: The Pride of the Swift-Growing South"

W hen John arrived at Tuskegee Institute, he was surprised to see that it was no more than a few buildings on dirt roads. On the day he began his duties, it was hot and dry, there had been no rain for some time, and the vegetation was parched and yellow. The unforgiving humidity encouraged flies and mosquitoes to compete for attention.

John found his way to the office of Tuskegee's treasurer, a man named Warren Logan. He was sitting at his desk with his shirt collar open, wiping the sweat from his face. John knocked on the open door to announce himself. "Mr. Logan?"

"That's me. How can I help you?" "I'm Dr. Kenney," John said, "and I'm reporting for duty, sir."

"Welcome, Dr. Kenney," Logan said, rising from his chair and crossing the room to shake John's hand. He was a distinguished looking man with a broad smile. "Come in; please have a seat."

"Thank you, Mr. Logan. It's nice to meet you. I received the letter you sent me last month, letting me know certain things before I arrived. You felt that one of the first things I should do is a general inspection. What are your concerns other than the 'slow fever' season?"

"I'll let you see for yourself, John. It's all right if I call you John?"

"Of course it is."

"Well, you never know, with some doctors. A few whom I've met recently behaved like M.D. stood for 'Magnificent Deity,'" Logan said, laughing.

John couldn't help but join in. "Well, my professor at Shaw cautioned us against that grandiose attitude. He said that self-importance is the anesthetic that numbs the pain of the fool. I don't stand on ceremony, Mr. Logan. I'm just happy to be here to help, and to do what I've been trained to do."

"Then we'll get along just fine. And please call me Warren. I'm going to take you over to the men's dormitory," Logan continued, "and get your hiring process started. The first thing you have to do is have a physical examination by the doctor who comes on a temporary basis once a week. After that, we'll go to registration and sign your employment papers. Then, if you don't mind, we have a few young men – and women – here today for their entrance exams and they will need physicals. Do you mind helping out?"

"I'll be happy to…Warren."

"By the way, and just out of curiosity, what is your marital status?"

John chuckled to himself and replied, "I am engaged to be married. I thought I would come and get settled first before I brought my betrothed here."

"Congratulations to you both. I think that was a smart decision."

When John had completed the hiring requirements, Logan took him to meet with some other school administrators and personnel. After assisting the visiting doctor with the student physicals, John decided to do an inspection of the developing campus.

Although he had no special training in public health work or sanitation, the results of the environmental inspection assured John that there was serious work to be done. The eager students from nearby rural areas who came to Tuskegee to learn were ignorant of proper hygiene, appropriate health practices, and sanitary requirements. John's job would be to treat the consequences of this ignorance, as well as teach the students how to prevent such life-threatening – and preventable – results. He had to ensure the health of the population at hand before he could feel free to request assistance from any of his colleagues, if he needed it, much less even think about bringing his future bride to Tuskegee.

First buildings on the campus of Tuskegee Institute

And there were health hazards galore! There were the absence of running water and a sewer system, the use of old wells with wooden curbs and a chain bucket apparatus, dirty and open swill carts, and contaminated swamps. Much too close to the campus of the school were poultry yards, pig sties, dairy barns, slaughter houses, stables, and "open earth closets." The night cart made the rounds in the morning to pick up the human waste from the night before, and the excreta was used as fertilizer to enrich the plots for the growing of vegetables. This attracted buzzards to the poultry yard and other food-bearing areas, and the atmosphere for infection was ideal.

The water source was not a good spring, but an infected stream and reservoir. The shallow wells had old oaken buckets more famed in song than safe in modern use. The wells were curbed part of the way down; and the buckets, drawn up by ropes or chains, upon which, when wet, the attendant liberally washed his hands (whether clean or dirty, and sometimes very filthy) into the oncoming bucket of water or back into the well. The prohibitions contained in any basic sanitary code were non-existent.

John wrote a report to the administration and summed it up by saying, "I now see the 'why' of your annual 'slow fever' visitations." He stated that the matter was urgent, and that conditions were ripe for a smallpox or typhoid epidemic. He gave Logan a copy and asked that he make sure the principal, Dr. Washington, received a copy as well. The report was pigeon-holed without acknowledgement.

John, Booker T. Washington and the Tuskegee faculty

Booker T. Washington was an imposing figure at Tuskegee, as much for his commanding presence as his stature. He was over six feet tall, handsome and charismatic, with piercing dark eyes. His father was a white man, and his mother a former slave. Washington had been born a slave, and had worked at menial jobs until his mother was freed. He was then given permission to seek an education. He had heard of Hampton, a school for coloreds, and he walked two hundred miles to get there. Penniless when he enrolled, he worked as a janitor to pay for his education. Inspired by the principal of Hampton, General Samuel Armstrong, Booker T. Washington developed a self-sacrificing spirit, a philosophy of self-help and moral improvement, and basic Christian values that he espoused and exemplified.

A few days after John had submitted his report, he was walking across the yard when he spotted the school's principal. John caught his eye, but Washington merely nodded John's way and kept on about his affairs. A short time later, however, he sent for John, requesting his presence at the principal's office. Nervously, John put on his coat and hurried to his appointment.

The door was open, and John could see Washington sitting at his desk, reading a book with his feet propped up. Washington glanced up when John arrived and greeted him with a warm "Good morning, Dr. Kenney." Before John could reply, Washington stated, "Every Monday, when I am at the school, I wish you to come in and look me over. Just stop in and let my secretary know you are here to check me."

"Yes, sir," John said respectfully. "I'll be happy to do that."

Washington sat down and went back to reading his book. John stood silently for a moment and then, sensing he had been dismissed, left the room. He made a mental note to remember to check on the principal every week.

John checked on Washington every Monday for the next few weeks. The principal was in good condition and had no complaints, and John began to wonder why the check-ups were necessary. There were so many other things he needed to do. As time went by, he grew careless and missed a few appointments. Before long, John got a message on a Thursday from the principal's office, saying that his presence was required. He hurried over.

Booker T. Washington was looking out the window when John arrived. He turned as John entered and said, "Dr. Kenney, regarding our Monday appointment, let's make it at two o'clock every week so that both of us know how to schedule our time. This way we will both be clear on our obligations." Still standing, and actually towering over John, Washington looked him squarely in the eyes, making sure that the young doctor understood him clearly.

John sensed that this was the last time he would be reminded. "I will be here without fail, Dr. Washington," he said resolutely, meeting the principal's gaze. "You can count on me."

John took seriously to his task, and not only did he see Washington on Mondays, but as the principal's schedule grew heavier, Washington had more frequent need of medical supervision and treatment. Many nights, John was called to his bedside to relieve his suffering, and John was grateful to have redeemed himself in his superior's eyes.

Washington became John's tutor in many things, and John his. They had a lot in common, and learned from each other. Both came from humble beginnings, were progeny of the legacy of slavery, and had worked hard and sacrificed to achieve what they had. And they had a common understanding of their mission in life – service.

Booker T. Washington was a practical Christian. He did not put nearly as much stress on the "Glory, Glory Hallelujah!" within those pearly gates, as he did on the everyday fitness of things on this side of the river. He believed in clean living with all that the term implied – clean morals, a clean body, a clean home, and clean surroundings. He believed in the toothbrush and the bathtub. He considered these two utensils the most advanced agents of civilization. He believed that in order to wear the White Robe in the Bright Mansions above, it was necessary to go through a little preparation in this mundane sphere. He believed in absolute cleanliness.

To make a point, Washington liked to tell a story to the students in chapel. His subject was an "old time" colored minister who was preaching from the pulpit. His subject was "Cleanliness is next to Godliness." Having announced his text, the minister leaned forward over his open Bible and, looking down over the rims of his spectacles at the chaotic mass of humanity before him, repeated the text with emphasis: "Cleanliness am next to Godliness. Dat's zackly what de Wurd sez. But if dat am true, dis congregation sho' am lost." With every telling, the chapel erupted in laughter as Washington imitated the "down home" preacher.

He may have told this story as a joke, but he was serious and deter- mined about its message, and one could tell by his demeanor that he expected only success. The raising of an eyebrow conveyed more than words. All who came in contact with him learned that he was a giant of a man because his expectations matched his reputation.

John was honored to be the physician not only for Tuskegee Institute, but for two of the most eminent gentlemen in the Negro race in America, Booker T. Washington and Dr. George Washington Carver. Dr. Carver was as self-effacing as Washington. He had discovered over three hundred uses for products made from the peanut and refused to patent them. He said of his inventions, "God gave them to me. How can I <u>sell</u> them to somebody else?"

George Washington Carver and friends

Finding himself in the company of these two esteemed leaders, John felt compelled to conquer the challenges and rigors of his new assignment. He had accepted the position of Resident Physician for fifty dollars a month, room and board. He was soon to realize that his duties would include a private practice, one that would cover a wide area of southern Alabama country, including the surrounding towns of Opelika, Tallassee, and Kowaliga.

This practice spanned a broad territory, generally extending at least thirty-two miles from the school. In those pre-automobile days, John would drive either a one- or two-horse buggy. For his nearby practice, he drove one horse, but for the fifteen to thirty-two mile trips, and when the road was "heavy," he drove two. Sometimes he had a boy with him, but often he rode alone.

He also had acquired a dog that would accompany him on long trips in the fields and woods, hunting or hiking. John believed that man had no more faithful companions than his dog and his horse – as long as they cultivated each other. So as long as John kept his horse moving, the dog would continue his expeditions in wide circles. If John got tired and lay down for a nap, the dog would cease his excursions and sit by him, his keen eyes and pointed nose surveying every direction until John's nap ended. This was, in John's view, an example of unconditional love between creatures of God at its best.

John's usual horses from the school barn were equally reliable. On many a night he found himself miles into the country, with the sky so dark that he could not see the road. At times, he knew that he was following the road only because he could see the faint light of the stars shining overhead between the treetops. He trusted his horses instead of himself and gave the reins to them. A spiritual communication between man and beast allowed them to rely on each other, and a mutual trust and dependency sustained them. Never once did one betray the other.

Under such conditions one dark and stormy night, John came upon a bridge. His horse snorted and stopped. John did not urge him but got out of the buggy, took a stick, and felt his way ahead until he reached the bridge, which was covered with water. With the aid of the stick, he explored the bridge, found it intact, and then returned to the horse and patted his nose to assure him that everything was all right. Taking him by the bridle, John walked by his head and they crossed the creek safely.

On another stormy night, his horses refused to take the flooded ford, and John sought out a nearby farmer who knew the "holes" and "shadows." After exploring the passage with his mule, the farmer came back and said to the horses, "Follow me." Instinctively, the animals trusted his voice and obediently followed him and the "dumb" mule through the water.

The farmers and their families who lived in places so far from towns that only mediocre care was available, looked to the country doctor to perform "miracles" in the face of overwhelming illnesses and intolerable living conditions. And John looked to God to help him.

One afternoon about four o'clock, a man came and asked John to attend to his wife, who was in childbirth. John arrived to find that her labor was very slow. He waited until eight o'clock and, with the aid of three midwives, prepared for the forceps delivery. The only light in the cabin was from the pine knots burning on the hearth, so the bed was drawn across the floor in front of the fire. There was nothing in which to heat the water but a skillet, which in those times was an iron contraption with three legs that was used for baking cakes, biscuits, and the like on an open hearth fire. The only containers for water were a two-quart basin, apparently as old as the mother, and a wooden tub.

John prepared his instruments. When he was ready, he assigned each of the three midwives her station and duties. Then he administered the chloroform. When the woman was asleep, he handed one of the midwives the chloroform bottle. He noticed that two of the women had retreated, and he now had only one to act as the anesthetist and the assistant. He applied the forceps and, with gentle pressure and guidance from above, the baby was delivered without major complications, other than a perineal laceration to the mother. John repaired this, and left the sleeping mother and child with the elated father.

Feeling blessed to have delivered a healthy soul into the world, John climbed into his buggy to make his way back to town. He did not have his faithful horse with him that night and, instead, drove a strange youngster whose behavior did not give him much comfort. The night was pitch black. There were no lights on the buggy. A field hand led John across the yard to the main road and said goodnight. As soon as they were on the road, the horse plunged for high speed; but from his actions, John decided that the tie reign was down and the horse was stepping on it. He brought him to a halt, got out, felt for the rein, and tied it up. But being as foxy as the youngster, he had kept the reins in his hands. No sooner did the horse know that the obstacle had been removed than he dashed forward, but John swung on the reins and brought him down.

In his turn, the horse danced and lunged, not letting John back into the buggy. There they were, in the black of night out somewhere in the country, and this horse was letting John know who was in charge.

From years of growing up on a farm, John knew he could match wits with a horse. He remembered, first of all, that horses were nearly always hungry. That was the solution. He led the youngster a little distance and turned him towards some grass on the embankment. That left an opening between the wheels. While the horse ravenously cribbed the grass, John jumped into the buggy.

It seemed that the horse became more riled and vile because John had tricked him. The animal tried to fly, and John prayed that the road was theirs at that time of the night. Positioning himself in the middle of the seat directly behind the horse, he applied his full weight and strength against the bit, but even then the horse fairly flew. John's only aim was to keep him in the middle of the road. With that speed, and with his will pitted against the horse's, they reached the barn in what must have been a record time, and John turned horse and buggy over to the night man. The next day, exhausted but victorious from the experience, John sent word to the barn inquiring as to how his "youngster" was doing. He was told that the horse had not gotten up yet – an indication that he too had been affected by their war of wits.

The work of country doctor was complemented by John's work as resident physician. This was a lofty title for a very primitive situation. At this point, there was no infirmary, and students who were ill had to be treated in their rooms. There was no central location for patients, and Tuskegee did not have the funds to begin any construction. John had started a nurse training program in another building, but he needed a training facility where the students could get "hands on" experience. Then Washington, traversing the country to solicit philanthropic contributions to continue his work, inspired a Mrs. Bennett of New Haven, Connecticut, to step forward and donate funds for a small, two-story frame hospital – Tuskegee's first!

The building had a small room used as a business office, a slightly larger room set up as an infirmary with enough space for about six patient beds, a kitchen, another room for staff, and an operating room.

The operating room was a ten- by twelve-foot wooden room, with large windows to provide adequate sunlight and allow proper ventilation for the pot- bellied stove. A few months later, as John was becoming acclimated to his position, the school built a small addition to the little hospital and made a few other changes. This structure became known as Pinehurst. At that time the only patients were students and, vary rarely, teachers; no "outside patients" had ever been treated at Pinehurst.

With the addition of the campus hospital, John's confidence in his ability to handle certain illnesses increased, and he was satisfied that this facility would provide the training his nursing students sorely needed. He was still worried, however, about the possibility of a more widespread outbreak of illness. There were several persons who were pockmarked from a past outbreak of smallpox, and John took hold of this evidence and continued to hammer the importance of avoiding, or at least containing, this dreaded disease. He preached health and sanitation. He ordered the removal of manure piles (fly breeders), and other rubbish and accumulated filth. He urged a program of "clean up!" Clean up everywhere! Clean and drain the swamps; and clean out the breeding places of flies and mosquitoes. Since the "earth closets" were a necessity, they were improved by cleaning and fly proofing. He urged the extensive use of screens, but he knew that these measures were like putting a bandage on a ruptured blood vessel. They would never hold.

As the school year opened, vaccinations against small- pox were mandatory. Dormitories were cleaned and fumigated, and many helpful improvements were instituted, but they were too slow.

In John's second year, his medical skills were tested. He became suspicious when he was called to the dormitory of a sick student who, he was told, was hiding in a closet and wouldn't come out. John went to his room to investigate this strange behavior. He walked into the room where the shades had been pulled down, and where there were no sheets or pillows on the bed. The fluid-stained mattress was certainly the source of the offensive odor that permeated the room. John heard some rustling in the closet, and he opened the door.

Tuskegee Health Wagon

"No! No! Close the door," shouted a voice from the darkness. John could see a figure covered with the bed sheets, and clutching the pillow as if it were a baby.

"Son, I am Dr. Kenney. I am here to examine you. I need you to come out."

"Leave me alone. I am being punished. God told me not to come out because I have sinned. I am a snake in the Garden of Eden, and I will shed my skin. Then I will get the word."

John could tell that the student was either out of his mind or, perhaps, delirious with fever.

"Son, you will have to come out now, or I will have to come in and get you. I'm here to help you."

"All right, I'll come out. You tell God that you told me to. He won't be mad at you."

The figure began to undrape his sheet. As he emerged from the closet, John could see that he was covered in his own waste. He took the boy's arm to assist him from the floor. His skin felt hot and sweaty. By touch, John guessed that his fever was over 103 degrees. The patient was totally disoriented and agitated. John made him sit in a chair by the window so that he could get a good look at him. He was taken aback. The student's mouth and tongue were covered with red spots and foam. He moaned constantly, as if he were in great pain. John knew at once that this might be the precursor to full-blown smallpox.

He called for some of the other students to get a stretcher and some facemasks, so that they could help him move the patient to the hospital to be quarantined. John snatched the linen curtains off the window to cover the boy from head to toe so as not to frighten the other students, and to protect them at the same time. He made sure that no one touched the patient. Even so, living in such close proximity had put the other students at risk, and it was probably already too late to stop the disease from spreading.

"You gentlemen go back to your rooms," John said once the patient was settled in an empty room at the hospital. "We'll take care of him now. I need to know at once if anyone else has symptoms of any kind, understand?"

"There are two others on the third floor who are sick, Doc," one student said. "I think they have the measles."

"Let's go see them," John said. "I need to see them."

An examination of the two additional students revealed the same symptoms. John was beginning to foresee a campus-wide epidemic, but he didn't sound the alarm yet. He knew that the only treatment was isolation and prayer, and the hope that the immune system was more powerful than the disease. He informed the administration of the possibilities, and the students were asked to remain in their rooms until further notice. Everyone had to be quarantined until the staff could separate the sick from the well.

The next day it was clear. The dreaded smallpox epidemic had arrived. One of the quarantined students was covered in pustules where there had been only a red rash the day before. He was hallucinating, and had to be restrained to prevent self-injury or the chance of his injuring someone else. John wasn't sure that the boy was going to make it.

More and more students and teachers became ill. John felt the pressure of numerous lives in his hands. He knew how dreadful the outcome could be. His stalwart staff took shifts in the dormitory, and they rotated the patients to different floors based on their severity. For three weeks, they battled the disease. Those who had not been affected were moved into other buildings. Those who were recovering helped to nurse those who were sick. The recent improvements with respect to sanitation and hygiene helped to stem the spread of the disease, but not to prevent it. Vaccinations were given wholesale and, by isolation and quarantine, the school emerged with twenty-three cases and no deaths.

The town of Tuskegee had only one case. Local officials asked that he be admitted to the school's quarantine station. It was agreed, and the patient, who was confined to his bed, had to be transferred. John ordered a school carriage and driver to go to the patient's house to pick him up. As they were preparing to depart, the driver discovered that they were to pick up a smallpox patient, and refused to complete the mission. Disgusted, John said that he would go and get the patient in his own buggy. The sheriff of the town offered to accompany him, but when John got within sight of the patient's house, the sheriff virtually disappeared.

John drove up to the house and went inside. The patient was asleep and had his head covered with a sheet. As he heard John approach, he let his covering down, and the sight and the odor were so offensive that they initiated flashbacks of John's traumatic memories of cleaning the vat at Hampton. "I'm Dr. Kenney," John said, taking deep breaths to control his reaction. "I'm here to help you. Stay right here; I will be back."

John got into his buggy and drove to the school barn. There he ordered a one-horse wagon loaded with straw bedding, and then he drove to the quarantine station. He asked for one of the patients recuperating from smallpox to accompany him. When he reached the house this time, he told the convalescent to go in, get the patient, and drive him to the quarantine station. Thus he was able to get his mission accomplished without exposing himself or anyone else to the disease.

There were approximately 1,800 students enrolled at Tuskegee, and the staff had to work night and day to round them up for smallpox vaccinations. Ignorance surrounding the disease had some people believing that they could get it from the vaccination. Others, not having experienced an epidemic before, did not realize the seriousness of the matter and the need to be vaccinated, even after this outbreak. John and his helpers had to go to classrooms during the day and make the rounds of the dormitories at night. One evening, they went to the men's dormitory, and the occupants would not open the door. Although they heard muffled voices, they could not elicit a response. John looked around and spotted a fire hose hanging on the wall. There was an open transom over the door, and John told one of the male nurses to hoist the hose to the top. On a given signal, they turned the hose on full force, and the "wet rats" finally emerged. That was the last time John had to "convince" any students how important this was, or had to take such drastic measures to save lives.

This was Tuskegee's last smallpox epidemic, and the outcome was better than John had expected it to be. The community was finally becoming health minded, but progress was slow. While major advancements were made in sanitation and health care, the school was still very vulnerable. Even so, they had come a long way, and John felt that it was safe enough now to bring Alice to Tuskegee Institute as Mrs. John Kenney. They had a small wedding in Forest Depot and took the train to Tuskegee on the same day.

Alice had no qualms about coming to Alabama, and to an area even more rural than her hometown in Virginia. She had been teaching some local youths in Forest Depot, and offered to help with Booker T. Washington's efforts in any way she could. Her sweet disposition made her a favorite in the Tuskegee community, and John could not have asked for a more loyal companion or tireless helper. She never complained about the long hours he had to put in at the school, or about his traveling around the countryside. She would often say, "I knew the sacrifices that I would have to make being married to a doctor. I was not naive when I said 'I do.'"

While John was doing his job, Alice was keeping their home, assisting at the school, and working in the community to acquaint people with her husband's health initiatives. Then, shortly after her arrival in Tuskegee, John received word that his beloved mother had passed away. He and Alice traveled to Virginia to bury her.

The train ride to Virginia gave John time to reminisce about the woman who had charted the course for his future. Even though in recent years they had lived miles apart, Caroline's unconditional love was always close, and her spirit had sustained him on many an occasion. What was it in her that made her know he needed to leave the farm to achieve his greatest potential? What had she seen in her life that allowed her to think so freely – especially since she had been born in slavery? The realization that both of his parents were gone, and that now he was alone in the world, was sobering. He reached over and took Alice's hand. *She is my family now*, he thought.

Caroline was buried next to the house that she loved, and beside the cherry grove that John had planted for her. Alice and John returned to Tuskegee, where John immersed himself in his work to numb the pain of his loss.

During one summer, John traveled to Chicago to do some post-graduate work. Alice remained in Tuskegee to continue her tutoring, not wanting to interrupt her work with some local elementary school students, and to allow John to concentrate on his courses unfettered. It was a refreshing change for John to be in a city that had more sanitary conveniences, and made health care services available to the population in general. He was able to focus on his studies and not worry about open earth closets and rural inconveniences. He had a reprieve from the reality of what he had chosen to do. Just as his training ended, John received a telegram from his head nurse at Tuskegee. She wrote, "Sixteen cases of slow fever in the hospital." He wired back: "I knew it would come. I'm taking the first train for Tuskegee."

Upon his arrival, he found eighteen undiagnosed cases of an illness he did not have a definitive diagnosis for, and they were still coming. The patients had fevers, stomach pain, and weakness, and some exhibited a flat, rose-colored rash unlike the smallpox pustules. He knew that, at this rate, they would not have enough space in the hospital to quarantine everyone. He had extra cots set up in the hospital, including in the staff quarters, to hold as many patients as possible. The overflow would have to be housed in outside quarters in the grove adjacent to the hospital.

The weather was hot. The hospital was overcrowded, and the tents and cots in the grove were full. The patients were placed between two sheets without any other clothing for easy access and sponging. It seemed as if they had just broken one fever when another patient spiked an even higher one.

"Get that basin over here nurse; this one is 104! Send for a new set of sheets; these are soaking wet." John suspected that this epidemic would be worse than the last, but he kept his thoughts to himself to avoid widespread panic. "Someone bring me some fresh water, now!"

Before he could finish his sentence, someone handed him a bucket of water. As he looked up to receive it, he realized that it was Alice who was helping him.

"I'm sorry, honey, I didn't know you were here. How long have you been working?"

"I've been here all day, John. I didn't want to distract you, but I wanted to help."

John would have insisted that she go home, but she had already exposed herself to the disease. She wore a mask and gloves, and he prayed that the precautions had protected her.

John had read a paper from one of his colleagues touting the use of Cupric Arsenite, a new treatment for typhoid fever. He began giving the most severe patients one-one hundredth of a grain every four hours. He gradually increased the dose every four hours, depending on tolerance, and began to see improvement in some of the patients. There were others who had severe constipation, and those patients were administered boric acid enemas to keep the bowels clear. For those who could tolerate food, John ordered a diet of beef extract, milk, strained soup, and lemonade. Yet, some of the patients John thought were getting better seemed to relapse into an even more detrimental state. He surmised that they must have experienced some kind of re-absorption of the deadly bacilli for this to happen so quickly.

The head nurse, who had begun sponging an unconscious patient, looked worried and whispered quietly to John, "Dr. Carver sent word that he thinks the problem started with the food preparation in the dining hall. There were some fruits and vegetables from a new farm, and he feels that they were not washed properly. He also noted that the screens in the kitchen needed replacing and that flies were contaminating the food also."

"We need a definitive diagnosis," John whispered. "I will have to report this to the state authorities immediately. I think it may be typhoid."

The nurse stood silent at the sound of this word, and made the sign of the cross. "Lord help us," she said as she went back to her work.

John looked up to see a few bodies covered with sheets. He counted five and said a silent prayer to God. Please let that be all of them.

That same day, he reported the epidemic to the State Health Officer, and soon a bacteriologist from Mobile was sent to verify the diagnosis microscopically. The health officer arrived to inspect the cases, of which there were now about forty, and as he toured the premises, the grave look on his face foretold his recommendation. John took the gentleman to report to Booker T. Washington, who listened quietly as the epidemiologist listed sanitary deficiencies and verified that the illness was indeed the dreaded – and deadly – typhoid fever.

"Dr. Washington," the inspector stated, looking grave, "I have made a tour of all of the facilities on the campus. I agree with Dr. Carver that the problem started this time in the food hall. The produce was contaminated, and I am not sure that the food handlers were as sanitary as they needed to be. However, you have other serious health violations also. Your water supply is possibly contaminated. There is too much manual handling of the water, and it is too open to the environment. All of these things contributed to the outbreak. I will have to issue a citation."

Washington appeared calm and unmoved throughout this report, and when the officer was finished, he replied, "Yes, Doctor, everything you have told me is true, and it has already been pointed out by

Dr. Kenney. We have been so busy with other developments of the school that we have not given his recommendations the attention that they obviously should have had. We have been neglectful."

True to the honest and virtuous man that John knew him to be, Washington made no excuses, nor any attempt to divert responsibility or place blame. This completely exonerated John and reaffirmed Washington's confidence in his resident physician. John knew that here was a man he would continue to admire – and trust.

The effect of this epidemic was instantaneous. The Board of Trustees took steps to ensure the correction of the evils John and his staff had been fighting. The night soil cart was replaced with a garbage bin, and the wooden curbs on the wells were replaced with terra cotta. Eventually, the water buckets were replaced with pumps, and the tops of the wells were sealed. Many hours were spent in meetings and lectures held in the chapel and at Sunday schools, public forums, and any other venue John could find in which to teach health and hygiene to all who would listen.

With its new water supply, sewage system, bathhouses, and swimming pools, along with isolated slaughter houses for animals, a new Tuskegee campus was established. A few summers later, when John examined a patient and recognized a possible typhoid case, he immediately quarantined the man and his family and requested a curfew for the students until the disease could be identified. The patient had come to Tuskegee from Opelika a few days before, and John determined that this locale was the source of the illness. Based on the education that the Tuskegee public had been given, and the sanitary measures they had taken that were now bearing fruit, Tuskegee had only fifty-six cases of typhoid and no deaths.

John received praise and congratulations for the changes that had been made, and his reputation for excellent care spread within and outside of Tuskegee. Alice was proud of her husband and the progress that was being made in Tuskegee, even though she worried that he was immersing himself too much in his professional duties. She reminded him that one should balance the professional and the private life, and he promised her that he would – soon.

As advancements were made at the school and its reputation for a broad education gained respect and popularity, Booker T. Washington commissioned the poet Paul Laurence Dunbar to write a song in 1906 that expressed the sentiments and character of Tuskegee. Dunbar titled his work "The Tuskegee Song":

Tuskegee, thou pride of the swift-growing South
We pay thee our homage today,
For the worth of our teaching, the joy of thy care,
And the good we have known 'neath thy sway.
Oh, long-striving mother of diligent sons,
And of daughters whose strength is their pride,
We will love thee forever and ever shall walk
Thro' the oncoming years at thy side.

Chapter 9

The Word Spreads: A Real Hospital!

With all the improvements to the school's medical services, confidence in the hospital's medical capability grew rapidly among members of the Tuskegee community. More and more patients sought medical services, and John began building relationships with new colleagues in the medical profession.

Two white physicians, brothers Ludie and Frank Johnston, were practicing medicine in the town of Tuskegee and providing care to the local white community. Believing themselves guardians of the public health, they pledged to do charity work in the colored community. Ludie heard about John's efforts at the John A. Andrew Hospital and went to the campus one day to meet him. Ludie was disconcerted by the small building that served as a hospital for the colored people, and he said a silent prayer of thanks to God for the privilege of being born white and on the other side of town. He arrived at John's small office and announced himself to the woman who served as both secretary and the nurse on duty.

"Excuse me. My name is Dr. Ludie Johnston. I am here to meet Dr. Kenney. Is he available?"

"Well, sir, he has a surgery in an hour," she replied slowly, not looking up from a medical chart, "and that means that he will be coming back from the woods in about five minutes."

"Excuse me?" Ludie asked, surprised at her explanation. "The woods?"

"He always walks in the woods before an operation. That's just his habit. Have a seat; he'll be here in a minute." The secretary went back to her work never noticing Ludie's incredulous expression.

Ludie took a seat. He had a feeling that this colored doctor was practicing a different kind of medicine from what he had been taught. He remembered the "root-docterin'" of the old colored woman who had raised him, and he began to feel uncomfortable. A few minutes later, John appeared at the door looking refreshed and relaxed.

"Dr. Kenney," Ludie said hesitantly, standing up and holding out his hand, "I'm Dr. Johnston from Tuskegee proper. I am here to introduce myself."

"Welcome, Dr. Johnston," John said. "Please come into my office. Have a seat."

"Your secretary told me that you were in the woods, Dr. Kenney?"

"Oh, yes, Dr. Johnston. It's a habit I got into growing up on my family's farm in Virginia. Whenever I have a pressing matter to contemplate or a complex procedure to think through, I take a walk in the woods, appreciating the cycle of life and its inherent importance. I spend some time meditating with Mother Nature, and this gives me the confidence to hold the life of another human being in my hands. It's just a spiritual habit that keeps me grounded."

"Oh, I see," Ludie said in a guarded tone, rethinking somewhat his initial opinion. "I'm happy to meet you."

"Likewise, Dr. Johnston," John said. "Let me show you around our little hospital."

Ludie couldn't believe his eyes. The operating theatre was a ten-foot by twelve-foot space with plaster walls and wooden floors. A little wood-burning pot stove provided the heat. A wash boiler on the kitchen stove was used as a sterilizer. The operating table was placed near a large window with no shade in order to gain adequate light, as there was only one bare light bulb hanging from the ceiling. Ludie looked out of the window to see the secretary-nurse running to take the white sheets off of a laundry line ahead of the approaching rain. "Lord have mercy," he said to himself as he absorbed the primitive conditions at Pinehurst. He began to feel as if he might be getting in over his head by offering his assistance in these backward conditions, but he quickly decided to do what he could.

"Dr. Kenney, I am here not just to meet you, but to see if we can work together. I've been practicing here for many years and know the people and the territory. I may be of help to you."

"I'd be grateful for any help you have to offer, Dr. Johnston, and please call me John."

"And I'm Ludie."

After that day, John and Ludie conferred on several cases and began to develop a mutual respect. John appreciated the counsel, and Ludie felt that he was helping a backward people as God had ordained him to do. Their relationship, a first for that time, did not go unnoticed on either side of town.

Ludie was visiting John on campus one day, when their medical discussion was interrupted by a shriek from John's secretary. As they rushed out of John's office to her side, they encountered three students; one bloodied and held up by the other two. The injured student had his hand bandaged in a towel, and appeared to be losing consciousness.

"What happened here?" John asked, as they laid the partially delirious student on a table. The bandage was rapidly turning from red to crimson, as blood from the wound seeped into the towel.

"He cut his hand with a saw in the machine shop," one of the boys said. "He almost cut his fingers off! It's bad, it's really bad!"

"We'll have to operate right away," John told his nurse, as he unwrapped the hand for a better look. "And send for my medical students right away!"

As the complexity of the injury became clear to both physicians, Ludie felt compelled to make a reluctant offer.

"Let's take him to the hospital in Montgomery. My buggy is right outside. I think I can get him in the ambulatory room through the back door of the hospital and do the surgery myself. He can be brought back here to recuperate."

"There is no guarantee that the white hospital will take him," John said, "even if you make the trip. And the trip will take too long. He's lost too much blood already." He reached into his bag and found a strap that he applied to the student's arm as a tourniquet. "This boy needs surgery *now*."

Ludie was dubious that the surgery would be successful in such a limited surgical environment and without the proper equipment, but he acquiesced. He was as curious to see how John would handle this surgery, as he was eager to avoid a commotion in Montgomery by bringing a colored patient to the white hospital.

"All right, I'll assist you by giving the anesthetics," Ludie said, taking off his overcoat. "Let's go."

John had one nurse present in the surgical suite, as well as two medical students in training from Meharry Medical College. After making sure that the suite was scrubbed and cleaned meticulously, John ordered the room sprayed with a carbolic acid solution from a compressed air tank to ensure sterility. He explained to the student interns every step of the process from beginning to end so that they could understand not only the surgeon's responsibility, but the correct protocol for everyone involved. Ludie listened quietly.

The patient was brought into the operating room, and placed on the table in the supine position so that Ludie could begin to anesthetize him with ether. John continued his teaching while the patient was being sedated.

"Gentlemen and Nurse Gibbs," he began, "surgical technique reduced to its simple analysis is just plain, everyday cleanliness, plus surgical cleanliness. The first consideration in surgical technique is to get clean and keep clean. No one can contemplate aseptic surgery against filthy conditions. Location is of the first importance and must provide good drainage, healthy surroundings, sunlight, and fresh air. Also important is the absence of foul odors, dust, smoke, and dampness."

John could see that Ludie was nodding in approval, and even though a mask covered Ludie's face as he administered ether to the patient, his wide eyes revealed his surprise at John's thoroughness with antiseptics.

"In spite of all that is known of infection and immunity," John continued, "there are yet many things unknown. We know, or think we know, that we will get an infection of our wounds if we permit their contamination with non-sterile extraneous material. It is generally accepted surgically that certain observances are necessary in our operative work in order to get satisfactory results."

By now all eyes were on John, including those of the guest surgeon, who was staring intently. John felt a bit like a Shakespearean actor in the round with a captive audience.

"In preparing for an operation, it is necessary to trim the nails short, push back the cuticle, and, with no sleeves present below the elbow, scrub the hands with a strong laundry detergent or green soap, hot water, and a stiff brush. This is the most important part of the preparation and should receive due time and attention. Five minutes and more are necessary.

"Strict attention should be given to the cleanliness of the roots and ends of the nails and fingers and the flexures of the fingers. After rinsing, this procedure should be repeated, followed by a ninety-five percent alcohol rinse to dissolve away the fats from the soap. Then we will soak in a one to three-thousand bi-chloride solution, followed by immersion in an iodine solution. Don't consider the antiseptic solution some kind of holy water that you only have to pass through to be made clean. You must dwell in it five minutes or more for contracted effect, and then follow with another rinse in sterile water."

"Excellent surgical prep and antiseptic precaution," Ludie remarked to no one in particular. He looked up at John questioningly.

"I studied antiseptic conditions during my internship at Freedmen's Hospital in Washington, D.C.," John said, anticipating the question. "Under circumstances like these it becomes more important than ever."

"Are you ready for your gown, Dr. Kenney?" Nurse Gibbs asked.

"Yes, Nurse Gibbs." John held out his arms, while still explaining the procedure.

"As you can see, during the hand preparation, a nurse or an attendant puts on the head piece and face mask for the operator. At no stage should the operator touch or pick up a non-sterile object, such as turning on the water or handling soap containers, dirty soap, or a brush. After the final rinse in sterile water, he is ready for his gown. A sterile nurse opens it for him from the front, and he slips his hands and arms through the sleeves, like this, and a non-sterile nurse ties the strings from behind. Are there any questions so far?"

"Your hands are still wet," remarked one medical student.

"Very observant, young man," John replied. "The nurse will now give me a sterile towel to dry my hands. You notice that I do this after the gown is on and not before. I will then have my hands dusted with sterile talcum powder, and will put on the sterile gloves. The doctor should touch nothing that has not been sterilized, and whoever does so at any stage of the operation has broken his technique and should immediately re-sterilize. There is a reason for every step, and this technique is ample for any surgical procedure.

"Nurse Gibbs," John said, turning to her, "few things are more annoying to the operator than to stand helplessly with sterile hands and wait for nurses or other assistants to perform their duties. The faithful, trained, capable nurse will see to it that this seldom happens. She goes carefully over all regular preparations and prepares for any eventualities."

"Yes, doctor," the nurse agreed.

John looked at Ludie directly, while continuing to address the entire group.

"My maxim is, not one drop of ether more than is absolutely necessary for the patient. Patients do well and recover quickly, other things being equal, in proportion to the amount and depth of the anesthetic."

"The patient is ready," Ludie said quietly, "and I'm in complete agreement with your anesthetic maxim: it is better to err on the side of caution."

"Deportment in the operating room is a most abused part of our technique," John added, not stopping to acknowledge the doctor's remark. "To me, the operating room is a sanctum – the holiest of the holy. It seems to me that with the life of a human being hanging by a thread, as it were, where a few drops too much of anesthetic or the slip of the knife by a sixty-fourth of an inch may prove fatal, all seriousness should prevail. I consider it a crime for the doctor or the anesthetist to engage in running conversation and jocular methods during the performance of their duties. This is about as close to our maker as it is our lot to get on this mundane sphere. Without doubt, many of our cases will recover with less elaboration than I am outlining, but why take the chance?"

By this time John sensed that Ludie, who was listening as keenly as the students, was duly impressed and reassured.

"Precision, delicacy, and gentleness count for so much in operating," John instructed. "Avoid roughness and pulling as much as possible. The patient today is a twenty-year-old, right-hand-dominant, mechanical studies student. He was working with a bow saw in the shop, and he caught the tool on something. According to witnesses, the saw kicked back, catching his right hand. He presents with near amputation of the index finger, an open wound with fracture of the middle finger, and lacerations to the thumb and ring finger. The index finger will likely require amputation, as it is poorly vascularized and there is signif-icant bone loss."

"How much bone loss do you estimate, John?" Ludie asked.

"There is about fifty percent of the middle phalanx missing, and significant loss to the distal phalanx as well," John answered.

As he proceeded, he noticed that there was only slight blood flow to the injured finger and no vessels left intact. This was not a good sign.

"What are you going to do?" Ludie asked, waiting to weigh John's decision against his own opinion.

"I am going to have to amputate. Please tighten the tourniquet for hemostasis and ex-sanguination," John ordered.

Ludie nodded his approval and marveled as much at John's innovative approach as at his skill and dexterity during the procedure.

Ludie's initial doubts about his colleague's qualifications gave way to obvious respect, as he observed a technique that even he might not have been capable of.

John cleaned the wound, amputated the index finger, then sutured a piece of incised skin to the middle phalanx stump and closed the wound. The thumb was prepped and sutured. John suspected a nerve injury, but it was more complicated than he had anticipated, and there was only so much he could do. Lacking the appropriate equipment and unable to repair the nerve, he closed the additional lacerations and released the tourniquet. The digits were checked for suffusion of blood into the fingers, and the operation was considered complete.

At the close of the surgery, Ludie laid both of his hands on top of John's shoulders and said, "Well done, John. I will be honored to operate with you anytime."

Since Ludie Johnston was one of the state's most recognized physicians and a leading surgeon in Macon County, John felt proud to have earned his praise. They became a team, and this drew even more members of the community to the school's hospital. Soon the word was out that the medical care offered at Pinehurst was the best around, and people began to seek John out to ask his advice on a variety of health issues.

With the hospital attracting serious interest as well as curiosity, John received a questionnaire from a surgical firm in Montgomery, Alabama, desiring to know if Negroes suffered from appendicitis. It was not long before the hospital's surgical files contained records to support an affirmative answer.

One such case added a touch of humor, and it illustrated just how much some locals continued to fear surgery. John, having operated on a patient stricken with appendicitis, was doing post-operative rounds the next morning. He had ordered the patient, an old farm woman who had been brought in from the cotton field, to get out of bed and sit up, but she had not done so.

John went over to her bedside and looked at her directly. "Mrs. Webb," he said, "I gave orders for you to get up and walk about the floor, but you are still in bed. Why have you not gotten out of bed?"

"I ain't got no clothes," she said.

"Well, where are your clothes, Mrs. Webb?"

She looked at John as if had asked a stupid question. "I dun gi' 'em all away," she said. "I didn't think I was gwine need 'em no more."

"Well, young lady," he teased, "I will tell the nurse to bring you some new clothes. You are going to need them, because your operation was a success and you are going to live a long time!"

The old woman grabbed John's hand and gave him a toothless grin. "Thank ya, Doc," she said. "I is so grateful to you an' to God."

Successes like this were achieved almost in spite of the meager surgical resources John had available. Later, as the community utilized the hospital more, it was necessary to build a two-story wing. This included a well-lighted operating room with a tiled floor and wainscoting, sterilizing rooms with high-pressure sterilizers, anesthetizing and recovery rooms, and a few private rooms. Because this little hospital now served a community that previously had had to travel great distances to get medical care, Pinehurst soon had to expand even more, with the addition of a nearby annex that was used for some medical cases. And still the patient load and the hospital's reputation continued to grow.

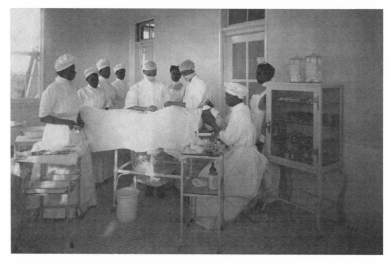

Hospital operating room

With both his duties at the hospital and his private practice, John was extremely busy. He arrived home late one day, just as Alice was putting away the dinner she had prepared.

"I'm sorry to be late, Alice. I know I said I would get home on time, but a lad came in with lockjaw and I had to take care of him. He cut himself in the barn a week ago and should have come in then. I don't know how to make the farmers understand the dangers they face if they don't come in and get medical help. This boy was lucky – not like my father."

"It's all right, John," Alice said with a resigned sigh. "Dinner may still be warm. I already ate; you were taking so long." She proceeded to unwrap and serve the food.

"Its fine, Alice. Now sit with me, and let me tell you about this case. This is one for the textbooks."

It was at times like these when John most missed the camaraderie and counsel that he had shared with his colleagues in medical school. Alice was often his only sounding board, and while she always listened patiently to his recitations of case studies, it wasn't the same as conversing with another physician. Although a colored physician was practicing in Montgomery and another in Opelika, Alabama, there were miles separating one from the other, and not much opportunity to fraternize or caucus. Little did John know that colored physicians all over the country were sharing his sentiments – and already doing something to remedy the situation.

The NMA, Personal Tragedy, and Progress

John and Ludie were sitting in John's office at the hospital one spring day, discussing an interesting surgical case they had just completed, when John's secretary arrived with the mail. Casually, he thumbed through it, and unfolded a rather large, orange-colored piece of paper.

"Hmm, look at this," John said with interest. "This is an announcement for a meeting of the National Medical Association coming up in November in Nashville, Tennessee."

"I haven't heard of that group before," Ludie replied.

"You probably haven't heard of it because it's an organization of Negro physicians. This is the first attempt on the part of the Negro medical profession to form a national organization. I'm impressed with the creed printed on their flyer. It speaks to the reason the organization came together. Read this for yourself."

John handed the flyer to Ludie. Printed at the top was the following affirmation:

"Conceived in no spirit of racial exclusiveness, fostering no ethnic antagonism, but born of the exigencies of the American environment, the National Medical Association has for its object the banding together, for mutual co-operation and helpfulness, the men and women of African descent who are legally and honorably engaged in the practice of the cognate professions of medicine, surgery, dentistry and pharmacy."

"That's excellent, John," Ludie said, duly impressed and handing the paper back. "Why hasn't your race affiliated as a group before now?"

"Well, from a historical perspective, the early Negro doctors only recently emerged from the wilderness of slavery, superstition, and poverty, and have been too engrossed in the experience of practicing medicine to give much heed to the mechanics of organization. With their training and licenses in hand, they practiced their art largely among their own people and were achieving splendid results – professionally, socially, and economically. Eventually, however, organization claimed their attention, and the association was born. It came together loosely at the Atlanta Exposition in 1895. Then it was called the National (Negro) Medical Association of Physicians, Surgeons, Dentists and Pharmacists."

"Are you a member?" Ludie asked.

"No, I have not had the opportunity of joining or going to a meeting yet."

"Why don't you go to the meeting this time, John?

"I guess I should give it some thought. I like that the goal of the organization is the advancement of Negro medicine, and it's a very good forum to foster communication between practitioners from different areas of the country."

"By all means, go, John. I'll cover your duties while you're away."

"If I went, I'd like to present a paper, but I don't think I have anything worthy of bringing up before that esteemed body."

"But this could be a great opportunity for you, John. You're more ready than you think. You've been studying the subject of shock and its clinical manifestations. Why don't you do a paper on shock?"

At Ludie's suggestion, John promptly prepared a paper, focusing on surgical shock from anesthesia since he had witnessed it and believed that practically all of it was due either to incompetence or carelessness. John was soon on his way to Nashville, called "The Athens of the South," to attend his first meeting of the NMA, which was held at

Meharry Medical College, with the surgical clinic held at the private Mercy Hospital.

John entered the auditorium on the first day, humbled and in awe of the large number of Negro physicians assembled together in one place. Also present were a goodly number of students from Fisk, Walden, and Roger Williams Universities, and an audience of public citizens who could intelligently appreciate the meeting. John had not felt so impressed with an assembly of Negro physicians since medical school, and he regretted not having joined the group earlier.

The meeting was presided over by Dr. F. A. Stewart of Nashville, a polished scholar and dignified gentleman. Given that John was a presenter, he was asked to sit on the dais with Dr. C. V. Roman, Dr. Daniel Hale Williams, Dr. E. P. Roberts, and some other notables. Their presentations were scholarly, humorous, and inspiring, and he wondered if his paper was too simplistic, too bookish. He was lost in thought when he heard Dr. Willis E. Steers of Decatur, Alabama, call his name and introduce him as the "kid of the Association."

John rose, approached the podium, and opened his paper. As he looked out at all of his colleagues watching him with interest, he found his courage. Clearing his throat, he began his talk. "I will now speak to you on surgical shock and its clinical manifestations."

John's paper detailed the history of anesthesia, covering the discovery in 1831 of chloroform and, in 1842, of ether and their uses up to the present time. To illustrate the inconstant properties of anesthetics, he included an anecdote he had read in medical school – a tale related by J. Marion Simms, one of history's early physicians: "In 1839 in Anderson, South Carolina, a number of youths were exhilarating themselves one day with the seductive vapor of ether. In their excitement, they seized a young Negro who was watching their antics and compelled him to inhale the drug from a handkerchief, which they held over his nose and mouth by main force. At first his struggles only added to their amusement, but they soon ceased as the boy became unconscious, stertorous and apparently dying. After an hour or two of anxiety on the part of the spectators, however, he revived and was apparently no worse for his alarming experience."

John got a few knowing chuckles from the audience with this story. He then chronicled a number of operative cases that he had observed, and many of his own experiences with anesthesia and its consequences. He ended his paper by saying that most deaths by anesthesia were avoidable; and added that in patients free from organic disease, death was most often the result of carelessness, incompetence, or recklessness.

As he finished his paper, his audience clapped appreciatively. Dr. Daniel Hale Williams, *the first surgeon of record in the world to suture the heart of a living human being*, stepped to the podium and clapped John on the shoulder.

"Well done, Dr. Kenney," he said into the microphone. "Let's give Dr. Kenney another hand for his excellent paper."

"Congratulations!" echoed Dr. Roman, who joined them at the podium.

John received more accolades as he passed through the assemblage on his way to some of the clinical sessions. He was immersing himself in the fraternal and scientific spirit emanating from the group, certain that from now on he would take a more active part in this grand organization.

In notes he took during the clinical sessions, John recorded that among the men who demonstrated their surgical skill and precision were Dr. Daniel Hale Williams of Chicago, Illinois, "the premier Negro surgeon"; Dr. W. A. Warfield, the careful, "skillful and successful surgeon of the Freedmen's Hospital"; Dr. N. F. Mossell, "the profound, able and learned chief surgeon" of the Frederick Douglass Memorial Hospital, and Dr. John E. Hunter of Lexington, Kentucky, the "erudite, painstaking and skillful" physician and surgeon.

Following the NMA meeting, John met with Dr. Williams, who had presented a paper on penetrating wounds of the thorax just prior to John's paper on shock. Williams seemed as impressed with John's paper as John had been with his, and invited John to visit his hospital in Chicago. This was the beginning of a friendship destined to be of great help to John in his surgical career. Williams was so impressed with John's service as an anesthetist during the clinical sessions that he arranged with Dr. G. W. Hubbard, the president of Meharry Medical College, to let John spend a week at Meharry each year in order to administer all the anesthetics for Dr. William's annual clinics. John would also give a course of lectures on anesthetics to the senior medical and dental students.

After the clinical sessions, Williams again approached John, who was preparing to return to Tuskegee.

"I would like to invite you to Chicago in April to work with me at my hospital. Your work is admirable, John, and I think this would be good experience for you."

"I would be delighted," John said, overwhelmed with excitement at the invitation. "Just let me know the exact dates, and I'll schedule it on my calendar."

The following spring, John made a visit to Chicago to work with Dr. Williams at the Provident Hospital there, making this John's second trip to that city. The two doctors made rounds together, and John observed Williams' skillful surgical techniques during several operative procedures. He was impressed with Williams' pathological and bacterial units and his sterilization techniques. John was also extremely impressed by his colleague's own personal history, which Williams shared openly, revealing the many hardships he had turned to his advantage, experiences very similar to those of John's early life.

"I have heard of your work in Tuskegee with the school's hospital," Williams said as they toured Provident Hospital. "I opened this hospital in 1891 with only twelve beds, and we served as many members of the community as would come, much like your experience at Tuskegee."

"Yes, I know what that feels like," John said, awed to be in the presence of such a distinguished and revered member of the profession. "At first people don't trust your motives, and you have to prove yourself before they will come."

"That's exactly what you have to do. When the community did start coming here the first year, we averaged an eighty-seven percent success rate with medical treatments. The morbidity rate was extremely low so, little by little, people gained confidence in our abilities."

"I am also working on the development of a nurse training school like you did, and we share the notion of using physicians of all races to contribute to our efforts, a notion not respected in all circles," John said.

"That's true. But in all cases you have to remain true to your beliefs and principles. That's the secret to success."

"Thank you, Dr. Williams. You are a man after my own heart."

"And I'm impressed with your work, John. We need more dedicated and optimistic leaders in our organization. When we meet at Lexington, Kentucky in the fall, I'm going to nominate you for the position of secretary of the NMA," Williams announced.

"I'll serve in any way I can, sir."

This ungrudging benevolence bestowed on John by such an esteemed physician was the impetus for a lifelong dedication to the NMA. The two men became best friends, and John benefited from the association with a man who expressed great confidence in his work, and who gave him constant encouragement.

The next NMA meeting was held in Lexington, Kentucky in October of 1904. Lexington was one of the most beautiful cities in the Blue Grass region, and the members were royally entertained by their hosts. The opening lecture was given by a Dr. Stuckey of Lexington, who opened the session with the following statement: "Gentlemen of the National Medical Association, the practice of medicine knows neither race, color, nor creed; brains count!" This set the tone for the meeting, which had the largest attendance of any before it. In addition, two hospitals under white management opened their doors to the NMA, resulting in white and Negro physicians working side by side in mutual respect and admiration.

During the last day of the Lexington meeting, elections for officers were held and, true to his promise, Dr. Williams nominated John for secretary of the organization. The current president, Dr. C. V. Roman, presided over the elections.

Feeling nervous and not at all sure that his reputation and accomplishments were sufficiently well known in the group, John couldn't keep his insecurities from spoiling the moment. As the ballots were passed out, he wondered how he had let himself get talked into this situation.

After the ballots were collected and tabulated, Dr. Roman rose to announce the results.

"I would like to announce the members elected to a term of office for the upcoming year. For president we have the esteemed Dr. John E. Hunter of this fair city of Lexington. Congratulations to Dr. Hunter." Applause followed all around the meeting hall.

"And for Vice President, the honor goes to Dr. R. E. Jones of Richmond, Virginia. Congratulations to Dr. Jones."

Dr. Jones rose and acknowledged the applause he received.

"The position of secretary will be filled by Dr. John A. Kenney, of Tuskegee, Alabama!" Roman announced. "Let's all thank him for the excellent job he did acting as anesthetist for all of the surgical procedures. Congratulations to Dr. Kenney."

The election results and the hearty applause confirmed for John that, indeed, his reputation and his accomplishments had not gone unnoticed.

The next meeting was held in Richmond, Virginia, capital of the Old Dominion State, in 1905. Even more successful in scientific discussion and surgical innovations and techniques than the previous meeting, there was standing room only in most of the sessions. John was again elected to represent the organization as secretary.

As the NMA grew in size and importance, its members became more self-confident. Sporadically knocking on the door of organized medicine, they requested admission into its folds. The recalcitrant American Medical Association, the eminent organization for white physicians, continually rebuffed the efforts of Negro physicians in the North and the South to be recognized as equal colleagues. In an issue of *The Journal of The American Medical Association* in 1907, a report listed the classifications of all medical colleges in the United States, with all of the Negro medical schools placed in the third, or lowest, class or left unclassified. This dichotomy, and the standards and practices of the

AMA in general, resulted in many heated discussions among members of the NMA.

John and some of his colleagues, incensed at the report, expressed their anger and disgust at an executive committee meeting prior to the annual NMA meeting.

"We need a committee to investigate and refute that report," John argued. "We must take that up at the next annual meeting."

"Make no mistake," Dr. Hunter, the NMA president, declared. "That will be first on my agenda, along with the membership requirements. They stipulate that to become a member of the AMA, you have to live above the Mason-Dixon Line. How ludicrous is it that an imaginary line stretching in an easterly to westerly direction across part of the continent determines the fitness for membership?"

"But," Dr. H. F. Gamble, John's cousin, added sarcastically, "in the spirit of discrimination, every white physician who lives south of the line and who has met the professional requirements is eligible for membership! Just think about it. If someone like Daniel Hale Williams lived below that line, he could not join the American Medical Association."

"Even though they let some of the northern Negro physicians into their fold, they put 'c-o-l' beside their names so that everyone will know they are 'colored.' And Negroes in the South have no possibility of joining – because segregation won't let them join the southern medical professional societies so they can meet the AMA requirements. Anyone see any discrimination there?" John asked in disgust.

"It's as plain as day, John," Dr. Hunter said with a sigh of resignation. "It's a ridiculous state of affairs, and that's just another battle we will have to continue to fight. Life is a battle – you might as well don your helmet!"

Despite these indignities from white organized medicine in general, there were instances where philanthropic white benefactors aided Negro causes on individual levels. Tuskegee Institute became an example of this kind of benevolence. In conjunction with one of the regular board meetings, a wife of one of the board members, Mrs. Elizabeth Mason from Massachusetts, visited the hospital at Tuskegee and was extremely impressed with the results that were obtained, despite the handicaps that confronted the staff. She invited Dr. Washington to visit her and her husband in Boston the next time that he traveled up North, and he accepted. When he later made the trip and met with Mrs. Mason, she offered to help build a modern new hospital at Tuskegee.

When Washington returned to Tuskegee and, with great satisfaction, announced at the next annual meeting that Mrs. Mason had agreed to give him twenty-five thousand dollars for a new hospital, everyone applauded. John, however, was reminded of his old teacher, Mr. Jackson, and his mantra, "Do not be afraid to ask for what you need." Thus, when Washington surveyed the room, his searching eye found John's dissatisfied expression.

"What's the matter, Dr. Kenney?" he asked. "You don't seem so pleased."

"I congratulate you, Dr. Washington, on what you have done," John replied, "but you have not gone far enough. If we are going to build a hospital at this stage of our development, we should build not for the *now* only, but for the future, and twenty-five thousand won't do it."

Although Washington showed that he was a little hurt, he was still game. "Well, I can't ask her for more, but if *you* think you can get her to give more, I'll make an appointment for *you*!"

"Accepted!" John replied.

Shortly after that meeting, John met with Mrs. Mason at her spacious estate in Hingham, Massachusetts, near Boston. She welcomed him politely and listened attentively. When he had finished, she said, "Leave the papers here, Dr. Kenney. When my husband comes home tonight, I will talk to him and send word of our decision."

Dr. Washington was spending time at his summer home in New York, and John took the night train from Boston to report to him. It was Washington, however, who reported to John.

"I have a telegram from Mrs. Mason that she will give fifty thousand dollars. Now let's go build that hospital!"

John and Dr. & Mrs. Washington at groundbreaking for new hospital in 1911

Thus, the John A. Andrew Memorial Hospital was built, named for Mrs. Mason's grandfather, the Honorable John A. Andrew, war governor of Massachusetts. The building was constructed largely with student labor, including the making of the bricks that formed the walls. Once the medical equipment was installed, the plant was worth well over one hundred thousand dollars.

With the hospital completed, a formal groundbreaking ceremony was held. In his address to the community, Booker T. Washington, in his usual good-hearted style, gave John the credit for getting the second twenty-five thousand. Mrs. Mason's generosity did not stop there. She kept up with the work of the hospital and made other donations and improvements. She also provided funds for fireproofing, for an elevator, and for the erection of a building in which medical clinics could be held.

It was through these cumulative efforts that Tuskegee came to produce the greatest medical and scientific meetings ever held. It was because of the generosity of this patron that a decision was made to hold annual medical clinics at Tuskegee, and this endeavor was named the John A. Andrew Clinical Society. At the time, John said to Washington and the staff of Tuskegee, "The day will come when the best men in the profession will feel honored to be invited before this society."

John was soon meticulously formulating plans for Tuskegee's medical clinics. Various clinics and refresher courses had already been held in several cities around the country, but he wanted Tuskegee, through its clinic and scientific meetings, to be the bastion of opportunity for the Negro medical profession. It was while serving as secretary to the NMA, however, that he began some of his most arduous work for the Negro medical profession. He began publishing the minutes of each annual meeting and reporting on the proceedings of the organization for that particular year, something that had never been done before. His reports covered the meeting in Richmond in 1905, in Philadelphia in 1906, in Baltimore in 1907, in New York in 1908, and in Boston in 1909. It was during this time that John conceived of an idea that he hoped would further legitimize the NMA as a scientific body in the eyes of the world.

John A. Andrew Memorial Hospital

In 1908, John's cousin, Dr. Gamble, became chairman of the Executive Board of the NMA. John wrote to him about the possibility of starting a medical journal. Their correspondence went back and forth until John said he had some plans in mind and asked if he could present them to the executive board at the next meeting. Gamble wrote back, "Go to it."

At the next executive board meeting in New York City, John presented his ideas.

"Gentlemen," he said with enthusiasm, "I herewith propose the idea of founding a medical and scientific journal for this organization. It will benefit progressive Negro physicians of the North, South, East and West. It will not only be theoretical, but it will be practical. It will not only be intellectual, but it will have literary worth. Its scientific discussions will provide continuing medical education for a population of Negro medicos attempting to make ourselves known in the medical world."

"That's an excellent idea, John," Dr. J. E. Hunter said, clearly excited. "The American Medical Association has its journal, which is widely read and supported by its membership. We certainly can have our own."

"Without a doubt," Dr. N. F. Mossell agreed. "As I have stated before, the future of the NMA lies in our integrity, our intelligence, and our wisdom. Our own journal can demonstrate all of these virtues for the medical community at large, not only in America, but internationally!"

"Do you have any ideas for a publication staff?" Vice President Howard asked.

"Yes, I do!" replied John emphatically, spreading out his plans on the table. The atmosphere of the meeting had gone from mundane and businesslike to one of excitement and optimism; the prospect of an organization-wide project that all could contribute to was provocative and compelling. Everyone suddenly had ideas and opinions on how to proceed – until the president reminded them that they needed to approve the proposal by a vote of those present. After establishing that there was a quorum, the board passed the proposal unanimously.

Thus, the *Journal of the National Medical Association* was born. As soon as John returned home from the annual meeting, he made a trip to Nashville to induce Dr. C. V. Roman, whom he considered "the most distinguished scholar among us," to be the first editor. Roman had a doctorate and a medical degree, and was known to quote philosophers and scholars to make his point. At the annual meeting in Philadelphia in 1906, John had been impressed with Roman during his presentation of a paper to the NMA on the study of the ear. In acknowledging the hardships faced by the Negro physician, Roman stated eloquently, "Negro slavery in America is conceded by all impartial and disinterested observers and investigators to have been, on the whole, the most fiendish oppression of one people by another that has ever disgraced the annals of civilization – since man first found the power to make his brother mourn." John believed that this impassioned orator and scientist would be the perfect person to man the helm of this new venture. Roman accepted the job of editor, and he and John began a lifelong friendship working on the *Journal* together.

It was decided that John would act as managing editor or editor-in-chief; Dr. W. G. Alexander would serve as business manager; Dr. W. S. Lofton as dental editor; and Dr. Amanda V. Gray as pharmaceutical editor. The subscription rate was fifty cents per issue, and the January-February issue – the first *Journal* – appeared in 1909.

It was at the Boston meeting in 1909 that John had the privilege of becoming a member of the first Negro surgical team to do an exploratory abdominal surgery in that city. The surgery was done at Plymouth Hospital, the private hospital of Dr. C. N. Garland. Dr. Garland had bought a building and converted it to a hospital in 1908. The facility was already successful, having been the site of two hundred and thirty- three surgical procedures, many of which were abdominal surgeries.

The chief surgeon was Dr. John E. Hunter of Lexington, Kentucky. John and his cousin, Dr. H. F. Gamble of Charleston, West Virginia, were the assistants. Dr. Mitchell of the Freedmen's Hospital in Washington, D.C., was the anesthetist. This procedure was a daring pursuit, and the white establishment was watching to see how these doctors did.

The doctors assembled at the hospital to review their case. They were not intimidated by the expectations, positive or negative, of those awaiting the results of this surgical first. They knew that, while it was critical to know when to operate, it was frequently more critical to know when *not* to operate. That rare, impalpable something called surgical judgment often, very often, determined the issue. But John knew that by surgical judgment, a doctor did not mean that one should not operate merely from fear of losing the patient – for that was not surgical judgment but surgical timidity. That was the white feather in surgery.

"EDITORIAL STAFF" OF THE JOURNAL OF THE NATIONAL MEDICAL ASSOCIATION

First editorial staff of the *Journal*, Dr. C.V. Roman, seated.

The patient brought before these Negro doctors was a thirty-eight year-old female, who had experienced severe abdominal pain and distension for two days. She had been transferred from another hospital where the attending physician determined that she didn't need surgery, just palliative treatment and observation. Her family had disagreed, seeing their loved one in such agony, and the hospital had transferred her to Plymouth. If she died, it wouldn't be on the first hospital's rolls.

The team of NMA doctors examined the patient and formed their own conclusions.

"Every surgeon wants to protect his mortality list, but it is cowardly to attempt to protect one's record at the expense of a life," Dr. Hunter said, scrubbing for the surgery.

"Yes, that's true," John added. "In my opinion, the deciding factor in these cases, after bringing to bear every available help, is whether or not there is a chance for the patient's life. If it is better with surgery, then go to it, regardless of the outcome."

"And this patient will not survive without this surgery," Hunter said. "Let's begin."

The physical examination had been very disturbing. A pre-operative diagnosis was made and a ruptured, suppurating appendix was suspected, complicated by a fibroid uterus, a right ovarian cyst, and possible general peritonitis. The prognosis was not at all favorable. What a case for the world to watch!

The operation took several hours, and members of the NMA paced the operative gallery as the clock ticked on. They had hoped for a less complex case for their first effort. If this patient did not survive, it would not be because she didn't have the best surgeons available performing the surgery – but just try to convince the onlookers that that was the case.

Complexities arose with the first incision made, just below the umbilicus. The patient's intestines were severely distended and congested, with many loops held together with fibrous adhesions. The operative conversation was brief and concise. The situation was grave.

"Scalpel," Hunter said.

"Retractor," Gamble added.

"Bleeder!" John warned.

"Clamp!" Gamble ordered.

The surgeons worked together in synchronous collaboration, a first-time team with a dual mission at stake. They were oblivious to the galley above, which continued to fill with spectators wanting to witness this historic moment.

"Look there," Hunter warned, "the appendix has ruptured, and it looks gangrenous."

"The uterus is also inflamed. And where is all that pus coming from?" John asked. "Looks like an additional tube rupture down here."

"We're going to have to do a supra-vaginal hysterectomy and an appendectomy," Hunter decided. "The infection is too great."

The operation proceeded slowly and methodically. As they neared completion, the pelvic toilet was made, the entire abdominal cavity was irrigated with normal salt solution, and small tubes called cigarette drains were put in place.

"Pulse one hundred," Dr. Mitchell said. "All other vitals are in normal range."

For the first time since the surgery had begun, the optimism in the operating room was evident. Dr. Hunter's eyes sparkled with excitement as he finally exhaled. "Great job, doctors," he said. "Today we have accomplished our mission, gentlemen, despite all odds." He removed his mask and gave a salute to the gallery, where the viewers erupted into applause.

"God was with us on this one," John said, beaming and giving his cousin a handshake.

Dr. Hunter left to let the patient's family know that she would be fine. After delivering the good news, he added, "If you had waited another few hours to transfer her here, she would not be with us today."

The elated doctors left the operating room to meet the public and discuss their case. Their excited colleagues crowded around them with questions and congratulations.

"We've made history here in Boston today!" one colleague shouted.

"In the annals of the NMA, this will be one of our grandest moments!" another proclaimed.

Several newspaper representatives were waiting with other hospital officials for interviews. The surgery was a success story, and with it, the Negro physician was beginning to make a mark – impressively so – on the profession. The obvious doubt was giving way to a grudging respect that further motivated the race to strive to be the best. Faith and unity in a common purpose was beginning to pay off.

*   *   *

With John now fully involved in the activities of the NMA, Alice chose to travel with him to the annual meetings where she participated fully in the ladies auxiliary programs. She was accustomed by now to seeing her husband immersed in his professional duties and obligations and actively sought out activities of her own to fill her time.

In Boston, she busied herself with the women's sightseeing program, visiting many interesting places in a city called "The Athens of the Western Hemisphere." Boston was home to most of the leading intellectual and cultural powers in America, including Harvard College, the Boston Public Library, the New England Conservatory of Music, Bunker Hill, Paul Revere's home, and many other equally historic and significant landmarks. Between sightseeing trips, Alice read the *Boston Tourist Guide* and discovered a romantic restaurant called "The Aura" that she wanted to visit. She decided it was time she had an evening alone with her husband, and when he returned from a scientific session, she presented her idea.

"I've found a quaint New England restaurant, John, and I thought we might go there for dinner. It features seafood, and you know we can't get that in Tuskegee. Shall I ask the hotel to make a reservation there for us?"

"I'm sorry, darling. I have an executive committee meeting tonight. Everyone is excited about the February edition of the *Journal,* and they want to make it a quarterly publication. We got a good review in *The New York Age*. Do you know what they said? They said the *Journal* contained interesting material, and should prove a successful publication. The paper also said that it was dignified in appearance, as well as conservative, and the articles are of high merit. Isn't that great? We need to cement plans for the next edition. Perhaps we can go to the restaurant another day?"

"All right, John," Alice said with a sigh. "We'll try another time. Just let me know when your schedule will permit it." She gave him a peck on the cheek, and silently reminded herself of the sacrifices that all doctors' wives had to make – perhaps admitting for the first time that the situation was not likely to ever get any better. Days later, in the spring of 1911, they left Boston without ever having dined at the The Aura restaurant.

John returned to his patients and Alice to her students, each of them assuming their duties after one of the best conventions on record. Shortly after their homecoming, Alice began showing signs of declining health. Her symptoms were vague at first: tiredness, shortness of breath, and general malaise. John thought that the trip had been too much for her, and he ordered her to rest from work for a while. After several weeks, during which she showed no improvement, he decided to take her to the Battle Creek Sanitarium in Michigan, which was known for diagnosing unusual conditions.

Alice was admitted, and had to remain there for several weeks. John stayed with her part of the time; and at other times he traveled, visiting hospitals and clinics in Detroit, Cleveland, Chicago, Minneapolis, and even the Mayo Clinic in Rochester, New York. He felt sure that Alice was in good hands, and he believed that what he was learning on his medical sabbatical would aid Tuskegee when he returned home.

On returning to the sanitarium, however, John realized to his dismay that, not only was Alice not improving, but she was also definitely losing ground. The two of them decided to return to Tuskegee. When the head of the sanitarium, a Dr. Kellogg, heard that they were preparing to leave, he sent for John and asked him if he could perform an examination of Alice before she left the institution. Based on his examination, he considered the kidneys the primary focus of the problem, rather than the liver, as others had suspected.

On the way back to Tuskegee, and without an appointment, John and Alice stopped in Chicago to see Dr. Daniel Hale Williams. Williams was out of town, but John left him a message regarding Alice's health.

Shortly after, Williams wrote John a letter saying that he was coming to Tuskegee to examine Alice. He noted that he was bringing with him Dr. F. A. Stewart, a professor of surgery at Meharry Medical College in Nashville, Tennessee.

When the doctors arrived, they examined Alice and decided to do exploratory surgery, with the liver as the possible offending organ. John went to Alice's hospital room to explain to her the decision the doctors had made. When he entered, she smiled at him; and, for some reason, this unnerved him.

"Darling, I'm so glad you're here," Alice said weakly. "Now I know I'll be fine."

"Yes, you will be fine, but Dan and Stu and I have decided that we need to take a look inside to see what's going on. We think you may have a small cyst or tumor, and if we can remove it, you will begin to feel much better," John told her, more with hope than confidence.

"I was hoping that I wouldn't have to have an operation, John, but if I must, I must. I know that I am in the best of hands with you three, and I am not worried. Just do it and get it over with so I can feel better again."

"We're going to scrub now, Alice. We'll send for you when we are ready." John kissed his wife lovingly and squeezed her hand, relieved that his esteemed colleagues were in Tuskegee to orchestrate the surgery.

The surgical suite was prepped for surgery, and two attendants brought Alice in and placed her on the operating table. She seemed relaxed and confident, looking up into the faces of her husband and Doctors Williams and Stewart as she was anesthetized.

Williams made the incision, opened the abdominal cavity, and began his exploration. It was not long before he made an announcement.

"There it is. Look at that. She has a large malignancy of the right kidney that is encroaching on the liver. From what I am observing, our only option is to remove the kidney. John?"

"Yes, yes, I concur," John said, alarmed by the size of the growth. "We don't have a choice." His heart was racing and his breaths came too fast, keeping up with his mounting concern.

"I'm going to have to tie off the renal artery to approach the kidney before I attempt to remove it," Williams said more to himself than to his colleagues. "Hold this retractor, Stu," he told Dr. Stewart.

Williams attempted to tie off several blood vessels, but the arterial walls were so deteriorated that they could withstand neither the clamping nor the tying. All of a sudden the doctors were faced with profuse hemorrhaging from several areas.

Blood gushed undiminished, despite their frantic efforts.

"Tie there!" Williams ordered. "Clamp here!" he barked, his heroic attempts continuing nonstop.

Stu and John followed orders as best they could, three surgeons working furiously to save Alice's life, even though two of them already knew their best efforts might not be enough. After some time, Williams and Stewart exchanged looks of resignation as John made frantic attempts to staunch the bleeding.

"There, tie that one!" he ordered loudly, making several attempts to no avail. "Hurry!" he pleaded.

Williams stepped back from the table and put his hand on John's shoulder. With Alice's condition already compromised by the tumor and its effects, he knew the shock and blood loss would be more than she could stand. Then Stewart put down his instrument and looked at John, who seemed oblivious that his co-surgeons had stopped.

"John, it's no use," Williams said softly. "She's lost too much blood. There is nothing more we can do."

John looked up, finally realizing the impact of his friend's words. He looked down at Alice, whose abdominal cavity was quickly filling with blood, and he knew. He pulled off his surgical cap in despair.

"I'll close her, John," Williams said.

John turned and left the room, his head in his hands.

Williams hurriedly closed the wound, and Alice, accompanied by the three doctors, was moved to her bed. John sagged into a chair at her bedside and stroked her face and hair, while his friends stood solemnly by his side. Alice's breathing grew labored and slow, her color sallow and pale.

"Alice, I love you," John murmured burying his face in her hair. He heard a raspy gurgling sound and looked up, realizing that she wasn't breathing anymore. "Oh no...Oh no," he cried. "Alice!"

"We'll wait outside, John," Williams said quietly. As he and Stewart went into the hall, Williams slammed his fist into the wall and said, "I vow that I will never ever operate on the wife of one of my friends again!"

John remained for some time at Alice's bedside, holding her close. When he left at last, he walked to his office and sat in the dark, dreading the dawn of a new day – a day without Alice. Thoughts of her and their life together filled him with remorse. She had sacrificed so much for a cause they both believed in – but for which he received most of the accolades. Too late, he realized that he had been too engrossed in his work, that he had failed to recognize her efforts, efforts that made his own accomplishments possible. He remembered times when he had been too busy with his own agenda to acknowledge hers. He agonized over the promised tomorrows that now would never come – and he cried.

Alice was buried near the hospital where she would be close to John. With her nearby, he felt he could commune with her spirit and, perhaps, recover from his loss. In the months that followed, he tried to make some sense of what had happened, but the exercise was futile. There was only one way he knew of to relieve his pain – to fill every hour of every day with work.

Healing the Pain, the Good Will Tours

After Alice's death, John tried to numb his loss with untold hours of work, but he found little consolation. Loneliness constantly reminded him of the beautiful soul he had lost. The revelation of his own neglect made him even more determined to justify his existence by rededicating himself to the work of elevating the Negro race, a mission he and Alice had shared. He owed it to his father, his mother and, now, to his beloved Alice.

He soon grew obsessive about his mission, focusing entirely on the development of the John A. Andrew Clinics, the NMA, and the *Journal*. Late in the summer of 1911, he attended the yearly meeting of the NMA at Dixie Hospital in Hampton, Virginia. At every turn, he was reminded of Alice and the days they had spent together in college.

His return to the Hampton area was bittersweet. He deliberately retraced their campus walks: the path past the water and to her old dormitory beyond, the routes to their favorite spot under the trees, and to the old building where they were in English class together. Part of the time he mourned, and part of the time he felt content reliving the happiest moments in his memory. There was something cathartic about this tour, and he left feeling grateful for Hampton and all that it had brought him.

It was at this meeting in Virginia that John got the idea of holding the next NMA meeting in Tuskegee. He contacted several of the organization's leaders, and they concurred. The next thing John needed in order to proceed was Booker T. Washington's permission. He placed a call from Dixie Hospital.

"Dr. Washington, this is John Kenney. I'm at the NMA meeting at Hampton. How is everything going in Tuskegee?"

"Everything is fine here, John. I'm just back from a relaxing fishing trip to Coden Bay, so I'm fine. What can I do for you?"

"I was just thinking…ah, I had a bright idea, and I hope you like it."

"What is it, John? You're not usually at a loss for words."

"I would like your permission to have Tuskegee host the fourteenth annual meeting of the NMA next August."

"That's an excellent idea," Washington agreed at once. "Of course you have my permission. It will be good for Tuskegee to have such esteemed physicians on our grounds, and it will be good for the NMA to see the work we have done in the public health arena here and to see our new hospital."

"Good; then I will propose it. I will give you a call later with the details."

"That will be fine," Washington replied. "And since you have been so strapped with your work for Tuskegee and the *Journal* lately, I will see if the budget can afford you a stenographer as you prepare for your meeting. That's the least we can do."

John was overwhelmed with this kind gesture. "Thank you so much, Dr. Washington. Your thoughtfulness and kindness are sincerely appreciated."

John worked feverishly to make the Tuskegee meeting the most memorable ever. As always, he had the cooperation of the staff of the hospital and the faculty of Tuskegee. Physicians in the region and NMA members from Decatur, Anniston, Mobile, and Opelika, Alabama supported his efforts on a local level. He worked night and day planning the program, calling for abstracts and papers, and soliciting speakers and participants, spurred on by his dedication and promise to those who had loved him and inspired him – his parents and Alice, who were never out of his mind.

As John prepared for the meeting, another idea came to him. He had long wanted to compile a history of Negro medicine and pay homage to the predecessors of the art. Now that he had some stenographic help, he felt he had time to write a small book to be presented to all who attended the meeting. As he did his research and uncovered history he had not been aware of, he became more and more excited about the book. He was surprised to learn that a James Derham of Philadelphia, Pennsylvania was the first Negro physician of record in the late 1700s, and he was astounded that such medical history was not common knowledge. He was convinced that if the profession and the race didn't know their own history, they were giving short shrift to the talent and genius that had preceded them. If they didn't know what their own accomplishments were at this point in history, how could they ever hope to be fully cognizant of the impressive gains they had made? The more history he uncovered, the more impassioned he became.

John titled his book *The Negro in Medicine*. It honored the early Negro medical pioneers with the following inscription:

"To my esteemed predecessors in the art of healing who have braved the prejudices and difficulties and laid the foundation so sure and so true, and to my worthy contemporaries who are building upon this foundation the bulwarks that shall stand for all time to come, this little booklet is dedicated."

The book listed some of the most successful Negro physicians of the day and included pictures of them, their homes and properties, and some of their wives. Many of those who would attend the meeting would be delighted to find themselves listed in this "Who's Who" publication.

As part of the opportunities planned for the visiting physicians, the rural population throughout the region was invited to come and take advantage of a privilege never before offered to area residents: to be cared for by two or three hundred doctors of their own race. People came, and for nearly a week the work continued until five hundred twenty-five cases had received attention: five hundred medical cases and twenty-five surgical operations. This clinic also provided health tutorials on the campus that brought physicians and interested citizens together. The assembly room at Douglass Hall overflowed with people straining to hear the lectures that gave instructions in public health and answered questions from eager participants.

Throughout the meeting enthusiastic NMA members complimented and praised John for his hard work.

"Excellent meeting, Dr. Kenney," Dr. J. E. Hunter told him. "You know, I said in the last *Journal* that the big Tuskegee meeting would be the biggest in our history, and it is!"

Dr. Balloch, dean of the medical school at Howard University, added, "The scientific agenda is top notch."

John thanked them both, obviously pleased with the results.

"I think that one effective way that we can elevate our racial status," Dr. Gamble added, "is by ethical demonstrations of our scientific knowledge through our achievements and through such organizations such as this. And by the way, cousin, where can I get a copy of that book of yours? I hear I'm in it," he said, laughing. John's book had become the "hot" item to have at the Tuskegee meeting.

The people of Tuskegee, on that occasion and always, threw themselves heartily into supporting the meeting by housing, feeding, and providing a warm welcome and unequaled Southern hospitality to their visitors. There was an all-pervasive "something" in Tuskegee that John called the "Tuskegee Spirit," a combination of love of humanity, support for community, and dedication to the common cause that bound the community irrevocably together. This closeness was the foundation upon which many endeavors were supported, nurtured, and accomplished. This bond allowed the race to work together, never to be daunted by what looked like an immovable object. Segregation gave them their raison d'être, and it was a constant reminder of the work still to be done, with Tuskegee at the forefront of this effort.

John was especially proud when Dr. Washington commended him publicly for a job well done. Not only did Washington enjoy having the NMA meeting in Tuskegee, but he knew that such prestige would enhance the school's reputation and, in turn, his own. As respect grew for

Tuskegee Normal and Industrial School, Booker T. Washington himself became known not only for the school, but for his stance on racial equality. To spread his message and educate people to his purpose, he decided to conduct tours throughout the South and North. He called John into his office one day to discuss this new venture.

"Now that your meeting is over and you are less occupied," Washington began, "I want to tell you about some good will tours I would like to conduct."

1912 NMA Annual Meeting postcard

"Yes, Dr. Washington, I heard talk about this at chapel last Sunday. The whole school is excited that you want to travel to promote your ideas and talk about Tuskegee and our success. How did this come about?"

"I realized that in so many parts of the South, many white people have never seen an educated Negro; they have no idea we could be such. They only know the hate that is passed down from generation to generation, and they don't really question it. I want to go and 'stir the pudding' as it were. I want to talk about racial inequality and hate, and put a name and a face to it. I want to start whittling down that barrier, word by word. Let's go into these southern towns and tell them what we've done here in

Tuskegee and what other parts of the South are doing. Let's go and cement friendly relations between the races – for the first time!"

"That's a very worthy undertaking, sir," John said. "What can I do to help you?"

"Well actually, John, I would like you to accompany me on these tours as my physician and as my friend."

"It's quite an honor to be asked, Dr. Washington, but I am not sure how I could do that and maintain my responsibilities here at the hospital."

"We'll work that out, John. On my most recent trip to Mississippi I had a spell of illness, and I could not find a doctor to tend to me. That will probably be the case in many of these towns that I will travel to, so I really do need you. I think the Johnston brothers will help us out, as well as some of your local colleagues."

"Then I will be happy to accompany you, sir," John replied, still trying to figure out how he was going to arrange all the details of his work.

John's colleagues readily agreed to take over his hospital duties while he was away. Dr. Ludie Johnston put it into perspective, offering John a compliment at the same time. "It is an honor to be the one who is asked to attend to the great leader of the Negro people. You can certainly handle that responsibility, my friend."

The following Sunday morning John, Dr. Washington, two local ministers, and four school officials headed to rural Georgia by car. Washington had been invited to speak there by the local white mayor, who had heard Washington speak at the Atlanta Exposition.

A convoy of town officials met them at the city limits, and offered to guide them. Halfway there, the cars passed a field with majestic oak trees. The cars stopped and the mayor jumped out and came back to Washington's car.

"See that big oak there in the middle?" he said to Washington, who stared out the car window, trying to differentiate one tree from another.

"Yes, I see it," Washington said with a tinge of doubt. "They're beautiful trees."

"Well, a nigra was lynched there just last week. Look, you can still see some rope where it was cut off."

"God rest his soul." Washington said solemnly, making the sign of the cross. He had no need to know the history of the lynching – he already knew the conditions of life that provoked it. That's why he was making this tour. The caravan started up again and moved slowly toward town.

When the party arrived at the local courthouse, word of the lynching spread among Washington's group. The tension was palpable. Inside the courthouse, the room was filled with townsfolk, mostly mountaineering people. Stares of curiosity, both from the whites and the local Negroes, greeted Washington's party as the well-dressed entourage took their seats. As at all of these gatherings, the whites sat on one side of the room and the coloreds on the other. The atmosphere seemed heavy, with some of the whites openly hostile. The audience was what John termed "frozen." Sensing this, Washington knew instinctively that he would have to break the ice and thaw these people out, and he had a whole warehouse of homely jokes for this purpose.

"Ladies and gentlemen," he began, "my name is Booker T. Washington, and I am the founder and principal of Tuskegee Institute in Alabama." The scanty applause from the colored side echoed in the room. "In today's world," Washington continued, "we must have both foresight and hindsight. That reminds me of the two frogs who fell into a bucket of cream. One frog had hindsight and the other one had foresight. The frog with hindsight swam for a little while, got tired, gave up, and drowned. The frog with foresight swam and swam all night, never giving up. In the morning he realized his swimming had caused the cream to turn to butter, and he got up and walked out on top it."

A few people in the audience smiled, but the mood changed very little. As soon as he began to speak seriously, Washington realized this group was not yet ready for him. He knew that he would need his best joke to move this crowd. He started again.

"And then there's the story of the Irishman and the Englishman. They were having a conversation about Frederick Douglass, the great Negro orator.

"The Irishman said, 'Who is that speaking?'"

"The Englishman replied, 'That is Frederick Douglass, the famous Negro speaker.'"

"The Irishman asked, 'Can a Negro speak that way?'"

"The Englishman said, 'Well, he is a mulatto. Kind of one-half a Negro.'"

"The Irishman replied, 'Well, if one-half a Negro can speak that well, what can a whole Negro do?'"

This joke provoked laughter from the entire group, and the ice was broken. Washington was then able to speak about hard work, education, health, and the benefits of all races of people working together toward the same goals. As he finished and was leaving the room, there were many in that "cracker" crowd who wanted to meet him and shake his hand.

A few days later, Washington's reception in South Carolina was as unfriendly as it had been initially in Georgia. He was scheduled to speak at the town hall, which became dangerously overcrowded. As his party approached the hall entrance, some townsmen blocked the door as if to prevent Washington and the others from entering, then stepped back menacingly and, at the last moment, let them through. Washington, if he felt any fear, never showed it. He entered the room and walked confidently to the stage.

"Good afternoon, ladies and gentlemen, my name is Booker T. Washington, and I am happy to be in the state whose motto in Latin is 'Dum Spiro Spero,' or 'while I breathe, I hope.'" This use of Latin underscored his liberal education.

As he looked around, he spotted out of the corner of his eye a white man walking around offstage. It seemed odd to see this man with his hat on, smoking a cigarette and pacing nervously, and Washington made a mental note to keep an eye on him.

"That motto expresses exactly how I feel about life," he continued, glancing back to see the man backstage move toward the fire bell, pull the rope, and run out the back. "Stop!" Washington called, but the man had already made his getaway.

Immediately a warning bell began clanging, and people jumped to their feet, scattering here and there, some even screaming and cursing. An elderly woman was knocked to the floor and several people tripped over her trying to escape, ignoring her cries for help. Chairs were knocked over and programs went flying. Washington, who was momentarily stunned by this turn of events, stepped to the front of the stage and held out his arms.

"Sit down!" he ordered, his bass voice booming. "Everyone sit down, now!"

The sound of his voice and his air of authority caused the crowd to pause. The frenzy died down as people looked up at him and, one by one, began to help those who had been knocked down. Those who had fled began to reassemble in the room, and when everyone was seated and quiet, Washington spoke.

"That was someone's idea of a prank to keep me from talking to you today," he started sarcastically, "but the joke is on him."

What could have been mayhem was averted. With the composure and calm of a resolute leader, Washington had showed his courage and natural ability to meet and handle an emergency. He proceeded to deliver his speech, and the tour continued.

In Tampa, Florida, the meeting took place in a theater that Negroes had never before entered, except as cleaners. Washington had been told when he received the invitation that all citizens would be invited, Negro and white, but upon learning that colored weren't allowed in the building, he thought he would have to preach to this issue in his speech.

The day of the meeting, his party entered the theatre from backstage, and as Washington made his way downstage, the taunts began.

"We don't allow niggers in here," a redneck yelled from the crowd.

"Lessen you is here to do some cleaning!" shouted another.

A group of whites standing near the stage shook their fists threateningly as the visitors took their seats. The atmosphere was menacing and volatile.

But Washington seemed not to have heard nor seen the insults. He stopped at the center of the stage and stood, silent and motionless, staring out at the audience. Stunned, he took in the incredible scene in front of him. White sheets hung from lines strung down the middle of the hall – with the white people sitting on one side and the Negro people on the other. Visibly affected, Washington strode to the front of the stage and, without a greeting or a smile, spoke adamantly.

"I have traveled all over this country and in many foreign countries, but this is the first time that I have ever seen the two races separated by a sheet. Now, before I speak, I want those things taken down from there." In less time than it takes to tell, the sheets were down and out.

"Now I will begin my remarks," Washington said, ready to address the crowd.

John turned and whispered to one of the ministers in their party, "Can you believe him? He is fearless! What other Negro do you know who could get away with that?"

Yet Washington did "get away" with that – and more. In his speeches, he appealed to the sensibilities of his listeners, exhorting them to search their consciences, and admonishing them in words full of emotion and compassion.

"Lawyers, judges, juries," he would say, "when you have a colored boy before you accused of a crime, before pronouncing sentence upon him, put your hand upon your hearts and ask yourselves, before God, has this boy even had a chance?"

Other times he would challenge people, saying, "Talk about social equality – General Robert E. Lee was not afraid or ashamed to go into the Negro church and teach Sunday school. There are distinguished Southern ladies who have done the same thing. If you watch closely, you'll find that the people who make so much fuss about social equality haven't got much social equality to lose."

A confirmed believer in self-reliance and independence, Booker T. Washington knew that he had to solicit support for his cause – financial and otherwise – in unorthodox ways. While he advocated social separatism, he believed in racial equality in other areas, and he knew he needed to attract the largess of philanthropists to support his vision of education for the colored person. Yet, to be successful, his vision of educating the Negro had to appear as if it were no threat to white society. He often quoted a passage from Matthew, in the Bible: "Be ye therefore wise as serpents, and harmless as doves."

The unequal apportionment of school funds also drew his attention and earned a novel approach. When he talked to educators, he explained the situation this way:

"Everybody likes to be complimented, particularly when it is deserved. But when you say that the Negro child has so much native wit, so much more ability, that he requires only three months of schooling per year while the white child needs eight months, you pay us a compliment that we do not deserve. Therefore we cannot appreciate it. Give the Negro child the same opportunities that you give the white child, and he will reward you with improved citizenship."

With just a wave of his hand and a huge broad smile, this six-foot tall, brown-skinned Negro orator left crowds applauding for more, and John learned from the master the power of the spoken word.

In Jacksonville, Florida, while Washington was speaking in a theatre, a mob tried to stage a lynching party. Certain outraged townspeople armed with guns and sticks crowded around the jail, determined to remove the prisoner, a Negro who had allegedly robbed and murdered a white shopkeeper. The sheriff and the deputies stood guard at the door.

"We want justice!" shouted one protester.

"Let that nigger go!" shouted another. "We got some wood waitin' for him."

The sheriff made an impassioned plea to the menacing crowd. "Everybody, listen up," he shouted above the clamor, "we've got guests in this town. We've got newspaper people here and out-of-town folks. Do you want to bring Jacksonville bad publicity all over the country? Now, calm down and go home before we are branded as white folks who don't have no sense. Just calm down and go home!"

The crowd slowly disbursed, and the prisoner was spared for the moment. Cooler and more determined heads had prevented a riot, but Washington and his party soon got word of the incident. Since the tour was near its end, some members of the party felt compelled to leave as soon as Washington finished his speech. Washington stayed, however, and was invited to tour the city the next day. At the great Jacksonville library, he made mention of the incident.

"I am proud to be standing in front of this great library funded by the Carnegie Family. Knowledge is the key to the past and to the future. I am sorry that I have been deprived of some of my party and that they are not here to visit it with me, but several of them received urgent messages last night to return home," he said with the hint of a smile and a gleam in his eye.

One of the city officials quickly apologized for the "unfortunate incident," hoping to counter the negative impact of almost having a lynching take place virtually under the nose of such a well-known speaker. Washington, in turn, took his own time to counter, diplomatically making his point.

"Yes, some of my party took the train out of here somewhat hurriedly last night. I hear that one of my group, an elderly Baptist minister, was late leaving for the station and almost missed his train. Now in the South, we all know that a white taxi driver is not supposed to drive a Negro in his cab, but the minister had no way to get to the station, so he rushed up to a cab driver who was white and asked to be driven to the railroad station.

"Of course the cab driver said, 'Uncle, I don't drive colored people in my cab.'

Ever resourceful, the minister replied, 'There is no use having an argument about it - just let me fix it. You get in the back and do the riding and I'll get in the front and do the driving.'"

The crowd howled with laughter, while Washington waited for them to finish. As the merriment died down, he finished his story. "In a few minutes they were both at the train station. The white man got his quarter, and the colored minister made his train. Now, we don't want to waste a lot of time debating who'll do the driving and who'll do the riding, but what we want is to build up our beautiful Southland and to pull together so that we'll all reach the train. God bless you all – and goodbye."

John returned home from the Good Will Tours, impressed and in awe of Booker T Washington. He would soon be presented with an even more important proposition from his "hero" – one that he couldn't resist.

Love Blossoms "Between the Lines"

It was a beautiful spring morning when John received a call that Dr. Washington wanted him to come to his office to examine him. The day was unusually clear and bright, the scents of honeysuckle and gardenia mingling agreeably in the cool air. John reveled in the freshness. The lush green campus and the manicured gardens belied the reality that most of Alabama was a mixture of red clay and sand, a dense landscape that was difficult to cultivate. When John arrived with his medical bag, he was surprised to see that Washington was feeling fine and seemed to be in a particularly good mood. He invited John to sit down.

"I have good news, John. I have hired a teacher from Boston to teach physical education to the female students. This teacher also has training in the arts, and can work with the students in that department. She comes well recommended, and we are so lucky that she chose to come to Tuskegee. She must be spirited to want to come so far – and to an area of the country that she has never been to before. This will be quite different from the city life she is used to, and we have to do our best to make her feel at home."

"That's wonderful, Dr. Washington," John said, wondering what this had to do with him.

"From her papers, I can tell that she has a strong commitment to educating Negro youth, which will fit our mission quite nicely.

According to her resume, she is the first Negro woman to graduate from the Sargent School in Boston, a smart lass at that! I can't wait to meet her. She is going to be here in a few days, and she will be a guest at my house until her quarters are ready," Washington explained.

"Very good," John said, now completely at a loss as to why they were having this conversation.

"Now, here is my plan. I know that you recently purchased a car from Detroit. It's one of the few in Tuskegee privately-owned, and I would like for you to orient our new teacher to the campus and Tuskegee proper when she arrives. Can you arrange some time to do that?"

"I will be happy to take her on a tour, Dr. Washington. If you will give my office a call when she arrives, I will re-arrange my schedule accordingly."

In spite of his willing response, John was miffed at this intrusion into his well-planned schedule and the interruption of his clinical work. "I don't have time for this foolishness," he thought. He had acquiesced only because the request came from Booker T. Washington, himself.

A few days later, John got word that the new teacher, a woman named Freida Armstrong, had arrived. John sent her a note by campus mail.

April 2, 1913

Dear Miss Armstrong,

Dr. Washington has asked me to give you a driving tour of the campus and the surrounding countryside. I am the Resident Physician for Tuskegee, and I would be glad to pick you up at four o'clock after I finish my clinic. Please let me know if you are available.

Cordially,

John A. Kenney, M.D.

John received a note in reply:

April 2, 1913

Dear Dr. Kenney,

Thank you for the invitation to tour. I am a little under the weather with the sniffles. I think I should rest tonight, but I will plan on touring with you tomorrow if your schedule permits.

Sincerely,

Freida F. Armstrong

John wrote back:

April 2, 1913

Dear Miss Armstrong,

I am sorry that you are under the weather. I will make myself available tomorrow after the clinic around 5:00 p.m. I am sending you over a tonic that may help your cold. Send me a note if you are unable to go tomorrow.

Cordially yours,

John A. Kenney

John was relieved not to have to fulfill his obligation that day and promised himself that he would be more enthusiastic the next, if required. He had been spending his extra time working on ideas for the *NMA Journal* and corresponding with other physicians to get their input on its direction. He was also working on the plans for the medical clinics at Tuskegee – emulating the success of the previous NMA meeting there. This required correspondence with doctors around the country, as well as many months of advance planning for each clinic.

Because of John's managerial, professional, and business responsibilities during the day, the great bulk of his editorial work had to be done in the wee hours of the morning, particularly between 4:00 and 5:00 a.m., after a few hours of sleep. He never exceeded six hours of sleep, because his vision for Negro medicine so occupied his mind that it often kept him awake. He visualized his colleagues one hundred years hence, a respected body of scientific men and women whose names would be emblazoned on the emblems of medical literature. These would be physicians whose erudite opinions and scientific skill would be sought by individuals of all races. John wanted to play a part in bringing that vision to life.

The next day, he received a note from Miss Armstrong by campus mail, saying that she would like to go with him for a tour. John arrived at the Washington's' home and was greeted by Mrs. Booker T. Washington, who showed him to the parlor.

"Miss Armstrong will be right down. Be sure to take her inside the chapel so that she can see the work the students have done," she instructed.

"Yes, I definitely want to see the chapel," said a voice from behind John.

Frieda Armstrong

Turning, he saw the most striking woman he had set eyes upon in some time. She was not beautiful per se, but she had an air of elegance and sophistication that made him feel that he should have put on his best jacket and shirt as opposed to the white coat he wore, looking as if he were there to see a patient. He felt chagrined by his country doctor appearance, and intimidated by this obviously high society Bostonian who exemplified loveliness. He was at a loss for words.

"Thank you so much for coming, Dr. Kenney. Let me get my wrap, and I will be ready to go."

John left the house in a state of bewilderment. He had not taken a woman out in his car since Alice had died, and for a moment the image of her sitting in the front seat flashed through his mind. On some level he was saddened that Alice was no longer with him, but on another level he felt strangely comfortable with this woman whom he had just met. Even so, his attempts to put together intelligible sentences brought forth laughter at his obvious incompetence, and coherent conversation eluded him. He was reeling from the vision of this exquisite apparition in his car and the scent of her intoxicating perfume.

Freida was excited to see all of the progress that Tuskegee had made, and for which it was becoming quite famous. She told John that she was happy to be a part of Dr. Washington's work and his plan for the survival of the race. She talked about her plans for physical education for the students as part of the health curriculum, and she was also looking forward to working with the music department to plan pageants and plays. All that John could do was listen. There was something about her that calmed and comforted him, and it had been some time since those feelings had stirred. He was reminded of what the comfort of a woman means – and of the void he had not been able to fill with work.

He returned Miss Armstrong to the Washington's' home and asked her if she would accompany him on a drive again in the near future. She said that she would be pleased to do so if he could fit her into his busy schedule. John told her that she would be hearing from him soon. He was already rearranging his sleep schedule in his head.

The next day, John inquired about Miss Armstrong and was told by Mrs. Washington that her guest had already immersed herself in classes with the students. Apparently, she was fine-tuning the senior play that had been in rehearsal for some time. A few days after that, John sent a note inviting Miss Armstrong to go driving again.

She replied:

April 9, 1913

My dear Dr. Kenney,

I am sorry that I will have a class at 6:30 p.m., and I will be busy with the rehearsal of the senior play after that this evening. But I will be pleased to go with you some other time if agreeable.

Gratefully,

Freida F. Armstrong

To his surprise, John felt thoroughly undone that he was not going to see her that evening. Instead, he would have to resort to his now uninterrupted schedule.

The next day, he sent her a note asking her if she could go with him on Friday. She wrote back:

April 10, 1913

Dear Dr. Kenney,

As a rule I have Friday, Saturday, and Sunday evenings until chapel to myself, but on account of the senior play, which comes off on the nineteenth of this month, I don't have Fridays free as I call a rehearsal on that night. I will be very glad to go when agreeable to you.

You must come to the play. Don't forget the date!

Sincerely,

Freida F. Armstrong

Annoyed at this point, but admittedly eager to see Miss Armstrong again, John changed his tactic and invited her to a ballgame. He received a handwritten note in response:

April 12, 1913

Dear Dr. Kenney,

I will be very glad to go to the game this afternoon. I will be at Huntington Hall at 2:00 p.m. I'll see you then.

Gratefully,

F. F. Armstrong

P.S. Please excuse the pencil.

This time John gave more thought to his attire. He shined his shoes and put on his argyle sweater, a little more casual for the occasion. When he picked up Miss Armstrong, she was dressed in pale peach silk lace – more like a special doll you would put on a shelf and look at because it was so chic and delicate, but certainly not one you would toy with. John realized that people were staring at her whenever she came into view, and he had to confess that he was impressed with himself for having this unique and stunning woman by his side. It was clear that she was already special to both the students and the teachers, for everyone vied to get her attention. She smiled and waved, and seemed totally unaffected by this obvious adoration.

John's tickets entitled him to premium seats near those from which Mr. and Mrs. Washington usually observed the sporting activities. The tickets had been a gift from a professor for whom John had performed an emergency appendectomy. In gratitude, the patient had gifted John with his preferred seats, which provided a better vantage point from which to see the game, but also made the seats quite public. John, who usually spent the game on the sidelines or in the dugout tending to the athletes, had today left that to his intern. He felt quite important as he escorted the lovely Freida to their seats. He could feel the curiosity and imagine the envy being leveled in his direction, and he was basking in it.

"What great seats!" Freida exclaimed. "You must be very impor-tant to have seats so close to the Washingtons."

John just smiled and nodded. He looked up to see the Washingtons arriving for the game, and he tipped his hat in their direction. Booker T. looked at John approvingly and waved back.

The first inning was exciting, and everyone was enjoying the game until one of the players was hit in the head with the ball and knocked unconscious. John was relieved to see that the intern was attending to the player, and he was about to ask Freida if she wanted to get some refreshments when he felt a tap on his back. He looked up to see Washington, who greeted him briefly and then turned his attention to John's guest.

"Miss Armstrong," he murmured, "you're looking lovely today. Would you care to join me and Mrs. Washington in our box while Dr. Kenney tends to the injured player?"

Before John could protest, Washington had taken her hand and said to John, "It's all right; we'll take good care of her."

John thought it appropriate to do as Washington had suggested, so he made his way down to the field. When he was unable to revive the breathing but unconscious player, he prepared somewhat reluctantly to take the young man to the hospital for further examination and treatment. He sent a student to relay the message to Dr. Washington and Freida, and in return he received assurance from them not to worry; the Washingtons would look after Freida. John couldn't believe his bad luck, but uncertainty was the nature of his profession. Usually he accepted it graciously, but not this time.

After the game and after his patient was stable, John went to the Washington's' home and spent some time there discussing the game he didn't get to see. He returned home after dusk, still heady with Freida's company and the smell of her perfume, but before he could find a quiet moment to recall his time with her, he was summoned to the country to tend to a sick family. With a sigh, he packed his bag and drove miles to a remote farm.

There, he found all nine members of the family prostrate with influenza. In one large bed were four children, two with their heads to the head of the bed and two with their heads to the foot. Three adults were in bed in one room, and two in another. John treated them all and made it back to the hospital in the wee hours of the morning, just in time to take a catnap before starting his hospital rounds and patient clinic. He tried to take comfort in another of his mother's maxims: "It is better to wear out than rust out."

John often had to make these late night jaunts. Sometimes, he was so exhausted that he'd stop the car on the side of the road and snatch a few minutes sleep. Once he got out and flung himself on some pine needles, wrapped up in his lap robe, and slept fifteen minutes, just as he had planned. He found this much better than persisting when the flesh was literally screaming for relief. On one occasion, when he was fighting to hold on, he had waved a salute to a farmer whose place he was passing, and inside of a half-minute he and his car were in a ditch. He had gone to sleep that quickly. Thoroughly embarrassed, he was wide awake when the farmer came to help him out of the ditch. In the wee hours of this night, however, he lay awake with Freida on his mind.

The next day, John got word that Freida had taken a fall during one of the rehearsals for the musical program and, although she was bruised, was not seriously hurt. Even so, John sent his nurse Hilda over to look after her. Later Hilda returned with a note.

April 13, 1913

Dear Dr. Kenney,

I thank you very, very much for your kindness. I do not think there is anything serious, but aside from the one bad bruise that I sustained, I feel lame around my shoulder on the left side where I fell. I had it rubbed with liniment, and it feels somewhat better. I had the nurse you sent over take my pulse, etc., as I felt so restless, but I am sure I will feel better tomorrow, don't you agree? Hilda has promised to come and look after me again when she comes from chapel. Thanking you again for your kindness.

Sincerely,

Freida F. Armstrong

Freida soon got better, and John had to juggle his time in order to see her between rehearsals for the play and her chapel duties. He was looking forward to the play so that he could admire her handiwork – and also so that it would be over and he could spend more time with her unencumbered. It had become clear to him that they shared a passion for service, his in medicine and hers in education, and that they were mutually compatible. She was as avid about her calling as he was, and he was becoming more and more attracted to her.

The night of the big production finally arrived, and students and teachers and some community locals crowded into the Children's House Elementary School to watch. All eyes were on the students as they sang and danced and recited their lines.

Freida, standing left, and the women faculty of Tuskegee Institute.

John's eyes were on Freida. She stood at the bottom of the music pit, out of sight of most of the audience but where the students could see her. She had told John that she had written a special song for the "two of us" and incorporated it into the production. It was called "Between the Lines" and would give him some clues.

John managed to get a seat in the bleachers so that he could look down and see her singing, conducting, and coaching her performers.

The program indicated that the song would be sung after the first inter-mission. John was all ears when the soprano began:

> "If you could read between the lines,
> You'd see what I am trying to say.
> Between the lines you'd see
> The games that I play,
> The things that are so hard to say,
> Whenever we're face to face...."

John tried hard to "get it." What was she trying to say? Between what lines? Was she talking about their conversations or their letters? And games, what games? He listened harder:

> "And you would know the things you'd have to do,
> The things that would make our love grow.
> And I'd know, too, the things that I'd have to do,
> Things done just for me and you,
> If you could just read between the lines."

John's medical education did not help him to understand the machinations of the female mind. Why didn't she just come out and say what she was thinking? Why this guessing game? He could get it right – or he could get it very wrong. He decided to wing it. He would tell her that the production was wonderful, and the music tantalizing. Then she would have to figure out what he was trying to say, and whatever conclusion she came to, he would agree with it.

Unfortunately, they had little time for conversation after the show. The musical was an absolute success, and Freida was swamped with compliments and congratulations, and received an on-stage testimonial from Booker T. Washington himself. He told the students that their education would not be complete without an education in the arts, and he spoke of the importance art played throughout history, as well as in the present day. He admonished the students to look respectfully at each other, because out of their group could come some of the famous artisans of the day. A self-supporting community would need accomplished citizens at all levels in order to be viable, and Washington implored them to use their talents to be of service to whatever community they chose.

Later, as John drove Freida home, she said she was too exhausted for conversation and had a sore throat from all the singing. John controlled his curiosity about the song she had written and instead sent her flowers the next day – a bouquet of roses studded with white magnolias to congratulate her on the event. Eager to see her again, he included an invitation to a patron's supper. Her response both disappointed and encouraged him.

>April 20, 1913
>
>My dear Dr. Kenney,
>
>First, let me thank you for those beautiful flowers you sent me. I think they are just lovely, and I thank you very much, although I didn't sing as well as I would like to have as my throat was troubling me somewhat. I am so glad you thought the play a success, and I thought the students deserve much credit too.
>
>Doctor, I prefer not to go over to Mrs. Seale's to supper, but I thank you just as much.
>
>By the indications of the weather now, I daresay we will not be able to drive this afternoon, as it would undoubtedly be unpleasant. I will not look for you this afternoon, but if you wish, you can come over to Mrs. B. T. Washington's tonight around 8:00 p.m. She is going out – but I will be here.
>
>Sincerely,
>
>Freida

Excited about having some time alone with Freida, John was ready to decline his invitation to supper. Then, thinking that this might be inconsiderate, he decided to stop by Mrs. Seale's home briefly and then leave before dinner. When he arrived, he was surprised to see Mrs. Washington, who immediately took him aside to discuss the health issues of some incoming students. She wanted to devise a plan to introduce a curriculum for proper hygiene to educate the new students, as they were coming from areas that were primitive in sanitation matters. John tried to come up with some excuse to leave and go to her house, but she had him cornered. Instead, he found himself at the dinner table, eating without tasting anything, and explaining his ideas to Mrs. Washington between mouthfuls. As soon as he could, he excused himself, saying that he had to see a patient on the hospital ward. As he prepared to leave, Mrs. Washington grabbed his arm and stopped him in his tracks.

"Dr. Kenney, I am excited by your ideas. Won't you drop me at home so that I can relate all of this to Freida? My husband will be home around eight this evening. Why don't you come over after you see your patient, and we can share this with him?"

"I'll be happy to drop you," John said with tongue in cheek. "I will send word later whether or not the state of my patient makes it possible for me to stop by."

John dropped his passenger off, much to his chagrin, and returned to the hospital, where everything was as fine as he had left it. He did some paperwork and then sent word to the Washington home that he would come by briefly to discuss his ideas. When he arrived, he could see the disappointment on Freida's face, and he was certain that it registered on his, but at least they cemented some new guidelines for student health. John left, promising to send word to Freida later. The next day, he sent her a note inviting her for a drive.

April 21, 1913

My dear Dr. Kenney,

I am not feeling so well today. Still, I feel better now, and I thought I would stay in today, but I would like to have my throat tested. Couldn't Hilda do it when she comes over to dinner? I am so sorry I have to stay in on this pretty day. I hope you are feeling okay. My throat is not feeling quite as well as I would have it.

Freida

Frustrated, John realized that more often than not his mind was focused on Freida and on seeing her without interference from Mrs. Washington, Hilda, her students, or any other distractions. To make matters worse, he knew that Freida had befriended Mrs. Washington's neighbor, Mrs. Owens, and that the lady moved her curtain to peep out every time he drove up to get Freida. Between the two matrons, who felt they needed to protect propriety for appearance's sake, John and Freida rarely had any privacy regarding their plans.

Taking a new approach, John suggested that Freida go with Mrs. Washington and her party to the Southern shore, as it would do her good to get some sun and enjoy the water. He knew the train ride would be long, so he suggested that he drive them. He was looking forward to having some time with Freida, even in the presence of the other ladies, when Mrs. Owens offered a suggestion. Her boy worked down south, and he could meet them halfway so that John would not have such a long drive. His plans thwarted again, John resigned himself to what remained. With all parties agreed, John arranged to pick up the ladies the next morning.

The drive was uneventful, and John was happy to have Freida in the front seat again, even though they had to indulge the other riders' chit-chat. The time fairly flew, and John knew the ride home alone would seem much longer. Mrs. Owens' son, Scott, met them at the halfway point, and John reluctantly parted company to get back to his clinic. The next day Freida wrote:

June 16, 1913

My dear Dr. Kenney,

I am so anxious to know whether or not you reached home free from accident of any sort. We arrived safely about twelve o'clock and, of course, Mrs. Manley was surprised to see us so soon, thinking that Scott had to go to the depot to get us. Oh, I enjoyed the trip so much. Especially the first part until we changed cars.

I was very happy at the thought of you coming all the way with us. But after we left you, and seeing the rough road and long distance we had to go, I felt glad that you didn't make it; and then, too, you would have had such a long trip back. I fear I would have been tempted to return with you.

This is a beautiful place here and the air is free. After having dinner, we were so sleepy that we couldn't hold our eyes open, so we took a nap and later went out for a walk before it stormed. After supper I gave a little concert, and we didn't retire much before eleven, but we hope to do better than that tonight.

I daresay you are very busy today. When do you think you will get away? Are you operating today? You see, I want to know all about you and what you are doing every minute. Is it curiosity? I don't think so, because I don't think I am a very curious little girl, do you?

Well, they have teased me about leaving my lunch in your car. Did you see it? It was quite a joke, but it happened just the way I wanted it to. If I had known it was going to turn out that way, I would like to have had a hand in preparing the lunch, but Rosa at Mrs. B. T.'s put it up for me on a very short notice, and it wasn't prepared as nicely as she wished because she couldn't get any good bread. However, I hope you enjoyed it. They teased me enough about it, telling me that I meant to leave it in your car, etc. It was useless to try to convince them otherwise.

Well, I won't bother you any longer because I know you are busy. Write me when you have a few spare moments. With much love,

Yours,

Freida

John was elated. He kept repeating her closing words over and over to himself: "with much love," "with much love" – she actually wrote "with much love." At last, he felt pretty certain that Freida had the same feelings for him that he had long since held for her. That acknowledgement left him smiling all day long. He was truly happy – with a different kind of happiness that he had known only once before.

After Freida returned from the shore, John was able to steal moments with her from time to time, but their schedules often conflicted. The most consistent communication they seemed to have was their cross-campus letters, delivered by school mail on a daily basis. John kept them all in a box on his desk, often re-reading them to validate the progress their relationship was making. They served a purpose, but left him with a longing that would not subside until she was in his presence.

John had grown tired of cross-campus courting, and he was certain that sometime soon he would ask Freida to become a permanent part of his life. When he learned that she would be going to go back to Boston during the summer to spend some time with her family, he decided to propose before she left. He wrote to Tiffany's in New York and requested a catalog of their engagement rings. He had overheard Mrs. Washington say that Tiffany's was renowned for its quality and workmanship in jewelry, a pearl of wisdom she had dropped one day when she was showing off her ring in his presence. John knew that Freida had spoken highly of the ring her mother had, and that it had also come from Tiffany's. The ring choice was one thing he knew would be right – the answer to his question was another.

John ordered a beautiful diamond solitaire ring in eighteen-carat gold with platinum points. Once the ring arrived, he contacted Mrs. Washington's housekeeper Rosa. He wanted her help in creating a special evening.

"This dinner must be special in every way, Rosa," he explained. "I have asked Miss Armstrong to come over on Saturday, and I'm certain you will know how to make this evening special."

"I'd be happy to help you, Dr. Kenney. We can duplicate the anniversary dinner I prepared for the Washingtons, if you like. Miss Armstrong brought her best cookbook with her from Boston, called

Antoine's. Her favorite recipes are marked. She helped me with the menu for their party. I prepared a corn chowder, codfish cakes and hominy, fresh braised vegetables with salt pork, and plum pudding. Miss Armstrong told me this menu made her feel like she was at home."

"That will be fine, Rosa."

TIFFANY & CO.
FIFTH AVENUE & 37TH STREET
NEW YORK

August 13th, 1913

Dr. John A. Kenney,
    The Tuskegee Normal & Industrial Institute,
        Tuskegee, Alabama.

Dear Sir:

Complying with your request of the 10th instant, we are pleased to send you under separate cover our 1913 Blue Book, containing information concerning our general stock with range of prices; and, herewith, engravings and prices of our first quality, perfect diamonds mounted as women's solitaire rings in 18 carat gold with platinum points, together with a ring size card. The cuts show the styles of the mountings and the sizes of the stones, although we can furnish either larger or smaller diamonds at almost any price from $20. upwards.

Should the enclosures not supply the information you wish, and you will kindly advise us more definitely regarding your requirements, stating the price you contemplate paying, etc., we shall be pleased to send other cuts.

Very respectfully,

WJF

Tiffany & Co.

Tiffany letter

"We can get some fresh flowers from the greenhouse and get some of Dr. Carver's homemade wine. It will be special, Dr. Kenney, I promise," Rosa said, smiling excitedly as if she sensed something special was about to happen.

Rosa went about her duties gathering ingredients and attending to the small details. She arrived at the house with rose-scented candles that the students had made in the home economics department. She also brought a bouquet of white roses with one red one in the middle, and Mrs. Washington sent over her elegant crystal and fine china for the occasion. John wasn't sure how these women were "on to him," but he really didn't care.

As John left to pick up Freida, he could hear Rosa singing in the kitchen. When he returned with his guest, the candles were lit, the wine poured, and the flowers arranged in an elegant crystal vase. When Freida entered the room, her eyes sparkled with delight.

"John," she said coyly, "it's not my birthday. How sweet of you to go to all of this trouble. What's the special occasion?"

"It is a celebration of us, Freida," he replied. "I thought it time that we talked about the future and our intentions."

"Oh, really?" she questioned. "What is it you are trying to say, John?"

John was getting hotter under the collar, and he loosened his tie. His heart was racing and he felt a drop of perspiration trickling down his temple. He couldn't help thinking, "What if she has changed her mind? What if she doesn't have the same feelings for me that I have for her? What if she says 'no'?" Nervousness threatened to overwhelm him, and his hands shook as he handed Freida a glass of wine. "Just be a man and speak your piece," he told himself, but his throat felt swollen and his mouth full of cotton. He cleared his throat, and immediately regretted making such a sound.

"I, uh, have noticed that we have a lot in common, Freida. Our goals for ourselves... our desire to, uh, see our race uplifted," he stammered.

Freida remained silent, looking at John questioningly as she sipped her wine.

"We seem to enjoy each other's company when we are together, and, well, even more so when we can go for a ride alone," he added.

"Yes, John," she said. "That's true."

John wished for more information from her, some signal that would help him know what to say. Her perfume was intoxicating, her closeness dizzying. He wanted to take her in his arms and keep her there forever. Heart pounding, he took her hand in his.

"Freida, I've grown very fond of you," he blurted out. As soon as he used the word "fond", he knew he had taken the coward's way out.

Freida frowned and gave him a puzzled look.

"All right," he said boldly, "let me speak plainly."

He walked over to his desk and took out the distinctive little blue box. Freida's eyes widened in recognition. John plucked the single red rose out of the bouquet and handed it to her. He opened the box and took out the Tiffany diamond ring. He saw tears welling in her eyes, and this gave him the courage he needed to continue.

"I have fallen in love with you, Freida Armstrong, and it would honor me tremendously if you would be my wife. Will you marry me?"

Freida set her wine glass down and held out her left hand. "Yes, John, I will marry you."

John put the ring on her finger and took her in his arms. They kissed lightly and then more deeply, at last able to acknowledge their feelings for each other. They held each other for several minutes, their bodies intertwined, their passion stirring hot and forceful, straining to be recognized.

Were it not for the tinkling of the dinner bell coming from the kitchen, John would have had great difficulty in letting Freida go. Rosa appeared from the kitchen a few moments later with a silver tray and proceeded to serve dinner. The longing to be with Freida had dampened John's appetite. All he could do was gaze at her in the candlelight, anticipating what lay ahead.

New Beginnings and a Requiem

John and Freida made plans to be married in Boston as soon as it could be arranged, sharing their secret only with the Washingtons and Rosa. Even so, John suspected that meddlesome Mrs. Owens knew. Every time she saw John, she tried to pry information out of him. One morning, she seemed to appear out of nowhere just as John neared the Washington's front door.

"Good day, Dr. Kenney," she called, trotting up the steps to the porch.

Startled, John turned and caught his breath, struggling to maintain his composure. "Well, good morning, Mrs. Owens. Ah…lovely morning, isn't it?"

"Oh yes, it is. But you're here early. Is everything all right?"

"All is well. I'm here on business," John answered, turning toward the door.

"I'm sure you are," she said with a sly grin. "It wouldn't be marriage business, would it?"

"Whatever do you mean, Mrs. Owens?" he asked, knowing exactly what she meant.

"Oh, nothing, doctor. I was just thinking out loud," she said with a smile, not owning up to the gossip she had undoubtedly shared with neighbors.

"Well, I'll leave you to your thinking then," John said. "Good day."

Mrs. Washington must have been listening, for as soon as John knocked on the door, she opened it and, without even a greeting, declared, "I swear I haven't told her a thing, Dr. Kenney, not a thing! Now you come on in and let me know the latest plans. I'm just so excited."

"But remember, this is confidential," John said seriously, knowing it was almost impossible to keep this kind of secret in Tuskegee.

One reason for the attempt at secrecy was to give John and Freida time to inform her family before a public announcement was made. They had decided that Freida would go to her parents' home in Boston to begin the planning, and John would join her as soon as his schedule allowed. His job, in the interim, would be to locate larger quarters for the couple to move into after the wedding.

While Freida was in Boston, she wrote to John constantly to help ease the gloom he felt with her away.

2989 Washington Street

Roxbury, Mass.

August 26, 1913

My dearest Dear,

Well, at least I reached home safe and sound, but very worn and tired as you might imagine. I often wished during the trip that I had planned to go straight to New York and from there home, and if I had known we were going to be so well looked after as we were from Cheehaw to Danville, I surely would have chosen that route. The porter was especially kind and attentive, and was very nice to me. He let me use the drawing room in the morning and looked after my every want. When I reached Danville, I had a wait, but I met a friend, Laura, who used to teach with me at Tuskegee. We were surprised to see each other, but also relieved. She was making the trip also, and now I had good company for the duration.

The trip from Danville to Norfolk was something terrible! I hope I shall never take it again. It was the dirtiest trip I ever realized and such uncomfortable seats. When we reached Norfolk, of course we felt wretched. We had some time before the boat came, so we went over to the M&M T. Companies office to see about getting staterooms. We couldn't get an answer, as the boat was coming from Baltimore and they couldn't assign us until it reached there at noon. We started over to Hampton to get something to eat, as we were starved. I called on my friends, Mr. and Mrs. Barton White, but they were away - so we went to Mrs. Holmes' house in Phoebus where we rested and cleaned up, and had a lovely dinner. Then we started on our journey with renewed energy and feeling fine.

We left Hampton for the boat from Norfolk, and when we reached the wharf, we were assigned our rooms. With more time to wait, we went shopping in Norfolk. We then boarded the boat, rested, and had a nice supper. After strolling on the deck for a while, we retired. Got up in the morning feeling fine, ate breakfast, and not a bit seasick. I ate heartily at dinner, but after that I felt rather shaky and turned in. I couldn't eat any supper as I was afraid to get up, but it was well that I didn't try because I was taken with vomiting and couldn't keep anything on my stomach. As soon as I took the spirits of ammonia, it all came up at once. I had a time of it for a while, but I managed to get off to sleep and woke in the morning feeling pretty good. My friend enjoyed the trip and did not get sick. She ate everything and enjoyed the sail.

We should have reached Boston at 9:00 a.m., but another boat from the same company ran into something and sprang a leak, so we had to go very slowly so as to be near her, which delayed us for up to two hours. When we reached Boston, I was feeling fine and glad to say I did not look sick at all, and Papa and Mama looked well. I saw Papa on the wharf before the boat landed, and I could hardly wait to get there. I am happy now and being feted like a princess.

My Aunt Martha came up from Magnolia to see me, but she is returning tonight. All of my folks ask about you and send their love. They are all excited about our plans, and I have so much to do to get started. The weather is delightfully cool here.

I wish I had brought some okra to Mama; she seemed so disappointed that I didn't. Do you think you could send some if it isn't too much trouble? I hope to hear from you real soon.

With lots and lots of love,

Freida

Freida's request for okra gave John a warm feeling of pleasure and usefulness. Here was a chance to both please and impress her family. Although he had left the Kenney farm in his youth, he had never disassociated himself from farming. Tuskegee was no exception. Farming was his first love and, whenever there was an opportunity, he went back to it. He had bought a plot of land near the hospital where he cultivated his own garden, as well as grew his own vegetables. He believed fervently that the way to good health was to eat as "close to the way God made it" as possible.

By now, John had become recognized as one of the foremost gardeners at the school, notwithstanding the fact that "The Wizard of Tuskegee," as George Washington Carver was called, had gained national notoriety as an agriculturist and scientist. John would often go to him for advice or with a problem, and Carver would tell him scientifically how to correct it. He was *always* right, and John's garden flourished. His okra, as well as his other vegetables, were his prized possessions, and he dutifully shipped some to the Armstrong's in Massachusetts with a written reply:

July 30, 1913

My Dearest,

I am so glad that you reached home safely. I hope that the time will pass quickly and that the wedding will be here before we know it. Given my hectic schedule here at the hospital, I won't have much time to think about it. I just want you here by my side as Mrs. John A. Kenney. Regards to all of the family.

And all my love to you,

John

Before long, Frieda sent another letter.

September 15, 1913

My dearest "D,"

Now, who knows what that stands for but me? They might guess, but I know they would never strike it. May I call you that, my "D"? Mama received the okra, and we had a splendid gumbo. That was so kind of you since we cannot get good okra in Boston. Have you used "my car" much? Don't let it get rusty; you must take your friends out, and you need the recreation also.

I'm so glad you enjoy my letters. I hoped you wouldn't find fault with them. I like to write to you just as if I was talking to you and had to do all the talking myself. You see, if you were allowed to interrupt me now and then, I would be forced to say something that I wouldn't write otherwise, so we will leave all that until you have the opportunity to interrupt me, which of course will be extremely agreeable to me. Ha! Ha!

Mama and I went to the moving picture show the other day and then later to Chinatown to eat some chop suey. I wish you had been with us. Have you ever eaten the stuff? I like it, but I have to be good and hungry to eat it. I will take you down there when you come to Boston.

I have been looking at wedding bands, but I haven't settled on a style. I am going downtown this morning, and I will send you some catalogs that I got for wallpaper for the house. I will send you a picture of some furniture, or perhaps I'll ship it in this letter and mail it to you from downtown.

People up here know I am engaged, and there are so many rumors here about our wedding. I know they will be anxious to attend it. I never saw such gossip mavens in my life. Papa and Mama say don't worry about a stopping place when you come to Boston because you have a home here now, and we will be delighted to have you with us. They want you to know that you are perfectly welcome at all times.

I hope you are well, my dear, and not working too hard. Have a good time in Nashville and be as gay as you want to, because, well, never mind why, ha! ha!

Lovingly,

Freida

P.S. I have just had my dress measurement, and size 5 is just right.

Tiffany price list

John was happy to have this correspondence. He had no idea what kind of decorating Freida wanted him to do. He wanted to start off right and make sure that she had exactly what she wanted. He had learned – even from his limited vantage point – that you endear yourself to a woman by giving her what she wants, not what you think she wants. He had found an apartment near the hospital that would be spacious enough for the two of them to live in after they were married.

Mrs. Washington had shared some decorating ideas and, since the Washingtons were planning a trip up North to do some fundraising for the school, had offered to take sketches to Boston to give to Freida. Once there, the Washingtons would have the opportunity to get Freida's opinion of the designs and to meet her father.

"Look here, Dr. Kenney," Mrs. Washington said with assumed authority, trying to solicit his opinion, "I've had my man in Montgomery make up these drawings for you. Look at this. In this room, the oak fireplace mantel and the sawn oak hall seat will match. Throughout the house the wood is oak, but all in different designs. Do you like that?"

Having no idea what he liked, much less what Freida would think was appropriate, John explained, "I've never thought about things like that. I really don't have any expertise in these matters."

"Look at this picture," she persisted, ignoring his comments. "The inlaid table and chairs would be perfect for the dining room. What do you think about that style?"

"That's nice, I think," John replied, rapidly growing restless and bored with such details.

"Well, let's see what Freida says about the sketches and the wallpaper samples; I got some of those too. You just go on back to the hospital and do what you do best. Let us women figure out the decorating."

"That's fine!" John said, getting up to leave. "I'm out of my league in that arena."

Once the Washingtons arrived in Boston, the women quickly finalized the details and decided that they would purchase the furniture from Atlanta because of its proximity to Tuskegee and the varied selection available there. Freida liked the sketches and picked out wallpaper and antique chandeliers for the dining room and the hall entrance. Everyone was pleased with the results, and Freida was sure John would like the plan.

John had already planned a trip to Boston to speak with Freida's father. Feeling quite lonely with Freida gone, he was eager to move things along, and at the end of the month he traveled north to meet with Judge William Armstrong to formally ask for his daughter's hand in marriage. While he had heard from Freida that her father was pleased that he had proposed, he also knew that the judge was a stickler for tradition and wanted to be considered.

Judge Armstrong was perhaps over six feet tall, an imposing man with silvery white hair and a bushy, turned-up mustache that was his trademark. A well-known retired judge, he soon had John feeling as if he were on trial and the unexpected verdict about to be pronounced. The two men were standing in the library of the judge's home when John said, "Judge Armstrong, I would like to ask for your daughter's hand in marriage."

"Dr. Kenney," the judge replied, "my daughter is a delicate girl. She is sweet, she is smart, and she would make someone a loyal wife. However, she was a sickly child, and even now she is sensitive to the elements, often catching cold and feeling poorly. I suppose that marrying a doctor would give me the assurance that she would be taken care of – in sickness and in health. She seems to be smitten with you, and from what I hear, your reputation is clean. Therefore, I give my blessing to this union."

Freida and John were married in Boston a few months later at Saint Andrews Episcopal Church. The wedding was prim and proper, and John felt out of place amidst so much formality. He had married Alice in a country church with only his mother and her parents in attendance. It had been so simple. In Boston, however, they were in a huge church with several hundred people dressed as if they were attending a presidential inauguration. John was decked out in a long, black suit coat with tails and a stiff white collar that scratched his neck. His shiny new shoes were tight and squeaked when he walked, something like a duck quacking. All he wanted to do was to get the wedding over with – until he saw Freida walking down the aisle. His discomfort vanished, and he focused on his beautiful bride.

Freida had never looked more glorious. She wore a fitted, snow-white silk gown embroidered with fine silk thread and Chantilly lace. Her headpiece resembled a crown encrusted with pearls and rhinestones, and a veil trailed behind her to the floor. She carried a bouquet of white orchids tied with silk ribbon that matched her dress. John was mesmerized and intoxicated by this woman walking his way, step by step, with eyes only for him. He didn't remember much about the ceremony afterward and only hoped that he had done everything as rehearsed.

The reception was held in the undercroft of the church, and all of the invited guests crowded around to examine this interloper who was taking one of their most eligible debutantes away. The newlyweds were surrounded by many of the Negro elite who attempted to replicate the high-society ways of their white counterparts. John was amused by conversations he wasn't supposed to hear.

"Who are his parents?" sniffed one homely matron.

"It doesn't matter, dear," retorted her counterpart. "He is a doctor!"

"Oh, I see. He is rather attractive with his reddish hair and greenish eyes."

"I hope the children will turn out... well, you know..." whispered the counterpart.

"Me too!" whispered the matron.

John paid little attention to this foolishness. He had lived long enough to know that this kind of thinking was the result of years of propaganda, brainwashing, and insecurity. He knew that, as a people, Negroes could be their own worst enemy. The only remedy for this would be the creation of a strong Negro society that could stand on its own merits, not just imitate the white society that his people would never be a part of anyway. John was determined to help create an independent society whose citizens represented the best of what his ancestors had stood for – determination, hard work, and the will to survive. He believed that out of the genius of the Negro people would arise everything needed for them to prosper and flourish, and this independence would sustain the race well into the future. That would be a society that the world could emulate, if everyone adhered to the common goal – excellence in all that was done and service to mankind.

Soon after the wedding, John and Freida Kenney returned to Tuskegee and resumed their work with Booker T. Washington. John was encouraged that, as a team, they could be even more effective in leaving a legacy for Tuskegee and in making a difference.

*   *   *

As 1915 warmed into a typical Southern summer, John became concerned that Dr. Washington seemed to be losing his usual vigor and vitality. Headaches and dizzy spells required more frequent treatment, and during the fall, when retrograde changes were obvious, John spent a good deal of time near his mentor. Then Washington was invited to go on a fishing trip to Coden, on Mobile Bay, as a guest of a Mr. Allen of Mobile. Eleven days were so spent, and Washington brightened up considerably.

On his return to Tuskegee, he felt good enough to take a speaking engagement in New Haven, Connecticut, and John was surprised – pleasantly so – when Washington said he felt good enough that John need not go with him. Washington also planned to go from Connecticut to Petersburg for the meeting of the Negro Organization Society of Virginia.

It was during this trip, while taking a tour of New York City, that the great leader was stricken in the streets. Immediate medical help was summoned. Some of the trustees came to his rescue and had him moved to the Rockefeller Institute, where he was examined and various tests were made. He was then moved to St. Luke's Hospital.

At this point, Washington yearned for his wife and his own Dr. Kenney, saying, "They can relieve my head as they have done so often." Mrs. Washington was called by wire, and shortly afterwards John received a message to come at once. He immediately boarded the train at Cheehaw, fearful that "our star" would not shine again.

When John arrived in New York and walked into the hospital room, Washington looked up, extended his hand, and then turned and buried his head under the sheet. They both knew that the "game was lost." After a few days, in keeping with Washington's oft-expressed wish that he would die in the South, arrangements were made for his last trip home. He was in a coma most of the time. Even so, John advised him from time to time of the progress they were making. Finally, when they reached the station, John said, "We are at Cheehaw."

"Ah, Cheehaw," Washington replied with a weak smile.

Loving and willing hands lifted him from the train to the ambulance, and when he was at home in his bed, John told him, "Dr. Washington, we are at Tuskegee."

"Tuskegee," he quietly whispered, and that was his last word. In three hours he had passed away.

John left the Washington home and walked across the campus to the hospital. The staff had gathered to await word. They knew from John's demeanor and expression that their hero had passed away.

John addressed the staff and quoted an applicable scripture: "Know ye not that a great man this day hath fallen in Israel."

John went home to give Freida the news. She immediately began getting ready to go to the Washington home to be with Mrs. Washington.

"You know, Freida, the Negro medical profession had no more staunch supporter or better friend than Booker T. Washington. His unwavering support for the John A. Andrew Medical Clinics and the National Medical Association gave us the advantage of his association," John mused.

"I know, and he proved his confidence in you by choosing you as the personal physician for himself and his family. His attitude was 'if he's good enough for the students, he's good enough for me and my family'."

"I remember operating on his niece and his nephew when they had appendicitis. I often wondered how I would feel if I had to perform surgery on Booker T. Washington himself, and I'm glad it never came to that," John said.

He knew that his association with this great leader had inspired him and benefited him in numerous ways. They had been physician and patient, mentor and student, gentlemen and friends. John learned firsthand the difference that one man can make in the lives of a vast number of people, and the ways one's influence can ultimately change the landscape of life's experiences. Little by little the walls can come tumbling down. In a similar way, John wanted to make a difference in the field of Negro medicine and to implore other Negro physicians to join the quest. He felt that, as a whole, they could set a standard the whole world would admire – one man at a time.

Booker Taliaferro Washington died on the campus of his beloved
Tuskegee Institute on November 14, 1915, and was buried beside
the chapel that his students had built, brick by brick. A statue was
eventually erected on that spot, a gift from one hundred thousand
appreciative Negroes from all walks of life. This statue portrayed
Booker T. Washington *"lifting the veil of ignorance"* from a kneeling
Negro citizen.

Presdient Calvin Coolidge at the Booker T. Washington Monument.

A Personal Challenge for the Kenneys

Spring of 1916 was in the air as the faculty of Tuskegee, in full academic dress, filed into the chapel. Teachers took their seats on the stage, ready to inspect their student charges. The sun, adding its glow to the pomp and circumstance, shone majestically on the parade of marching students coming to take their places for the inaugural celebration. The Tuskegee band, resplendent in maroon uniforms with gold epaulets, led the way along the winding campus thoroughfare. The fanfare of polished brass horns and the deafening beat of huge silver drums pulsated and reverberated off the pavement, announcing the band's arrival and lending excitement to an already auspicious occasion.

The young women students marched behind the band's percussion section, a sea of white dresses and white cotton gloves, patent leather high heels clipping along rhythmically to the staccato beat. The young men brought up the ranks in proper Southern fashion. In their black suits and hats, and their starched white shirts and shiny black shoes, they were ready to pass muster after repeated rehearsal and instruction. Townspeople, young and old, lined the roadway, smiling and impressed with the scholastic atmosphere of "their" students.

Although Tuskegee still mourned the passing of Booker T. Washington, a new successor had been named principal of the school. Robert R. Moton, formerly the commandant at Hampton Institute, was prepared to follow his predecessor's tenets to assure continued philanthropy to the school, although there was speculation among the faculty and the townspeople as to how he would perform.

"I heard that he is more like DuBois than Booker T. Washington," whispered one of the English professors to the colleague sitting next to him in the chapel.

"I heard that it depends on what way the wind blows," said another.

"Well, he has big shoes to fill and time will tell if he can walk in them. Here he comes now. Let's see what he has to say."

Dr. Moton sat quietly on stage, waiting for the hall to fill and the late arrivals to take their seats. Next to him, an empty chair symbolized Booker T. Washington's presence in spirit. As Moton stepped up and took his place at the rostrum, the chapel grew deathly still with expectation, every listener ready to pronounce sentence if the verdict wasn't convincing.

"I thank you all for the hearty welcome that you have extended me. I come to you like Booker T. Washington and John A. Kenney, as a proud graduate of Hampton."

He smiled confidently as he surveyed his audience. "It is no coincidence that the money borrowed to start Tuskegee Institute was borrowed from Hampton Institute. You all are aware of that fact, aren't you?" A few people in the audience nodded affirmatively, while others wondered where he was going with this topic.

"It is not a coincidence that we are all sitting here in the same room with the same mission. God has ordained all of this, and it is now up to me to lead the way. I promise you that I will continue to do Dr. Washington's good works, and together we will continue to make Tuskegee a model for the entire South."

An audible sigh of relief could be detected as the atmosphere relaxed, and people sensed that the status quo would remain.

Mrs. Washington, dressed in black mourning garb and surrounded by her children, smiled at the reference to her late husband, and Dr. Moton acknowledged her. "I assure you, Mrs. Washington that this school will continue in the tradition that your husband started, and your counsel and your experience will be invaluable to us as we move forward." ·

The audience applauded with appreciation, and Mrs. Washington lifted her veil and nodded her approval.

"When Dr. Washington left us," Moton continued, "he left us with an endowment of almost two million dollars. I plan to take that and double it, and then triple it," he declared authoritatively. "We will acquire more land and expand the grounds. We will build more buildings and dormitories and make this the most beautiful campus in the South! We will increase enrollment from the two thousand we now have – to as many as want to come here to seek an education."

The audience stood and applauded this last remark. Dr. Moton symbolized the beginning of a new era, but Tuskegee's citizens felt safe knowing that this would be a continuation and not a change.

Under Dr. Moton's leadership, Tuskegee made considerable progress over the next few years. It was remarkable to see what had initially been a few small dwellings on a dirt road continue to expand into a half-mile stretch of modern buildings and dormitories. The apex of this development was the John A. Andrew Hospital, with its circular drive studded with magnolia trees. Their perfumed essence permeated the atmosphere, giving solace and comfort to all who entered the hospital's doors.

Tuskegee Institute Campus

During this time, John and Freida started a family. Their first, second and third children were boys, to John's delight. John, Jr., or "Jack," Oscar, and Howard were the sons that John had always wanted. His "little soldiers" as he called them were the army of the future. He wanted to add one more soldier, and was shocked and surprised when Freida delivered a girl, Elizabeth, who would expose John's sensitive nature. He had known a girl was possible, of course, but he never really considered it. Elizabeth, the image of her lovely mother, quickly became the apple of his eye and the one he couldn't resist. For some reason, a girl made him conscious of his own mortality in a way that the boys did not.

These family responsibilities meant that Freida did not have much time for her work with the students, and preferred to do her own schooling at home with her children. Both parents were adamant that raising a family was part of the master plan, and they took their task seriously. While their joint mission focused on the future, John felt his role was to set an example, not only for his family but also for his race and profession as well. He took to heart the saying of Descartes: "If humanity is ever to be made perfect, the means of doing so will be found in the medical profession."

Freida understood this and felt that her job was to empower her children to survive and succeed in the world by developing their intellect and character. This, combined with their father's example, should put them in a position to continue the work long after she and John were gone. Although she loved her work with the students, she and John felt that the family was the backbone of a productive society and, without such stability, the foundation would be compromised. When a choice had to be made, their children came first.

This was just as well, because Freida still seemed vulnerable to bouts of tonsillitis and respiratory problems that often left her weak. John had tried everything he knew of to affect a cure, but her symptoms persisted. Lately, he had been thinking of sending her to Boston for a rest and to give her a break from the children for a week or two. She had seemed to grow a little less resilient with the birth of each child, although her spirit remained indomitable. Now her life revolved around raising the children and creating a strong family unit – what she felt she was born to do.

Jack, Elizabeth, Oscar, and Howard Kenney

One Sunday morning, she and John were relaxing in the study. She had a wool blanket wrapped around her, even though it was early spring, and was trying to shake a cold that had been hanging on for a few weeks.

"D," she said to John, who was reading a paper, "do you think if I make a trip to the warm baths in Virginia that it will make me stronger?"

John knew that this would not have much of an effect, but he humored her. As a physician, he knew that the palliative suggestion was just as important as the prescriptive cure. The necessary element was optimism, and that almost always affected the outcome.

"If you feel inclined to go, I will be happy to send you," he replied, not looking up from his paper.

"John! I am asking for your medical opinion. You are the physician. I am not trying to be happy. I'm trying to be well," she said in an exasperated tone.

"Let's try that new salve Dr. Carver has developed for rubbing on the chest, and let's use that tonic twice a day instead of once. If that doesn't help, I'll make the arrangements for the trip up to the springs."

John's heart sank each time Freida suffered a new episode. He had done everything he knew to improve her condition, but to no avail. That, he admitted, was the irony of practicing medicine. He was trained to heal, yet with all of his medical knowledge and surgical skill, he could not relieve what seemed to be a basic medical problem that threatened her immunity further with each attack. He often felt helpless and less of a man in her eyes because he couldn't accomplish what he was trained to do – heal. He considered this his biggest challenge.

"I'll try it then," Freida said. "I trust your advice, John, and I know God will strengthen me in His own time. I have total faith in Him – and you!" she added with total conviction.

Freida's complete confidence in John – combined with his inability to resolve a simple medical problem – left him feeling totally inadequate. When Jack came running into the room, followed by Howard, Oscar, and Elizabeth, he welcomed the interruption.

The children had just returned from their Sunday morning walk with Dr. Carver, who was teaching them about botany and the world of plants. They thought they were just playing a game. Little did they know they were receiving their first scientific lessons from "the Wizard" himself – Dr. George Washington Carver.

"Look at my leaf, Dad," Jack said excitedly. "Dr. Carver said mine was a spatulate leaf. It's shaped like the tool mother uses for cooking."

"And this is a serrate – like a serrated knife," Howard added, not to be outdone.

"And look at mine, Daddy," said Oscar. "Mine is acute…like Libby!"

They all laughed at his interpretation, as Howard and Jack tumbled around on the floor trying to grab each other's leaf specimen. It was at times like this that John was most proud of his family and the love that bound them together – he and Freida called it "Kenney love." It was one of a kind and would weather many a storm, although sooner than John expected.

Freida's change in medication did not improve her condition, and John decided to send her home to Roxbury, the suburb of Boston where her parents lived, to rest until she was stronger. His colleague in Boston, Dr. Garland, promised to refer her to a local practitioner. After John arranged for childcare with Mrs. Owens' help, he put Freida on the train to Norfolk.

Freida knew that she needed some time to rest, but she promised herself that she wouldn't stay away too long. John and the children needed her, and she wasn't going to let this malady hold her back. She took the boat from Norfolk to Boston, fantasizing that she was on a huge ship traveling to foreign ports – a woman of independent means. Traveling alone always gave her that feeling of independence and freedom she had loved as a young student in college. She was standing on the deck as the boat pulled into Boston harbor. It had been some time since she had seen her parents, and the thought of them meeting her at the dock filled her with excitement. As the boat got closer, she saw her father standing on the wharf. She wondered where her mother was, but her father's smile and the thrill of being home quickly absorbed all her attention. She ran into his open arms, feeling safe and sound and the center of his attention, "Daddy's little girl" once again.

"How's my baby?" Judge Armstrong asked, hugging his daughter tightly.

"I'm fine, Daddy. I…" Freida began, and then seemed to choke on her words. "Just one moment…." She took her handkerchief out of her pocket and coughed forcefully, spitting politely into the cloth. "I'm sorry, Daddy, it's that stupid cough and sore throat again. Where's mother?"

"Mother's a little under the weather. She told me to come and get you, and she will see you when we get there."

Freida looked alarmed.

"It's nothing serious, honey. Let's find your bag and get the car. We've missed you."

They crossed the busy wharf and found their way to the lot where the car was parked. The judge smiled as Freida expressed delight at the sight of his shiny new car. He opened the door and helped her in.

Freida opened the car window and let the fresh air blow on her face. She took off her hat and unloosed the hairpin from her chignon, letting her hair blow in the wind. Her father looked at her and started laughing. "You never did like confinement in any way, did you? You look just like you did as a young girl: spirited, unorthodox, and with a mind of your own."

Freida didn't immediately reply. She was enjoying the ride, all of a sudden homesick for all the sights she was seeing, sights that she hadn't realized she missed so much. On the outskirts of Roxbury, she saw that everything was just as she had left it in 1913, but now, she was the one who had changed.

She remembered how it used to thrill her to ride the electric trolley around the city with her mother, discovering this world that used to seem so foreign to her when she was a young child. The factories and warehouses dotted the skyline, their smokestacks spewing grey and black smoke and giving the air a sooty hue. As they drove further into the city toward the downtown area, the air cleared and Franklin Park, with lush green grass and lovely gardens, gave the impression that the city was more spacious than it actually was. The business district was thriving with hotels, department stores, banks and movie theaters that bustled with weekday business. The car passed the historic district with its buildings made of puddingstone, a local building material, and soon reached their neighborhood of row houses built of wood and stucco near the intersection of Washington and Warren streets.

"It's so nice to be home, Daddy," Freida finally said as she got out of the car and ran up the steps to the house. She opened the front door, while her father retrieved her bags from the trunk of the car.

"Mother, where are you?" she called, throwing her purse and hat into a chair. "Mother?"

"Freida, I'm upstairs in my room," her mother answered, straining to be heard.

Freida ran up the stairs and found her mother in bed, a hot water bottle on her forehead. Alarmed, Freida went to her side. "Mother, what's wrong?"

"I'm okay, honey," she said in a weak voice. "It's just these darn headaches I've had lately. The doctor was here yesterday. He gave me some buffered powder, and I am some better. I'll be fine."

"Well, you look pale and drawn. I don't like it. I want to talk to that doctor, and he can look at my throat at the same time. I can't seem to shake my cold. Some pair we are, huh?" Freida questioned with mock disgust.

They both laughed, and Freida lay down on the bed with her mother. "It's so good to be home," she said again as her mother stroked her hair, reminding Freida of the love that had always embraced her. They talked and laughed, and after some time they both fell asleep. The last thing Freida remembered was someone covering her with a blanket.

The next day Freida awoke feeling rested and somewhat better, other than having slept in her clothes. She looked at her mother, who seemed to be resting peacefully, and then tip-toed out of the bedroom. She bathed and dressed and went down to the kitchen, smelling breakfast as she approached. Her father was there with her Aunt Martha, who was busy cooking.

"Aunt Mar, how good to see you!" Freida exclaimed as she hugged and kissed her favorite aunt. "Morning, Daddy," she added, kissing her father on the cheek and playfully tweaking his turned-up mustache.

"It's good to see you too, Freida dear, though you look a little worn out," Martha said, looking over the top of her glasses and surveying her niece with a look of concern.

"I'm fine, Aunt Mar, really. What are you cooking?" Freida opened the oven to take a peek. The rolls were golden brown and crusty and looked as if they were almost ready to "pop," a sign that they were done. Freida loved to tear the steaming bread open and slather it with melted butter.

"I'm cooking a fine New England breakfast that will make you stronger. Spoon bread, codfish cakes, grits and popovers," she said. "Okay, the grits are a Southern product, but they go so well with the codfish cakes."

"That sounds yummy. When can we eat?"

"It's almost ready. Have a seat." Aunt Mar took the popovers out of the oven and piled them on a plate in front of Freida, who immediately began to butter one.

"This is so good," she muttered as she ate one and reached for another.

"After breakfast, I thought we'd go downtown so that I can show you what's new in Ferdinand's store," Aunt Mar said, serving the grits. "Maybe we'll have lunch and then come back home. The doctor will be here by then, and you and your mother can be examined."

"Okay. That sounds great, Aunt Mar." Freida paused between bites of codfish cake. "We'll do that if I can stop by the park for a moment. I want to take off my shoes and stockings and walk in the grass in my bare feet like I used to. We can't do that in the South, you know?"

"Lord, chile," lamented Aunt Mar, "I thought marriage would have settled you down. You're still as rambunctious as ever!"

"I hope so," Freida said, laughing, as her aunt feigned disapproval.

Freida and Aunt Mar took the electric trolley downtown, just like the old days. They visited several department stores and took a stroll in Harriswood Crescent, another historic park in Roxbury. Freida walked barefoot in the grass, trying to get her aunt to be more liberated, but Aunt Mar adamantly refused. After lunch, they took a taxi back to the house so as not to miss the doctor's appointment. As they approached the house, they saw an ambulance pulling off and Judge Armstrong hurriedly getting into his car. When he saw them getting out of the cab, he shouted, "Hurry! Get in the car. It's your mother. I couldn't wake her!"

Freida and Martha jumped into the judge's car and followed the ambulance to the hospital. When they arrived at the emergency room, the nurse told them in a flat voice that Mrs. Armstrong was being tended to by the doctors, and they should have a seat in the family waiting area.

After what seemed like an eternity, the doctor on call came out to talk to the family, approaching the judge with a grave expression. "I'm sorry, sir. We did everything we could. We worked on her for almost an hour, and we couldn't revive her. We won't know until we get the autopsy results, but I feel certain that she must have had an aneurysm. I'm very sorry."

The family stood in stunned silence, the reality of the message not registering. Judge Armstrong sank into a chair, putting his head in his hands. Freida began to cry, and put her arms around her father. Aunt Martha reached into her purse and took out her rosary. She closed her eyes and, with shaking hands, started passing her fingers over each bead, praying: "Hail Mary full of grace, the Lord is with thee. Blessed are you among women and blessed is the fruit of your womb. Holy Mary, mother of God, pray for us sinners now and at the hour of our death."

The hospital priest soon arrived and ushered them into a small room with a cross on the wall and a few chairs. He asked the judge if he would like to see his wife, and both father and daughter said yes. Aunt Mar declined, asking to remain alone in prayer.

Freida and her father were led to an examining room where the body lay draped in white sheets, except for the face, which, illuminated by a ray of sunlight from the window, no longer looked pale and drawn. Seeing the peaceful smile on her mother's face, so unexpected after having been told of the heroic attempts made to revive her, Freida felt strangely comforted. In fact, she thought her mother looked angelic, even beautiful, in death. The scene was so ethereal that Freida stopped crying and stood in awe at her mother's bedside. A sense of calm came over her, and the longer she stood there, the more convinced she became in her soul that this was all right. She just *knew* everything was as it was supposed to be.

Judge Armstrong orchestrated a beautiful funeral for his wife, with Freida giving the eulogy. She spoke of inheriting her mother's strong will and spirit, which gave her the capacity not to be afraid of taking on new risks and challenges. She told the mourners that it was her mother's faith in God that had sustained the family during many trials and tribulations, and that faith was sustaining her now. She held up well throughout the service and burial, but she collapsed with exhaustion at the repast that followed.

John had not been able to make travel arrangements from Alabama in time for the funeral due to the weather and distance, but the local doctor had sent John a telegram confirming that Freida was in his care. A day after the funeral, John called his father-in-law to express his condolences and to inquire about Freida. "Aunt Mar called and told me about the service," he said. "She said it was magnificent and that Freida gave a beautiful tribute to her mother. How are you holding up?"

"I'm holding on, son, doing the best I can. Thank you for the lovely spray of flowers you sent for the casket; they adorned it beautifully."

"You're welcome, Judge. How is Freida doing? I'll talk to her in a few minutes, but I wanted to get your opinion first."

"The doctor was here today. He said she is exhausted due to the ordeal and has some rheumatism, but nothing serious. I am insisting that she remain in bed, but you know how she is. I wish you could have come for the funeral. I think you know how to handle her, John; she listens to you."

"I wanted to be there, but it was not to be. Besides the weather, we have upwards of forty patients in the hospital, some of whom have come from quite a distance for special treatment. I also have several post-operative patients who have had surgeries in the last few days, and I am obliged to see them through. As far as Freida is concerned, it is not out of the ordinary for inflammatory rheumatism to follow tonsillitis. If she does what the doctor says, she should be ready to come home as soon as she feels better. Why don't you come down here for a spell? It would be good for you under the circumstances. Then I can keep an eye on both of you."

"Thanks, John. I need to be near home for a while, but give me some time and I may take you up on your offer."

Freida returned home four weeks after her mother's funeral. She finally felt better, and seeing her children gave her the boost she needed. Everything returned to normal in the Kenney household, although the mood of the country was anything but normal.

The unrest in Europe over the past few years had at last embroiled the United States in World War I. By 1917, the conflict had left its "second-class citizens" feeling homeless. Negroes had as much patriotism as any other Americans, even though they were denied the rights of basic American citizenship. They were all the more loyal because of their need to show that the brotherhood of men was far greater and more important than the divisiveness of prejudice, especially in wartime. They were willing to postpone their fight against racism in the name of national defense, but their help was unwanted and their faithfulness eschewed.

Who could have predicted that the war overseas would be the catalyst for a "war" in the United States – a war between the races – one that would shock the entire country?

A Brewing War

John was working in his office at the hospital one Sunday morning, enjoying the beautiful fall day just beyond his window, when the telephone rang.

"John!" Judge Armstrong bellowed into the telephone, "thank you for the guinea fowl and the canned food stuffs from your summer crop. We can't get those things here this time of year in Boston, and we really appreciate it. How are all the Kenney's, and especially my Freida?"

"We are all well, Judge. Freida and the children are at Sunday school, and I'm finishing my clinic. I will meet them at the chapel at eleven. We are having a service to pray for the troops at war. It's so damn frustrating! We are not able to do our part to serve the country. Our people only recently attained freedom. This makes us want to serve even more!"

"Get used to it, John," the judge said with resignation, "and then you don't worry about it. Don't spend energy worrying about what you can't change. The chief thing that bothers me now is the high cost of living. I'm not deeply interested in the war. I'm concerned only so far as it affects my pocketbook, chiefly because the colored man is not a desirable participant as far as this administration is concerned. If the war continues long enough, however, the people who are sending their sons to the front will demand a change. They will declare that life is more important than prejudice, and at that time we will be called to serve. Expediency – not humanitarianism – will demand it. Mark my words."

As Judge Armstrong predicted, colored men were called to serve in many capacities. Prejudice and segregation still abounded, but the colored soldier served diligently in whatever capacity to which he was relegated. Nonetheless, those soldiers who sustained injuries and illness during the war were often kept in basements, attics, or other undesirable places in hospitals. Some were even kept in jails.

As one of the prominent physicians in Macon County, John was called on to administer to some of these soldiers in various towns and cities. On one of those trips, he traveled to Montgomery, Alabama, to a makeshift hospital near Camp Sheridan, a military facility, to look after some veterans' home from the war. He arrived at a building that had formerly been a correctional facility. Once deserted, it now housed twenty or thirty Negroes who called this place home. Some church missionaries brought food, water, and supplies during the day, but the men were left to their own devices most of the time. Most had been treated at military facilities until they were stable enough to be dumped at this location.

When John went inside, he couldn't believe his eyes. Many of the soldiers were sharing what used to be cells, sleeping on stained pallets atop rude wooden benches. It was revolting to see these heroes who had served so honorably treated no better than prisoners of war. He was so angry and disgusted that he was at a loss as to what to feel. How could this country be so mean-spirited, so inhumane, and so cruelly callous? Here were men who had put their lives on the line overseas, and had come back to conditions at home that put their lives at more risk. Here was blatant proof of what Dr. Roman had once said: "The history of mankind is full of cruelty – in fact, the history is almost written in blood."

John stopped to treat an older man who appeared to be sicker than the others.

"I'm Dr. Kenney," he said. "I'm here to look after you. How are you feeling?"

"I'm breathin', doc," the soldier replied. "That's 'bout all I can say. Don't do no good to complain. Nobody's gwine do nothin' anyway."

"Let me check you over. You look dehydrated. Somebody bring me some water," John called.

"There ain't no water comin' till mornin', doc. They already been here for today," another soldier shouted from his cell.

"Excuse me for a while, gentlemen. I will be back."

"Sure you will," a voice said sarcastically.

Quietly John picked up his hat and medical bag and returned to his car. He drove down the road until he came upon a country store next to a farm. He had some money with him and intended to spend it, but the moment he entered the store, he saw that the proprietor had a large and probably painful abscess on his neck. John offered to treat it in exchange for supplies. With a deal struck, John efficiently drained the abscess, loaded up his car, and drove back down the road to where the veterans were housed. He walked in loaded down with bags and boxes.

"Doc," the older man said with a grateful look, "we took bets on whether or not you would come back. I knew you was a man of your word. I told 'em you'd be back."

John passed out the supplies and took care of those who needed medical care. Then he went back to Tuskegee and informed everyone of what he had seen. Even some of his white friends were embarrassed by his story, and vowed to alert the people in government who could change this situation. The National Medical Association also addressed this inequality of care regarding black servicemen home from the war, and eventually the newspapers published articles assailing such practices. Stories of the soldiers' heroic exploits overseas helped to bring the issue to a head.

As the service of these men became more widely recognized, the Veteran's Bureau in Washington sought to establish a facility to care for disabled Negro soldiers. At the end of the Civil War, President Lincoln had decreed that America was dedicated to "…care for him who shall have borne the battle and for his widow and his orphan…." In this spirit, the United States Treasury Department established a hospitalization committee to investigate providing for black soldiers who needed ongoing medical care. The result of the committee's survey revealed that no place existed in the South where these soldiers could be cared for properly.

The Congress then authorized another committee to study the feasibility of building a hospital for the 300,000 black veterans scattered throughout the southern region. President Warren Harding, along with other government leaders, felt that the solution was to build this hospital on the grounds of Tuskegee Institute. They contacted the school's officials, who hailed the proposal and saw it as an employment opportunity for young black physicians and nurses.

Tuskegee donated over three hundred acres of land for the project, and the government bought an additional forty acres of land from a local white woman. The hospital was named the "Hospital for Sick and Injured Colored War Veterans" and was built at a cost of $2,500,000. It had six hundred beds, and was the third largest hospital in the country to be erected by the government. It was suggested that this facility would be a means of employment for young black physicians, as well as a training center.

Mr. Williston, the school's landscape artist who had done so much to beautify the campus, secured the contract to convert the barren hilltop where the new hospital stood into a Garden of Eden. His job was to transform approximately four hundred acres of land with twenty-seven permanent buildings adjoining the Tuskegee campus. The grounds became a place of beauty and a monument to Williston's artistic genius. The entire town was excited to have a facility of such grandeur in its midst.

A dedication ceremony was held on February 12, 1923, on President Lincoln's birthday. It was a great day for Tuskegee. Vice President Coolidge was the principal speaker, and several government officials came with him. The governor of Alabama, William Brandon, was in attendance, as was Colonel Robert H. Stanley, a Southern white man. It was soon learned that Colonel Stanley would be named the temporary head of the hospital, news that angered many of the Negroes who had envisioned a colored director and who also believed this white man had ties to the KKK, or Ku Klux Klan, an organization of whites that had gained strength from the escalating opposition to the Negro race. Yet, in spite of the tension provoked by Stanley's presence, the ceremony went off without a hitch, and a plan was made to petition the president for a full Negro staff. The Negroes were sure Stanley's involvement would be a temporary situation.

Veteran's Hospital Gates

Dr. Moton had invited all of the local townspeople to the dedication celebration. It was a grand event, starting with a parade through the campus and a caravan of cars and wagons winding along the back road to the new hospital site. The workers busily pruned and manicured the landscape and decorated the grounds with balloons and colored crepe paper. The Tuskegee choir sang and the school bands played. The home economics department prepared a feast replete with southern fried chicken, potato and hog maw salad, collard greens, and crackling cornbread. Tables of homemade cakes, pies, and other desserts lined the driveway under the oak trees. The children enjoyed drinking punch and bobbing for apples, and Dr. Carver's dandelion wine for the grown-ups quickly livened up the festive occasion. This hospital would honor the efforts and sacrifices of the more than 300,000 Negro servicemen in the South, and would stand as a concrete example of bravery and courage.

The jubilance was short-lived. The president and the Republican administration in Washington ordered that this colored facility be staffed with all white physicians and nurses. Perhaps no single interracial issue had so rocked the South since Booker T. Washington dined with President Roosevelt.

The Tuskegee faculty was having a staff meeting when the news went public. One of the secretaries came running into the staff room carrying a radio. "Excuse me, Dr. Moton," she said urgently, "the director of the Veteran's Bureau is speaking on the radio. He is saying that the president is going to staff the V.A. hospital with a white staff."

Everyone in the room looked stunned. As reality set in, they began to ferociously condemn the administration. Moton jumped up and called for order. "Quiet, please, everyone. Turn on that radio and let's hear for ourselves. I don't believe it!"

The secretary turned on the radio and turned up the volume. Everyone in the room crowded around to listen. A spokesman for the Veteran's Bureau was speaking:

"The government has awarded four hundred and forty-six million dollars in disability benefits for our ex-servicemen. The president has allocated two million dollars of this for the veteran's hospital in Tuskegee, Alabama, and as of now it will be staffed with white personnel."

"Blasphemy!" Mr. Logan shouted, outraged.

"I don't believe we have been deceived by President Harding himself. This can't be possible," Dr. Moton muttered in disbelief.

"Ladies and gentlemen, we have a crisis," John said, realizing the impact that this announcement was going to have nationally. "We're going to need help to solve it."

"You know the bureau is beset with scandal and the president has put his cronies in his cabinet. Who can we trust?" Logan asked.

Word of the decision spread like wildfire. All over the country, telephones were ringing, radios blaring, and telegrams criss-crossing the nation to deliver the bad news.

The Negro community was outraged and argued that since this was to be a training ground for Negro professionals, then the hospital should be staffed totally with Negro personnel. It had been intimated, since the inception of the hospital proposal that the institution would be for Negroes and by Negroes. Why else would they donate land for this project? The word that the government had misled them spread quickly through the colored community, and evoked protests from Negroes nationwide who demanded that the government reverse its decision.

The National Medical Association, regarding the situation as a gauntlet thrown down, jumped in and snatched it up. The Association's first move was initiated by Dr. George E. Cannon, who wrote a letter to President Harding on April 11, 1923.

My dear Mr. President:

As Chairman of the Executive Board of the National Medical Association composed of organized Negro physicians, dentists and pharmacists in the USA, I have been requested to write you as follows:

The report both by rumor and press has come to us that a plan is on foot to man the Veteran's hospital in Tuskegee, Alabama with white physicians and nurses. This, to us as a group of medical men, constitutes a serious situation since this hospital was established for colored veterans.

As men of the medical profession, we are deeply concerned in this matter, and I have been requested to write and ask for an appointment with you so that the officers of our medical association may talk over the situation with you. We are desirous that the best thing be done in the manning of the hospital and feel that the conference asked would be helpful to all concerned. I hope that you will see your way clear to give us this conference at as early a date as possible. I would be pleased to know of a date for the appointment at least four or five days in advance so I could notify the officers in different sections of the country.

Trusting that you will give this request your favorable consideration, I am

Yours truly,

George E. Cannon

Dr. Cannon received the following reply:

The White House

Washington

April 16, 1923

My dear Dr. Cannon:

Your letter of April 11th has been received and I have laid it before the President. It will not be necessary for you to go to the expense and trouble of a visit to Washington for the purpose to which you refer, as I can assure you that the hospital in question is to be organized with colored personnel.

Sincerely yours,

George B. Christian, Jr.

Secretary to the President

With this information in hand, the NMA officers were assured that the president would make an official announcement, although he didn't do that right away. The second move was to begin negotiating for the National Medical Association to be recognized in the same manner as the white American Medical Association, which represented organized medicine. This move further antagonized white factions.

Soon the tension in the South was as palpable as the unyielding temperature scorching the entire region. Tempers flared. Where there had been civility between the races, there was now outward hostility. From the pulpit to the newspapers, white preachers and politicians denounced the idea of a government facility staffed by blacks. White cities held rallies and marches to protest this unthinkable idea. Black churches and newspapers spread the word that on this issue the Negro population had to stand its ground. State and local officials who had campaigned on popular segregationist platforms to get elected now complained that this hospital situation represented Negroes trying to segregate themselves – and surely this must be against the law.

The white community was adamant. Someone in the government had indirectly proposed to them that they offer a compromise, suggesting that the hospital staff would be all white, except for colored nursemaids. Since it was against the law in Alabama for a white nurse to actually touch a black patient, the nursemaids would do the touching. Many of those in favor of a white staff felt that there were not enough well-trained colored physicians and nurses to adequately staff the hospital anyway. This compromise insulted blacks, and their reaction infuriated whites.

The issue of which race should staff the hospital was debated all over the country. The closer one came to the Northern states, the more liberal opinions became. The deeper into the South one ventured, the more attitudes about the matter disintegrated into an ugliness that defied human nature or logic.

John's NMA members kept him informed as to the national sentiment. A colleague of his in North Carolina, Dr. Charles Shepard, called him about an article he had read in the *Greensboro Daily Newspaper*.

"Hey there, Pudding Head," he quipped, using a nickname from John's medical school days. "How are things going in Tuskegee?"

"We are holding our own right now," John replied, not amused by Charles' joke.

"No, seriously, you know we are with you. I wanted to tell you about this article in a local newspaper. It states that 'the ability and the management capabilities of Negro physicians cannot be questioned, and the selection of white men to staff the hospital was a mistake'. It says that this *mistake* was probably made by an individual or a small group, and that it was perhaps a bureaucratic blunder made in Washington."

"Go on," John said with renewed interest. "This is good to hear."

"It says that 'the decision resulted in a storm of protest from the educationally advanced, highly race-conscious Negroes of the whole country, and whether this may be mistake number two is debatable. If it was a mistake, it was the mistake of a race, growing out of the blunder of persons in officialdom.' That is a quote directly from the article. A mistake, huh?" he asked.

"We think our protest was anything but a mistake!"

"Well, you know I agree with you. The article further states that 'the highest medical authorities would say that Negroes in the profession are able to furnish perfectly capable medical and surgical skill, although the percentage of able doctors in proportion to the Negro population is relatively small'."

"That's why we have to be allowed to do what we can wherever we can."

"The conclusion is that, while the president may be persuaded to rescind his decision to employ white physicians, it is not always easy to undo a mistake."

"The atmosphere in Tuskegee is proof of that," John said. "But we have reason to believe that he has changed his mind. The announcement should be made anytime now."

Perhaps hoping to head off any such announcement, Governor William Brandon of Alabama had sent a telegram to the president asking him not to take any action to staff the hospital with Negroes until the governor's office could investigate the situation. Brandon intimated that the institution, if located in the South, would not serve its mission and would only lead to racial violence. Unfazed, President Harding rescinded his order and stated that the hospital would be staffed with Negro personnel. The ensuing uproar threatened government stability.

OPPOSED TO NEGROES AT HEAD OF HOSPITAL

Governor Brandon Wires President to Delay on Tuskegee Officers

Expressed in terms which clearly set out his unalterable opposition to the reported plan of President Warren G. Harding to place negro officers in charge of the new government hospital for negro soldiers at Tuskegee, Gov. William W. Brandon in a telegram dispatched to the president, Saturday evening, requested the president to take no action along these lines un- til he has carefully investigated the situation.

Alabama's chief executive stated to the president, that it is his opinion that the placing of negro officer's in charge of the government hospital at Tuskegee might tend to racial trouble which does not now exist. He reminded the president also that the Tuskegee Institute is located in the heart of the South, and stated that if the reported plan is carried out the hospital would not serve its mission.

Brandon's Telegram

Governor Brandon's telegram follows: "Press dispatches indicate that you will officer hospital at Tuskegee with nergo. Let me respectfully urge that you do not take such action without careful investigation. In my opinion the institution would not serve its mission it being located in the heart of the South. Placing of negro officers in charge might tend to racial trouble which does not now exist. I plead that you make a careful survey of situation before you take action."

Dispatch from Washington

News dispatches from Washington, D.C., published in the press of the state Saturday afternoon, were to the effect that Roscoe Simmons, of Chicago, Il., editor of a negro newspaper, had discussed Saturday with President Harding, plans to make the personnel of the new government hospital for Negro soldiers, at Tuskegee, wholly negro. It was also stated that both the president and the federal board of hospitalization have for several weeks had under consideration plans to turn over the hospital completely to negroes. Simmons, the negro editor, was reported to have stated upon leaving the White House, that he had been assured the change would take place within 30 days.

Once before it when it was rumored that the president was planning to place negro officers in charge of the Tuskegee hospital for negro soldiers, Governor Brandon filed his protest against such a step. He was joined in this protest by General R.E. Steiner, of Montgomery, State Commander of the American Legion. An effort was made Saturday evening to communicate with General Steiner, but he could not be reached over the telephone.

Newspaper article on Alabama Governor Brandon

Considerable communication flew back and forth between officials in the Alabama State Government and the Veteran's Bureau, while as much or more conversation passed between local whites and their white sympathizers all over the country. General Frank T. Hines, Director of the Veteran's Bureau in Washington, who had been selected to staff the hospital, consulted with Governor Brandon, who wanted to avoid any violence. In one telephone conversation, the governor urgently expressed his fears in a breathless voice. "General Hines, I know you are under pressure to follow the President's order, but you must realize what kind of commotion it's causing down here in Dixie! The KKK is up in arms, the citizens are hopping mad, vigilante groups are forming, and the coloreds are getting bolder by the minute, defending the right to staff that hospital with Negroes. Are y'all tryin' to start another war on top of the one we've already got goin' on?"

"Calm down, Governor," the general responded in an even tone. "It's just a matter of keeping your folks under control and not letting things get out of hand. The president is aware of the situation, and he is giving you authority to call out the National Guard if you have to."

"Well, it may come to that," Brandon warned.

Shortly after the president rescinded his order, John received a newspaper article from his colleague, Dr. Charles Cater of Atlanta, Georgia. It had appeared in the *Enquirer Sun News* of Columbus, Georgia and stated that the president was being swayed by the Negro constituency above the Mason-Dixon Line, and wrongly so. This kind of press further antagonized relations between the races below the Mason-Dixon Line.

The Enquirer Sun News, May 20, 1923

Over the protests of the governor and other prominent citizens of Alabama, and over the earnest and urgent request of Dr. Robert Moton, president of the Tuskegee Institute, the great Negro institution founded by the late Booker T. Washington, President Harding seems determined to organize the new two million dollar hospital for Negro veterans of the world war with a general staff of Negroes. This action of the president follows or will follow an unwise effort on the part of some Negroes, principally in the North, to have the president pursue this course.

The hospital, when finished, will be one of the finest in the world, and the inmates will be men who made sacrifices for their country. Presumably, therefore, they are entitled to the best, to the most skillful medical and surgical treatment. "The Negroes, in demanding a full Negro personnel and control of the institution," says the *New York Morning Telegraph*, "means that color and not competence would determine selection."

It is an absurdity. It assumes that the colored race, despite handicaps for which it is not responsible, but handicaps of a most weighty nature, has advanced as far in sixty years of freedom as the white race has advanced in thousands of years.

When the contract was let for the erection of the hospital building, it went to whites because there was no contractor or construction company, composed of Negroes, financially able to handle it. The main point is that of giving such service to those Negro veterans as they deserve, which is the best the government can give. If those Negroes who have demanded a full Negro supervision and control of the institution believe they have among themselves men who can give the best service the government can afford, they display great ignorance. They ought to know that they have not possibly learned as much in the few years of opportunity that they have had afforded them as the whites have learned in the thousands of years they have been studying and equipping them-selves for just such work as will be required of those in control of this institution. And for them to insist upon their demand shows that they are, unintentionally though it may be, not willing to give the men of their race the treatment they deserve – the best the government can afford.

There should be neither politics nor racial feeling in the matter, but everything should be subordinated to the good of these unfortunate men. In order that this may be done, those best fitted and equipped to do it should be chosen for the work, and there is no argument when it comes to determining the question as to who is the best qualified for it. This does not mean that there should not be Negroes engaged in the work in every place where a Negro can do it. The *Enquirer-Sun* has often called and will continue to call attention to unfair and unjust treatment of the Negro by whites; and it will also not fail to warn the Negro when he seeks to put an injustice on himself by stupid and foolish acts, of which this demand is one.

Dr. George Cannon and Dr. Michel Dumas, prominent members of the NMA, called a meeting to propose that John be named an active candidate to head the Tuskegee Veteran's Hospital. After the vote, they phoned to give John the news.

Freida stopped him just as he was going out the door to attend a strategy session at the chapel. "John, you have a call from George Cannon."

John gave Freida a peck on the lips as he turned and took the telephone.

"George, how are you? Is everything all right?"

"Yes, John, all is well. I am calling to let you know that I have just met with Doctors Dumas, McNeil, and Curtis, and we have gone over the situation at Tuskegee. We have reached some conclusions that we want you to be aware of. We are writing General Hines a letter requesting that you be appointed to the Tuskegee post."

"I don't know what to say," John said, taken aback. "This is a surprise and an honor." He turned to Frieda. "They want me to head up the hospital." She squeezed his arm, nodding.

"We are letting them know the regard in which you are held. You don't know this, but our group is practically unanimous in support of your selection. Your qualifications both from your training and your experience are impeccable. You are used to managerial responsibility, and your administrative ability is proven."

"Thank you, my friend," John said, humbled by the compliment.

"Dumas is here with me," Cannon said. "He wants to tell you something else."

"Kenney," Dumas said without pausing, "things here have taken such a turn in the last few days that they may truthfully be designated in the old phrase 'confusion worse confounded.' Everyone knows that we petitioned for a complete colored staff at the hospital, and that was not an easy task to accomplish. But we did it. Now we know we have an uphill battle with the whites, but we're determined. We just need to know that you are the man to head up this mission."

"I'll give this my utmost consideration, Dumas. Let me mull this over for a bit; this is so sudden. You know I'll do whatever I can."

"I'm going to have the Veteran's Bureau send you the application. We are definitely counting on you," Dumas declared.

John hung up the phone and turned to Freida. "This is one of the highest honors I have ever received," he said. "To be voted on by my peers to represent the Negro people in an issue of this magnitude and importance is overwhelming."

"Of course you are the one to do it, D."

"I've got mixed emotions, Freida. I'm honored, but you and I both know that the escalating volatile tensions here in Tuskegee are straining civility, and I'm afraid of what might happen. We had better be ready."

"You will be, my dear," Freida remarked as she handed John his hat.

"Well, this meeting tonight should at least help us get ready. I'm going to make rounds afterwards, and then I'll be home. Think you can wait up for me?"

"Of course, D, I'll be waiting."

John walked over to the chapel thinking about how Dr. Washington would have handled the situation. He was reminded of the power of the spoken word and how Washington had used it to defuse many a dangerous situation.

Dr. Moton had called the emergency meeting of the faculties of the Tuskegee Institute and John A. Andrew Hospital. By the time John arrived, Moton had stationed senior students at the windows and doors for security. "Let me know if you see anyone approaching or anything out of the ordinary," he had urged the students. "We need to expect the unexpected."

In this atmosphere, Moton addressed those gathered in the chapel. "Gentlemen and ladies," he began, "we are facing a crisis. The entire country is taking sides in this hospital affair, with a number of them being on the other side. Here in the South we are totally outnumbered, and I fear that the forces of hatred are mobilizing and we need to be ready. It is imperative that we all stand as one, that all of our voices echo the same truths. This hospital for colored war veterans must not be jeopardized. I have heard from many of our friends up North who support us, but they are unable to help us outside of some financial assistance. We must rely on the federal government to stick by its decision and to help us if there is any violence. We must formulate a plan of action, and everyone on this campus and in this town will have a role to play. The board of trustees and I will communicate with the government and ask for help in case there is violence."

At this point one of the students motioned that someone was coming. Everyone remained quiet and still. The door opened and the treasurer, Mr. Logan, walked in, surprised to have all eyes upon him.

"I'm sorry I'm late," he announced, almost tripping over one of the lookouts. Laughter relieved the tension, and Moton, breathing a sigh of relief, continued.

"Teachers, you must talk to the students and the townspeople and make it clear what the issues are."

"Students," he said, "you must conduct yourselves appropriately when you go in town and not be taunted into disobedience. Dr. Kenney, you and the hospital staff need to be ready for any medical emergencies. You gentlemen from Tuskegee Institute need to form a committee to patrol the campus as a security measure. Now let's break up into groups and formulate our plan. Everyone needs to know what everyone else is doing. Our lives depend on it."

After the strategy meeting in the chapel, John got advice from many sources regarding how he should proceed in the hospital matter. Everyone seemed to have an opinion, and all the harsh words and strong emotions made it hard to imagine how a satisfactory solution could ever be found.

The National Medical Association petitioned the government, asking that officials not be swayed by the outcry from the white community. The Association also sent documentation supporting the ability of Negro physicians to manage the hospital. Numerous newspaper articles fanned the flames by alternately printing articles for and then against the movement, and the publicity only made the situation more volatile.

Dr. Moton began hinting at some sort of compromise to avert violence. This stance angered white people who did not want to see any coloreds in positions of authority, and it angered some Negroes who felt that he was caving in to the pressure.

The NMA also protested to the War Department that the "Jim Crow" laws were unconstitutional. These laws prohibited Negroes from riding in railroad cars with white people. Negroes were relegated to the back of the train in crowded and often dirty cars where they received little or no attention from the railroad personnel who serviced the "white only" cars. The NMA presented a resolution to the government on behalf of the Negro veteran that read as follows:

> "As loyal and patriotic medical men, we have offered ourselves to the nation, now in the throes of a great national crisis. Approximately one hundred physicians have been commissioned into the armed services, and there are hundreds of others who want to serve their nation and who are being denied. This is deplored, and an appeal is made to the war department to right the injustice of the present policy and to give us a fair representation of commissioned officers. We are inconvenienced, humiliated, and abused by the "Jim Crow" passenger system in railroad cars. It is out of keeping with the tenets of the American government, for which the world is now bathed in blood, that the government itself should operate such a passenger traffic system. It not only debases a patriotic class of citizens, but it breeds a discontent and deprives citizens of fair compensation for money invested in railway tickets. An appeal is made to abolish the law as a war measure to the end that twelve million faithful citizens may be rewarded for their devotion."

In the midst of this turmoil, John's colleagues, Ludie and Frank Johnston, came to see him. They were concerned about their association with him and with the hospital. On the one hand, they were white physicians who wanted to treat all patients regardless of color. On the other hand, because they were white physicians who practiced in the white community of Tuskegee, they could be in harm's way if they did not take a stand in opposing the decision.

"John," Ludie said, "this situation is putting us in a dangerous place. Anyone who is in agreement that the hospital should have a colored staff is fair game. I can't tell you how ugly it's going to be if the president doesn't change his position. As for us, we will have to cease our consulting privileges here at the hospital if we want to protect our homes and families from harm."

"I know you understand," Frank piped in. "You know this is not personal."

"It's about as personal as it gets, gentlemen," John said earnestly. "This is about right and wrong. It is not right to want to staff a hospital for Negroes with white personnel when there are competent Negro physicians to take care of them. It is not right to have white nurses trailed by colored nursemaids who actually touch the patients because the white nurses won't. It is not right to make these patients feel that they are outcasts or lepers. That's just plain wrong!"

"I know, John, but we still have to cut back our visits here for the time being," Frank said solemnly. "If things get any worse, we will have to stop coming altogether. I'm sorry, John. That's just the way it is."

It was hard for John to believe that all of the hard work had come to this. Tuskegee, a town where two different races had coexisted in polite friendship for years, was now a potential battleground for a race riot or worse. The existence of the school was in jeopardy, and longstanding "friends" were deserting the ship.

In this climate of controversy, resentment, and jealousy, activities carried out at the hands of some whites had given renewed birth to the dreaded Ku Klux Klan. The organization's objective was to preserve white supremacy, especially in the political arena. Estimates put the national membership at between four and five million. Members were organized in every county and township where they could be recruited, and membership in the South was growing at a rate of thirty-five hundred a day. The Klan was rapidly turning into a power that nothing could stop, and its tactics of hatred and vengeance caused great fear and trepidation among those Negroes who chose to speak out for what was right and fair. The KKK represented the antithesis of the principles that the country had been founded on – equality and justice.

The growing support for the Klan made it clear to John that many Southerners still harbored a resentment that had begun when the slaves were freed. Akin to an infected carbuncle, this historical wound still had the potential to become inflamed, irritated, purulent, and malignant. In the current turmoil, many Negroes believed that this condition would recur like an infection, resistant to treatment; if not properly resolved, it would become chronic. These people saw that blame for the situation was directed at the Negro, who was seen as the source of the problem.

In this atmosphere of fear, the sinister tactics of the Ku Klux Klan, the secrecy of its agenda, and the methods its members used to instill fear thoroughly terrified the Negro population. Marauders on horseback appeared in the dead of night dressed in white sheets and cardboard cone hats, their identity concealed. They burned huge wooden crosses and, by the light of the rising flames, they dragged unwitting, sleeping Negroes out of their beds in the middle of the night. Torture, beatings, and murder were their weapons. Their strategy was succeeding.

The Klan in Tuskegee openly included some of the leading white citizens of the town. For that reason, John was not surprised when Dr. Moton received a letter saying that a committee of appointed white citizens wanted to meet with the principal faculty members of Tuskegee to discuss the situation. Moton agreed, and the meeting was set for the next day at three o'clock. The committee members said they would come to the campus, which gave the Tuskegee faculty cause to hope there would be no violence. Even so, they planned to be ready for any eventuality.

Taking the Heat, Taking a Stand

ompkins Hall was the perfect place for the historic meeting between the Tuskegee faculty and the committee of townspeople. The building housed the campus dining hall and was centrally located on a hill overlooking the grounds. The location afforded the faculty various escape routes in case of any untoward events. Dr. Moton, Mr. Logan, John, and seven other faculty members assembled in the main hall to await their guests. The tension in the air was at an all time high as everyone realized this climactic meeting would result in massive change – one way or another.

The day was hot and sultry, and the "sweat bees" were swarming all over John. He took out his handkerchief and wiped his brow. Word came from one of the student lookouts that a caravan of cars was slowly approaching. Soon the drumming of many footsteps drawing closer and closer could be heard outside on the stairs. John's heart raced, and his breath came fast and shallow. Several of the group exchanged nervous glances and then looked apprehensively toward the door.

The faculty members remained in their seats until the first of the committee stepped over the threshold. Then the teachers rose in unison, standing tall and still as the group filed in. At least twenty members of this truculent committee fanned out across the room, quite a few more than the faculty had expected, but the teachers showed no sign of the nervousness or anxiety they all felt. The members of the citizens committee stared at the Tuskegee faculty with varying degrees of contempt and hostility, but the school officials remained unmoved.

Senator Powell, one of the most vocal political representatives, identified himself as the committee spokesman. Dr. Moton invited everyone to sit down and then welcomed Senator Powell to take the floor to express his viewpoint.

"Gentlemen," the senator opened, pacing back and forth in front of the sitting faculty, "we have a serious problem before us, but I am sure that we can come to a satisfactory conclusion for both sides."

He looked around, gave a nervous and insincere smile, and continued.

"The citizens of the town of Tuskegee have been considerate and generous for a number of years, allowing the colored to come to town and buy things that you don't have over here. We know you have learned to do certain things for yourselves, but your lives would not have been so comfortable without our kind generosity," he declared.

"We are indeed indebted to your generosity," Moton agreed in a conciliatory tone.

"We let your women folk work for us in our own homes, and we even trust our children to you. We have left you alone and not interfered with your learning. We have been good to your people," Powell went on, scolding the group of educated Negro gentlemen like disobedient servants.

"Yeah, that's right!" chorused some fidgety members of the group.

"We have been good to you people!" the senator said more defiantly, confident in the support of his backers. "When the government wanted to build this here hospital for coloreds, we allowed it. We knew this would bring money and jobs to our town. We didn't have to support it. You should be grateful for that."

"Senator Powell," Moton began, but was rudely interrupted by the senator.

"Just let me finish, *Mr.* Moton," Powell interjected, feeling in control of the encounter.

John clenched his jaw at the obvious lack of respect for *Dr.* Moton.

"Our people stand ready to staff and manage this facility for your people. But how do you show your gratitude? You want to protest to the government and make them have all colored people running this hospital. We were not led to believe this would happen when we supported it. Then we read in the paper that the president said the hospital would have colored personnel. This cannot happen, not in Tuskegee, not in Macon County, and not in Alabama!" Powell shouted, turning bright red in the face.

The committee of citizens jumped up and down, slapping each other on the back and applauding their speaker. The men representing the school remained seated, silent and resolute. As they looked around the room at the angry crowd, they knew, with chills up their spines, that they were looking at some of the faces that rode under the white sheets at night.

"It is audacious that you think we would let this happen," the senator proclaimed. "Your school was founded on the ideas of Booker T. Washington, and if I understood him, that meant goodwill, friendship, and toleration by the white people in this community. I have heard dozens of his lectures. He told us that if our citizens desired and determined it, they could stop the proceedings of the school at any time they chose. If this was not true, then we have been misled."

"No, you were not misled, Senator Powell," Moton answered. "We stand by the words of our late leader."

"Mr. Moton, I understand that you are willing to broker a compromise and that you are willing to consider a white person as the head of the hospital, along with a colored doctor named to the staff. Who told you that you are in a position to compromise?" Powell asked with assumed authority.

One committee member called out menacingly, "Yeah, who do y'all think ya are?" Several of the group moved closer to their comrade as if proximity enhanced their solidarity.

Without waiting for Dr. Moton to respond, Senator Powell continued. "The citizens of Tuskegee have determined that they will not permit the government or anyone else to come down here and put anything over on us. We will not have it – we are united in this." He cleared his throat and raised his hand, one finger held up for emphasis. "We won't permit it, not now, not in the next ten or fifteen years, not in the future, and not in our times. Do you understand me?"

Again the committee loudly applauded and congratulated the senator, while the faculty kept silent. Moton did not dignify the senator's tirade with a response. When the commotion died down, the rhetoric turned insinuative and threatening.

"We have friends in Montgomery, Opelika, and all around us asking us what we are doing over here," the senator began again. "They have offered to come over here and handle the situation themselves. If you continue to insist that the Negroes man the hospital, the burden of what will happen will be on you."

At this point, the room became deafeningly quiet. All eyes turned toward the school officials. Moton rose from his seat and spoke quietly and with dignity.

"Senator Powell, representatives from Tuskegee, let me say this. Tuskegee Institute and the John A. Andrew Hospital were both built with the generosity of many patrons and the hard work of Booker T. Washington and Dr. John A. Kenney. While the spirit of cooperation has been good between the citizens of Tuskegee proper and the citizens of Tuskegee Institute, we have managed to build and grow a school and a hospital with colored staff and colored management. We feel that we are quite capable of taking care of the Negro veterans as they would want us to do. We feel that Negro doctors and nurses would welcome the opportunity to contribute to the war effort by being able to do this. I have conceded to a white commander…"

"You're right about that!" someone shouted, and several others echoed the sentiment.

Moton continued. "I would also like to see Dr. Kenney appointed to the staff. At some point later on, other colored doctors and nurses will be added to the staff. I have sent letters and telegrams to the department at the Veteran's Bureau, and I have made my position clear. I am open to an initial compromise."

There was grumbling among the members of the citizens group, but no interruptions. Then Logan stood and began to speak.

"Senator Powell, members of the citizens committee, I want to confirm that the faculty of Tuskegee is in agreement with Dr. Moton's compromise, and we also want you to know we would like to continue the friendly relations that we have enjoyed with you in the past. The faculty and the Negro community will sustain Dr. Moton's position."

Some members of the committee nodded, while others glared. As Logan nervously sat down, John rose to face the citizens of the committee, many of whom were by this time even more incredulous and outraged. Struggling to compose himself, he began as civilly as he could. The visiting entourage looked at him with suspicion and menace, but he refused to be daunted.

"Gentlemen of Tuskegee," he said, "I will agree to assist Dr. Moton if that will affect a compromise. However, I feel that I must express what I feel deeply in my heart."

Moton and the members of the faculty eyed each other nervously, shifting in their chairs.

"I am not overestimating the situation, and I think that we are facing one of the most momentous crises in history, and certainly the most momentous of my career. I am a Negro born in the South, and what little education I have, I have gotten in the South. For nearly twenty-one years, I have labored in the South. I came here as resident physician for Booker T. Washington, and I was instrumental in helping to build the John A. Andrew Hospital and in starting the John A. Andrew Medical Clinics. Physicians of all nationalities and from all over the country come here to study and share the latest health discoveries and innovations. I have excellent relations with the white physicians in Tuskegee, and in Alabama for that matter, as well as with the business people in Tuskegee."

The faces of the crowd looked confused by this information, as if they were not sure what John was trying to say.

"As a Negro, I have the same aspirations and ambitions that you do, and I am working nationally and locally toward my goals. I have not asked anyone to make a move for me in this hospital matter, but my name has been presented to the Veteran's Bureau and I have been asked if I would take this position."

"You'd better not!" one man hissed.

"Let's go," said another. "Ain't nothing going to be accomplished here. These darkies need a lesson." With this threatened suggestion, three or four of their crowd departed.

"Since Senator Powell has been allowed to speak his mind freely, I think it is fair that I be allowed to do the same," John said, his tone expressing a statement of fact, not asking for permission. "I will tell you what I told the Veteran's Bureau. I can take no other position than to favor a staff of Negro personnel in that hospital."

The committee members protested loudly among themselves, arguing as to whether they should stay or go.

John could hear Moton clearing his throat, trying to get his attention. He heard Logan calling his name in a whisper. He ignored all of the signals to retreat.

"When the hospital idea was first presented, the colored people had no desire to staff it, since we did not even think that was a possibility. The conditions changed when the President of the United States proclaimed that he would put Negro personnel in charge. That being true, I am compelled to support his decision."

The racket began again, and John held up his hand for silence. Steeling himself, he walked around to the front of the table, which put him closer to the opposition. He could feel their hatred growing like wildfire: scorching, unpredictable and visceral; and impervious to the winds of justice and fairness.

"Now, I know Southern white men and their ideas," he said seriously. "You have set forth your position, and I know you well enough to know that you are not going to have colored staff in that hospital. I know it would be foolish for me to buck against you, and I have no desire to do so, but that does not prevent me from letting you know my opinion and how I stand in this matter. I will say to you further that, in keeping with Senator Powell's statement, if there are any of us here who are not with Dr. Moton, or any who by our attitude would create race friction and break up harmonious relations between the town and school, if I am that person, I am willing and ready to leave now. I do not have to remain at Tuskegee to practice medicine. I have elected to practice here. I am registered in other states. I can go to Virginia, or I could go to Michigan."

Some of the committee looked at him in amazement. For them, it was not in the realm of possibility to think that a Negro would have these kinds of options. There was a hushed silence.

"I believe that by reason of my relations in the profession, I would have no trouble getting reciprocity in any state in which I elected to practice. If conditions here are such that I cannot remain here and practice in a government hospital run for Negroes, by Negroes, then I would rather leave."

"Guess you better get going then," remarked one bystander.

John could hear sniggling and undertones from the group, but he ignored them.

At this point Bobby Lee Edwards, one of the committee representatives, jumped up and yelled, "I want clarification for the record!"

He looked at the entire Tuskegee group, and then he looked specifically at John. When John did not sit down, Edwards walked over to where he stood. Reeking of alcohol and stale cigars, Edwards stood uncomfortably close, but John did not flinch.

"We've been told that some of you are not with us for a white personnel in that hospital out there," Edwards said. "If that's true, you had better get out of this county, because we don't want no Negro personnel in that hospital," he shouted. "We are not going to have it! We can cut off your town privileges, and we don't have to sell you any goods for your school. We can send all your mammies and your maids packing, and you can do without the good will we have shown you in Alabama. Maybe you'll decide to go up North with your friends who want to tell us what to do down here. And if that don't work, we can call in all of our friends who are now standing by, just waiting for the call, to enforce what we are saying here today. Do you know what I mean?" he taunted with a finger too close to John's face. John clenched his fists to keep from reacting physically.

Another committee member, a Mr. G. B. Edwards, got up from his chair and called for a vote of confidence and support for the senator.

"Will all y'all who do not want Negro personnel in that hospital out there stand up and be counted? If you stand, you agree to do whatever is necessary to prevent it."

Each and every one of the white citizens stood, and the motion was unanimously carried. They sat down, but John remained standing, more determined now than ever. He began to speak with full control and with measured words.

"This is the most critical moment of my life. I have served the National Medical Association for many years. They have recommended me as their choice to head the hospital. I don't know yet whether I want to accept the position, but I do demand the right to speak for myself. Deep down in my bosom…"

Ripples of laughter and guffaws pierced the air as soon as the word "bosom" was uttered.

"Oh, he has a bosom. We damn sure don't have to worry about him!" someone yelled.

"Deep down in my soul," John rephrased, raising his voice to get their attention, "are the same impulses, the same desires, and the same ambitions that are in yours. If this organization wants to honor me, it should be my privilege to decide. All of these terrible things that you have threatened I know that you can do, because you have the power. But that does not prevent me from letting you know my position in this matter."

The senator rose from his chair and walked over to where John was standing. He had a strange expression on his face, a cross between a smile and a menacing grimace. He looked directly at John while speaking to the entire room.

"Dr. Kenney does not have to leave here. We know Dr. Kenney. He can go to the hospital and practice and have the respect and protection of every white citizen of this community." He pointed his finger directly into John's face and added, "But mark you, it will have to be under white management!"

The white citizens erupted into applause, and then a man with whom John had done business, a Mr. Wiley Parker, stepped up from the group.

"I have known Dr. Kenney for twenty years. He has not done himself justice on this occasion." He spat a wad of brown tobacco and saliva onto the floor.

Moton and the rest of his group looked ashen and shaken, but John pretended not to notice. The Negroes had no time to caucus.

"Gentlemen," John said in a calm, clear voice, pausing for a moment to make sure he had everyone's attention, "I have been speaking to you for several minutes. I thought I had made myself clear. If I have not, I want to thank the last speaker for the privilege of doing so. Your question is – do I favor a total Negro personnel in that hospital?"

The assemblage looked on in amazement as he raised his clenched fist in the air and brought it down emphatically on the table with a loud bang!

"Most emphatically I do!" he shouted with enough volume to startle the men in front of him. "Anything less would make me a liar and a traitor!"

Senator Powell looked at John in disgust. His comrades stood by him, waiting for an order. He turned his back and addressed his committee members in a low voice that shook with anger. "We will meet about this later at our usual place." When he turned back, he glared first at John and then let his cold stare sweep over the entire group.

"Gentlemen," he thundered in anger, "this meeting is adjourned!"

No Promise of Tomorrow

"There is no promise of tomorrow,
and yesterday is done.
We'll make the most of each new day,
Living one for all, all for one."

Senator Powell and his followers stormed out of the room, knocking over chairs and slamming doors. The Tuskegee group sat silently for a few moments, gathering their thoughts. Dr. Moton spoke first.

"Well, John, they certainly have no doubt as to how you feel. I was hoping for a more conciliatory resolution."

John had little doubt that Moton would have liked to curtail his speech if he could have stopped him. John knew they were in for trouble, yet he also knew that, had he done less, his entire life would have been blighted, and nothing he could ever do would wipe away the stain.

In the onerous atmosphere that followed this meeting, the Klan grew more active. There was word of secret meetings held in the middle of the night and, on one evening, Klan members rode past the campus dressed in full garb – hooded sheets with slits for eyes. They burned a cross near the chapel and threatened to leave a bloody trail throughout Tuskegee. They threatened Moton's life, as well as John's.

After the Klansmen left the campus, they rode onto the grounds of the V.A. hospital and were served dinners in the hospital dining room. It was discovered later that the sheets they had covered themselves with had come from the V.A. hospital's supply, with the approval of Colonel Stanley.

The entire campus went on alert. Stalwart students did around-the-clock security duty. Male students were stationed at possible entry points around the perimeter of the school, while female students coordinated a schedule to make sure that each security shift had coffee and food. The women also brought information from each outpost to the command center so that the channels of communication remained open. John would often accompany the young women to make sure that there were no medical problems among the guards.

One evening, he was called to the back gate of the campus to assist a guard who had stomach pains but would not leave his post. The women were distributing food, but this man was too sick to eat. After diagnosing appendicitis, John knew that the guard needed to be replaced. With his patient in tow, he headed back to campus to see who was available, following a road that was being cut through the forest and would eventually connect the school with the new hospital. The night was pitch black, but John's headlights illuminated the dirt road ahead, allowing him to navigate the rugged terrain. The sudden appearance of a hooded figure in the glare of his headlights set his heart pounding, but this hooded apparition was dressed in black, not white. John breathed a cautious sigh of relief. All the same, he stayed on guard. As he slowed the car to a halt, a woman's voice called out to him.

"Dr. Kenney! Dr. Kenney!"

Too stunned to answer, John peered into the darkness. He recognized nothing about the shadowy figure slowly approaching. As the apparition came closer, it removed its dark hood and John could make out the face of a woman – a white woman.

"Dr. Kenney, it's me – Miss Lillie, from the corner store downtown. I need to tell you something."

A suspicion flashed through John's mind that this white woman had been sent to trap him, but he had done business with her for years, and they had always seemed to hold a mutual respect. He stopped the car and started to get out. He still couldn't see her face clearly, but he did recognize her voice.

"Miss Lillie," he called out, "what in the world are you doing out here at this time of night by yourself? You know what is going on and how dangerous this is."

"Don't get out," she called in warning. "I came to bring you a message. You need to leave town now. The committee is having a meeting about you. You are not safe in Tuskegee, and you must leave before it's too late! They're planning to do something awful to you. Please go now!"

Before he could respond, she disappeared into the darkness. His sickly passenger, now sitting up straight in his seat, looked as if he had seen a ghost. John reassured him that they were okay, and they headed toward the lights of the campus. In spite of the strange warning, John felt there was nothing he could do but go on with his activities until something happened – one way or another.

The next morning, he was writing in his operative ledger when his secretary rushed into his office.

As she came through the door, she announced with some agitation, "You have a visitor, Dr. Kenney. I asked him to wait but…"

Before she could finish her sentence, a man burst through the door. John was surprised to see that it was Wiley Parker, the gentleman who had put him on the spot during the meeting with the white citizens committee.

"Good day, Mr. Parker," John said. "What can I do for you?"

"I am here representing the committee, Dr. Kenney. We are giving you one last chance. We demand that you retract your words in writing, and we are going to print your response in the *Daily Advocator* newspaper so that everyone will know you have come to your senses." He handed John a pen and a pad of paper.

"I cannot and will not do that, Mr. Parker," John said in a stern voice, locking eyes with the angry intruder.

Parker asked with sarcasm, "What shall I tell the committee then, Dr. Kenney? I know you must have some last words for them!"

John didn't even blink as he said, "Tell them anything you please, Mr. Parker, but tell them I will not retreat from my position."

"Well then, I am embarrassed. You know I have known you for twenty years and I was always a friend." Parker seemed to imply that his friendship had been a favor, one that needed to be repaid, now.

"Yes," John said without emotion. "That seemed to have been true."

"And if anything happened to you, you'd expect me to befriend you," he said.

"Yes, I certainly would, and I would have done the same for you."

"Well, things have changed now, Dr. Kenney."

He offered his hand, and John shook it. Then Parker said goodbye and left, shaking his head in disbelief.

Stoically, John sat back down at his desk and decided he had better get his affairs in order. There was no telling what might happen to him now. He made sure that most of his medical reports were completed, and then he reviewed his will to see if he needed to make any changes.

Finally, he wrote a letter to Senator Powell to see if they could resolve the situation without the violence that was sure to come. Again, John assured Powell that the stand he had taken on the hospital matter had nothing to do with his being designated the medical director by the National Medical Association. He said that he had documents to prove this and that, even if he were not the candidate selected, he would still support the President of the United States, who had given his verbal and written statement that he would put Negro personnel in charge of the Veterans Hospital at Tuskegee. There had been no change in the president's position, or in John's.

John reminded the senator that the Veterans Bureau had also adopted the same stance, and that eliminating him would not change the circumstances one iota. He argued that it made more sense to work together and to select someone who would most nearly represent the interests of both the white and colored people of the community. He reiterated that he had done nothing to bring about his appointment other than to devote himself to providing adequate medical care for his people over the past twenty years, and to serving the Negro medical profession faithfully.

As he wrote, he began to feel that the situation was hopeless. Even so, he went on to remind the senator of the model community that Tuskegee was for the nation, and of the good history of race relations that had existed until now. He mentioned that the open threats of violence toward him and the school were clearly understood, and that was why everyone needed to work together to find a mutually agreeable solution. He again stated that if he were the stumbling block in the current circumstances, then he would leave the community.

John received no answer to his letter that night, but by morning a number of firebombs littered the campus and his front yard. The thought of being the object of this violence and the cause of possible harm or destruction to the hospital was an unbearable burden. Since he was the most obvious target of the white people's hatred, a part of him thought he should leave. Yet he also wanted to stay. He didn't care what people said about him, but he knew that he could not let everything he and Dr. Washington had built be destroyed. They had come too far.

Angry, frustrated, and desperate for an answer, he left the campus early and went home to be with his family. Freida had cooked his favorite meal, hoping to alleviate his stress, while trying not to show her own. After she had put the children to bed, she joined John on the front porch for a cup of coffee. They sat in silence for some time, neither knowing how to comfort the other without causing additional alarm.

"It's late, John," she said with resignation. "Come on to bed. It doesn't do any good to worry like this. I have faith that everything will be all right."

"I have some editing to do," John answered, knowing sleep would be impossible. "You go on in and get some sleep. I'll be in shortly. I just need a few more minutes out here." He tried to sound calm and unaffected, even though he felt his dinner rising in his throat. He took a swallow of coffee to regain control.

"Okay," Freida said without argument. "I'm going in."

John kissed her and, stifling his worry, watched her as she walked into the house. When she was gone, he put his head in his hands and prayed. "Please, God, protect my family from harm. I am ready to accept whatever you have planned for me, but please protect my family."

After several minutes, John went inside and sat at his desk. He opened his satchel, removing a medical journal and began to read an article on "Multiple Stab Wounds of the Abdomen". He wasn't able to shake the feeling of anxiety that the events of the past few days had planted in his gut. Why couldn't humans live in peace, making character, values, faith, and morals the rules by which they co-existed? Why couldn't man just love his brother? These warring thoughts were racing through John's mind when the telephone rang.

"John, its Warren. I'm calling to warn you. You've got to get out of there. The Klan is on its way to torch your home!"

A Critical Choice

W arren's words had launched a waking nightmare for John and his family. Rousing the children, packing food and clothing, fleeing through the dark night – it had seemed almost unreal – until they reached Cheehaw station and witnessed the delivery of guns to the Klansmen. Now, with Freida and the children safely on the train north, his gun on the car seat beside him, and the flames from his burning home glowing on the horizon, John accepted the knowledge that there were people who wanted him dead – and his family, too, he thought with a shudder. Yes, they had escaped – for now. But who could be sure of the future anymore? Who could know when the next crisis, the next threat, would come? And from where?

He was sure that for now he would find refuge at Tuskegee, if he could only get there safely. He drove without headlights, expecting hooded Klan figures to apprehend him at every bend in the road. His burning home, its fiery glow clearly visible against the lightening sky, was a grim reminder of just how narrow had been their escape. Thank God the train was now carrying his family to Boston, where they would be safe. Knowing that, he could focus on keeping himself and his work alive. Time was of the essence, he knew, and he had better be prepared.

He breathed a sigh of relief when he drove at last onto the grounds of Tuskegee Institute. He left the car outside his office and took sanctuary within its familiar walls. There was much to do, and he had little inclination to sleep in what was left of the night.

The next day, with his attention focused on tying up loose ends, he made a follow-up visit to a typhoid fever patient on a farm outside of Tuskegee. The visit occurred without incident, but before he left the farm, he advised the family to get another physician because his situation was precarious and uncertain. His resentment at having to say such a thing left a sour taste on his tongue. He had never before abandoned a patient, yet now his presence brought people more danger than medical assistance.

The atmosphere at the school and in the community continued to grow heavier and more ominous. Trouble was expected daily. Although John was relieved that his family had escaped, he now felt painfully alone. To dull his longing for Freida and the children, he immersed himself in steps to protect his work at the hospital. He was organizing files in his office one day when Warren Logan brought him a message from a committee composed of three of Tuskegee's leading white citizens, all of whom had been among the Klansmen who had previously visited the campus to deliver their ultimatum.

"I received a letter this morning," Warren said. "It has my name on it, but it is written to you. The letter asks that I bring this to you immediately."

"From friend or foe?" John asked, looking at Warren for an explanation, but sensing that this communiqué was not good news. "Well, what does it say?"

"It says that you are a marked man, and that you need to take your annual vacation. Now. They say they don't want to see anything happen to you, despite the showdown the other day. It also says, in bold black letters, DO NOT LEAVE THE CAMPUS FOR ANY REASON! It says you may get a call to tend to a patient out in the community, but for you not to go."

"Thanks for bringing the warning. I guess I may still have a few friends on the other side of town," said John with a touch of sarcasm.

Later that morning, John did get a call to go ten miles into the country to see a patient. He suspected that it was a trap, and he called his secretary in to witness the call. He held the phone receiver so that they both could hear.

"Yeah, Dr. Kenney, it's Mr. Wainwright at the old horse farm out yonder. He came down with something fierce and we need you to tend to him," said the man on the phone.

"Mr. Wainwright? I never heard of anyone named Wainwright," John replied, going over patient names in his head and trying to establish the veracity of the call. "And where is this farm you mentioned?"

"Well, Doc, it's kinda hard to get to. We'll have to have someone meet you out by Sandy Springs, and they will lead you the rest of the way."

John and his secretary exchanged knowing looks; this was the call they had been warned about. His secretary's eyes widened with alarm as she realized she was listening to someone with murderous intent. John felt the hair on the back of his neck stand up, and a cold shiver ran down his spine. If he'd had any doubts that certain people wanted to murder him to make a point, those doubts were now gone.

"I'll tell you what," John said, keeping his voice calm and even in order to sound sincere, "I have rounds to make, and that will take me about an hour or so. I will start for Sandy Springs after that. Now you be sure someone is there to meet me, and tell them not to leave until they see me. I won't know my way from there."

"Thanks, Doc, we'll be waitin' for ya'." With that pronouncement, the man slammed down the phone.

John hung up the receiver. "You'll be waitin' till hell freezes over," he said out loud, knowing that he was never going to take that ride.

That afternoon, a group of the school's leaders met with John to discuss what strategy they should take. Everyone was adamant that their opinion about whether John should leave or stay in Tuskegee was the right one.

"It doesn't make sense for you to risk your life or the future of this institution," Dr. Moton declared angrily. "I think the mood will change if the Klan knows you are out of the picture. Your remarks riled them up, and they know that, for you, a compromise is unpalatable."

"I have to disagree," Logan said. "We have let these crackers dictate to us for too long. We all need to stand our ground and fight if that's what we have to do. I think it's better to stand our ground and see what their next move is."

Mr. Robb, the comptroller, agreed with Dr. Moton. "There is no sense in having a bloody battle at Tuskegee Institute if we don't have to. This school is much too important to sacrifice if there are other ways to avert a crisis. Let John go for a while, until these hot heads cool off."

John pondered his dilemma, thinking while the others argued. Did it make sense for him to stay and possibly become a martyr for this cause, or should he leave for a while until the situation eased and tempers subsided? Tuskegee could do without its doctor for a few months, although not permanently. He knew full well the evil that was being directed against him. The irony was that for years he had been driving all over Macon County, attending to his practice under the aegis of the same men who had now turned against him. They had withdrawn their protection, and what did he have to gain by risking his life? Was it worth the destruction of Tuskegee Institute?

"I'm going to go," he announced with a suddenness that implied finality. The others could tell by his expression that his decision was unconditional. "We have too much to lose that can't easily be replaced," John declared. "I won't risk it." Turning abruptly, he walked out of the room without waiting for comment or looking back.

John's decision to leave emphasized the seriousness of the situation, and stiffened the rank and file members at Tuskegee. Throughout the crisis and in its aftermath, it was generally asserted on campus that if Klan members had ever left the main road and come upon the Institute's property, there would have been a serious interracial clash.

Two short days later, John was able to hop the same early morning train he had put his family on. He was the only passenger in the colored Pullman car. His body was limp with exhaustion, and he was emotionally spent. Yet, the discomfort of his body paled in comparison to the ache in his heart. Thoughts of his mother and father, who had endured slavery with courage and bravery in the hope that the future would be brighter for him, intensified his pain.

Sitting in his compartment, John paid silent homage to all those of his race who had perished in the quest for freedom, whether swinging in the wind from the old oak tree or dying with a bullet in the back as they fled to safer territory. Was this really America, the land of the free and the home of the brave? He was supposed to be a free man, but here he was, escaping – like a runaway slave. The yoke of slavery had metasta-sized into a vise of hatred and intolerance, becoming a cancer on the nation's soul. The disease was malignant and the prognosis at this stage was critical at best; at worst, the disease was terminal.

John hadn't eaten for hours, and hunger pains made his stomach growl. Knowing that he could not eat until the white travelers on board were fed, he waited, reliving the experiences of the past few weeks and trying to make sense of what was happening. Near Greensboro, North Carolina, he asked the porter to make up his bed while he went to the galley to get dinner.

Answering the third call for food, he took his time approaching the dining car to make sure that all of the white passengers had vacated the tables. When he saw that the car was clear, he took a seat. Once his hunger was relieved, the only thing he wanted to do was sleep – sleep and escape from the voices in his head and from his visions of the nightmare he had been living for the past few days.

When he returned to the Pullman car, he found a letter-sized sheet of white paper in the center of his bed, on which was written in heavy black letters: **Nigger, don't let the sun rise on you in here. KKK**. The drawing of a crude skull and crossbones on the note added a chilling effect. John stepped out into the hall to see if anyone was lurking about, but there was no one in sight. Just as he was closing the door, he heard a deep voice.

"Dr. Kenney! Just a minute."

John felt the doorknob turning slowly in his hand. He stood per-fectly still as the door opened wider and wider; then he suddenly yanked the door completely open, raising his fist to strike. He was surprised and relieved to see that it was only the porter on the other side of the door.

"I've turned your bed down, Dr. Kenney. Is everything all right?" His eyes opened wide at the sight of John's raised fist.

John let out a sigh of relief and dropped his hand. "I'm sorry, sir. I didn't mean to frighten you, but it seems I had some visitors when I went to the dining car. They left me this warning."

John showed the letter to the porter, whose face turned ashen. With shaking hands, he folded the letter and hid it in his uniform jacket. He was frightened and alarmed, but managed to remain composed.

"Stay in your room, Dr. Kenney, and lock the door. Do not let anyone in. I am going to show this to the conductor and the engineer, and we'll wire ahead to the next town for help. And don't answer the door unless you hear my voice. My name is James Johnson."

John decided that he would get in bed, but remain fully dressed. He didn't know what he might be facing, and he thought he would be more prepared if he were not in his nightclothes. He climbed into the berth and slept fitfully. He was eventually lulled to sleep by the rolling of the train and the twinkling stars in the passing night. A knock on the door startled him awake.

"Dr. Kenney, it's me, James."

John heard the porter's words somewhere through the fog in his head, just as the train came to a jarring stop.

He stumbled to the door and opened it with caution. James was holding the letter in his hand, and the conductor was with him.

"We have a railroad detective boarding the train at this stop. You will not have to worry about your safety. We're going to put him in the compartment next to yours," the conductor explained.

John looked down the corridor and saw a brawny, official-looking man heading toward them, smoking a cigar and carrying a gun in the holster strapped at his waist. John said a silent prayer that this was really the detective, and not a KKK member in disguise. The man flashed a badge to the conductor, nodded at John, and went inside his compartment without a word. John was again instructed not to open the door. The conductor and the porter vowed that they, too, would also be on the lookout. With that reassurance, John undressed and finally succumbed to sleep.

When he awoke, he opened the compartment door and looked down the corridor. The railroad detective was leaning against the wall, looking out of the window at the passing countryside, a cigar hanging out of the corner of his mouth.

"You don't have to worry no more. I got those two culprits, and they are tied up in the freight car. I'm taking them off at the next stop," he mumbled, nonchalant and unmoved by the events of the night.

"Thank you, sir," John replied, obviously relieved.

"Don't thank me. I'm just doing my job. If I was you though, I wouldn't get off the train at the next stop. We are still in Klan country, and you ain't safe till you reach the capitol."

John thanked him for his advice and assured him that he would be careful.

"Adios," the detective mumbled as he ambled toward the front of the train.

John decided not to go to the dining car for breakfast. He sat in the Pullman and looked out the window, watching the scenery flash by in a steady blur. The passing forests, lakes, rivers and towns became one swift panorama of images altered in time and place, and John couldn't tell where one scene started and another ended. He tried to focus, but his mind kept going back to the events of the past few months.

Even though he could not shut his eyes to what had happened and to the unfavorable conditions in the South, he was not ready to give up on all of its white people. Thousands and thousands of people in the South were as good as those in any part of the country. John counted among them the dark-hooded white woman who had warned him of the danger by way of the grapevine, and the white men who sent the message that he was threatened. And how could he forget to pay his respects to Dr. Frank Johnston and his brother Ludie, his associates. They had said at their first introduction that they would do anything they could to help John, and they had meant it. Frank Johnston, recognized at the time as a leading surgeon in those parts, and his brother had become professional brothers to John. Never once in their work together had there been a misunderstanding about a fee or a patient. Never once had John called for them to come to his assistance, whether day or night, that they did not come. Much of the advice he got from the elder Johnston in those early days had felt like lessons passed from father to son. John owed much to these two men, and he knew that such individual relationships were not unusual, even in those volatile years. They existed in some form in practically every community.

Many people of broad and lofty human sympathies offered support for the entire Negro race. Some took steps to improve interracial relationships, but others were deterred from taking a public stand by the potential repercussions. Yet, it was also true that sometimes a friend in disguise could be of greater help than if he wore no mask. Many of these masked friends lived and worked throughout the South. Had they not been there, what might have been John's fate?

Favorable liaisons like these modified to a perceptible degree the tension of interracial relations in the South. But would their influence be enough to salvage the situation at Tuskegee? Only time would tell.

The rest of John's train ride was uneventful and quiet, giving him time to ponder his immediate future. What should he do now? Should he expect to return soon? Or should he relocate somewhere else? If he went back, would he and his family be safe? All of these questions occupied his mind as the countryside rolled by, displaying scenery as transient as his thoughts.

When he reached Washington, D.C., he bought a newspaper and read it while he waited for a taxi. The headline in the *Dallas Express* was large and bold:

HARDING STICKS TO DECISION TO COMPLETELY OFFICER
VETERAN'S HOSPITAL AT TUSKEGEE WITH NEGROES

John was relieved to see this, even though he didn't know what it might mean in terms of retaliation against his comrades in Tuskegee. He quickly scanned the article to learn more.

President Harding has made a formal request of congress to support his decision to staff the V.A. Hospital in Tuskegee with Negro personnel. Last week a large delegation of white Alabamans conveyed by members of their congressional delegations called on President Harding to make a final appeal that the hospital should be staffed with white physicians and nurses and not colored personnel.

The appeal seemed more like a demand. The President thanked them for coming but politely let them know that he had made up his mind on this matter and that the Veteran's Bureau would be taking applications for the jobs from Negro applicants. The attempts by white Southerners to control the hospital caused controversy across the entire country and political lines were drawn. Senator Talmadge, a staunch supporter for Negro personnel, expressed himself, stating that he "couldn't see what white folks wanted to be nursing sick 'niggers' for anyway." This hospital would be the largest institution in the world manned by Negroes. It was expected to also be a test to see how well the Negro can manage a big enterprise when given the opportunity. The capacity of the hospital would be 600 beds. It would be built for colored patients only and would be the only one of its kind in the world. Persons who desire to apply for a position should request an application from the Civil Service Commission. Applications should be filed at once.

As John read the article, he tried to understand the nature of hate. He dissected the problem philosophically: Hatred served whose purpose? What was the purpose of racial, religious, or ethnic conflict and strife? Whenever different races had come together throughout the ages, there had been animosities; but what congenital anomaly in the inner sanctum of the human heart allowed hatred, greed, and corruption to spew into the arteries and veins of mortal men? Was this a question of right or wrong, or simply a matter of what *is*?

When the taxi arrived, John asked the driver to take him to 1817 13th Street, NW, the home of his friend Dr. Michel O. Dumas. As he settled down in the car, he took a deep breath and exhaled. The die had been cast and the whole country would be waiting to see how Negroes did at managing the hospital – if Congress approved the president's request. As the taxi pulled up to the Dumas house, John saw that his friend Dr. George Cannon was also arriving.

"John, how are you, my friend? I just heard you were forced to leave Tuskegee. Trial by fire, eh? I want to hear all about it," Cannon said after parking his car in front of the house.

"I'm alive and well, thank you…" But before John could elaborate, the front door opened and Dumas came down the steps.

"Welcome, gentlemen. Come on in. Dr. Alexander is here, along with Mr. Scott, the secretary-treasurer at Howard University. They are giving us a hand with this matter. We'll have to bring you up to date on what is going on. How was your trip, John?" Dumas asked as he took John's suitcase and carried it into the house.

"Other than being escorted by the KKK, I guess you could say it served its purpose," John said casually.

"What?" the doctors chorused in unison with expressions of disbelief.

"I'll give you the details inside," John said as he went into the house.

As the men listened to John's story, they realized that he had barely escaped the South in one piece. They were totally sympathetic to his plight, and the thought of his nearly being killed elicited vicarious fear and empathy. His recital emphasized the real danger that he had faced, and his friends were somber and respectful.

"We can't say enough how glad we are that you have reached here safely," Dumas said. "Now let me bring you up to date on what is going on. We are fairly certain that the Congress is not going to overrule the president, but that doesn't stop certain factions from still trying. The white Tuskegee paper *The Star* said yesterday that they had brokered a compromise with the government. It said that the medical director of the hospital would be a white man, as would be his two assistants, and the rest of the staff would be colored. Senator Powell then released a statement saying that those terms were unacceptable. He is most defiant and audacious as to what they would allow. You would think from the tenor of his speech that the federal government is in the position of supplicant, seeking favors at their hands."

"That's right, the enemy is very arrogant," added Scott, "and I want to say that it seems to me that some way should have been found to save you from being thrown to the Ku Kluxes of Tuskegee. I don't see how you could ever go back with any feeling of security."

"Well, I'm going to wait and see what happens," John replied. "I'm not making any decisions until I see if this hospital decision stands."

"There are several other things you need to know about, John," Dumas said. "Dr. Moton and a Tuskegee committee are still trying to broker a compromise to keep the peace down there, I guess, but the government is totally against that too. Someone from the *Washington Tribune* showed Cannon a telegram Dr. Moton sent to that white attorney Charles Hare. The telegram stated that Dr. Moton had seen General Hines, and that the instructions to the committee were to come and meet in strictest secrecy. Our group regards this telegram as a matter of sinister import. What is the significance of such actions? Are we being double-crossed?" he asked.

"Tell him the rest, Dumas," Cannon interjected.

"Well, there are some other secret meetings going on. You remember that fellow Crossland from the NMA? He has been engaged in some dirty work at the Veteran's Bureau. He wrote a little paper in a most truculent vein, praising the white man's superiority in experience, and he expressed a desire to go to the V.A. hospital under a white man. What he said would almost make you want to do him violence. The irony of the matter is, he was previously held up to ridicule at the Bureau, but his new position seems to insinuate him into the good graces of persons high up there. It would be little short of a calamity if he is sent there in any capacity," Dumas added.

"That's a lot to swallow, gentlemen," John said. "And what about Crossland? How can men stoop to such chicanery? You know the saying,

'The politician is an acrobat. He keeps his balance by saying the opposite of what he does.' Is this politics? If so, none for me!"

John paused while everyone laughed at his quip.

"And what about Senator Powell," he added, "saying that the government's new terms are totally unacceptable? If that's true at all, then for once we are in complete agreement on an issue, but with very different objectives."

"We have to have faith, gentlemen," said the taciturn Dr. Alexander, "faith that our moral precepts will lead us to victory over evil."

"You've struck the keynote," John said, "faith. And beyond that, we don't know anything. But why worry? I carry a copy of Bryant's 'Thanatopsis' in my pocket to remind me that life is ephemeral and transitory. I read it when my patients are facing a life and death situation, and the other day I read it when my life was on the line." John pulled the piece of paper out of his wallet, showing it to his colleagues.

"Remind me of it, John," Alexander asked, leaning forward with interest.

"It says, '… So live that when thy summons comes to join that innumerable caravan where each shall take his chamber in the silent halls of death, thou go not like a quarry slave at night, scourged to his dungeon, but, sustained and soothed by an unfaltering trust, approach thy grave like one who wraps the drapery of his couch about him and lies down to pleasant dreams.'"

"It was a very long time ago that I read that," Alexander said, "but I am still impressed by it. We do have faith, and we are living our lives with honor and dignity, trusting that we will prevail."

"With God's help we will," Cannon added. "We all just have to follow this hospital situation closely, keep in constant communication, and we will know where to go from here."

John left the meeting, thankful to have friends and colleagues who were loyal and steadfast to the same ideals that guided his life. Cannon gave him a ride back to Union Station to catch the evening train to Boston.

As John got out of the taxicab in front of the Armstrong house, Freida and the children rushed out the door and began hugging and kissing him until he had to hold them back. Judge Armstrong produced a bottle of vintage champagne, and herded everyone inside to toast the safe arrival of his son-in-law.

Freida filled her glass and held it up in salutation to John. "My husband has put his life on the line for our principles. Such honorable men are rare. I couldn't be more proud."

"Thank you, darling," John said, blushing and giving Freida a quick kiss.

"I'm relieved that you are out of there, John," the Judge added with indignation. "Those idiots down South don't deserve you! Perhaps you will give some thought to practicing medicine in Massachusetts. I am well connected, and I will help you get the best opportunity possible."

"I just need some time to rest and think, Judge. I'm not making any decisions right now, but I appreciate the thought."

John spent a few days doing nothing but enjoying his family. He couldn't believe that there had been a possibility he would never see them again. That made every moment all the more precious. He wrote Dr. Moton a letter to let him know where he had settled temporarily, and was surprised to get correspondence back almost immediately. Apparently Moton had also left Tuskegee at some point, and had gone to Virginia. Moton wrote:

Capahosic, Virginia

July 21, 1923

My dear Dr. Kenney:

Thank you for your letter, which I have just received. Mr. Holsey, who was here yesterday, left for Washington to see General Hines today or early in the week. I have no doubt that things will work out all right if we just sit tight. Our friends, white and black now, particularly the whites in the South, are pushing matters in a way that is most gratifying.

That Ku Klux Klan movement at Tuskegee was the very thing to defeat their own purposes; it has brought to us sympathy and a resolution on the part of the entire country that we had not had before. You are, of course, making no plan except to return to Tuskegee; at least I hope you are not. I hope while you are in Boston you will see Mr. and Mrs. Mason first, and go over the whole matter with them. They are very much interested, as you know, and we have no better friends anywhere in the world. Please remember me in kindness to Mrs. Kenney and the children, in which Mrs. Moton heartily joins.

Yours sincerely always,

R. R. Moton

John filed the letter away and tried to put the situation out of his mind. He and Freida decided that they would go to Aunt Martha's house in Oak Bluffs on Martha's Vineyard for some rest and recreation. The island had become a haven where Negroes could go to enjoy themselves without the constant reminder of the sting of racism. Martha's Vineyard afforded them an opportunity to enjoy a resort-like atmosphere, buffered and surrounded by miles and miles of the Atlantic Ocean. Many Negroes from across the country would travel there to reconnect with each other in a most idyllic setting. It was also a trip that thrilled the children.

The excitement of riding the ferry from Woods Hole, Massachusetts, on the mainland side to Vineyard Haven on the island side kept the children excited from the moment they got in the car.

"Where is Woods Hole?" asked Oscar. "How long does it take to get there?"

"It takes a few hours and it's on the coast of Massachusetts," Freida said patiently, wrapping a blanket around her legs.

"How long does it take to get to Oak Bluffs?" asked Libby, jumping up and down on the back seat of the car.

"After we get off the ferry, it will take us about twenty minutes, honey," John said. "Now sit down and be still, please. I don't want you to fall."

"But if I sit down, I can't see," Libby whined.

"Libby, come up here and sit on my lap," Freida said. "Then you can see."

"How come the boat doesn't sink if it carries so many cars and trucks?" asked Howard, looking puzzled.

"It is all based on science, Howard. You'll learn about it in school. Look at it this way: the ferry is mostly open, so it is very light, air going in and out of it. The ocean is thick or dense, and the lightness of the boat doesn't make it sink very deep. Do you understand that?"

"I guess so," Howard said, turning his attention to Jack, who was teasing him with a slingshot. "Hey, don't hit me with that, boy!" he warned.

"This will probably be the longest leg of the trip," Freida said with a laugh.

When the car reached Woods Hole, the ferry was already there, and John drove right onto the boat. The family went up to the top deck and found chairs on the starboard side, where they had the best view of the ocean. As the ferry got under way, Freida gave each child a few small pieces of bread so they could feed the sea gulls that swooped down to take the crumbs from their fingers.

"He bit me, Mama!" Libby yelled after one gull pecked her finger.

"Its okay honey, you'll be fine. Let's go inside and buy you some hot chocolate."

"I want some! I want some!" the boys yelled, following along like hungry kittens.

John and Freida loved spending time on Martha's Vineyard. Aunt Mar's house was within walking distance of the center of Oak Bluffs, overlooking a pond where they could go clamming, and near the harbor where they could go on the paddle-boats. Beside the pond were the "gingerbread houses," a historic cottage-city campground site where lovely Gothic-style Victorian houses decorated with bright colors and elaborate flower gardens delighted the tourists. Inside the campground was the Trinity Park Tabernacle, an open-air building constructed of wood and wrought iron, where religious services and concerts were held. A walk through the campground led to the main street of Oak Bluffs and down to the Flying Horses Carousel, the oldest in the United States. The children asked to ride several times a day, competing to see who could snatch the brass ring, the prize that marked the bearer as the lucky one to earn a free ride. The envy of all of the other riders and spectators was yours if you were the winner.

Fresh seafood was a delicacy not offered in Tuskegee. On the Vineyard, there was something about the saltwater and fresh air that kept one's stomach constantly craving attention. From clambakes and beach cook-outs to fishing trips catching lobster, shrimp, oysters and fresh fish, the dinner table was filled with offerings from the sea on a daily basis. Even the children loved these new foods, except when Aunt Mar served freshly boiled lobsters that still had the tentacles and eyes on them, which sent all four children running from the table. After that it was lobster tails "only," split in half and dipped in melted butter.

After a day on the beach and a seafood dinner, John often piled everybody into the car to go sightseeing. He drove out to East Chop and let the children climb up to the lighthouse. He took them to Chappaquiddick and, later, drove them out to view the sunset at Menemsha Park. The children loved to watch the high waves at South Beach knocking down experienced swimmers as if they were feather-weights, and John had to make sure that the children didn't go near the turbulent water. Sometimes he took them to Edgartown, Chilmark, or Tisbury to visit the shops and sightsee, and then drove back to the "Bluffs" and to Circuit Avenue to get some homemade ice cream or Murdick's fudge. This kind of unrestrained leisure helped to fortify the soul, a necessary element before re-entering the fray back home.

After a few months, John grew restless, and the family returned to Boston. He decided to do some traveling to solicit funds for the *NMA Journal* and to visit some of his association buddies. He also went to Jersey City to visit his friend George Cannon, who informed him that things were still pending with the V.A. situation, and that Tuskegee had "cooled down."

"Just be patient, John," George said, putting a hand on John's shoulder. "I know you want to get back to work and be of service, but the timing has to be right and your safety has to be guaranteed."

"I know you're right, George, and I will persevere. I always say that life is an adjustment of one's self to his environment. When that adjustment entirely ceases, and that other inescapable and inexplicable something occurs, death ends the scene. Whence we came or whither we go, no one knows, for no traveler has ever returned to tell, and right now, I fortunately don't need to know."

"Amen," George concluded. "Now let's pray that before we leave this earth, mankind will use its earthly powers to better the human condition – for everyone."

John also visited his friend Dr. E. P. Roberts in New York City. The NMA meeting was coming up in St. Louis, and the two doctors wanted to draft some resolutions on behalf of organized medicine to present to the president. During John's visit, Roberts showed him the copy he had received from George Cannon of a letter from President Harding's secretary, saying Harding still intended to staff the hospital with colored personnel.

Upon returning to Boston, John was faced with the decision he had been avoiding: whether to go back to Tuskegee now, or wait a few more months. He was sitting at the judge's desk in the library reading the newspaper, when Freida appeared at the door.

"John, here's a telegram for you that was just delivered. Do you want me to open it? It seems to be from Hot Springs, Arkansas."

"Yes, open it, please. I'll bet it's from Moton; he vacations there."

Freida opened the telegram and handed it to John. She noticed that his mood changed as he read the message.

"Here, Freida, read this."

The telegram read as follows:

AUGUST 18, 1923

PLEASE MEET ME TUSKEGEE...MONDAY AUGUST 20TH....FOR IMPORTANT CONFERENCE...EVERYTHING ALL RIGHT...YOUR POSITION IN COMMUNITY...WITH WHITE AND BLACK STRONGER THAN EVER BEFORE...

WIRE REPLY CARE JOHN L. WEBB...HOT SPRINGS ARK

"I guess my decision is made," John said, rubbing his forehead in resignation. "I have to go back now."

"But D, you can't be sure that it really is safe. I don't like it." Freida slammed the telegram down on the desk. "What if Moton's wrong? All you have done will be for nothing."

"He wouldn't ask me to come back if it wasn't safe. I'll start making my travel arrangements at once."

Freida knew that John's mind was made up. Just when they were ready to get back to a normal life, something always intruded on their plans. She reached for her book of prayer, searching for something that would give her solace.

Before he left Boston, John received a letter from Charles W. Hare, the white attorney practicing in Tuskegee who had sent John a message to leave Tuskegee when his life was threatened. John had learned to trust this man and listen to his advice. Hare wrote that it was safe for John to come back to Tuskegee under all circumstances. He also suggested that John not be too hurried in reassembling his staff at the hospital. John thought this was odd advice but decided to figure out what it meant when he got back to his old job.

He soon left for Tuskegee, choosing to leave Freida and the children in Boston until he could see for himself what the situation was like. He had befriended a white physician in Boston who had agreed to look after Freida in case she needed medical attention in his absence.

John expected to pick up where he had left off when he got back to Tuskegee, but once there, he realized there had been changes, some veiled and some patent. So much appeared to be normal, yet it was evident to John that things were very different from what they had been on that fateful day when he had fled, fearing for his life. Events would soon prove that this was no longer his Tuskegee of old.

"I've Been 'Buked...
and I've Been Scorned"

John got off the train and went immediately to Mrs. Booker T. Washington's home to let her know he was back. He knew she would spread the word, and the whole town would quickly know that their doctor was home.

"I can't tell you how glad I am to see you, Dr. Kenney! I haven't been able to get any proper care since you left. That old arthritis has got a hold of me, and I haven't had that medicine that you prescribed for me. I've been in such pain."

"Well, as soon as I get back to my office, I'll look at your file and send something over to you, Mrs. Washington."

"Thank God you're home, Dr. Kenney, that's all I can say."

John walked eagerly to the hospital, pausing at the front door to remember the small wooden structure that had served as the first hospital where his career had begun. Its transformation into such a modern facility still impressed him. With a warm feeling and a pleased smile, he entered the foyer and looked around. When he didn't recognize any of the staff he saw working there, he headed to the nurses' station to find his two favorite employees. A new nurse was manning the station.

"Excuse me, Miss, I'm Dr. Kenney, and I'm looking for Miss Booth or Miss Gibbs, the head nurse and her assistant," John said with hopeful expectation.

The new nurse eyed him coolly, taking her time before replying. "And I'm Miss Anderson, the new head nurse now," she replied, emphasizing the word *now*.

John sensed a hint of arrogance in her voice, but he held his tongue, deciding he would deal with her later. "Do you know where I might find Miss Booth or Miss Gibbs, Miss Anderson?"

"They don't work here anymore. They left town a few months ago." Miss Anderson looked at John as if he should have known this. She shrugged her shoulders and went back to her work, letting him know that she had provided all the information she had – or cared to.

Disappointed, John went to find Warren Logan. This was not the welcome he had expected. He needed to know what else was going on.

"A lot of things have changed since you left, John. Besides your nurses leaving, we couldn't find a medical director. We finally secured a young doctor from Washington, D.C., to help out, but he is a new medical school graduate, and he doesn't have managerial experience," Logan lamented. "He does know that you will be returning to your previous position, however."

After more investigating, John found out that the new doctor had brought two young interns with him, and that none of them were prepared for the task at hand. John had one big mess on his hands. Now he understood what Attorney Hare had been trying to tell him in his letter.

John immediately called a meeting of the hospital staff to let everyone know who was in charge. It was evident that his return had cast a pall on everyone's activities, and while the young doctors knew they needed direction, they also resented it.

At the meeting, John presented a hospital organization chart showing himself as medical director and Dr. Davis, the graduate who had been brought in as acting director in John's absence, as his attending physician. The two other rotating interns would assist Dr. Davis. He explained the protocol that he expected everyone to follow.

"This is the chain of command, people," John instructed the assembled staff. "All changes will go through me. If I have to be away,

I will signal who is in charge, presumably Dr. Davis. I have asked Miss Gibbs to return to Tuskegee to take up her old position as head nurse, and all of the nurses will take direction from her."

Miss Anderson looked at Dr. Davis as if he should say something about this decision, but he remained quiet.

"The foremost objective of this institution is to give service, and I mean excellent service, to our patients. We work to serve them. I am passing out to each one of you a pamphlet that I wrote about the John A. Andrew Hospital. It's titled 'Service of a Negro Hospital.' It details the history, objectives and purpose of this fine institution. I want everyone to read it and digest it, and then I think some of the lackadaisical attitudes around here may change."

The pamphlet was received with genuine interest by some staff and obvious indifference by others. John could readily sense which staff members he could probably count on, and which ones he would have to watch.

"I will add one last caveat regarding my attitude toward service," John admonished. "William Drummond said, 'The greatest thing in the world is love.' I think that, if with that love he has included service, then I agree with him. If not, then I'd say the greatest thing in life is *service*, active service, useful service, helpful service, service to one's country, service to one's day and generation, service to one's fellow man – and service to God!" John picked up his charts and announced, "This meeting is adjourned."

Sensing the seriousness of their director, the staff filed silently out of the room. John spent the next week going from one department to another, making sure that everyone understood the new rules.

Soon after the changes were implemented, things returned to semi-normalcy, although not up to the standard where John wanted them to be. Even so, the community began to feel more confident about the hospital now that it was operating more efficiently, and business began to improve. John was writing up a report on these improvements for Dr. Moton, when his secretary came running into his office.

"Turn on the radio!" she shouted, her voice full of hysteria. "The president is dead!"

John jumped up and took hold of both her arms. "What are you talking about, woman?" He stared in shock as she crumpled to the floor, sobbing. Quickly he reached for the radio and turned it on. By now other hospital employees were running into his office to see what the commotion was about. John fumbled with the dial until he could clearly hear the announcer's voice:

"Today, August 2, 1923, our venerable president, Warren G. Harding, was found dead of unexplained causes in a San Francisco hotel room..."

John didn't hear much more of what was said. He called Dr. Moton and then Freida, to mourn the loss for the country and, particularly, for the Negro people. He didn't know what this would mean for the Veteran's Hospital situation, but he knew it would probably mean a substantial delay. The entire country was in mourning, and Calvin Coolidge was quickly sworn in as president. There was nothing to do but wait and see what this event would mean on many levels. Meanwhile, life had to go on.

About that time, the Standard Life Insurance Company in Union Springs offered John a contract to do life insurance examinations for the students. This was a welcome opportunity that would supplement his modest salary, since his raise had not yet been approved. He would make about five dollars for each exam, and Standard Life would provide basic coverage for each student who passed the examination. In addition to these financial considerations, as medical director he would be the only one allowed to have a private practice on the side, one of the fringe benefits of his position.

With the income from these activities, John was confident he could soon bring Freida and the children home. He missed his family dearly, and was tired of making do with telephone calls and correspondence. Even though correcting the hospital situation occupied his days fully, his nights were empty, lonely affairs, and he planned to bring everyone home as soon everything at the hospital was in order. A few illnesses, however, made the decision worrisome.

John had returned to find three cases of diphtheria on the campus, and twenty-eight cases of La Grippe. He hadn't yet felt the need to discourage people from assembling, but if the infections spread any further, he would have to. He was just glad that Freida wasn't there to be exposed to the breakout, or to witness his struggle to put the hospital back on track.

When he had left Tuskegee, the hospital had earned a Grade A rating from the American Hospital Association. Upon his return, the institution was in danger of losing that accreditation due to disorganization and the downright incompetence of several departments. John had to constantly check to be sure that the improvements he had made were still in effect, and that people weren't slipping back into their old neglectful ways. At this point he didn't trust anyone else to handle that responsibility, although he looked forward to the day when he once again felt secure about his staff. He tried to focus on that result, but at times the strain was just too much. On some days, he even wondered if he should have come back to Tuskegee.

In the midst of his efforts to restore the hospital to its previous reputation, he received a letter from his friend Daniel Hale Williams in Chicago, explaining that he had missed the last NMA meeting due to the illness of his wife. It seemed that Dan and John had more in common than just their love of medicine. John could always count on Dan to boost his spirits by recognizing his accomplishments, and John was awed by Dan's humility regarding his own. Now here he was again, telling John in a letter, "You have done and are doing a great work single-handed and alone. None in our group has or ever can compare with you in progress and solid achievement. I am always and ever with you."

What was remarkable to John was that these words came from a Negro physician who was a pioneer and a hero in Negro medicine in his own right. The kind of support, admiration, and sincere esteem in which John and Dan held each other was a bulwark of the Negro physicians of the day. True, there was ego, but it was more of a communal attribute, a kind of shared respect, because they were all in the same fight to prove they were the best.

Being the best was part of the Tuskegee philosophy. Booker T. Washington taught it, and John was determined to teach it too. He had some ideas about adding two weeks of didactic lectures after the annual John A. Andrew clinic so that the medical students could extend and enhance their training. He decided to ask young Dr. Davis if he would help with the planning.

"Please come in and have a seat," John said as Davis arrived at his office and sat down. John, to avoid the formality of sitting at his desk, took the chair beside him. "I have an idea for a post-graduate course for the young physicians attending this year's clinic."

"That sounds like a novel idea, Dr. Kenney. What do you have in mind?"

"I thought that if we could offer something like this, especially to those aspiring to be surgeons, not only would it further their training, but we could offer certificates of completion, which would enhance their credentials," John explained.

"That's an excellent rationale. How can I help?"

John was pleasantly pleased with Davis's reaction. Maybe he needed to give this young doctor a little more time to prove himself, and maybe he had been too hasty in his assumptions. He decided to let Davis provide some input on the curriculum for the course, and see how he handled the responsibility.

John also needed to get the principal's approval for his project, so he headed over to the administration building and knocked on the door to the office of Dr. Moton's secretary. He stuck his head in and called "Good morning" in his usual cheerful manner.

The secretary glanced in John's direction, nodded, and went back to working on her typewriter.

"Excuse me, Miss," John said, sticking his head into the secretary's office. "I'm Dr. Kenney from the John A. I was wondering if Dr. Moton has a few moments to talk with me."

"He's busy now," she said curtly, her attitude disinterested and dismissive.

"It will only take a few minutes. May I please wait?" John asked.

"I said he was busy, sir," she replied more rudely than before.

"Then I will come back later," John said. "Good day."

The woman kept on with her work and did not reply. John shook his head in amazement at the woman's discourteous behavior, and made a mental note to speak to Moton about her. As he was leaving the administration building, John realized that he and Moton had barely spoken since John's return to Tuskegee. The letter John had sent inquiring about a raise had gotten no response. It dawned on John that perhaps Moton had not appreciated the unyielding stand that he had taken that day at Thompkins Hall when the white contingent from town had threatened them. Moton had never said a word, but his silence now left John wondering. Things were certainly not the same.

As John was going up the steps to the hospital, his secretary rushed out to meet him. "Dr. Kenney, you have a call from a Dr. Miller in Boston," she said quickly. "I saw you coming and asked him to hold."

John hurried inside to take the call.

"I'm sorry to intrude on your day, Dr. Kenney, but I need to talk to you about Mrs. Kenney," he said in a serious tone.

"What is it, Dr. Miller?"

"Your wife told me that she talked to you last night, but she didn't tell you that I have been seeing her regularly. She told me she didn't want to worry you."

"No, she didn't mention anything," John said, his alarm growing. "What's going on?"

"I have seen her several times since you left. Four days ago she was feeling no better, and I thought I had discovered some dullness at the base of her lungs and some rales."

"Did she have fever?" John asked, putting the clinical clues together in his mind.

"Her temperature for the past four nights varied from 100 to 101.6 degrees. This afternoon it was 102."

An icy feeling began to rise slowly from the pit of John's stomach, causing his heart to ache. Trying to push the fear from his mind, he began processing all of the possibilities.

"I'm sorry, Dr. Kenney, but that's not all," Dr. Miller added in a regretful tone. "She is also having some discharge from her left breast. My partner Dr. Breed and I examined her this afternoon, and we both feel that she has a fairly active tuberculosis process, with possibly some fluid affecting the breast."

In a moment, John's world shattered into billions of little pieces – a kaleidoscope of beliefs and emotions that vacillated from one feeling to the next. He was the doctor, the husband, the father, the lover – and all of these personae were demanding a piece of his wounded and broken psyche – all at the same time. For a moment he was too overcome to say anything.

"Dr. Kenney?" Dr. Miller asked. Like any physician, he hated to be the one to give a colleague bad news, especially over the telephone.

"I'm here. I am just stunned. We examined her together before I left."

"I know. At that time I did not discover anything, but there must have been something there. Dr. Breed insisted that she must go to bed, and she is doing that. Her aunt is looking after the children. She wanted to start for Tuskegee at once, but Dr. Breed felt it would not be right for her to do it while she is as acutely sick as she is now."

John fought to keep his composure. "I think we need to admit her right away."

"We wanted to make arrangements for her to go to the hospital, but she is averse to doing so. We feel that she should be where she can be well taken care of and where she can have an x-ray picture."

"I concur," said John with emphasis, "and I will make arrangements to get there as soon as I can."

"Your wife is quite a woman," Dr. Miller added with admiration in his voice. "She didn't want me to worry you because she said your work is too important to interrupt, and she wants to help you by doing her part to take care of herself."

"Yes, she is quite a woman, Dr. Miller. Thank you for calling. I will be there in a few days."

John pulled himself together and sent for Davis, who agreed to take over John's duties until he returned, assuring John that he need not to worry about anything at the hospital.

When John arrived in Boston, he took a taxi to Judge Armstrong's home. He arrived to see his children playing in the yard under the watchful eye of Aunt Mar. They were excited to see him, and as he hugged and kissed them, gladness and sadness filled his eyes and spilled onto his cheeks, creating a blur.

"Daddy, why are you crying?" Elizabeth asked with impish curiosity.

"These are tears of joy, Libby," he said quickly, wiping his tears on his coat sleeve. "I am so happy to see my family that it makes me cry. Now I'm going upstairs to see your mother. I'll be right back." The children resumed their game as quickly as he had interrupted it.

John climbed the stairs to Freida's room. She was sleeping peacefully, but looked thinner than when he had seen her last. Yet she was as beautiful to him as ever, and he sat down on her bed and gently took her hand. She looked up at him and smiled, as she reached to hug him.

"John, I am so glad you are here. I'm going to feel better now. Give me a few days and we can go home together," she said her face full of hope.

"Let me examine you, Freida, and then we can make some decisions. You are doing exactly what you need to be doing, and that is getting some rest. I know you, and you never think of yourself. Everyone else always comes first, and you take care of each of us, even when you are sick. Now we're going to change that. Let us take care of you for a change."

"All right, Doctor, I'll be your patient for today anyway," she said coyly.

John pulled out his stethoscope. He listened to Freida's lungs and examined her breast. He could barely keep his bedside manner professional. The tuberculosis had definitely affected the right breast, and the prognosis would be grim if he did not get her immediate treatment. He went back downstairs and called Dr. Miller, speaking in a hushed tone. The children and Aunt Mar had just come in from outside to get ready for dinner, and he didn't want to alarm them. "I see that my wife has a more sinister problem than was evident at the time we examined her. I would appreciate it if you would make arrangements for her to go to the sanitarium of your choice to get this under control. She needs to be away from others to ensure that no contagion occurs. I will explain this to her and the family, and I will bring her to you as soon as you make the arrangements."

"All right, Dr. Kenney, I will attend to it right away. I suspect that I can get her a room at the Sharon Sanitarium in Boston, and we can admit her this evening. I will give you a call back in a few hours."

John took the judge and Aunt Mar into the parlor and explained the situation. The judge was sober, but Aunt Mar collapsed in tears. While her brother-in-law consoled her, John headed back upstairs to have the hardest conversation he hoped he would ever have to have with his wife.

She looked at his face and asked her question with caution, "What's wrong, John?"

"Freida, your lungs are congested. The discharge from your breast is a symptom of a larger problem. Dr. Miller and I feel that you have a tubercular process going on, and you will need to go to the sanitarium to be treated…tonight."

"D," Freida cried, "I can't go! The children need me. You need me to take care of them so you can do your work. I'll just rest a few days and you'll see – I will get better. Just get me some pills and I'll be good, you'll see."

John couldn't believe what he was hearing; his wife was making no sense. She knew what tuberculosis was, and that it was contagious. Maybe the fevers were affecting her sensibilities.

"Freida," he said more sternly than he meant to, "you have to go to the sanitarium, and you will have to stay there a while. We cannot risk your father, the children, or your aunt getting sick. They have been exposed to this, and we will have to pray that they are not alread infected."

Faced with this reality, Freida seemed to submit to John's suggestion and turned her head toward the window. "I hope I will have a view like this one when I get there. I love looking at the clouds and the sun shining down on a pretty day. Even the rain brings me comfort. Can I have a room with a view there?"

"We'll do our best, my dear," John said stroking her hair. "We'll do our best."

John stayed in Roxbury for a few weeks, visiting Freida daily. Even dressed in the required sterile sanitarium garb, he couldn't really get close to her, but he thought his presence was reassuring. He took her a radio and some classical books that she loved to read; but, after a while, Freida sensed his restlessness and suggested that he go back to Tuskegee. She told him she felt better and there was nothing he could do anyway. John assured her that they would talk often and that he would be in touch with her doctors to monitor her progress.

When he arrived back in Tuskegee, Davis and the staff assured him that everything had gone as usual. There had been no calamities, and for this John was grateful. He was going through his mail when he found a letter from Mr. Aubrey Williams, the Standard Life Insurance agent, informing John that he had sent two applicants, a James Jeter and a Harry Carlos, to his office for insurance examinations. Williams seemed quite sure that they had both been examined, but he reported that the office in Montgomery had not received the examination papers yet. He offered as an explanation that maybe John had sent the papers to the home office in Union Springs instead of to Montgomery. He said that the applications were being held up until he got the results of the examinations, and if John would look into this, he would appreciate it. John didn't recognize either of the names, and he went to the clinic to check his books. When he couldn't find either name, he called Davis into his office.

When the young doctor arrived, he greeted John warmly and said, "I heard you wanted to see me."

"Yes, I do. I received this letter from Standard Life saying that we have examined a Mr. Jeter and a Mr. Carlos, and that no examination papers have been sent in on them. Do you know anything about this?"

"Uh…no, I mean, yes, I think I examined a Mr. Jeter while you were gone. But I don't know anything about a Mr. Carlos," he said hesitantly, looking down at his feet.

"Well, where are the examination papers?" John asked.

"I think I sent them in, sir," he said. "I will go and check my office to see if they may have been misplaced, but I really think they were mailed."

"Well, you go and check. We have always been on time with these examinations and never had an application held up, and I don't want to start now. We have a record of efficiency and accuracy, and your reputation is everything, you know."

"Yes, sir, I will get back to you," Davis said as he quickly backed out the door.

These young doctors, John thought. *They just don't have the discipline they need to follow through the entire process. They just make a stab at something, and they are too impatient to move on to the next task without finishing the one they started. What will medicine come to?*

Davis continued to scour his records for the next week or two, finally telling John that he had found the exam papers. Apparently they had been misplaced in the clinic, but he assured John that they had been mailed at last. John called Williams and apologized for the delay, assuring him that this would not happen again.

John had given the younger doctors permission to do the insurance exams in his absence so that they could get the experience, but he had made it clear that he was supposed to review the results and send in the vouchers for payment. When he sent in the voucher for this exam, however, he was told that it had already been paid – to Dr. Davis.

John sent for Davis again.

"Dr. Davis," he said sternly, "there seems to be a misunderstanding. I asked Standard Life if you could do some insurance examinations for me in my absence, which they agreed to. It was my understanding, however, that this arrangement did not change the basic process under which we work with the insurance company. Therefore, when you reported to me that you had made the examination, of course I sent in a charge for it. Now I'm informed that the charge has been disavowed. According to Standard, a voucher was sent in with your name on it, and the money was paid to you. It seems that you may have a different interpretation of how we operate. Is that so?"

"I guess I really didn't understand the process," Davis said somewhat sheepishly. "I will pay you back for the exam."

"I am sure you see the necessity of our having a definite understanding to prevent this kind of confusion. Are you sure that you don't remember a Mr. Carlos also?" John asked.

"I never saw a Mr. Carlos," Davis said defensively. "I told you all that I know."

"Well, Dr. Davis, I'll consider this matter closed. We will have a meeting next week so that I can explain to you and the other doctors what the procedure is."

At that moment, John's secretary stuck her head in the door to let him know that Freida was on the line.

Davis left the room, and John picked up the telephone. "Freida, how are you, my love?"

"I am doing much better, but you know how I resisted coming here."

"Yes, I do, but you know that it was the only realistic choice," John said in a paternal tone.

"If only I could have gone back to Tuskegee with you and have been hospitalized there. I guess this is a better treatment facility for this particular malady, but I hate to be away from you and the children. Father and Aunt Mar tell me they are doing well, and if things continue to go smoothly, I should be out of here in a few months. There is some good news, do you want to hear it?" she asked.

"Of course I do," John said feeling encouraged.

"I have met a wonderful friend here. Her name is Carrie, and she is from Worcester. She has given me a book called *Science and Truth*, and it is about how I can heal myself. Sickness can be mind over matter, you know?" she said, waiting to gauge his reply.

"A positive outlook always makes a difference," he agreed, trying to sound nonchalant. "Just focus on getting better and follow the doctor's orders and you will be fine. There is a lot of research being done around tuberculosis, and I am sure that in the future, sanitariums will be a thing of the past," John said, wanting to encourage Frieda about future possibilities, no matter how remote, to preserve her good mood.

"Oh, by the way," Freida continued, "one of Dr. Casey's boys died. He was taken with a hemorrhage right on the street, and Dr. Cook's daughter died last Saturday. She committed suicide, but they are keeping that quiet. She hung herself in her mother's closet. They are saying that she had heart trouble, but she really died of shame. Her mother was in Europe, having gone over there to see her other daughter marry a white man. This girl could not 'pass' like the rest of the family, and it drove her insane. I think the mother and father should be ashamed to lift their heads in public, don't you think, D?" Freida asked.

"What a shame."

"Well, I have to go now; they are bringing my dinner. Don't work too hard, and write to me soon. I love getting your letters. And I love you, John."

"I love you too. I wish you were here, but we'll see each other before you know it."

John's conversation with Freida left him despondent and emotionally drained. This was the price she paid for her decision to come to rural Tuskegee – convalescence in a sanitarium. If she had stayed in Boston in a more modern environment and with advanced medical facilities, she would not be where she was now. He felt partly responsible, being her husband and physician, and he had to admit that the process had gone on too long before she had been properly diagnosed in Boston. Were the lack of a proper diagnostic laboratory and updated fluoroscope equipment partly to blame? He had to admit the obvious and accept the responsibility. His heart was heavy with this realization. As he swiped at a tear that dropped on his editorial material, another knock sounded on his office door. It was Mr. Robb, the comptroller of the hospital. John picked up the papers quickly, pretending to be engrossed in his work.

"Dr. Kenney, may I have a word with you?" Robb asked.

"Of course, Mr. Robb, please come in and have a seat."

"This is not good news," Robb said. "It has come to my attention that your doctors may be treating patients under the table. The rumor has been going around for a few weeks, but I encountered two students today who told me that they had paid a fee to one of your physicians for negative venereal disease reports. And it is being said that students are receiving injections and medications and being treated, for a fee, in their rooms. I know this is against your agreement, and I thought you should know."

"Do you have any proof of this?" John asked, his mood changing from melancholy to frustration tinged with anger.

"Right now, it is only rumor and innuendo," Robb replied. "If it is true, we need to try to get some evidence so this can be brought to a halt."

"We need to inform Dr. Moton right away. I will do that if you will see whether you can get any physical evidence from your student. Keep me apprised."

"I will, Dr. Kenney. I'm sorry to have to bring you this news."

When Robb left the room, John put his head down on his desk. *How could anyone, given this great opportunity to make a difference at Dr. Washington's great school, do anything that would bring disgrace on our efforts and tarnish the accomplishments we worked so hard for?* he thought. *And for what? For five dollars here or there?* He had rarely felt so disappointed, dispirited, and bewildered, as if he were losing control.

He made an appointment to see Moton to let him know what they were up against. John waited in the principal's study for what seemed like an inordinate amount of time until Moton could finish his work, but John was too angry by now to feel slighted.

At last Moton invited John into his office. "Have a seat. Would you like a brandy?" he inquired, refilling his glass from a decanter.

"Yes, I would," John replied. "Perhaps that will cool my temper. I just had a visit from Mr. Robb, who informed me that he suspects our doctors are having a practice out of the dormitories and receiving monies that are not going through the hospital administration. He said that he had heard the rumor about Dr. Davis for weeks, and that it was verbally confirmed by a student he had questioned."

"Whoa now, not so fast," Moton said casually. "You know what Shakespeare said about gossip: 'Rumor is a pipe, blown by surmises, jealousies, conjectures…' Let's not be taken in too fast. I know Dr. Davis well. He was just here earlier, and he seems to be an honest man. The other two boys idolize Dr. Davis and would never do anything without his approval, so I think what we have here is a rumor, and just that. What else can I do for you?"

John could not believe that Moton was treating the matter so lightly, and even questioning John's motives in the process. This was not the Dr. Moton he thought he knew. Something had definitely shifted in Moton's attitude toward John.

"I feel this problem is more than rumor," John said, "but I will do some investigation on my own and then present it to you. My intention in coming here was to make you aware of a potential problem whose ramifications could be serious. I see that you will require absolute proof, and therefore I won't take up any more of your time." John rose to leave.

As he was heading out the door, he stopped to add, "By the way, I hope you have considered my request for a raise, as my finances are tight."

"We'll consider it when we review the budget, but things are tight here too," Moton replied as he opened a book.

John was incredulous, but he wasn't going to waste time fretting over Moton's response. Instead, he would watch his colleagues for the next few months for any signs of irregularity. Then he would come back.

Everything seemed to go well for the next few months. John instituted some new protocols to ensure better record keeping at the hospital, and he had more regular staff meetings so that all staff would be aware of the new policies. He was planning for the upcoming John A. Andrew Clinic when Mrs. Gaillard, his secretary, called him from the hospital.

"I'm sorry to disturb you, but I have been going through Dr. Davis' log," she said in a tone that John knew meant trouble. "I find that he is not keeping it up, and I'm not sure what months he is doing certain cases. I think he has gotten lax again."

"I'll talk to him," John said, hanging up without a goodbye. Angry to have to pick a bone that he had thought was buried, and too furious to talk, he sent Davis a letter through the campus mail. He advised him that the secretary had found his posting book in disarray and, that having examined it himself, John too had found it delinquent. He explained that this caused problems for the accounting process and caused the hospital to send overdue bills with back charges, which made the hospital, seem administratively incompetent. John also advised him to include all of the names of the patients or insurance applicants so that they could account for all charges. In addition, John wanted to review and sign his book on a regular basis, and wanted to sign all insurance examinations personally. He let Davis know that the only time this procedure would differ was when John was out of town. The last thing he said was that he wanted a response to his letter immediately. To John, having to go behind grown men, and doctors at that, to secure a commitment to excellence was blasphemy.

John was expecting a letter the next day, but Davis showed up at his home instead. The housekeeper ushered him in and offered him a seat.

"Dr. Kenney," Davis began with obvious annoyance, "I note that you are overanxious to receive an answer from me. Despite the fact that I have a very busy day, I am taking time from my other demanding work to give you an answer now. I must admit that, from several of the questions you have asked me from time to time, you seem unsure of my position regarding our personal work."

Careful not to show any emotion, John looked at Davis and waited for him to continue.

"I know that I have been absolutely square with you, as the people in Tuskegee all know. I have done your work with just as much earnestness as I would do my own. You surely must know that I certainly did not want to beat you out of any money. I am not crazy about money," Davis said, his tone changing from indignant to arrogant, "simply because I do not have to be. I tell you, Dr. Kenney, it has never been my policy to let anyone do any more for me than I can do for them."

"Dr. Davis," John said as he stood up, "we have had sufficient meetings and discussions for there to be no ambiguity. I see that you do consider yourself a regular examiner for Standard Life Insurance Company. Will you kindly advise me how long you have felt this to be true? On what date did you start, and from whom did you get your authority to do this? And while you are at it, tell me what circumstances brought about this understanding on your part?" John leaned down in front of Davis and made eye contact, speaking with the disillusionment of a father for a son who refused to be contrite. "I think that for some time you have been laboring under the wrong impression."

At this point Davis stood up and walked a few feet towards the door. "Dr. Kenney," he said, "I have not had a private practice in Tuskegee, but some of your patients that I treat ask me if I have my own practice. I tell them no and that they must stay with you. I have not done anything that was not in our agreement, and unless you have proof, I think we have discussed this enough."

Davis's departure left John wondering why, in the midst of all that needed to be done – producing a medical journal, planning a medical clinic, and managing the health affairs of a hospital and a college – he had to deal with this crisis too. What had become of the commonality and camaraderie between colleagues? He didn't have time to ponder this conundrum any more than he had time to do an investigation of Davis' activities; but he knew that he would do one, nonetheless, and that at some point things would come to a head.

The cumulative effect of all of these events left John feeling despondent. His wife's illness, the problems with Davis, and the lack of support from the principal were almost too much to bear. He decided to go to a concert given in the chapel by the Tuskegee Choir. They were singing William Dawson's spirituals, his favorite music. He hummed along with the choir as they sang:

"I've been 'buked and I've been scorned…

I've been talked about – shows you born,

'Dere is trouble all over 'dis land...children
Ain't gwine lay my 'ligion down, children.

That was exactly how he'd been feeling since his return to Tuskegee: rebuked, scorned, and talked about. But he wasn't ready to lay his religion down, either, not yet.

Besides, he had a lot to be happy about. Frieda was doing much better, and Dr. Miller had given her a clean bill of health. His family was coming home, and in anticipation of their arrival, John was having the house repainted a bright white. The school had planted magnolia trees, her favorite, along the driveway, and John had secured an aide for her from the home economics department. He had even rearranged their bedroom furniture so that the bed was by the window where she could have a pleasant view, day or night.

As he drove to the train station, the excitement of the reunion was overpowering. He could hardly contain himself. This was just what he needed. His heart seemed to expand when he saw Freida step from the train. She looked much stronger, and there was a calm about her that was quite extraordinary. John couldn't put his finger on it, but there was an element of peace about her that he had not seen before. She kept talking about spiritual healing and mind over matter, but he didn't care what it was as long as she was getting better.

The children had grown and matured more than he expected – this thanks to their great-aunt, who was a strict disciplinarian. Yet, they all acted like children when they got home. The reality of being together again as a family was the only thing that mattered. The house felt as joyous and festive as if it were Christmas Eve, and for the reunited Kenneys, it might as well have been.

John decided to put all of his worries out of his mind and focus on getting his family back to some sort of normalcy. Over the next few months, he felt satisfied that he had accomplished this and let himself settle into the lull of complacency. He had no way of knowing that this was the calm before the storm.

King Jesus Is A'listenin'

John's prayers had been answered. His family was back home, the hospital management was under control, and he could get back to his old routines.

The Kenneys settled quickly into their familiar habits. Freida enrolled the children in Children's House, the elementary school on the grounds of Tuskegee Institute. This gave her the opportunity to substitute teach, and also to resume her work at Saint Andrews Episcopal Church near the campus, where she had been one of the founding members. Even though Freida was now firmly embedded in the Christian Science religion, she continued her work at Saint Andrews, because she knew that the same tenets formed the foundation of many different faiths.

John dedicated himself wholeheartedly to hospital improvements and developments. The knowledge that he had had to send Freida away to get a level of medical care that Tuskegee could not offer was never far from his mind. Embarrassed that this deficiency existed within his domain, John was determined to resolve it. He began to upgrade the x-ray department, but quickly realized that the hospital could not afford the necessary radium. He had no choice but to approach Dr. Moton.

"I know you're aware that I've been upgrading certain departments," John began. "We now have a new x-ray machine, but Warren Logan tells me that we cannot afford the radium. I was hoping that there was an account you could draw upon to help us out."

"Right now we are under strict budget constraints, Dr. Kenney," Moton replied. "I appreciate what you are trying to do, but right now you will have to use the old equipment."

"That is unacceptable!" John said more vehemently than he had intended. "We cannot continue to get Grade A ratings without the updated equipment. Our patients deserve the best there is to offer. Furthermore, sir, I cannot begin to tell you what it feels like to have to send my wife away to Boston for medical care because we can't accommodate her properly right here!"

"Calm down, Dr. Kenney," Moton said. "I can empathize with you, but I cannot appropriate funds where there aren't any. We can make radium a line item on the budget for next year, but there is nothing I can do for now."

John left Moton's office determined to find a way to do what needed to be done, and damn the obstacles. He did some research to find out where he could get a loan to buy the radium now, and then he talked with Warren Logan to find out if he could be reimbursed for this purchase during the next fiscal year. He was quickly approved for a loan and immediately sent for the radium, even though he had not yet gotten the okay for reimbursement from Logan. But that didn't matter at this point, John decided. He would find a way later.

Eventually, Logan confirmed that John would be repaid, which gave John the confidence to tell Freida what he had done. She was not pleased.

"I know you were thinking of me and your other patients when you bought the radium, but we can't afford another expense. You haven't received the raise you requested last year, and we're still trying to pay off the medical expenses I incurred in Boston. Sometimes, I think you act before you think."

John was downcast at Freida's appraisal of him. It was not the response he had expected. "I just want to be able to take care of you here, Freida, at my hospital," John pleaded. "How do you think it looks to others when you have to leave here to get treatment? I'm the medical director, and I can't even take care of my own wife! That's ridiculous. I won't have it."

"How are we going to afford the loan payments?" Freida asked, softening her tone to keep from upsetting him further. She understood and admired her husband's intentions, but sometimes she wished he were more patient.

"I'm going to get some additional money from the insurance examinations," John said, "and if I have to expand my private practice, I will," he added, sounding somewhat tenuous and unsure. "Don't worry; I'll take care of it."

At the same time, John was also trying to make his case to the administration for another urgent upgrade Tuskegee needed: to have its own clinical laboratory. The existing hospital laboratory was entirely too small, not sufficiently equipped, and had no full-time laboratory technician. All of the blood work for the Wasserman tests for syphilis, for example, had to be sent to the Board of Health Laboratory at the state capitol, a time-consuming process. To have tissue work done, doctors had to send specimens to a private laboratory out of town, and pay five dollars for each examination. John decided to try to correct the situation by drumming up support from the medical community.

The urgency of the lab issue was clearly emphasized for John by a case where the findings were such that he was not able to say whether the patient operated on had syphilis of the stomach, tuberculosis, or carcinoma. A specimen of blood John sent to the laboratory at the State Board of Health returned a result of four-plus positive Wasserman, indicating the presence of syphilis. A specimen sent to another lab, however, was negative. The ambiguity meant John had to rely on his best guess in prescribing treatment, something he found irresponsible, unreliable, and completely unacceptable.

All of this was troubling John's mind as he prepared to start his clinic. He put on his white coat and hung his stethoscope around his neck, catching a glimpse of himself in a nearby mirror. His serious expression reflected his mood, and he forced a fake smile. "Can't see patients looking like this," he said to himself. As he walked down the hall to the clinic, an intern handed him a medical chart.

"Here is the report for Mrs. Brown, Dr. Kenney. Her examination was positive. She is ready for you in room number two."

"Damn it!" John said, startling the intern. "This is just what I was talking about."

Upon entering the examination room, he gently took the patient's hand and delivered the unwelcome news. "There are several lumps or nodules evident in your right breast, Mrs. Brown. Now, this could be something as simple as a fibrocystic problem, or it could be something more serious, like a malignancy." John's manner was caring and calm.

The woman's eyes widened in fear at the mention of the dreaded word. "You mean cancer?" she gasped.

"Yes, there is a possibility. It could be benign, but I'm sorry to say it could also be cancer."

"What causes cancer?" she asked, tears gathering in her eyes. "Is it something I did?"

"No, Mrs. Brown. In fact, the medical establishment at this point does not know what causes cancer, but research is being done to find out. There is one thing I can tell you, however. Cancer sometimes starts in one small area, and then continues to grow very slowly. This is a most important fact, because herein lies the advantage for the sufferer as well as the physician. If the symptoms are heeded in time, there is ample opportunity to bring to bear the proper measures in order to completely eradicate it and cure it while it is localized." Realizing that this explanation may have sounded too clinical, John asked if she had understood him.

"I understood you, doctor, but are you sure it might be cancer? I don't have any pain," Mrs. Brown said.

"That's good news, actually. With cancer, pain is one of the least prominent symptoms. There is no pain early in the disease, and when the patient does experience pain, the disease is more advanced," John explained.

"Well, what do you advise that I do, Dr. Kenney? What is the treatment?"

John was uncomfortable in explaining the options, a feeling compounded by the fact that the hospital wasn't properly equipped with laboratory facilities. "We can take a biopsy of the breast tissue, and send it to an outside lab for analysis," he began, clenching his fists in frustration. "Unfortunately, because we're in Tuskegee, this process will take a few months for a definitive diagnosis. If it is malignant, this is not good, since the cancer will have had time to spread. Or…we can remove the breast, a prophylactic measure, and that will be the end of it."

The woman burst into tears upon hearing these options. "I don't want to die, doctor. I have a little baby at home, and I want to live to see her grow up. Just take the breast; take it and let me live."

John comforted the young mother as best as he could. It was cases like these that were so frustrating and emotional, and there was nothing he could do. He scheduled the woman for surgery, and a few weeks later he removed her breast.

After a couple of months, she returned for a follow-up appointment, concerned that she might have cancer in other parts of her body, and that the breast was just an obvious site. John reassured her that this was not the case. Opening her pathology report, he took a deep breath and began to read.

"So you see," he admitted after reading her the results, "the report shows that you did not have cancer, Mrs. Brown. It was a benign fibroma."

The woman's face went blank, and she collapsed to the floor. With insufficient information and fearing death, she had given up a healthy breast.

Not long after that incident, John was examining Freida according to a timetable that he and Dr. Miller had agreed upon, and discovered that Freida had had some additional discharge from her breast.

"How long has this been going on?" he asked in a casual tone.

"Oh, I don't know, honey. Sometimes I'm so busy I really don't have time to pay attention."

John's breath caught in his throat. Freida was being far too cavalier about this discovery. He knew she was very much into her new philosophy that the mind was the true healer, and that every challenge could be overcome with faith, but he knew the gravity of the situation.

"You've got to start paying attention to these things," he urged. "If not for yourself, then do it for me. I don't think that's too much to ask, is it?"

"No, it isn't," she said and got up to get dressed.

Her perfunctory answer didn't reassure John that she would comply. Concerned, he went to his office and called Dr. Miller in Boston to discuss her condition.

"Good to hear from you," Miller said upon hearing John's voice. "Is everything all right with your wife?"

"Her lung condition is much improved," John told him, "and her spirits are good. But she has been studying that book her friend gave her, and she thinks that she can cure herself, so she is not paying too much attention to me. The breast problem is worrisome and doesn't seem to be resolving, and I would appreciate your counsel on that matter. While we are making strides in Tuskegee, this is not the best place for her to be treated with this condition."

"I am glad to hear that her lung condition has improved, but in my opinion, and I hate to say this, the best thing to do at this point is to have the breast removed."

"I was hoping against hope that it would not come to that."

"I'm sorry, John. The encouraging news is that it would probably not be necessary to take the muscles or dissect the axilla, just remove the breast itself. I should think that a discharging nodule in a tuberculous breast would be a constant focus of absorption, and would tend to keep her from improving beyond a certain point."

"I know you're right. I'm just wondering how this will affect her respiratory condition," John said vacantly, his mind focused on diagnosing and treating Freida's symptoms.

"If she were in the proper place, this could be done with gas – oxygen, without any ether," Miller said, "and there would be practically no danger of aggravating her lung condition. I don't know how you feel about this, and you are, of course, the only one to judge, as you see her every day. But the time will come, if it has not come already, when the operation will certainly be advisable."

"Yes, I agree with your assessment. While we are making great strides in Tuskegee, I regret to say that I think she needs to come back to Boston. Do you agree?"

"I honestly do agree, John. Anything I can do to help you, I shall be most glad to do. I will make all of the arrangements, of course."

"Thank you," John said. "I appreciate your kind assistance."

"I know that it seems she has had enough trouble without putting this on top of it," Miller said. "But on the other hand, it may be that she will not get back to normal health until this is done."

"You're right. I'll talk to her soon," John added, resigned to having to convince Freida that this was the right course to take. He didn't expect the conversation to be an easy one.

"And by the way, I got your correspondence regarding the hospital laboratory and the need for expansion," Miller added. "I will be glad to write Dr. Moton a letter supporting this project, and will see if I can find some additional funding from some benefactors up here."

"Thank you so much, Dr. Miller. I am indebted to you on many fronts. I will get back to you as soon as possible."

John slumped in his chair, remorse gripping him. A dark cloud of helplessness brought on a rain of tears. His temples began to throb, and he could feel the pressure pulsating in his head. Here he was again, helpless, useless, a doctor unable to cure the sickness in his own wife. He dreaded having to discuss Dr. Miller's recommendation with Freida, and was almost relieved that she had embraced a mind-over-matter philosophy. At least it offered her some optimism.

As the sky grew dark, he stayed in his office, praying for the strength to persevere. Reaching for his bible, he opened it and found a passage he had marked in St. Luke, where Jesus was telling a disciple how to pray:

"Ask, and it shall be given to you; seek, and ye shall find....for everyone that asks shall receive and he that seeks will find; and to him that knocks, it shall be opened."

John got down on his knees and asked God to preserve and protect the life of his wife. Still not ready to return home, he took out his journal and wrote that he knew this thing called life was an enigma. "We do not know whence it came nor 'whither it goeth,'" he wrote. Yet, he truly believed that the hand of God was man's only hope and salvation. He needed to bring that hope home to Freida.

At last, he left his office, sure that by this time the children would be in bed. When he got home, he found Freida reading her book quietly in the library.

"Hello, Mrs. Kenney," he said, teasing her, "how are you doing?"

"Oh, I'm fine, John, just musing on some new thoughts. How was your long day?"

"What thoughts?" he asked, not answering her question.

"Well, it says right here that 'disease is a latent illusion of the mortal mind.'"

Oh, Lord, why in the world had he asked that question? "Have you had any more leaking from your breast today?" he said, trying to stay in control of his emotions.

"Just a little. And listen to this: it says, 'Damp atmosphere and freezing snow empurpled the plump cheeks of our ancestors. They were as innocent as Adam, before he ate the fruit of false knowledge, of the existence of tubercles and troches, lungs and lozenges,'" she quoted with enthusiasm. "Our ancestors survived without the medical knowledge that we have today. It's surely divine power that saved them from their own worry. They didn't know about the diseases that could annihilate them, and therefore, in their minds, they were free. If sickness and disease is an illusion, then if we don't visualize it, we won't become victims of it."

John poured himself a brandy and dropped into his chair, thoroughly deflated and depressed. The dark cloud of helplessness threatened to descend again, but he knew he had to keep up appearances, at least for now.

"I talked to Dr. Miller today," he said, keeping a casual tone. "He was concerned about your breast."

"It will be fine; I am working on visualizing healthy tissue." Freida continued to turn the pages of her book, barely looking up.

"Freida," he pleaded, trying to stay calm, "we're worried about you… you must not take this lightly. It could be serious."

"John, darling," she said, putting down her book and coming over to put her arms around him, "I am a doctor's wife. I hear all of the cases you discuss with me, and I know the scenarios. You want to tell me that I might lose my breast. I know that. I'm not worried, and I don't want you to worry. We are in God's hands."

John started to speak, but was overcome with emotion at the thought of Freida worrying about him.

"Not another word, Dr. Kenney. Come have your dinner," she said, kissing him on the cheek.

They ate their dinner silently, and John examined Freida one more time before she went to sleep. He didn't like what he found, and he lay awake for a long time, worry and fear robbing him of sleep. Before dawn the next morning, he called Dr. Miller.

"I gave my wife another examination," John told him, "and the lungs still are clear. But, contrary to my previous report to you, last night's examination suggests there is a definite axillary involvement of at least one gland and perhaps more in the entire axillary space – causing a lump about the size of a partridge's egg."

"That's quite a worrisome finding," Miller replied.

"The breast is not discharging much, but it is larger. I am wondering if carcinoma is definitely ruled out." John questioned.

"It was the last time," Miller said. "The path report was absolutely negative."

"I know you will recheck this later when you see my wife, and I am still positive that the gland was not there at my prior examination. But since this breast is decidedly more enlarged with the presence of this gland or glands, it is very definite that the condition is progressive – and progressing very rapidly."

"When do you think she can get here, Dr. Kenney? I'm concerned about the progression."

"She's planning to take a trip to see her cousin in Cleveland, and to come to Boston at some time in the near future to visit her father, but

I will ask her to change her plans. I can't leave right now. My assistant is temporarily out of town, and I have several patients on critical care." John rubbed his eyes, desperate to think of some way to manage everything without unduly alarming his wife.

"I will leave that to your discretion. Just let me know as soon as you do."

John's dilemma was now twofold. For one thing, he felt guilty that he was reluctant to tell his wife about his new finding. He was sure that the news, in Freida's eyes, would be another nail in the coffin for the practice of medicine. Her insistence on the validity of Christian Science, and its self-healing prophesies, made him dread having another discussion with her to defend the medical profession. The second, and for John, larger issue was the question that continued to plague him: Didn't having to send her away for treatment again emphasize the inadequacies of the very hospital where he was the medical director or, in other words, *his own* inadequacies?

John decided he would test the waters with Freida. He went home for lunch and, when they were almost through eating, found his nerve to broach the subject.

"I'm still concerned about you, Freida, even more so after last night's examination," he said, trying to sound nonchalant.

"There is no reason to worry when one believes in divine truth," she responded, with a look of absolute certainty. "Faith is the answer, and one's personal power is derived from just that. We have to just go inside and listen to our own bodies."

That was all John needed to hear. He tolerated her comment, which was the antithesis of his medical training; because he loved her and because he thought her belief might serve as a distraction for her. He wasn't sure whether she really believed all of this hokum or if it was just a reaction to the fact that his medical knowledge had not rescued her. Did she adopt these extreme beliefs to mock him? Of course not. What would make him think something like that? He felt ashamed that the thought had entered his mind, and he chastised himself for being so insecure and disloyal.

"Freida, you can 'go inside' and you can go to Boston at the same time," John said, "and you need to go fairly soon. Let Dr. Miller look at you. You may need some additional surgery, but maybe not as extensive as before. I will agree to your going on your trip, but you will have to be in Boston within the next week or so."

"But I wanted to spend some time in Cleveland with my cousin, John," Freida complained.

"You'll just have to forego that for now, and that's my last word on the subject," he said, putting an obvious end to the discussion. Unable to ignore his conscience any longer, John went back to his office and placed another call to Miller.

"I hesitated to make this call," he said, "but I am sure that, as a physician, this state of affairs is not foreign to you. I am in a bit of a predicament."

"What is it, Dr. Kenney?"

"Along the lines of our, uh, first conversation, I, uh..." he stammered, "well, I felt it better not talk to Freida about my findings yesterday. This may seem unnecessary to you, but I am asking that you keep this confidence for me. She knows she may need more surgery, but that's it. Use your own judgment, however, as to whether she is told before the operation. I do not want it known at some later time that I made the discovery by examination here, and failed to bring it to your attention or that I somehow overlooked it."

"I understand, Dr. Kenney. I will do my best to preserve your position."

"I find myself in a helpless state that makes it necessary for me to burden you, and I apologize for that. I did tell her that she needs to see you as soon as possible, but she is quite determined to detour to Cleveland first."

"I will still go ahead and put her on my schedule in the next ten days or so. Will that give her enough time?"

"That will be fine, Dr. Miller. I would also appreciate it if you would call her father, Judge William O. Armstrong, and let him know her condition. Tell him that you advised an operation and that I agreed with your advice. He should know that I recently examined her, and urged her to lose no time in getting into your hands."

"That's no problem. I will take care of it."

John didn't know what he was more ashamed of, not being able to cure his wife's illness or not being able to admit his helplessness to her. He felt himself a complete and utter failure, and he had no excuse. The dark shadows in the room surrounded him and, strangely enough, comforted him, shrouding his uselessness and keeping his secret hidden and safe.

The next morning, John began making arrangements for Freida's trip. He routed her to Cleveland briefly, so as not to worry her too much, and then immediately on to Boston. She was his number one priority, but he also had to find a caretaker for the children that she approved of. If he failed to do that, he knew she wouldn't go.

John's spirit suffered from the weight of the concerns pressing down on him. The matter with Dr. Davis was under investigation, and John might lose him as an assistant just when he was most needed to help with the impending meeting of the John A. Andrew Clinic. John had also misplaced an important manuscript he had been editing for the *Journal*, one that he had to find before the publication deadline.

"Freida, do you know where I put Dr. Dailey's submission for the next edition? I can't find it," John called as he searched frantically through his study. How could this happen? He never lost such important items.

Freida called down from the upstairs room where she was doing some ironing. "No, I haven't seen it, dear. Oh, I forgot to tell you, Mrs. Washington called to see how you were coming with the solicitations from the NMA. She said to remind your colleagues that the money is for the Douglass home in Washington, D.C., and that we owe it to Frederick Douglass, who did so much for us."

John had not yet had time to solicit any money, and he knew he needed to do so right away. He sat down at his desk to make some calls, but couldn't think who to call first. He would do it later, he decided, when he was not so distracted. For something to do, he began sorting through the piles of paper on and around his desk and found, under some old newspapers, a stack of unopened mail that contained unpaid bills. Exasperated, he put his head in his hands. "It's too much right now," he muttered to himself.

Absently, he fingered the stack of mail, and noticed a card from George Cannon asking what was going on with John and the V.A. situation. The card was three weeks old. How had John let himself get so far behind in managing his affairs? There were so many pressing matters he needed to address, but they all paled in comparison to Freida's health, making his life feel more and more out of control.

The next day, to John's relief, Mrs. Washington arranged to watch over the children with the help of her house staff. This suited Freida quite nicely, and John got no argument from her about going to Boston, only a reminder that everything happens for a reason. Even if one couldn't see the relevance at the moment, she assured him, the answer would be revealed in time.

After Freida arrived in Boston and underwent exhaustive diagnostic tests, Dr. Miller decided that a mastectomy would be the only way that she would have a chance to return to normal health. Not sure what her reaction would be, he broke the news to her gently while they were seated in his office.

"Mrs. Kenney, you have been struggling with this disease for some time, and you have put up a valiant fight. I think that the time has come, however, for us to be somewhat more aggressive."

"I was expecting that somehow, Dr. Miller, based on my husband's unusual behavior lately. He is very defensive about the profession you know, and he really doesn't understand my faith-based healing. But that's all right. I'm also a realist."

"Do you understand what I'm saying, Mrs. Kenney?" Dr. Miller asked cautiously, noting her lack of emotion. "We will need to do a mastectomy to stem the tuberculosis." He wanted to be absolutely sure that Freida knew exactly what procedure he was describing. He had never seen a woman receive this kind of news with so much control and apparent lack of emotion. He was amazed at her calm.

"I absolutely understand, doctor. As I told my husband, one cannot be married to a surgeon all these years and not be aware of medical consequences. Let's do what we have to do, and get on with it."

Bewildered by Freida's nonchalant attitude, Miller called John to see if this was her normal behavior. He was worried that she might be in denial about her illness, and might have some sort of breakdown after the surgery had taken place.

"Your wife seems unmoved by the predicament she is facing," he said, puzzled at the anomaly. "It's most unusual, and I'm not sure how to take it."

"It's her Christian Science faith, Dr. Miller. I think it has a lot to do with the power of suggestion. It's akin to suggestive therapy: the greater mastery one has of the art, the better the effect on the patient. Her religion teaches that the power of the mind and strength of your faith is all you need to heal yourself," John explained.

"Is it rather like placebo therapy?" Miller asked.

"Yes, like that wonderful effect of the sterile water on the nervous patient. And what of the patient who could not sleep unless the sleeping powder was on the mantel? I believe in suggestive therapy, and I believe the day will come when it will receive greater recognition in regular therapeutic curricula."

"I, too, am duly impressed by it," Miller said. "So 'as a man thinketh in his heart, so he is'?"

"Yes, I think so. If a man thinks he is sick all the time, there is nothing for him to do but be sick. A sick mind makes a sick body. If you want to be well, think health, act health. That is what my wife is doing."

"Then I feel more secure in doing her procedure. I will schedule it right away."

*   *   *

John was resigned to the potential reality of what lay ahead. Freida, however, kept saying that she understood the treatment was necessary, and knew she would be fine. If only John and Dr. Miller could be that confident. Although they knew they were following the appropriate medical protocol, they also knew they could not guarantee the outcome.

While waiting for news of Freida, John found it nearly impossible to concentrate on his work. Every ring of the phone sent him racing for the receiver. One call was from Judge Armstrong, and it was not what John expected.

"I want to know why you didn't call me yourself to tell me about my daughter's condition" he said without greeting. "I don't understand why Dr. Miller called me, and my own son-in-law didn't."

There was nothing John could say. His inability to tell Freida the truth up front had caused him to use bad judgment with others in the end. While his decision may have saved him from some hard words with his wife at the time, this accusation from his father-in-law was perhaps even more degrading.

"All I can do is apologize, Judge. I took the coward's way out."

Although the judge admired John's honesty, he was too protective of his daughter to let John off the hook.

"I don't expect it to happen again, son. *You* keep me posted from now on." He hung up without waiting for John to say a word.

When at last John heard Miller's voice on the phone, his knees went weak with relief, while his heart raced waiting for the news.

"The operation was a success," Miller exclaimed, "and she did beautifully!"

John sagged into a chair, feeling suddenly drained. Tears of joy and relief filled his eyes.

"She had just the average amount of discomfort," Miller continued, "and she was sitting up in a chair reading her book when I last saw her. That is remarkable! The wound was clean and in good condition when I dressed it this morning, and the x-ray of her chest showed that the old trouble has practically cleared up. It was a tubercular process, not carcinoma, as I suspected."

Even as John listened, the thought that kept going through his mind was that his Freida was through with her ordeal and could now get well. A piece of him wanted to run and leap and shout like a boy.

"I will let her go to her father's house sometime next week," Miller said. "I will keep a careful eye on her until she can return to Tuskegee, but I think it will be sooner than I expected."

Freida was indeed home within the month and, travel notwithstanding, she looked radiant and rested when John picked her up at Cheehaw. He thanked God for watching over her, and was grateful for the wise words of Jesus that had helped him to pray for Freida and for her well being.

Now his wife was safely home, and he could turn his attention to other worries. The goal of upgrading the medical services at Tuskegee was more relevant than ever. There was just one annoying problem, however, that demanded his immediate attention, and he needed to get that out of his way.

A Chapter Closed

John had had enough. His investigation of Davis' activities had given him the facts he needed to confront the doctor again; he called Davis to his office. Placing each piece of evidence he had collected on the table in front of Davis, John sat back, giving his colleague time to peruse it. When Davis looked up, John proceeded to present his case.

"I find it necessary to pursue this matter for several reasons. In a certain sense, I am on the defensive, although I should not have to be. I want you to know that I have no desire to do you any personal injury, but the law of self-preservation is basic here. I consider my future in medicine largely behind me. You are at the beginning. Your possibilities are limitless. I have patiently, and with great personal sacrifice, struggled for twenty years to build up a practice. At a time when my physical powers are on the decline, to sit idly by and permit unwarranted inroads that could break down that practice would be suicidal."

"B-b-but, Dr. Kenney," Davis stammered, trying to find the right words, "I, uh...

"Let me finish," John interrupted, pointing a finger in warning and getting up out of his chair. "I have made it known to all parties, that on the medical staff of John A. Andrew Memorial Hospital, there is only one person entitled to an individual personal practice. There has not been a time during these twenty years that I did not think this arrangement was misunderstood by the assistant doctors here, and by the community.

I have yet to see how any of you doctors could have gotten a different impression."

"Listen, Dr. Kenney," Davis interjected from between taut lips, "I gave you my word at your home that I would accept the facts of a scientific investigation into my conduct. If you have any evidence that I am receiving money from a personal practice, I will be glad to forward you my check for same, and thus avoid any further disturbance both to you and to me. I would rather not argue it any longer, because you are tired of it and so am I, and I want you to be relieved of that worry." Davis threw up his hands as if the matter was settled.

"Doctor," John replied, ignoring Davis's dismissive tone, "from what has been said by you and others, it would appear that your outside activities have been considerable. Now, whether some of these same people would go to some outside doctor rather than consult me is beside the question. Your professional duties are as my assistant, and because you are my assistant, I have placed the weight of my influence behind you. If we cannot work together, I am greatly disappointed, because I admit that until this situation arose, I never trusted any man associated with me in medicine as I trusted you. I had placed strong hopes for the future in you."

John rose from his chair and looked out on the beautiful grounds of the hospital, remembering the small wooden building that used to stand there. With his back to Davis, he continued, his voice restrained and subdued.

"You know I shall have to relinquish my position here someday. Did you not imagine there was a possibility of your taking my place? I needed assistance, and I feel no grief that I have reached the stage where I must relinquish something. I looked forward to a young, active, vigorous assistant who was willing to pay at least a part of the price of working his way up. I didn't expect him to pay the same price that I paid, but at least a small part of it. By such means, you could have helped me, you could have helped the public, and you could have built yourself up. I'm sorry it hasn't worked out that way." John's words were more emphatic than apologetic, and he wanted to make sure that Davis understood his meaning.

Turning to look directly at Davis, he declared, "There is nothing binding on either side with reference to your employment agreement. Whatever is done, I desire it to be final, for I cannot afford the aggravation that this has brought about, and the conditions that are the result."

Davis met John's direct stare without wavering, although his clenched fists acknowledged the tension he was feeling. The two men stood in silence for a moment, and then Davis spoke.

"I can easily see how you could be worried and angered by such a situation, because it has certainly worried me to think that we two doctors could not work together without all of these disturbances. We need to move on; I hope you will think about it and let me know what you decide."

John's serious expression did nothing to reassure Davis, who turned and left the room. John sat down at his desk and put his head in his hands, trying to decide his course of action. He felt emotionally spent, drained by the events of the past few months and the matter at hand.

This difficult decision was made more so by the fact that the largest John Andrew Clinic ever was scheduled to take place in just a few months. They were expecting two hundred and six registrants from twenty-three states. Fully one-half or more of the Negro medical men in the country had attended past clinics, as well as a large number of whites from the North, Midwest, and South. John's saving grace was the knowledge that he was expecting a new physician to arrive in Tuskegee any day, a Dr. Eugene Dibble, who had excellent qualifications that had earned him high rankings in the profession already. This was just what John needed. He had kept the news quiet, not wanting to tip his hat to Dr. Davis. The clinics showcased the talents and aspirations of the Negro medical professional and represented the doctors' commitment to provide service for the less fortunate of the Negro race. If Dibble arrived in time, he could take over at least half of the planning work. Without him, the full responsibility would fall upon John.

As important as the clinic was, John came to the conclusion that, as a matter of ethics, he could not let the matter drop with Davis. He had

to decide whether a matter of such serious and far-reaching consequences, not only to him but to the institution and the work it represented, could be justly passed over without bringing it to the attention of the
school's authorities. He had not been able to answer that question in the
affirmative, and he felt guilty for not doing his duty with respect to the
irregularities he had suspected. With regret, John decided he had no
choice but to bring the matter to the attention of Dr. Moton.

To ensure full documentation for the record, he put his observations in written form and then forwarded his report to Moton. Able at last
to put the affair out of his mind, he turned his attention to the John A.
Andrew Memorial Clinic.

Despite the fact that the hospital was short-staffed, that year's
clinic was one of the most popular ever. Dibble arrived, and had proved
his worth in short order. The young physicians attending benefited greatly from the course of lectures, and the older doctors were gratified and
encouraged to see their expertise passed on to a new generation.

At the end of the meeting, during the clinic evaluation symposium,
several physicians gave their assessment of the efficacy of the courses
and offered suggestions for upcoming meetings. Daniel Hale Williams
offered the first remarks.

"Those of you, who have been in touch with Dr. Kenney and his
untiring work in the development of the John A. Andrew Memorial
Hospital, and in the Training School at Tuskegee, have been in deep
sympathy with his efforts and success in bringing this institution to the
high standard of efficiency and recognition it now enjoys."

"I'll second that," added J. E. Hunter, a physician from New York.

"Literally thousands of men and women have been inspired and
benefited by his surgical skill and executive control," Williams continued. "Students and all fair-minded observers will be impressed with his
most recent departure that projects into the institution a post-graduate
course. It will bring to the doors of the hospital a large number of men
and women, not only from a limited radius, but from throughout the
entire country. Let us have, by all means, a post-graduate training school
at Tuskegee where there is found a 'Class A' hospital and a wealth of

material! This has been done by a man who has picked up his technique, training, and refinement at odd times from the best minds and workmen in the country."

Many Attend Tuskegee Club
(By the Associated Negro Press)

Tuskegee Institute, April 24. –The Words of Dr. John A. Kenney, Medical Director of the Institute, "that no institution is doing more for the health of the Race than Tuskegee" were born out by the stretch of 450 patients and the 60 major operative cases that poured into the John A. Andrew Hospital of Tuskegee for the 13th Annual Clinic of the John Andrew Clinical Society, March 31-April 5, which was brought to a close with a gala Health Parade "driving home" the techniques and dictums of the week. Over 100 physicians, surgeons and nurses from every section attended the clinic. The observance of the National Negro Health Week, which occurred during the same week, heightened to a considerable extent the attention and enthusiasm of this movement.

Many Attend Tuskegee Club
(By the Associated Negro Press)

Tuskegee Institute, April 24.—The words of Dr. John A. Kenny, Medical Director of the Institute, "that no institution is doing more for the health of the Race than Tuskegee" were born out by the streah of 450 patients and the 60 major operatives cases that poured into the John A. Andrew Hospital of Tuskagee for the 13th Annual Clinic of the John A. Andrew Clinical Society, March 31-April 5, which was brought to a close with a gala Health Parade "driving home" the teachings and dictums of the week. Over 100 physicians, surgeons and nurses from every section of the country attended the clinic. The observance of the National Negro Health Week, which occurred during the same week, heightened to a considerable extent the attention and enthusiasm of this movement.

John A. Andrew Clinical Society Meeting

"Let's all stand and give Dr. Kenney a hand," exclaimed Ulysses Grant Daily, one of John's colleagues from Chicago. The entire assembly stood and applauded.

John couldn't help but be humbled and gratified by these words. He had worked long and hard for this moment. He stood and addressed the group.

"Thank you, my friends. It has been of very great encouragement to me to receive the unstinted help of so many members of the profession, both Negro and white; and, as never before, have I been impressed with the possibilities for us right here in the South. I believe we are engaged in a great work. Let us keep level heads, keep our feet on the ground, work hard, think deep, and not depart from our original principles, and I believe success will be ours."

John shook hands with each participant, and waved goodbye as the last car pulled out of the parking lot. Feeling pleased and gratified, he started to get into his car when he heard Mr. Logan calling his name.

"Hello, Warren, how are you doing on this fine day?" John called back.

"I'm fine," Logan said, crossing the parking lot. "And you're going to be even finer when I give you the news."

"What is it?" John asked, already feeling fine now that the clinic was over.

"Davis has tendered his resignation. Just up and left Tuskegee."

John's mouth dropped open in surprise. He was relieved, but somewhat chagrined, that he had not had a chance to have the last word with Davis.

"I was wondering why I didn't see him at any of the sessions, but I was really too busy to worry about it. Well, I will just have to write him and tell him what I wanted to say in person."

"Just thought you'd want to know," Warren said, walking back to his car.

Thoughtfully, John watched Logan drive off, and then went to the business office where he got Davis' forwarding address. That evening, John wrote a letter to Davis, letting him know that he could never have the same confidence in him that he had had when they entered into the initial partnership agreement. John further stated that, as far as he was concerned, the resignation was acceptable to him; and for the good of all, the matter was now closed. He added with sorrow and regret, that the matter had been the biggest disappointment of his professional life, so far. Now relieved, John felt that he could mentally let the matter drop.

With that year's clinic out of the way, John was able to resume his regular work and address the sudden volume of tasks that needed attention. He had managed to keep up with his editorial responsibilities for the *Journal*, but he was behind in his duties as general secretary to the NMA and had not had time to focus on the V.A. hospital matter. Yet, now with the clinic behind him, he couldn't deny how exhausted he was. He needed a rest. He would take some time off, he decided, but first he wanted to touch base with the NMA on the veteran's hospital matter. He gave George Cannon a call.

"John," Cannon said after they exchanged pleasantries, "we've been waiting to hear from you. Several of our members tried to call you last week, but we couldn't get through to you."

"I apologize, George. The clinic was in session, and it was pretty time-consuming. Now I am exhausted and overburdened with my regular duties."

"I'm sorry to hear that..."

"On top of all that, my wife's health has been troublesome. I had to send her to Boston for medical treatment, due to our limited facilities here. She needed a surgical procedure, and I couldn't go with her, due to some critical patients in the hospital."

"How is she doing?" Cannon asked, sounding concerned.

"She's doing well, right now. I am also trying to get reimbursed from the school for some radium that I bought with my own money, and trying to get the school to raise my salary, something I've been requesting for several years. And last, but not least, I must admit that this stalemate with the V.A. was the easiest to put off. It is an honor to be nominated for the position, but, to tell you the truth; I've got my hands full." John ended this litany with a resigned sigh.

"I'm sorry you're dealing with so much, John. Perhaps, what I have to tell you will relieve some of your burden. Since we didn't hear from you and couldn't get in touch with you, we felt we had to find another candidate for the V.A. job. We thought someone with a military background would be attractive, someone the Veteran's Bureau would readily endorse. We have in mind Major Joseph Ward of Indianapolis.

He is a skilled surgeon, and served overseas in the medical corps as
well. We would like to put his name up as our choice. How do you feel
about that?"

John breathed a sigh of relief. "That's fine, George, just fine.
At this point it is enough to know that a competent Negro man will be in
charge. The fact that the government finally recognizes that there are
enough competent Negro physicians to fill the post is good enough for
me. That is what we have been fighting for all along."

"I was sure you would feel this way. We are all united in our goals.
That is the marker for success. You have forged a mighty legacy for us,
John. Now, we need to carry on with what you've established. Let us
know if we can do anything to help you."

"Thank you. I appreciate your offer – and your friendship."

Before hanging up, George also informed John that the *Journal*
funds were dwindling, due to administrative expenses, and he projected
a deficit if the situation was not rectified. If subscription prices were not
raised, the publication was in danger of being cancelled.

John hung up with a heavy sigh. There was always something to
worry about, it seemed, but this was particularly discouraging to hear.
The *Journal* had come such a long way over the years, and had
accomplished so much. John remembered pecking away on the typewriter with his index fingers to get the early correspondence out. Now,
although the annual NMA dues that had started at three dollars a year
had been raised to seven, the association was still unable to meet its own
financial needs, and couldn't be of any help in subsidizing the *Journal*.
It was left to John, who received a monthly allowance of only ten dollars
to cover his expenses as editor, to pay for the stenographer, postage and
mailing expenses, and any other associated services. When he had a
deficit, he covered it out of his own funds. Other editors did the same.
Even the NMA treasurer, who got a token salary of ten dollars per year,
had advanced hundreds of dollars of his own funds to help carry the
financial affairs of the Association from one annual meeting to the next.
This was the commitment Negro physicians were willing to make without hesitation.

For some time, John had been working with a committee to reconstruct the by-laws of the NMA, and to help develop more fiscally sound policies. His hope was that a solution to keep the *Journal* afloat would come out of this group. At the same time, he was struggling to keep his own finances solvent. Freida was good at stretching a dollar, but she knew that, given his position at the hospital and the amount of work he was doing, he was not being fairly compensated. She broached the subject one day as she was balancing their checkbook.

"Have you heard from Moton, dear, regarding your raise or a bonus?"

John knew from the tone of Freida's voice that what she really wanted was verification that he had indeed already spoken to Moton. He hesitated, and then replied in a subdued tone, "No, I haven't. I was sure that he would have responded to my memo by now."

"You need to go see him in person," Freida said in defiance, her anger lighting a fire in her eyes and her patience exhausted. "He knows that you paid for the radium for the hospital yourself. He knows you have a family to support, and that you can't underwrite the expenses of the hospital. I am furious that he is being so casual about this after all that you have done for him! I have a mind to go and talk to him myself." Freida slammed the checkbook closed, and rose to her feet.

"Freida let me handle this." John put a restraining hand on her shoulder. "I know that you want to go and visit your father in Boston, and I know that we need a new piano, so that you can continue the children's lessons. You have been asking me for some time, and I don't mean to ignore your requests. Now that the clinic is over, I will approach Moton again. I promise you, I'll take care of it."

True to his word, John stopped by the Moton's home one evening after supper. Moton was sitting on his front porch smoking a cigar, and looked mildly annoyed at John's approach.

"Good evening, Dr. Moton, lovely evening, isn't it?"

"It's my favorite time of day, Dr. Kenney." He looked at John with a guarded expression. "It's peaceful and quiet, and it offers time for solitude and reflection."

John, aware that he was interrupting Moton's mood, took an apologetic tone. "I am sorry to have to disturb your tranquility. I tried to contact you at your office, but your secretary told me that your schedule was unusually busy. I need to discuss a matter of utmost importance."

"And that is…?" Moton's tone implied that the last thing he wanted to do at that moment was discuss business. He extinguished his cigar and stood up, waiting for John to speak.

"My responsibilities at the school have been extremely heavy – in fact, too heavy. I have put a lot of my own money into hospital projects, and I've received no response from my memo asking for a raise."

"These things take time, Doctor. There is an administrative process that we must go through to consider these types of requests. I'll look into it next week. Now I think I'll retire and do some reading, if you'll excuse me?"

"Sir," John said quickly, making no motion to leave, "hear me out. After the turmoil of the past few weeks with Dr. Davis leaving Tuskegee, and now that the clinic is over, perhaps I can do something for the school at the same time that I am doing something for myself."

"What are you proposing?" Moton looked interested, but cautious.

"I was thinking that I could go to Boston for a short break, and visit Mr. and Mrs. Mason. They are such regular benefactors, and I could solicit another contribution for the school. I could tell them about our excellent clinic, and the additional graduate course. Of course, I will tell them about the advances the hospital has made and what our plans are for the future. That way I will get a reprieve, and if they agree, the school will benefit also."

Moton readily agreed to this suggestion, fully appreciating the Masons' past philanthropy and hoping for more. He and John had found some common ground to agree upon, and they shook hands as John left the porch.

Within a week, John took Freida and the children to Boston. He decided to let them stay there for awhile, so they could go to Oak Bluffs with Aunt Mar and Judge Armstrong. John returned alone to Tuskegee, eager to share the news that Mr. Mason had agreed to

galvanize fund-raising efforts among his colleagues, who had previously supported Tuskegee's cause. He had also advised John that Dr. Miller
in Boston, who had treated Freida, was interested in attending the next
clinic and bringing some of his colleagues to Tuskegee. They were doing
research at Massachusetts General, and they felt the clinic would be an
excellent resource for the program.

Upon arriving back at Tuskegee, John found correspondence from
Moton saying that he had decided to add another surgeon to the hospital
staff. This doctor would be called the "Consulting Surgeon."

"What the hell is Moton up to?" John thought to himself. "And
why?"

Feeling both troubled and annoyed, John called Moton to apprise
him of the Masons' fund raising efforts, and to ask about this latest
decision.

"I got your letter, Dr. Moton. What prompted your decision to hire
another surgeon?" he asked calmly, pausing to hear the rationale.

"Well, you have been so taxed. I thought it proper to give you
some relief. We must find a candidate who will work alongside you and
take some of the burden," he replied. For a moment neither one spoke;
each trying to gauge the others mood.

Trying to keep his voice from rising, John added, "I am sorry that
you undertook this effort without consulting me. If you pursue this,
I want you to be careful in your selection, because this person will have
a big responsibility to the race. He must be of high ethical and moral
standards and be a total professional in all of his undertakings. He must
respect the standards that Dr. Washington espoused and carry on his
work, as we have been doing for years."

"Of course, Dr. Kenney," Moton said. John thought he detected
a hint of sarcasm in his tone. "I hear you. With so many competent doctors in your organization, I am sure there must be another like you."

"Please keep me apprised as to your search." John hung up the
phone without waiting for a response.

He was confused as to how Moton could even consider hiring
another surgeon for the staff when the institution was not able to

reimburse him for the substantial expenses he had paid out of his own pocket. He called Freida to blow off steam.

"You won't believe what is happening now," John yelled into the phone, the veins bulging in his forehead, and his jaw clinched.

"What is it, dear?" she asked her voice full of concern.

"They are hiring another surgeon for the hospital, a consulting surgeon is his title, and I wasn't even apprised of this until today. How am I supposed to take this?" John paced back and forth in front of his desk like a sentry on guard, waving his hands and defending his position.

"John, you are going to remember your purpose for being in Tuskegee and think about all of the good that you have done for so many people," Freida scolded in a tone that made John stand still. "You have done your job already, and you can continue to do it if you choose. You'll be fine – just as you've already been – if you decide that's what you want to do."

He was too tired and disappointed to comprehend what Freida was suggesting. Over the next few days, he focused totally on deciding how he should react to these new developments, and what they meant. One morning, while writing everything down in detail, he was interrupted by a call from Dr. Miller in Boston.

"I have just seen your wife this past week," Miller said, sounding cautious. "I can find nothing wrong in her chest, but it does seem as if she is developing a tuberculous process in the other breast, the right one."

John's heart stopped. "I just talked to her a few days ago," he said in disbelief. "She didn't say a word." His head was swimming with this new news, and he had difficulty processing the information. Dizziness forced him into a chair, and he closed his eyes, his world spinning out of control.

"I have told her that I want to watch it for a few days, partly to decide whether I should do another operation and partly to give her skin a chance to clear up, as it has been irritated so much with the iodine." There was no reply. "John...are you there?"

"

Yes, yes..." John murmured, still trying to focus his thoughts. "What's your plan of treatment?"

"If, at the end of a week or ten days, she does not show any signs of getting better and if the condition of the skin is all right, I really think that it will be best to remove that breast, just as we did the other. She seems perfectly willing to have me do this. I have never known before of tuberculosis developing in both breasts, but it does seem as if that has happened."

"I don't know what to say..." John's voice trailed to a whisper.

"I'm so sorry to have to be the bearer of bad news again. I will have her chest thoroughly gone over while she is up here, and we will make sure that she is all right; although I examined her carefully, and could not hear anything wrong. I assure you that I will do everything in my power to get her straightened out, and I will keep you informed."

John was too shocked to talk. He could only thank Miller and ask him to call at any time, night or day, to keep him up to date.

This crisis was the last straw. John began to seriously consider leaving Tuskegee for a location that would be more conducive to medical treatment for his wife. He felt that much of his work in Tuskegee had been accomplished, especially now that the administration seemed reluctant to embrace his current ideas. And with the situation regarding the V.A. hospital resolved, he could finally spend some precious time with his family.

His previous call to Freida kept running through his mind. She had not once mentioned her predicament, expressing concern only about his. She deserved better than what he could give her in Tuskegee. Knowing her, and given her new attitude regarding self-healing, he thought that she might feel his heavy workload had caused him to neglect her. This Christian Science fascination may have been her self-defense. He desperately wanted to devote more time solely to her, and to his family.

He sat down at his desk and penned a brief letter to Moton. Dated July 15, 1924, it announced that he would resign as the Medical Director of the John A. Andrew Memorial Hospital, perhaps as early as September or October. He stated that he would begin at once to arrange his affairs, and since he still had one month's vacation that he had accrued over the years, he would use some of that time to find a place where he could relocate his family. Moton answered swiftly, accepting his resignation and expressing keen appreciation and respect for the work he had done at Tuskegee. John didn't know if Moton was being sincere or patronizing but at this point it didn't matter.

John was stoic about his decision and comfortable with it, until he got a call from Mrs. Booker T. Washington, who had just found out that he was leaving. "Dr. Kenney," she began in a teary voice, choking to get the words out, "there are times when the heart is too full for utterance."

"I know," John said, his voice beginning to crack and his eyes welling up.

"This is one of those times. I do not need to tell you how I feel about your leaving here and severing your connections with us all – I could not make you understand it if I were to try."

"This is very difficult for me," John admitted for the first time. "I didn't envision things coming to an end like this."

"You were always so loyal to Booker T.'s work, and so faithful to every trust and duty, that I cannot bear to think of your going. I do understand that you regard it as your duty to go away and make another home for your family, but it is a great loss for Tuskegee."

John waited for her to stop sniffling before he answered. "Right now, Freida and the children are first and foremost in my mind. There is nothing more important to me."

"And that's the way it should be, Doctor. I shall always follow you and your family with interest and affection, and if I can serve you at any time, you have only to call on me. I am anxious that Freida shall be well and strong again for the sake of the children, as well as for her own sake and yours. There are times, Doctor, when one cannot put into words one's feelings and thoughts, so I am not going to try."

"Goodbye," John said, saddened to be leaving a friend.

"Goodbye to you, Dr. Kenney," Mrs. Washington murmured, and hung up the phone.

John slowly lowered the receiver, unnerved by the call. Was he making the right decision, or had he been too hasty? The simplicity of a clear answer evaded him. He picked up a picture from the nightstand next to his bed. It showed his family frolicking on the beach at Martha's Vineyard, and it filled his heart with love. A painful jolt of emotion brought him back to reality – he was not in the picture. The realization hit him like a speeding train, and suddenly the answer was crystal clear. He was leaving Tuskegee.

Freida, the children, Judge Armstrong and Aunt Martha
on the beach at Oak Bluffs

Save Some for the Children

W_here on earth will I go_, John wondered. How could he be packing boxes in his office, while the people in Tuskegee were wondering what on earth they would do without their doctor? When the telephone rang, he resented the interruption and waited for his secretary to answer it.

"Dr. Kenney, it's Dr. Miller," she called.

Quickly, John put down the box he was holding and picked up the receiver. "Dr. Miller, I've been waiting to hear from you."

"I was just calling to let you know that we operated on Freida last night and removed her right breast."

"What?" John exclaimed, completely surprised by the alacrity of the decision.

"Well, her skin just opened up, and there was no use putting it off. The tissue showed diffuse inflammation and necrotic tissue from the tuberculosis. I'm sure that we made the right decision, and your wife insisted we get it over with. She is doing fine, and awaiting your arrival."

"I'll come at once," John replied, picking up the train schedule from the desk drawer. "Tell her I'm on my way."

Soon after John arrived in Boston, he moved Freida from the hospital to her father's house. She made it clear that this would be the last medical procedure she would submit to. She had embraced the Christian

Science religion with fervor, and John could barely convince her to take her medication. He grew even more concerned when, from another room, he heard her discussing her condition with her father and the children.

"Mother, are you going to have to be sick again, or are you well now?" Jack asked with childish innocence.

"Your mother is following the doctor's orders, Jack," Judge Armstrong cut in quickly, "and they are making her well." Jack looked hurt at the sharp tone of his grandfather's voice.

"I am not sick, son," Freida said softly, leaning down to take Jack's face in her hands. "I'm fine, and I will be fine, with God's help. God is in charge, and He makes everything okay through prayer to Him."

"Go find your brothers and sister now," the judge said, shooing Jack out of the room. "It's time for some quiet in here."

When Jack left the room, Freida turned to her father. "Daddy, you know that I don't believe in sickness or pain anymore, in the traditional sense. Those feelings are signals to alert us to elevate our thoughts to another plane, to a higher consciousness, as it were. The cure lies in connecting with this universal intelligence, this divine power, the immortal mind. When you connect with spirit, you learn that the façade of illness only exists in the mortal mind. Therein lies the truth – and the healing."

"Freida!" the judge said, throwing up his hands in frustration, "your husband is a doctor. He has trained for years on illnesses and diseases. He knew enough to send you here to Dr. Miller for treatment, and now you will get well. You will undermine his spirit if you keep this up, and you will confuse the children. They all depend upon you for guidance."

"Father, this *is* valuable guidance. With my spiritual beliefs, John's medical expertise, and our positive attitudes combined, we are indomitable." Ready to belabor her point, Freida looked at her father for his response.

"There's no use discussing it anymore," he said with an air of defeat, and left the room.

John chuckled to himself. It wasn't just anyone who could silence the judge. Still, though he had to admit there was some wisdom in Freida's words, he also believed that this illness, with its attendant surgeries, had been more traumatic for her than she had let on. She needed time to recover, so he would take some time too, and return to Tuskegee only when she was strong enough to travel. There was no need to rush back anymore.

With time on his hands, John pondered the future and where they would go next. He and Freida discussed the possibilities.

"We could stay with my cousin in Cleveland, John. You could see if you like the city. I think the only thing that might bother you is the cold of the winter season. You're not used to that."

"No, I'm not at all ready for that much winter. You know my cousin in West Virginia still wants me to practice with him; that's always a possibility."

"And don't forget that, while we are here in Boston, you can talk to Dr. Miller about opportunities right here in my home town," Freida reminded John with a sly look. She loved her hometown; its liberal attitude and sophistication defined her. She knew that John did not have the same affinity for her city, in part because it already had a fair number of Negro physicians, and her husband wanted to be of service in an area where the need was greatest.

Finally, John decided to make a tour of a few states to solicit money for the National Medical Association, while also looking for a place where the Kenneys could make their new home. He knew that Freida, who was recuperating nicely under Aunt Mar's care, would need to remain in Boston for a few more weeks before returning to Alabama, and the tour seemed a good use of his time until then. Even though he realized that his life's work was not to be completed at Tuskegee, he still wanted to leave a legacy for the race. And he needed to make sure that his family would be financially secure, wherever they chose to live.

At that time, Detroit and some of the other northern centers John visited on his tour, had become destinations for thousands of migrants from the South. On a train traveling northward, he saw one old man with five husky sons, each bearing a burlap sack filled with all of their earthly possessions.

The conductor asked the old man, "Where are you going, Uncle?"

"We is going up to Destroit, Michigan," was the answer.

From their rugged and determined looks, John thought that they gave the impression that they might make considerable headway in "destroying" a big part of Michigan. But John could not find the kind of opportunity he was looking for in Detroit.

From there, he visited New York City, and stayed with his friend E. P. Roberts. Astute in both medicine and real estate, E.P. was generous in sharing his knowledge and experience. He was partial to the Northeast, and thought that the region offered John excellent professional possibilities.

"It doesn't make sense for you to go to Michigan," he advised, thankful that John had not found an opportunity there. "Your family and most of your friends are on the East Coast. If you are between Boston and Washington, you will be closer to the best hospitals for your wife, as well as being better off logistically for your work with the NMA. New Jersey offers some interesting opportunities. A lot of our people have relocated to Newark from the South, and several wards are deficient in medical services, especially the third ward. They call it "The Hill" and they're hundreds of migrants living there with little or no medical care. Just the kind of challenge you like." E.P. smiled and gave John a knowing look.

"I hadn't really thought about New Jersey," John said with a mischievous grin, "but the idea is intriguing. Perhaps I should go and visit."

"Some of our colleagues are doing good work there. Let's drive over and you can get the lay of the land," E.P. suggested.

The visit to New Jersey offered much of what John was looking for. E.P. acted as tour guide, and shared his excitement about Newark's proximity to New York. "I'll be close enough to help you get situated," he volunteered.

The city of Newark teemed with a burgeoning Negro population, and had a myriad of health care needs. The third ward was just as E.P. had described it; dirty, dingy and squalid, a perfect storm for sickness, disease and their predictable outcomes. John felt a twinge of sadness in his chest as he surveyed his people in obvious squalor; but he knew that this was where he needed to be.

"I thought Boston had a lot of traffic," John said, shaking his head in disbelief as they headed downtown, "but this city is far busier."

E.P. stopped for a red light at Market and Broad Streets. "They say that this is the busiest intersection in the world. This city has seen an influx of Negroes from the South, and some areas of it are open to the change. Not all, though, but it won't be hard to start a practice here. The migrant class is growing by leaps and bounds, and that's the group that needs help."

They drove past rich neighborhoods and middle class ones, dense areas of high-rise buildings and other more spacious areas with quaint New England-style homes. John was intrigued. The city seemed a melting pot of cultures, and had a certain character he couldn't quite put his finger on.

When they passed the Coleman Hotel, E.P. pointed out, "That's where Billie Holiday stays when she comes to town."

John found he especially liked New Jersey because it was near the Atlantic Ocean, and he knew how much Freida loved to be near the water. Newark, he decided, was a definite possibility.

John returned to Boston, after having been well received by medical professionals in St. Louis, Chicago, Detroit, Cleveland, Boston, New York, Philadelphia, Baltimore, and Washington, D.C. He had raised five hundred dollars for the NMA in memberships and subscriptions to the *Journal*, and he had seen several cities where he believed his practice would make a difference. Now he and Freida would have to decide where they wanted to live.

John was leaning toward Newark, and weighing the pros and cons. It was closer to Boston, so Freida could visit her father more often, something she had mentioned now that he was advancing in age. But John wasn't impressed with the school system there; he thought it was inadequate in some areas. If they decided on Newark, they would have to decide what to do about that.

"They call Newark 'Brick City,'" John boasted to Freida, "because there are so many tall buildings. It's quite metropolitan, and transportation facilities are readily available for reaching other parts of the country, which makes traveling more appealing. Perhaps we could vacation a little more often." John looked at Freida expectantly, hoping his description sounded appealing to her.

"I'm not opposed to Newark, John. And knowing you and the way you work, if we still get away once a year we will be lucky. If you feel that it would be wise to open your practice there, then that's where we should be." Freida paused for a moment, a mischievous grin on her face. "Besides, I'm used to life in the city – you're the one who'll miss the sound of the rooster crowing in the morning." They both laughed at her joke, which had more truth in it than John wanted to admit.

Freida, once recovered from her surgery, was eager to help with the challenge of relocating to a new place. John decided that he would ask her to look for properties in Newark, while he returned to Tuskegee to close his practice. He knew that she loved a challenge, and had a sixth sense when it came to making important decisions.

"Try to find something near some of the hospitals so that I can pursue getting privileges, if possible," John advised. "We should have about fifteen thousand dollars from the sale of our Tuskegee home, and we should stick within that budget so I won't have to make a loan. You know I don't like to owe money to anyone! Now, I will go back to Tuskegee and begin to look for a buyer."

"That's a great idea!" Freida crowed. "I shall go forth and find the Kenney family a home!"

John sent Freida with two blank checks to Newark to investigate a lead E.P. had gotten from a real estate agent, who happened to be white. She spent several days traveling with the agent, who offered little encouragement about being able to show her what she wanted to buy.

"We are looking for a property near a hospital," she told the agent, "because my husband is a doctor. He must be able to admit patients when that becomes a necessity. He will need to get privileges."

The white agent looked at her questioningly. "There are certain areas that I can show you," he said. "Most of the hospitals are private, and it may be difficult to get, ah, colored patients in."

"We'll worry about that when the time comes," Freida replied with confidence, not acknowledging the insinuation. "Just show me everything you have."

They toured various locations in and around Newark, looking for just the right place. When she didn't like what she had been shown, Freida began investigating on her own, and found a beautiful property at 134 West Kinney Street in Newark. She contacted another agent in the area, and arranged to meet with him to discuss the home.

"I found this lovely house with the right number of bedrooms," she told the agent, "and not too far from one of the main hospitals. Here is the flyer with the address on it. I need to know how much it is selling for."

"That's a good buy," the agent said, examining the paper. "It's only eighteen thousand. The price has been reduced recently, due to the need to settle an estate. You should make an offer as soon as possible to hold it if you like it. I'll take you to see it."

When they arrived at the house, Freida requested the blueprints, after examining the house thoroughly. She asked to see the utility bills, and inspected the property tax documents. Satisfied that this was indeed a good buy, she prayed over the matter. She knew that the house was seven thousand dollars over her budget, but she also knew this was the one she wanted.

"I'll take it!" Freida told the startled agent. She opened her purse and, with the spirit of an entrepreneur, sealed the deal with a check.

"Here's your receipt, Mrs. Kenney," the agent said. "Too bad you can't purchase that lot next to the house also."

"I didn't know it was for sale," she replied, her eyes surveying the beautiful lawn adjacent to "her house." She imagined what it would be like to have another buyer building something so close to theirs. Something came over her, an intuitive feeling of some kind, and she knew she needed to acquire this other property too.

"How much is that lot?" she asked summoning her courage, wanting, yet not wanting, to hear the answer.

"It's going for seven thousand dollars, ma'am." The agent closed his briefcase, waiting for his client to indicate that she was ready to leave.

Freida stood still and pondered for a few minutes. Her temples pounded, and her heart raced. She remembered her husband's often quoted motto from Hampton: "Find a way or make one." It was now or never.

"Let's make a deal, sir. I will give you another check right now for five thousand dollars. That's two cash sales in one day. We will not even have to go to the bank for financing; this deal will be finished right now." Freida held her breath.

"I'm not sure my boss will accept that," said the surprised agent. "We're not supposed to reduce the prices."

"All right then, I will not take either one," Freida said definitively. She closed her purse, and began to walk toward the door.

"Wait a minute, hold on, Mrs. Kenney; let me make a call. I'll be right back."

The agent disappeared around the corner, while Freida pulled out her book and pretended to be absorbed in it. The agent came back running, flushed, sweating, and red in the face.

"My boss said if we get the other check right now, we can make that deal."

Freida reached into her purse for another blank check. She enjoyed her moment of triumph! She signed the check, accepted the deed, and then began to feel sick. How was she going to tell John that he would need to make a loan?

She made her way back to her rooming house, alternately feeling powerful, then faint, as the weight of her action hit her. She took a hot bath, followed by a brandy. The stress of her decisions sent her to bed with a terrible headache. The headache accompanied her on the train ride back to Tuskegee, and increased in degree the closer the train got to home.

When John met Freida at the station, he was eager to hear the outcome of her trip. Instead, she fiddled with her purse, and made rambling small talk while he drove back to the house. "The trip was good, D, but it is always good to come home. How are the children?"

"They're all fine. Now tell me about the property," he urged. "I want to know everything."

"You're going to love the house. It is a beautiful structure and will accommodate our family quite nicely. The children will have lots of room to play and exercise, and we can even get another pet. And best of all this will be a great inheritance for our children!"

"Well, where is it, and how much did it cost?" John demanded, trying to hold his impatience in check.

"It's in Newark and not an undesirable distance from a hospital. You will be able to take care of patients and perhaps have some sort of privileges there," Freida said, trying to change the subject.

"Excellent! Now, how much did you have to pay for it?" The tone of John's question let Freida know "the game was lost."

"Well, it was a little over our budget, D," she said softly, her stomach tied up in knots. She was afraid to tell him what she had done, but she knew it had to come out.

"Go on. How much over?" John's teeth were clenched at this point, and Freida noticed his hands gripping the steering wheel tightly.

"I paid eighteen thousand dollars for it, but I had to, it just seemed right!" Freida's words ran together, and it took John a moment to decipher what she had just said. She looked straight ahead, not wanting to see his expression.

He said slowly, "You paid eighteen thousand dollars for it, and it just seemed right? Is that what you said?" Perspiration began to form on John's forehead.

"Yes," she whispered, not daring to look at him.

John took a long swallow, and managed a weak smile. He didn't say a word.

"The lot next door was also for sale," she added in another hurried flurry of words, as if, now that she'd begun, she wanted to get everything off her conscience as quickly as possible. "I negotiated the price down by two thousand! I wrote a check for another five thousand dollars.

For a beautiful house and an entire lot next door, I feel that we did quite well, and you are going to love it. That lot may prove to be important someday, John." Freida still couldn't look at her husband, who drove on in silence.

Afterward, John was amazed he hadn't collapsed when Freida told him what she had done but, how near to it he was, she never knew. Yet, even though the news was quite a blow, he approved of her decision once he had time to think about it. If he had to make a loan he would pay it back as quickly as possible.

When Freida recovered from her headache, John commended her on her good judgment, acumen, and foresight. Somehow, he felt that fate had played a hand in her decision. He also knew that this property would be the legacy he would leave for his children.

As soon as he could, John closed his practice and sold the small farm he had bought in 1902. The money helped to buy the properties in Newark. The family shipped their furniture to Newark, and bid Tuskegee farewell. Everyone was excited about the move "up North", but John's excitement was tinged with sadness as he left his Tuskegee for good.

*   *   *

On the first day of September, 1924, John arrived in Newark with his family and entered the practice of medicine. Post-war money was plentiful, and he found no difficulty meeting his notes on the properties. His practice grew by leaps and bounds. The house that Freida had purchased was a two and a-half story frame house with four bedrooms, and a large basement. It was perfect for their active family, and the lot next door was perfect for the boys, who played football and found their recreation right beside their home.

Industrial activities were humming, and people were making good incomes. Colored workers and the doctors who treated them seemed, if not completely welcome, at least well tolerated. For about two years, John was extended the courtesy of practicing at the Community Hospital in Montclair and, for a somewhat longer period, at the Newark

Post Graduate Hospital; as well as, on one occasion, the Presbyterian Hospital in Newark. All of these were white facilities. At times, he had as many as five or six operative patients in the Newark Post Graduate Hospital at one time.

After a time, however, changes began to take place. There was evidence that the work of the colored physician was not as welcome as it once had been. John grew discouraged by the limited hospital facilities that were still open to colored doctors, and by the inability to give his patients the care they needed. An idea began to form in his mind, but he would need help.

Kenney Memorial Hospital

John gazed out his dining room window upon the spacious lot adjoining his house. He pulled out his diary and wrote, "I shall build a hospital on that lot." It was a bright, sunny New Year's morning in 1926. As was his practice, once he decided on something, whether in the inspiration of the moment or after long consideration, he was eager to get busy and do it. But by New Year's morning of 1927, still nothing had happened to move his hospital closer to reality. Again, he took out his diary and wrote, "I shall build a hospital in Newark, because I can't help it." This time he made a silent promise to himself to move forward.

John toyed with various names for his hospital, knowing that he wanted the Kenney name to live on as a legacy for Negro medicine. He wrote to his friend Dan Williams, and asked his advice on naming the facility the John A. Kenney Private Hospital. Williams wrote back with sage advice, for he had gone through this process himself. "The John A. Kenney Private Hospital," he said in his letter, "is in every way permissible, if the name will not react against its success with envious doctors. This is the greatest outstanding factor that you will have to keep in mind. I have had so much experience with that, and I am a little dubious. I enjoy your kind remembrance, and I think you are the most trustworthy and diverse man in the profession."

John decided to give more thought to naming the hospital, for he certainly did not want to resurrect the "green-eyed monster" again. He asked his father-in-law for advice.

"I want to do something for my people and for my family," John told him in a phone call. "I want to leave a legacy for both, but I don't want to alienate people. Dan felt that calling it the John A. Kenney Private Hospital might stir controversy. What do you think?"

"I understand his apprehension," the judge answered. "You have to remember that your community did not support this idea. You want to leave a legacy for your family, but you want to do it in a circumspect manner, so that your motives will not be questioned. If you memorialize it, the name will be evident. Why don't you dedicate it to your parents, perhaps?"

John realized that this conciliatory advice had solved his problem. He would dedicate the hospital to his mother and father.

His next move was to individually visit four selected Negro physicians, to find out whether they were willing to listen to his plans, with a view to cooperating with him. He needed the support of physicians who were respected by the people. He had been told that a Dr. Wolfe, who had a small but profitable practice out of his home, would be just the man to help. John went to his office to solicit his cooperation.

After they exchanged greetings, John got straight to the point of his visit. "I am interested in getting the cooperation of the Negro physicians in the North Jersey area to finance and build a hospital for our own people."

"That's an interesting idea, Dr. Kenney. How did you come to it?"

John thought that the answer should be obvious, but he explained in a polite tone.

"Since I arrived in Newark, I have had very limited privileges for my operative patients at the Newark Post-Graduate Hospital on North 12th Street and at the Community Hospital in Montclair. I also operated once at the Presbyterian Hospital, using courtesy privileges. These institutions are making it clear, through their inaccessibility and a general attitude, that they really do not welcome our business. I am sure that you have had the same experience."

"Well, I have been here longer than you have, and I am well known, but I can relate to what you are saying," Wolf said, with a hint of arrogance that John silently recognized and tried to ignore.

"Our people are in dire need of a facility," John continued, with emphasis on the *our*, "that will serve their health care needs in the same manner that the white physicians take care of their own population in their hospitals."

"I can see where that would be a good thing, but can we accomplish this in reality?" Wolf said with the same smugness. "It's such a lofty idea."

"We are quite qualified to do this," John said, more adamant than before. "We just need the vision and the foresight to accomplish it. We need to form a coalition to make it happen, and not be confounded by the 'doubting Thomases.' For the health and longevity of our people, I can't see any other solution."

"I like your idea, Dr. Kenney."

John tried not to show his surprise.

"I will support it," Wolf said, "and do what I can to make it happen. I have connections. This would also mean that our doctors and nurses would have a place to get proper training and credentials, so I see your point."

"Absolutely!" John agreed, happy that the man was finally getting the message.

"This is one area where we get held back in not having hospital privileges," Wolf added, "and doctors shouldn't have to worry about such things. We have enough on our plate as it is."

"Exactly," John said, "that was my thinking also. To present my plan, I am going to call a meeting next week of as many of us as I can notify. I hope you can fit it in on your schedule, Dr. Wolf."

"Call me with the date and time. Here are the names and numbers of three of our colleagues: Dr. Palmer, Dr. Hilton, and Dr. Burke. They will help you notify others." He handed John a piece of paper with the information.

"Thank you, sir. I look forward to seeing you next week."

John left the office, chastising himself for initially misreading Dr. Wolf. Soon after, he visited the offices of the physicians Wolf had recommended and, to a man, they supported the idea. John announced a meeting to be held at a recreation hall the following week, and expected approximately twenty of his colleagues to attend.

On the day of the meeting, John received a few calls expressing regrets regarding attendance. Several people had medical emergencies or family obligations. That evening, as he sat in the hall waiting for arrivals, he realized that his audience was going to be smaller than he had anticipated. In fact, only ten doctors showed up. Undaunted, John explained his rationale for a Negro hospital. He presented a detailed organizational and financial prospectus, and then asked for comments.

"You know, I've been thinking about this thing," Wolf said. "A hospital for Negroes is tantamount to segregation. We don't want to take steps backward. It took us a long time to get off the plantation, and a long time to get where we are in Newark."

"That's right," echoed Dr. Palmer. "We just need to work harder at getting privileges at the existing institutions. They are already established, and wouldn't cost us anything. We just have to show that we are as good as they are."

John couldn't believe his ears. The very physicians who had promised him their support were the very ones now disavowing the idea.

"Sometimes it's not good to rock the boat," another said with a sheepish grin. "We just need to keep sailing on as we are, and sooner or later we will find land."

"Gentlemen," John countered as he mentally prepared his defense, "my statistics show that there is a very high Negro morbidity and mortality rate in Newark in the Third Ward. There is a necessity for concentration of our efforts to improve the health conditions in our city. These figures are given without animus, bias, or feeling. This is simply a straightforward and honest presentation of existing conditions affecting the health of the Negro citizens of this community. The need is so apparent for a hospital by and for ourselves in this city that, to me, it is quite strange that there should be any controversy about it at all."

"We have heard your argument, Dr. Kenney. Let's take a vote on the matter and call it a night." Wolf stood to count the hands.

A vote was taken, and there were three in the affirmative, five in opposition, and two abstentions. John could see that his work was going to be more difficult than he had anticipated. He was dumbfounded at the apparent change of heart among his colleagues, and also very disappointed.

Unwilling to give up so quickly, John decided to send out a mailing to the entire North Jersey Medical Society. He posed several questions. "Should we not have a fifty-bed hospital to supply the needs of the people of New Jersey? Do not the physicians of North Jersey occupy a sufficiently strong financial and business position to supply this demand? Would you participate financially in such a venture and, if this seemed too stunning, would you give moral support and patronage to a smaller venture?" When he received only sporadic answers to his mailing, he decided to address the entire organization at one of its monthly meetings.

134 WEST KINNEY STREET
Newark, N. J.

November 29th. 1926

To the Physicians of North Jersey Medical Society:

1. Allowing due credit for all pre-existing efforts, should we not have a 50 bed hospital to supply the needs of North Jersey?

2. Do not physicians of the North Jersey Medical Society occupy a sufficiently strong financial and business position to supply this demand?

3. Don't you think this could be done for about $100,000?

4. Are you willing to participate financially in such a venture?

5. If this seems too stunning, would you give moral support and patronage to a smaller venture?

Dr. JOHN A. KENNEY

North Jersey Hospital Flyer

John was given a place on the program towards the end of what turned out to be a long and laborious agenda. He waited patiently for his turn, listening to financial reports, committee reports, and organizational issues. By the time he was allowed to speak to the assemblage, he could see that everyone was weary. As he looked around the room, he realized that many of those assembled were poised to go. Some men had their hats in their hands, and others were standing, seemingly ready to run for the door. Only a few appeared to be waiting to hear what the new doctor in town had to say. Already apprehensive, John did his best to summon up some enthusiasm.

"Good evening, colleagues. I promise that I won't keep you long." A few men sat back down in their seats. "I have a proposition for you. I would like to offer the idea of a joint venture with this organization to build and operate a hospital for the Negro people of Newark, New Jersey. The revenue from such a venture could underwrite the cost of the hospital, as well as establish a revenue source for this organization." Several attendees got up and headed for the door. John felt the need to make his point quickly.

"Who has heard of the North Carolina Mutual Insurance Company in Durham?" Several hands went up. Others, who had appeared disinterested, now began to perk up. "My good friend Charles C. Spaulding is the president of that company owned by Negroes. His business is based on racial self-help, uplift, and philanthropy, and has become such a national success that the president can go away to Europe on a trip without any business worries. In fact, under his direction and guidance, the business makes even more money when he is away."

"What's that got to do with us?" shouted one listener, ready to be adjourned.

"That is the perfect example of what we could do if we work together to establish and run our own hospital. The Society can help the hospital and vice versa." John said, feeling sure that his explanation would impress the group.

"We've already heard this plea before, doctor. Why don't you take an aspirin and call us in the morning?" The audience laughed at the play on words, and another group took this as their cue to leave. An elderly doctor sitting in the front row raised his hand to speak, and John acknowledged him.

"Yes, sir, what is your question?"

"Dr. Kenney, many of us have other projects that are more immediate, and rather than putting our money into something that could be years away, we want to stick with what we have."

"Gentlemen and ladies," John said, mounting a last-ditch effort, "let me offer you a final proposal, one that I hope will allay your fears of a long-term commitment. I will ask of each of you a personal loan of one thousand dollars."

The auditorium became quiet at this request. All eyes were on John. Some people looked incredulous at his remark, others sat upright in their chairs, and a few more got up and left the room.

"I am asking for a loan from each of you that will fund the idea of a hospital. I will pay back each loan, with interest, in one or two years when the hospital is profitable. For many of you who don't know me, I have brought copies of my curriculum vitae, which documents my work with the John A. Andrew Hospital at Tuskegee Institute in Alabama. I have here in my hand a pamphlet called 'Service of a Negro Hospital,' which is about the creation of that hospital, and how it became successful. I have copies for all of you. I worked with our esteemed leader, Booker T. Washington, to solicit money and build the only hospital for Negroes in the area, and one of the first in the country. This can be accomplished, but it will take the cooperation and investment of all of us."

The president of the society asked that John pass out his credentials, and said that they would take up the proposition at the next regular meeting. The meeting was quickly adjourned, but a few people stayed afterwards to get more detail on the hospital project, giving John hope that some interest still remained.

A week or two later, as John was getting into his car to make a morning house call, the mailman hailed him. "Dr Kenney! I have a special delivery for you." He held out a letter, and had John sign for it.

The return address was that of the president of the North Jersey Medical Society. John opened the envelope. The message was curt:

"This is to inform you that your proposal was brought before the body again and the motion did not carry."

John's astonishment at the decision turned to rage, and he tore the letter into tiny pieces, scattering confetti to the wind. *Idiots*, he thought, walking aimlessly around and around his car; *why do people have to be so unintelligent?* Would he ever see such behavior change in his lifetime? He was doubtful. At last, he got into his car, slammed the door, and drove off.

Although John's latest proposition had also failed, he knew he wasn't going to give up the hospital idea. In fact, during all of his various efforts, he had had his architect at work on hospital plans and specifications. He had experienced failure before, and it had opened the door to opportunity. He would not be defeated. *I will build the hospital myself, if necessary*, he decided. In a few weeks he had in his hands a drawing for a small hospital on the lot next to his house and, in his mind, an even bigger dream.

"Find a way, or make one." That motto had always appealed to him. Up until now, he had not found a way, so it was necessary to make one. The motto of his class at Hampton was, "Use what you have." Well, he had the desire, he had the initiative, and he had the courage. But did he have the ability? Time would tell. He decided to take what he had, and make a way.

Once his drawings and projections were complete, John went to his banker, a Mr. Seinfeld, and presented his plan.

"Here is my architect's rendering, and here is my business plan. All I need now is a loan to make it all happen," John explained. He eager-ly laid a stack of documents on Seinfeld's desk.

"Dr. Kenney, I'd like to help you, but I can't carry that form of risk. The industry won't allow it, but I will refer you to my friend at a mortgage company. He may be able to help you."

"Thank you, sir," John said as he folded his papers and tried to cover his astonishment at the speed of the refusal.

His next appointment was with a Mr. Klondike at the Newark Mortgage and Guaranty Company. He again explained his mission, this time holding his folded papers under his arm.

"I'm sorry, Dr. Kenney," Klondike said quickly, "we just cannot make that kind of loan to a … someone who doesn't have a credit history with us."

By this time John was becoming discouraged, but he was all the more determined. He went into conference with his most supportive strategist – himself. *There must be a way*, he thought, *but what?* Then it occurred to him that building another hospital in Newark, even a small one, would mean more sales for hospital supply houses. Maybe he could interest some of these businesses in helping him finance his project.

He presented a letter of proposition to several of them. All responded favorably, and it was through this avenue that the light appeared. One of the dealers, a Mr. Sedgewick at the Montclair Medical Supply House, came to see him.

"I received a copy of your solicitation from one of my colleagues," Sedgewick told John. "I'd like to help you as much as possible. What is your most urgent need?"

"Right now I am trying to raise funds to break ground. Any help you can give me at this point is critical," John said, his hopes rising.

"Let me make some calls. I'll see what I can do." Sedgewick asked if John would step out in the hall while he made a private call. After several minutes, he called John back into the room.

"Dr. Kenney," Sedgewick said looking disappointed, "I am not going to be able to personally finance your project." Sedgewick handed John's papers back to him.

John's heart sank. *Not again*, he thought. *Where will I go from here?*

"But I have a good friend who is president of a bank, and he is most interested. If we could arrange a meeting in the next few days, he'd like to talk with you," Sedgewick said, a mischievous grin on his face, as he watched John's reaction.

John's startled look turned into a grin of his own. At last, a breakthrough that was sorely needed. The two men set a date for the following day.

John arrived at the bank building ten minutes early. He wasn't going to be a victim of that old adage about colored people and time. He walked into the Broad and Market Bank in Newark with his financial prospectus and his architectural drawings under his arm. He had on his best suit and a new shirt Freida had made for him. He knew that this presentation would be the most important of his life, and he was totally prepared – and very nervous.

He was ushered into a spacious office overlooking the city. Mr. Bloom, the president, was at his desk signing vouchers. Sedgewick sat in a chair in front of the president's desk.

"Have a seat, Dr. Kenney," Bloom said, "and tell me about your project."

John sat in the chair across from Sedgewick, who smiled confidently in John's direction. With a deep breath, John opened his folder and explained his plans. Every few minutes the president interrupted, saying, "All right, I understand this facet; move on to the next part." John finished with his proposal in record time. He wondered if he had been thorough enough.

The interview lasted less than ten minutes. After a brief and, for John, tense silence, Bloom announced, "This is a good thing. It is much needed, and I believe you are the man to put it through."

John was astounded. Not only had this white man had the vision to appreciate the significance of what he was trying to do, but he understood it in a matter of minutes, and granted John the loan with no collateral except his and Freida's endorsement of the note. The irony did not escape John. He was getting assistance from the very people whose beliefs had created the problem and necessitated the loan. And while satisfied with the financial obligations, he was also curious why a white man could embrace his vision, when his own people were blind to their obvious need. He could get no support from the colored people who would benefit most from this endeavor, but he got essential support from those who would scarcely benefit at all.

Thoughts like these had troubled John before, and now, even though he arrived home elated, his elation was tempered with regret – regret that his own people were so conditioned to fear risk that the present repugnant circumstances were more acceptable that trying to do something new.

"What's wrong, dear?" Freida asked as she took his coat and hat, and ushered him to his chair by the fire.

"I am just trying to make sense out of the Negro consciousness of today. Why can't our people see the value of this hospital? If only they would realize that we can continue to be victims of circumstances, or we can take responsibility and do whatever it takes to help ourselves. Why do we keep sabotaging ourselves?"

"There are times when you can't worry about anything except your purpose in life, John. If you wait for other people to catch up with you, you may not accomplish your goals. You just set the example, and those who are ready to emulate you will be motivated and will act. Those who don't see the vision still have their own lessons to learn. Don't let them hold you back."

"You're right, honey. You're always right." John smiled and pulled his wife into his lap.

"I guess that means you didn't get the loan?" she asked as she snuggled in her husband's arms.

"Oh no... I mean, yes, I got the loan. It was much easier than I thought," John replied sheepishly. "We'll soon have the money to start building the hospital. But I'm puzzled that these white men can appreciate what I am trying to do when our own people offer no encouragement, much less any help."

"Oh, John! Why didn't you tell me the good news first?" Freida playfully punched John's arm. "I was feeling bad for you! Well, anyway, let's celebrate your accomplishment right now! I'll get the champagne. We must always proclaim our victories! In today's world they are hard to come by."

Freida, who always had a way of putting things in perspective, had once again helped John focus on what his goal truly was. If other people supported him, fine. If not, that was fine too. Maybe this was the lesson he was meant to learn.

Freida's advice proved accurate, when John found himself in immediate need of fifteen thousand dollars for construction. As evidence of the bank president's good faith, Bloom made the loan in about three minutes, taking John's note in exchange for the money. Of all of the debts John ever incurred, he considered this one the most binding, for it was granted on his reputation, and he considered it an "honor" loan.

In February 1927, the steam shovel rolled up and began digging the foundation for the hospital that would be dedicated to his parents, John and Caroline Kenney. The children raced around, playing out their excitement to the noise of the digging. John put his arm around his wife and hugged her. "Congratulations, my dear, on your fine business acumen. Buying that lot was a work of genius, and we will now have a hospital!"

Freida glowed. Seven months later they had a building and they began to ready it for the public. On September 18, 1927, the doors of the Kenney Memorial Hospital opened to serve the Negro population of Newark, New Jersey.

Kenney Memorial Hospital on left, at center is the Kenney Family Home.

You and your friends are cordially invited to attend
the formal opening of the

Kenney Memorial Hospital

at 132-134 W. Kinney St. Newark, N. J. from 2 p. m.
to 10 p. m., Friday October 14, 1927

There will be short programs of music and addresses
by distinguished visitors; among them City Officials, Ministers, Physicians, Business Men and others at 4 p. m.
and at 8 p. m.
This hospital is thoroly fire-proof thruout and is modernly
equipped for services in general medicine, surgery, obstetrics,
gynecology and a complete line of physio-therapy including
X-ray and radium.

John A. Kenney

Invitation to Hospital Opening

Help for My People and the Great White Hope

John and Freida stood on the sidewalk holding hands, and looking up at their hospital. Excited and awed that their dream had become a reality, they reveled in the accomplishment.

"Look at it, John, it's so beautiful. The architect drew it exactly to our specifications, even down to matching the stone face with a brick front."

"We did it, we did it," was all John could say as he looked up. The sting of disappointment at the lack of his colleagues' cooperation was all but obliterated by the sight of the new building in front of him. He felt validated.

"I'm so happy with the staff we hired," Frieda crowed. "We have a secretary, a stenographer, a matron in charge of the seven graduate nurses, and two maids. We've even budgeted enough for three orderlies. And, of course, the most dedicated medical director that ever existed is in charge. I'm so proud of you!"

"I'm proud of *us*, Freida. I couldn't have done it without you." John hugged his wife, and gave her an enthusiastic kiss. "Now we just need some more of the local doctors to join the staff. I'm sure when they visit, they'll be impressed and the word will get out." John walked up the steps, and held the door for Freida.

"They'll come," she assured him, walking into the lobby of the hospital.

She spoke as if the deed was already done, and John admired her unshakable faith and confidence – no matter what obstacles they confronted. It was as if she knew something that he didn't, that by simply uttering the words, the desired result was achieved. John frowned at his own speculation. His scientific training precluded these metaphysical thoughts. Suddenly uncomfortable, he changed the subject.

"I'm expecting Dr. Walter Darden from Montclair to visit today. I met him at the Wright's Sanitarium the other day. He is very well established, and has a lot of contacts."

"What time is he coming?" Freida began to reposition some of the lobby chairs.

"He said he'd be here at ten o'clock," John answered, straightening his medical school diploma, which was hanging a bit askew on the wall.

Promptly at ten o'clock, John saw Darden parking his car in front of the hospital, and went out to greet him.

"Welcome to the Kenney Memorial Hospital, Dr. Darden. We are happy that you took time out of your busy schedule to visit us."

"Thank you, Dr. Kenney," Darden said, smiling and offering a handshake. "Please call me Walter. I passed by the construction a few weeks ago, and I was very interested in your design. Now that I see the finished product, I am even more impressed. It's a most needed facility for this ward and for Newark. Congratulations!"

"Thank you, Walter" John said warmly. He liked Darden immediately. The man's sincerity seemed genuine and authentic, unlike some of the physicians John had already dealt with. And he knew that if Darden approved, then other Negro doctors would also be more likely to visit. "Please, let me give you the tour," he offered.

"I'm looking forward to it," Darden said, following John into the building. "I've heard a lot of good things about what you are doing. I hope to be of assistance in any way I can."

"Let me show you the architectural plans," John said, spreading the papers on a table. "Here is the original blueprint. As you can see, the building is modern and fire proofed in its construction. We followed the recommendations of the Newark fire department, and we have fire-proof materials and specific evacuation plans for such contingencies. We have fire hydrants down the block on each corner, and our distance from the fire house is only a mile."

"Excellent," Darden said, clearly in awe as they climbed the stairs to the first floor.

"This area is divided into small wards. There are semi-private and full private rooms for thirty patients. The first floor contains an outpatient clinic, a detention ward, the kitchen, and the boiler room," John continued, hoping that his visitor was appreciating the hospital's capabilities.

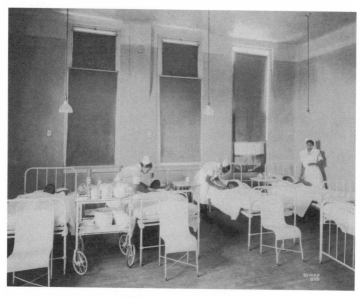

Kenney Hospital Ward

"You've maximized the space that you have," Darden commented, admiring the interior design. He walked into each area, nodding in approval as John continued to explain.

"And let me show you this." Beaming, John opened two wide double doors leading to another part of the hospital. "This portion of the building is connected to an office building by a corridor built over a nine-foot automobile driveway, thus making the two buildings the hospital. That was my idea."

"That was a stroke of genius. To have the administrative offices separate from the hospital itself is much more efficient for business purposes, and you also maintain the privacy and quiet needed for patient care."

"Let's go up to the second floor," John suggested, leading Darden to the staircase. They ascended two flights, arriving at a brightly lit corridor with a small patient waiting area. "Here we have the male ward, the nursery, and the female ward. The building is complete with gas and electric sterilizers, automatic oil heating, and electric refrigeration. We also have an outlay of physiotherapy equipment that will be a special draw for the hospital." As John pointed out each feature, he took pride in how far he had come since the unspeakable and unsanitary conditions of his first primitive hospital.

"You've thought of everything, John. I'm again impressed. I also think it was fortuitous of you to realize that this hospital is what the community needs. We had become so immune to the obvious inequities, that we were just doing the best we could. I think your fresh perspective on the situation was required to remind us that we needed our own hospital, and this building is proof of that. "

"I appreciate your comments, Walter, and I hope you'll consider joining our staff. We cover multiple specialties: general medicine, surgery, gynecology, obstetrics, physiotherapy, and x-ray, including radium."

"I didn't know what to expect before I came, but having seen this excellent facility with my own eyes, I can tell you that I will be happy to join your staff. I think when the word gets around, you'll have more staff than you can handle."

John laughed appreciatively. "I hope you're right. Now, let me show you the operating room." The two men headed upstairs. John was about to reveal his pièce de resistance.

Pausing before a small suite with wooden double doors, John inhaled the smell of fresh paint that still hung in the air. "Look there," he said with obvious pride, pointing to a shiny brass plaque mounted above the doors. It was engraved in elegant copperplate calligraphy and read: "The Daniel Hale Williams Operating Room."

"That man is a hero to all of us," Darden murmured in approval. "His skill and courage in surgery catapulted Negro medicine to the forefront, whereby it was impossible for the white medical establishment to ignore us."

"You're absolutely right. Dan is my longtime friend, and advised me on numerous occasions about how to implement my hospital plan. As you are aware, I'm sure, the Provident Hospital in Chicago is the institution he founded, and his experience was invaluable to me."

"What an appropriate tribute for the most esteemed surgeon of our day," mused Darden with obvious appreciation. For the first time in a long while, John's trepidation gave way to optimism. He began to believe that the Negro physicians might actually come together to make his venture a success.

From 1927 to 1929, the hospital had a liberal supply of help. The building housed more than thirty patients a day, and the outlook was encouraging. Freida kept the administrative records and reported to John, excited and proud of her findings.

"John, do you know that we are averaging nearly thirty patients a day... already?" she asked with unbridled glee. "If we keep on going like this, we may have to find some space for additional beds. Whoever would have thought we would be this busy?" Her enthusiasm caused John to smile.

"Well, it certainly has helped that the community has supported us so well. I think they are relieved that they now have options other than the white hospitals that don't want us there anyway. This is a safe haven," John replied, "where our people know they will receive the care they're entitled to, and deserve."

Soon, John began to receive queries from all over the country as to how he had accomplished his feat. His secretary, Mildred Dixon, could hardly keep up with the inquiries. Arriving at his office one fall morning, he found her with the telephone in one hand and two telegrams in the other. Flustered by continuous requests for information and appointments, she rolled her eyes in dismay when she saw John. She finished her call and looked up at him, exasperation on her face.

"Dr. Kenney, you have no idea what you have started. I have not had a moment to do my regular work for some time, what with the phone ringing, correspondence to be answered, and the telegrams coming. I've made two appointments for doctors who run their own hospitals, and want to visit from D.C.; Dr. James Dowling of Dowling's Private Hospital, and Dr. Simeon Carson of Carson's Private Hospital."

"That's wonderful. When are they coming?" John asked, clearly pleased with the response.

"They're coming in three weeks, and that's not all. You have been invited to speak to the medical students at Meharry Medical College. And Howard University Medical School wants you as a commencement speaker. And…"

"Where is my calendar? I want to make sure that we have every-thing scheduled properly so that we don't have any conflicts. This kind of interest in our little hospital is important, and if we succeed in this venture, we will influence others to do the same in other parts of the country. This reaction is more than I'd hoped for."

"Here is your calendar…and as I was saying, requests for infor-mation have come in from the Nebraska Negro Medical Association and the Missouri Pan-Medical Society. I didn't even know there were Negroes in some of those states." Mildred looked both puzzled and amazed at the revelation.

John laughed at his young secretary's naiveté. "You'd be surprised where we can be found. Is there anything else I need to know before I make rounds?" he asked as he headed for the door.

"There is a reporter coming from some newspaper to interview you. I'm sorry, I have the note somewhere," she said as she fumbled through the stacks of papers on her desk, looking confused.

"All right, Mildred, I've got to run now, but I'll check back with you later." Before she could get another word out, John was gone and the telephone had started ringing again.

A reporter from the *Newark Daily News* showed up at the hospital as John was finishing his rounds. With pad and pencil in hand, he walked around taking copious notes, but stopped in his tracks when he saw John. "Are you Dr. Kenney?" he asked, with neither greeting nor friendliness.

"Yes, I'm Dr. Kenney. How can I help you?" There was something about the man that made John uncomfortable and cautious. He waited for the reporter to speak again.

"I have been asked to do a story on your hospital. How did you do it? There's a lot of talk about it. I hear you didn't get any help from your own people, and you had to build this hospital by yourself. How did that make you feel? How are you going to react to that?"

The barrage of questions annoyed John. "What you need to know," he said, "is that I am fortunate to be a Negro in America where color is not a barrier to business, where the economy is good, and where an individual is free to provide for the needs of his community without political interference. That's how I feel, and you can print that." John had stated his feelings with pride, sensing that for this "story" the reporter was hoping he would denounce his own people.

"But how do you feel about your colleagues who would not help you? I want to know about that. Can you colored men work together, or is it every man for himself?"

"Look around, sir," John said becoming angry at the interrogation. "I have some of the finest Negro physicians in New Jersey on staff here now, and I am happy to have them. We are working together for the common good. Now, if you'll excuse me, I have a surgery." He was not, under any circumstances, going to buy into this man's need to print something divisive.

Not getting the story he was after, the reporter left, looking somewhat disgusted. For the moment, the little hospital was serving a dire need in the community, and people were working hard to make it a success. There was no bad news to print, and everyone knew that good news does not sell newspapers.

At the same time that the hospital was flourishing, the NMA was gaining more stature from a growing membership and from the *Journal,* for which wide recognition was evidence that it was an excellent scientific publication. The effort to keep continued pressure on the American Medical Association to admit Negro doctors was also still in force. The editorial Board of the *Journal* continued to meet for several days prior to each NMA convention to discuss ways to keep the struggle at the forefront of their readers' consciousness. John had suggested that they all write about the problem of exclusion, speak about it, and bring the discussion up at every public opportunity, escalating the tension and forcing the AMA to respond. Calling one such editorial board meeting to order, he opened the discussion on the Negro and organized medicine.

"Gentlemen," he said, "organized medicine, as generally understood, is represented by the American Medical Association. The subject we are discussing implies that we are not a part of this organization, in spite of the fact that we do very much wish to be so."

"We have been fighting the battle for so long that the discouraging results have made many of us want to abandon the fight," Dr. Dailey summed up, "but we must never do that!"

"It's a pity," added Dr. O'Donnell in a resigned tone, "but it's true that few of our men seem to know or care about either the necessities or problems of our national organization. Must it ever be so, that 'a prophet is not without honor, save in his own country'?"

"Well said, O'Donnell," John added, "and that is why we must keep the discussion current and demand action. Those of us who understand the significance and the ramifications of the problem, and who have railed against it for years must find ways to resolve it."

"Let's write yet another proposition to the AMA," offered Dr. Dumas, "but a more forceful one this time, asking them to allow membership and participation by the Negro physician in their organization, with all the rights assigned thereafter. The NMA has many exceptional men in its membership who would benefit the AMA as well."

"Exceptional men are the milestones of advance," the erudite Dr. Roman added with the patience and understanding that always matched his seniority. "That's who we are. And, personally, I believe in a purposeful evolution of things. I confidently look forward to the time when men will evolve a creed that will control conduct, as well as establish a government that will do justice."

"Then with clean conscience, let's appear before the poll of public opinion and the AMA with a front that is above reproach, and knock louder and longer until our voice is heard," John said with conviction. "We will demand to be heard."

"Let the NMA be the inspiration of confidence and esteem, the medium of influence and service, and the assurance of integrity and accomplishment," O'Donnell agreed. "Now let's get that proposition written. Timing is everything. The country is doing better than ever, and we have opportunities as never before."

In fact, the booming economy had spurred a renewed interest in politics at the local, state, and national levels, especially in northern communities. Negroes reentered mainstream electoral politics, making it known that their votes could affect the outcome of elections. For once, their political might could be a factor, and the white political establishment began to pay attention. The country was gearing up for an exciting presidential election, the outcome of which could affect the right of all citizens to do what John had done – become an entrepreneur without undue rules, regulations, and government scrutiny. Optimism was in the air.

In 1927, President Coolidge made a historic announcement: "I do not choose to run for President!" The presidency had been thrust upon him when President Harding died unexpectedly; and while the country had seen impressive economic prosperity, the taint of scandals, complaints of cronyism, and accusations of excessive stock market speculation during Harding's tenure had followed Coolidge into his administration and dimmed his enthusiasm for another term. With the presidential election up for grabs, the country was abuzz with anticipation over who might be the new president. Many hopefuls entered the fray, with Alfred E. Smith eventually garnering the Democratic Party nomination, and Herbert Hoover being nominated to represent the Republicans. Many Negroes believed that Smith was too embedded with the labor unions to care about their issues, and they saw Hoover as more of a humanitarian. They felt that he would be more sympathetic to the plight of the Negro, and that they would fare better under his administration.

In this climate, Mr. Bloom, the bank president, called to congratulate John on what he had accomplished. His voice boomed from the phone with an enthusiasm that startled John. "Dr. Kenney, I had faith in your plan to build a hospital for the Negro people, and I hear that the community is supporting you. Well done!"

"I appreciate your confidence, sir. And I couldn't have done it without your support." Elated at this unexpected commendation from such an influential white businessman, John smiled to himself. Whoever would have thought this man would champion his cause?

"Listen," Bloom said, "I have nominated you to participate in a radio show in New York City on the twenty-eighth of October. As one of a new breed of self-made businessmen and a Negro, you can comment on the political climate with reference to the upcoming election. I hope you'll be willing to do this."

More stunned than ever, John managed to stammer, "Of course I will do it. Just apprise me of the particulars."

The invitation, John felt sure, had been prompted by the success of the hospital. To be asked to speak for a majority of the Negro people through a national radio audience was an immense honor. John knew that he had to express the Negro's point of view, and at the same time, resolve to be a part of the political landscape in no uncertain terms – and this meant demonstrating that votes equal power.

"Just give the country an idea of what your position is and what issues are important to ...ah... people like yourself," Bloom said.

"I would be pleased to share my views on this subject, Mr. Bloom. You can count on me. I'll start work on a position paper immediately."

On the twenty-eighth of the month, radios throughout Negro and white communities were tuned in to the New York broadcast. Newspapers and radio ads had announced the event, and John had heard from many of his NMA colleagues that they would be listening. Bloom called to say that powerful people in the government would be listening to see if a Negro understood politics in general, much less what the outcome of the upcoming election could mean for colored people.

John could almost hear the radio knobs clicking on across the country as the time for the show drew near. He was determined to stuff his nervousness in his back pocket and "step up to the plate." He took a sip of water and stood up. The studio audience applauded as he approached the rostrum and spoke into the microphone. He began his remarks by letting everyone know in no uncertain terms which candidate his race supported, and why.

"Ladies and gentlemen," he began, "as an ex-president of the National Medical Association, the secretary for over eight years, and the editor of the NMA *Journal*, I count it a privilege to express what I believe to be the crystallized sentiment regarding the political situation as it exists among these 6,000 professional men and women, representing the greatest aggregation of intelligence, wealth, and scientific achievement within the race. Speaking for the medical profession as American citizens, I believe that I express their sentiment when I say that we shall support the Republican Party because it is the party of progress."

The assembled group broke into enthusiastic applause, and he continued, more confident with this approval.

"During the past seven and a half years, under a Republican administration, the country has enjoyed such prosperity as has never been known. We believe that the Republican Party should continue in power with Hoover at its head, because he has declared himself in favor of the Coolidge policies under which this prosperity was obtained, and in which we all have shared – big business and little business, capitalists and wage earners. This period will go down in history as the era of Coolidge prosperity, and under the administration of Herbert Hoover, we have every reason to believe this prosperity will continue. During this era, American dollars have not only kept the wheels of industry revolving at home at a speed never dreamed of before, but they have overflowed our national boundaries to the tune of billions, and furnished sinews for creating and reviving business in almost every land under the sun. Under this Republican administration, New York, the metropolis of our great nation, has become the center of the money market of the world during this period.

"With the existing evidence of satisfaction, contentment, and happiness on the part of the people as a whole, why should we make a change? Some corrections are necessary, but would it not be better to have them made by the party now in power rather than enter upon a period of experimentation? As American citizens, we favor the election of Herbert Hoover because of his sanity, his poise and breadth of vision, and his grasp of public affairs, domestic and foreign, which stamp him as the most outstanding figure on the American continent today. We favor him because he more nearly typifies the real American spirit than any other man in the public eye. We favor him because of his veneration for, and love of, home. To him, the American home is the most sacred of its great institutions. We are for him because he favors equality of opportunity and individual freedom. We favor him because of his 'unmistakable repudiation of all intolerance – religious, social, and political.' His address in Madison Square Garden on the night of October twenty-second, stamps him a statesman incomparable; and his address, replete with sane philosophy, unbiased and unemotional, will be given rank as a classic among American state papers."

At this point, John had to pause while the audience stood and applauded his remarks. He was surprised at the enthusiastic reaction, and found himself smiling.

He continued: "We are for Hoover because he is opposed to the bureaucratizing of the business of our country. In other words, he is opposed to the government ownership and dictatorship of American industries. We favor him with Federal control of all of our natural resources. We are for him because we believe, with him, that government ownership of business is inferior to individual ownership. As a boy in the grocery business, I often heard the expression, 'Competition is the life of trade.' It was true then. It is true now. Government ownership and dictatorship prevent competition and repress individual initiative and adventure. It is individual endeavor and accomplishment that has made America, our nation, great.

"On the night before last in the Hotel Astor in New York City, there assembled one of the most remarkable groups on record. It was called the ten-billion-dollar banquet, because two thousand men and women had assembled to do honor to nine men whose combined interests represented that figure. They were all individual pioneers in their chosen fields – Edison in science and invention, Schwab in steel manufacture, Eastman in photography, as well as Rosendale, the merchant prince, Ford, the automobile magnate, Firestone, the rubber king, and Wright, the mercantile. These were pioneers who Mr. Schwab said in his address 'had not only blazed the trail, but had kept on it, clearing and widening it for progress.' Could any such picture be duplicated in a communistic or socialist government?

"Only one Lindbergh flew the *Spirit of St. Louis* directly across the Atlantic to Paris and, in doing so, centered the eyes of the world on the American nation. There is no place for socialism or communism in the American economic structure. Mr. Hoover has witnessed personal evidence of their failure in his observations and activities abroad. For instance, in Russia, where the introduction of communism produced a decline in the peasantry farm production, he saw the extent to which the nation was bordering on starvation. No better example of the failure of our government in business need be sought than the collapse of our railroads under Federal administration, as was necessitated by the Great War. On the other hand, note their return to prosperity since they were given back to their rightful owners.

"We are supporting Hoover because he favors limited immigration, with a consequent full dinner pail for the American laborer and a protective tariff that will enable American industries and agriculture to survive.

"Thus far, I have spoken only as a citizen of the United States. Would that I might stop here, but the exigencies of the American environment over which we have no control make it seem best that I tell you why, as a race of twelve million people comprising about one-eighth of the population of the United States and with a voting strength now estimated at five million, we believe that the Republican Party with Herbert Hoover at its head should be returned to power."

At this remark, the audience stood again and gave him a resounding ovation. Feeling "righteous" by this time, John was ready to make a case for the Negro people.

"Speaking for the medical profession, I believe that I express their sentiment when I say that we believe that our united support should be given to the Republican Party because it is the party of Abraham Lincoln, Ulysses S. Grant, and Charles Sumner – the party of Theodore Roosevelt, Frederick Douglass, and Booker T. Washington. We believe that we should support the Republican Party because Abraham Lincoln was the Republican president who wrote the Emancipation Proclamation, and it was his party that wrote into the Constitution the thirteenth, fourteenth, and fifteenth amendments. We believe that the interests of twelve million Negroes will receive greater consideration in the Republican Party under the wise leadership of Herbert Hoover than they will at the hands of any other party that now exists. To say that we are for Hoover because he abolished segregation in the Department of Commerce in Washington may appear, in a manner, selfish. However, self-preservation yet remains a fundamental law of the universe. There are some of our number who believe that our vote should be divided between the two great parties. It is our firm belief that in state and local elections we should cast our ballots according to local conditions; but as yet, with the South remaining solidly Democratic, we should in a national election present a united front for the Republican administration.

"Of those who are calling for support of the Democratic Party in the coming election, we ask: Can you forget so soon? Have you already forgotten the Wilson administration? Do you not recall that one of the first and most impressive acts of the administration was departmental segregation in Washington? Have you forgotten that the Democratic Party is responsible for the ignominious Jim Crow car laws that make travel for respectable colored persons almost intolerable in the South? Have we so soon forgotten that it was a Democratic Party in the South that made the greatest inroads against the fourteenth and fifteenth amendments by introducing the 'Grandfather Clause', and disenfranchising almost the entire Negro electorate in the South? Have we forgotten the expression so often heard during the Wilson administration that the South is in the saddle? How can we so quickly forget such mortal blows, and help to return to power the party responsible for them?

"That there is house cleaning necessary within the Republican Party we do not deny. Not only is there the smell of oil, but there is also the taint of racial discrimination. We admit that the Grand Ole Party stood by and saw the war amendments remain a part of our sacred organic law. However, we ask the question, Can house cleaning be better done at home or in the enemy's camp?

"Now, ladies and gentlemen, with malice toward none, with charity for all, with a desire to reflect the light as God gives me to see the light, with no selfish ambitions, financial or political, but with an intense desire to be of the greatest usefulness to my country and particularly to the race I represent, I have presented what I believe to be the overwhelming sentiment of the Negro medical profession affecting the present political situation in this country. On Tuesday, November sixth, 1928, we shall, with comparatively few exceptions, march to the polls and cast our ballots to elect Herbert Hoover, the man of destiny, destined to be the president and leader of all of the people of this great country. Thank you."

John's speech was well received in all quarters, and much ado was made about the fact that a Negro doctor understood politics as well as medicine. The awe with which he was being regarded reminded him of the punch line Dr. Washington used to tell about the mulatto making a speech: "Well, if one-half a Negro can speak like that, what can a whole Negro do?" He guessed that now people knew.

The development of radio communication had made it possible for information to reach the masses instantaneously. The public could hear daily that the 1928 economy was booming, inflation was low, opportunities for employment were good, and people's incomes were increasing in these good times. The general optimism among citizens was at an all time high, and the pace of technology was aggressive. At the polls, Herbert Hoover was elected president, and he declared, "We in America are nearer to financial triumph over poverty than ever before in the history of our land." America was truly "The Beautiful."

John, too, enjoyed a share of the national euphoria. As he gained more confidence in his own financial management, he felt quite comfortable continuing to invest his savings in the stock market.

Lessons learned from Mr. Inge had always impacted his decisions in a favorable way. He perused his portfolio, and decided the time was right for some additional investments. Returning to the hospital from the bank on an especially profitable day and smiling broadly, he went to his office.

"Mildred!" John called out, startling his secretary, who was typing a letter, "call my broker at Halsey, Stuart and Company. Tell him I want to know the current value of shares at the Potomac-Edison Company and Central Power and Light. Get that information for me and bring it to me on the floor. I want to do this before the market closes today."

"I still don't trust the stock market, Dr. Kenney. My grandmother always told me that your money is safer under the bed than it is in the stock market, or even in the bank!"

"That kind of thinking is based on fear, and on not really under-standing what the stock market is," John lectured. "Stocks and bonds, or in general terms securities, are nothing more than IOUs - a certain amount of money I am loaning to an entity to conduct a legitimate business and for which they agree to pay me, under certain stipulated conditions, an agreed upon sum called interest."

"What's secure about that?" she asked. "They have your money and all you get is interest on it?"

"No, Mildred. Interest is paid on bonds or stocks at certain fixed intervals, and at the end of a stated time my money will be returned to me."

"Uh-uh, sounds too risky to me, too much of a gamble," Mildred said, shaking her head in disagreement.

"What is life but a gamble, Mildred, from the beginning to the very end? Who knows if the expected child is going to be born alive or, once it is, what's in store for it?

"I guess no one really knows," she admitted as she shrugged her shoulders.

"We are all gamblers. Who is a bigger gambler than the farmer? Even though he spends thousands of dollars to put that seed into the ground, he does not know what the outcome will be. He is gambling with nature. Labor conditions, drought, floods, animals, and pests are all possibilities. It is a gamble. You can see gambling going on in some form every day, everywhere."

"Maybe I'll try to learn more about the stock market. If you think it's a good way to invest money, then maybe I'll do it, but don't tell grandma!" Mildred pressed her fingers to her lips in confirmation of their secret. "My lips are sealed," she mumbled.

Laughing at Mildred's humor, John added, "It is not quite as simple as I have tried to explain it. So for absolute safety, since you have never been in it, I advise that you watch your step warily, or better still, stay out of Wall Street until you learn everything you need to know about it."

John went to bed that night confident and happy, never knowing that his fortune was about to "turn on a dime."

A Crisis of Economic Proportions

October arrived with its cool days, cold nights, and colorful fall leaves. John had just finished a surgery when Freida came running, her frantic, worried expression stopping him in his tracks. He knew at once that something was terribly wrong. *Please don't let it be one of the children* was his only thought.

"John!" Freida said, taking a moment to catch her breath, "you just had a call from your broker. The stock market has crashed, and he is warning all of his clients. He doesn't know what it means for you personally right now, but he'll get back to you later."

John's face turned ashen. He dropped into a nearby chair, feeling lightheaded, and for a moment he wondered if he were dreaming. Had she really said what he thought he'd heard? He started to ask, when Mildred suddenly appeared around the corner, running toward him. "Dr. Kenney, Dr. Kenney, something terrible has happened. I heard it on the radio. Wall Street has crashed!"

"I know," John said, still absorbing the shock. "Let's go listen and find out what's really happening."

They headed to John's office, where the announcer on the radio confirmed John's worst fears. The crash would create a banking crisis, which would create a cash flow crisis and threaten the country's survival.

Unable to reach his broker in New York or get through to bank president Bloom, John could do nothing but wait.

The headline in the newspaper the next day stated the worst: "Prices of Stocks Crash in Heavy Liquidation; Total Drop of Billions." On October 23, 1929, the economic bubble had burst. With the stock market crash, "America the Beautiful" had plunged into a disastrous financial quagmire. The article cited excessive and inflated stock prices, and blamed the Federal Reserve for a recent rise in interest rates.

As frightening as the news was, John and Freida knew that the worst was yet to come. Together, they tried to prepare for the outcome. "We will have to reduce the wages of our staff immediately, Freida. And we'll have to lay off at least two of the orderlies and a few of the less senior nurses. We just can't afford them right now."

"I know, John, but I cannot stomach it; these people are just trying to make a living like us. We will all have to pitch in and do whatever it takes. We'll reduce our fees and take whatever people can pay us, and I hope it will be enough to keep us in business."

The economic picture got worse, not better. Fortunes and lives were lost, and the ideology of liquidation became the mindset for survival. With the country traumatized, the panic grew, as did the murder and suicide rates. Many of those who had lost fortunes took their own lives, and others took the lives of those they deemed responsible for their predicament. Factories began to shut down, banks closed, savings were lost, and millions of people found themselves without jobs.

To make matters worse, the government raised interest rates and taxes. Real estate values plummeted, and relief organizations stepped in to help the growing numbers of needy and destitute. Soup wagons became commonplace, feeding the many hungry citizens who could no longer afford even milk. The plea, "brother can you spare a dime?" became the supplication of the day.

The Kenney Memorial Hospital teetered on the brink of failure. Freida's administrative report for John was worse than depressing, and she delayed giving him the news as long as she could. He finally demanded the information.

"The cash payments have dropped from eleven thousand dollars in 1929 to six thousand dollars today. If it doesn't pick up, we will have to let more staff go. We are already as bare bones as we can be, John. I don't know what else we can do."

"We'll do whatever it takes, Freida - this I do know," John stated, with no show of emotion. Yet he wondered how he was going to back up his statement. He tried to put the problem out of his mind, but when he had to let one of his favorite nurses go, he had to face the truth. He called Nurse Cobb to his office, despondent and dreading the conversation.

"The hospital is not making enough money to support payroll," he said, acutely aware of her suspicions. "I am extremely sorry, but I have to lay you off, even though your work has been exceptional. The head nurse has been here for a year longer than you, and I cannot afford to keep you both."

"Dr. Kenney, you always said that the duty of every individual is to support himself and those dependent on him. How am I going to do this with no job?" she asked, putting him on the spot.

Realizing that this was not going to go as smoothly as the last employee layoff, John offered, "I hope you will contemplate private-duty nursing, Miss Cobb. I will suggest your services for any patients I feel need home care, and I will ask some of the other staff to do the same."

"I don't see how they are going to be able to pay me when they can hardly pay you, but I thank you for the thought," she replied with moist eyes. "Well, good-bye then, Dr. Kenney. I hope we all survive."

"So do I, Miss Cobb, and thank you for everything." John watched her walk away, all expectation and hope vanishing with her as she turned the corner.

Before John could adjust to this latest calamity, a former patient who had been doing part-time maintenance work for the hospital came to see him. "Your wife told me my check was going to be a few days late, Dr. Kenney. That's no good. I have to pay my rent."

"I'm sorry, Joe. Everyone's check will be late. Several patients couldn't pay for their surgeries, and I have some partial payments coming due in a few days. I have no other recourse."

"Well, I do," Joe said. He handed John a letter. "A white doctor 'cross town asked me to work for him. Even though it may be fifty cents less, I figure I will always get it on time. You ain't gonna make it here anyway. I quit!" John placed the unopened letter in the expanding file of "former employees" and went home to his family. The outlook couldn't have been grimmer.

The hospital continued to struggle. Freida helped however she could, and even though her health was much better, she had her hands full with housework and the children. John worried that the increased strain would bring about a relapse, especially since she was relying more and more on her "book" for strength and had nearly discontinued the pills and vitamins she was supposed to take on a regular basis. The two of them were working in John's office one winter morning when Freida started sneezing.

"Honey, you're going to catch a cold if you don't fortify yourself with the medicines the doctors have ordered for you," John admonished, taking advantage of the opportunity.

In typical fashion, Freida said, "I'm fine, John. It's just a little drafty in here."

"But you've been doing so well and working so hard," John persisted. "I just don't want to see you get sick again. Why don't you follow Dr. Miller's recommendations and take your medicine like you're supposed to?"

"Do you know how much money I am saving us by not buying that medicine? I am using the savings to buy groceries for us and some for the hospital," she said proudly. "Besides, I have *declared* that I am going to be well, and I truly believe it."

"Not taking your drugs is tantamount to risking a relapse of your condition. This is not optional. Your medicine is the insurance you need to protect yourself from further illness."

"'A scientific mental method is more sanitary than the use of drugs, and such a mental method produces permanent health,'" Freida quoted. "That comes directly from my book, and it proves what I have said before. This is divine science, or medicine, as it were. I am using my mind to entertain thoughts of wellness, of healing, and you can see for yourself that it is working. How do you explain my progress so far? Especially since I am not taking any medicine?"

"I think Lady Luck is with you right now, but I wouldn't advise you to keep rolling the dice," John said, frowning.

"I have found that the answers are within, John. It's really that simple! There are basic truths that we are born with that guide our lives. We have only to access them to get whatever it is we want. We must learn to get still, be quiet, and focus our minds on what we want to create in our lives. And it's not luck; it's God and His universal intelligence flowing through us and revealing what we already know."

"What's flowing through your mind is conjecture, assumptions, and a notion of treatment based on some naturalist's psychic philosophy. There is nothing scientific that it can be traced to," John countered, trying not to sound defensive.

"Please let me try things my way, John. I have listened to you and followed your advice through myriads of medical treatments and procedures. And I don't doubt that they saved my life at the time. But now I want to embrace a way of thinking that seems so right for me, and it seems to be helping me."

"What is helping you is all those things that we did in the past to get you through to today. If you stop your medical treatment for too long a period, you will probably have a relapse of some kind." John shook his head in frustration.

Freida walked over and put her arms around her husband. "Listen, "D", I want to try to create thoughts of healing and wellness in my own mind, and I believe my body will follow. I can't do that if I take drugs, because it would be an admission that I am ill, which would defeat what I am trying to create."

John didn't react to her tenderness; hoping instead to show her how opposed he was to her beliefs. Given the history of her illnesses, however, he didn't believe his argument would do much to change her mind.

"I know it's not your way, John, but we have to allow each other our differences. All people should allow each other that. We all perceive life differently – each one of us has our own interpretation. It may look the same: we are born, we live, and then we die. But what happens to each one of us in our own lifetimes causes us to shape different opinions and become unique individuals in our own right."

"Freida, that's just not right." John frowned at his wife's obstinacy.

"There is no right way or wrong way – there are just different ways to do something." Freida took her arms from around John and shrugged her shoulders. "It's about allowing – and allowing without judgment. I do respect your medical training, darling, that's obvious; but I need you to also respect my spiritual intuition."

John knew when to hold his cards and when to fold them – and this was a time to throw in his hand. With no idea how to get through to his wife and make her listen, he chose to let the subject drop, feeling secure that the next time she had to take to her bed with a fever she would realize he was right. He knew, without a doubt, that the time was coming.

*   *   *

As the Great Depression deepened, both Kenneys remained determined to keep the hospital open, because now more than ever people of their race needed a place where they could have their health care needs met. With so many out of work, without homes, and often without sufficient food, diseases – both physical and mental – were rampant.

To save money, they reduced the wages of the hospital laundress from $14 per week with board, to $12 in late 1929. Not long after that, Mildred, his secretary caught up to John as he was leaving the ward.

"Dr. Kenney!" she began, almost out of breath, "Mrs. Brown in the laundry just quit. She said there was too much to do, and she wasn't getting paid enough. She just walked out. There are piles of laundry everywhere. What are we going to do?"

John took a deep breath to retain his composure. "Calm down, Mildred. When you encounter problems in life, it does no good to overreact. There will always be difficulties. It is how you face them that determine whether you are going to work your way out of them or not. Let's go downstairs to the laundry and see what we need to do." It was becoming an effort to practice what he preached.

When they reached the laundry room, they found dirty linens threatening to take over the landscape. Soapy water had spilled on the floor as if it had been deliberately splashed about, and the hot water had been left running.

"Lord, help me now," John muttered under his breath, and rushed over to turn off the tap.

"Okay, we have a problem," he said to the young woman standing wide-eyed beside him, "but there's always a solution. We just have to be creative and use what we have."

"How, Doctor?"

John gritted his teeth and didn't say a word; afraid of what might come out.

Taking off his white coat, John got busy, finally saying, "Put those dirty linens in the cart so I can mop up this mess. Then bring me more soap and some bleach from the storeroom." Grabbing a mop from the corner, he attacked the floor. Soon Mildred returned with the supplies, and helped John load the washtub with blood-stained sheets that had been used during surgery. John added bleach and left the sheets soaking in cold water.

"It's time for me to be upstairs in the clinic, Mildred. Go on back to your duties, and I will tend to this later."

Grabbing his coat, John headed upstairs to find three patients waiting. He took several deep breaths as he entered the clinic, attempting to regain his usual calm demeanor. "How is everyone today? I will be right with you."

The patients greeted him warmly, but as he entered his office, he thought he heard one of the ladies giggling. Composing himself, John took a sip of water, put on his white coat, and opened his office door to send for the first patient. A set of watery footprints led up to his office door. Looking down, he saw his sopping wet shoes and became aware of the damp cold wrapping itself around his feet. With a sheepish smile, he called the first patient.

After examining a number of patients, John took off his coat and slipped out the back door of his office to head back downstairs to the laundry room. The sheets were ready for a hot soaking, so he moved them to another tub and refilled the first with a new load. Back upstairs in his office, he put on his coat and opened the door to greet another patient, wiping away the telltale beads of sweat on his forehead. This scene would be repeated over and over in the coming days.

*   *   *

The closest John came to embarrassing himself in front of visiting dignitaries occurred the day that the board of trustees and the state inspectors visited the hospital. John had slipped downstairs to handle the laundry chores, and had donned the galoshes and overalls he now wore to protect his clothes while putting sheets through the wringer. A surgical cap and face mask hung loosely around his neck. At that moment, the sound of Freida leading the visitors into the laundry room to show off the facility froze John in his tracks. Keeping his back toward the group, he pulled the mask up over his face and continued to work.

"This is the laundry, Superintendent Collins," Freida announced. "We had to let the laundress go due to our budgetary restrictions, but we hope to get another one as soon as the economy improves. For the time being, everyone tries to help."

John put the wet sheet down and turned around. His eyes wide with warning, he grabbed the mop standing by the wringer in the hope of mopping his way out of the situation. Freida recognized him and gave a little start.

"Oh my!" she exclaimed, trying to cover her discovery, "it does feel a bit crowded, doesn't it? Here, why don't we go over here so I can show you gentlemen how well the mangle works? It saves the cost of an extra employee to do the ironing."

Freida moved past John to the machine with the guests following. John, head down and mopping frantically, scrubbed his way to the door, leaned the mop against the wall, and scooted into the hallway. From the laundry room, he heard someone say, "Excellent facility, Mrs. Kenney; now let's go see Dr. Kenney and let him know we are satisfied."

John raced up the back steps, struggling to pull off the rubber galoshes over his shoes. Both went flying, and he left them and his coveralls stashed in the stairwell. Grabbing his white coat from the back of his office door, he shrugged it on and straightened his tie. He had barely taken a seat at his desk when he heard a knock at the door.

Attempting to appear composed; he suppressed a gulp and called, "Come in."

The door opened and Freida entered with the guests. She smiled knowingly. "We have taken the tour, John, and everything is satisfactory. We even inspected the laundry room."

"I don't see how you keep such an efficient organization, Dr. Kenney, with the staff shortage and all," the superintendent commented with a satisfied smile.

"We use what we have, sir. I learned that long ago. Everyone pitches in, and there is no job too great or too small for our hospital family."

"Just be glad that you are the doctor and are spared from all of those mundane chores," the superintendent quipped. "Position does afford us some privileges, thank goodness. Can you imagine men of our standing having to do menial work? We'd be the laughing stock."

The guests all laughed at the thought of such a hilarious sight, but John was remembering what Booker T. Washington had always said: "No race can prosper till it learns there is as much dignity in tilling a field as in writing a poem."

In keeping with that advice, it was John's practice to fill in for any staff vacancy in the hospital, whenever and wherever necessary. He even took his turn as the night nurse, with the arrangement that he would awaken the registered nurse when she was needed. During these shifts, he would edit *Journal* material to keep himself occupied and awake.

After they lost the hospital cook due to diminishing revenues, Freida stepped in to take her place and helped prepare meals for the patients. Although she often corralled one of the secretaries for assistance, John still worried about her overworking. For her part, Freida refused to let him take on the kitchen work, and often enlisted the children instead to help her with minor details. She used these sessions to teach them about the importance of healthy eating. One Saturday morning, John came upon them assembled in the kitchen.

"Daddy!" the children called in unison, running to greet him. Freida looked up from her kneading and shot him a look of disapproval for diverting the children's attention away from their lessons.

"I was talking to the children about making bread," she said with a proud smile. "They are fascinated with the process of adding yeast to make the bread rise. They think it's magic."

"You kids go on back to your lesson. And make sure you help your mother as much as you can. This is a lot of work. I hope we can get a real cook soon."

Freida shot her husband another look that made him realize what he had said. "You know what I mean, darling," he apologized, looking away from the glare in her eyes. "I just don't want to work you too hard. Your cooking is superior to anyone else's, and we are lucky to have you." The kids laughed at their mother's expression, and then she too broke into laughter.

"If you're looking for more work, John," she said, giving him a coy smile, "look at the hospital floors when you go back upstairs. They're quite dingy and need some attention."

With his full schedule and the shortage of hospital workers, John had been too busy to notice the floors. Now that he did, he could see that the shine had worn off. The paint on the walls was also beginning to chip, and he knew that if he didn't tackle that job sooner rather than later, he would have to paint all of the wards. A look at his watch revealed he had just enough time to run by the laundry and do some mangling before he was due in the clinic.

As he walked back through the hospital corridors to the laundry room, John wondered when he would have time to catch up on all the maintenance work. After regular hours would be the most likely time, he thought. Sighing, he folded the linen and took it to the shift nurse on the way to his office. She chuckled when he handed her the stack of ironed and folded sheets.

"What's so funny, Nurse Thomas?"

"Nothing, Doctor," she said, grinning. "It's just strange to see a surgeon doing the laundry."

"My mother always taught me that you do what you have to do – until you can do what you want to do. You can take that advice to the bank!"

After the night rounds, when the hospital was empty and quiet, John cleaned the hardwood floors in the administration building. After they were dried, he put on one coat of shellac and went to bed, planning to get the boys up early to put on a second coat and some wax before opening time. As for the painting, he had decided to get the part-time janitor, who worked two days a week, to help him.

A few days later, John waylaid the janitor, an elderly man named Josh, and asked him if he would stay that evening and help with the painting after hours. When Josh agreed, John explained his plan.

"You get a pail and some water, Josh, and wash the hallway walls down to the wainscoting. As each portion dries, I will follow with the paint."

"Okay, let's git to it, Doc," he drawled in his Mississippi accent.

By early morning, they had cleaned and painted the lower section of the hallways on both the second and third floors. While they waited for the paint to dry, they hung up wet clothes in the laundry and then returned to complete the final task, painting the semi-private rooms and one ward. By the time they finished, they had to open all the windows due to the fumes. In the morning, when the sun came streaming in, the hospital looked like new.

As John surveyed the newly painted walls, he gave thanks that he had been able to install oil heating in the administration building. He had chosen the heating system because there was no dependable fire service in the area, but now the decision meant that he didn't have to worry about a furnace dispensing soot and grime throughout the hospital.

With all of his maintenance work, including responsibility for making sure the fire hoses were in working order, John's reputation for being a "jack of all trades" spread quickly among his close friends, especially those on the editorial board of the *Journal*, including Doctors "CV" Roman, Ulysses Grant Dailey, and Edward Perry. On one occasion, after all four doctors attended a meeting in Chicago; John's three friends began to tease him about his expanded abilities.

National Medical Association Meeting, Chicago, 1933

"Is it true you're doing the handy work at that hospital of yours?" Roman asked with a sly grin.

"And I heard that you're as good with a chisel as you are with a scalpel," Perry chimed in.

John doubted that his friends realized just how much money he was saving by doing things himself, and his pride in his effort to keep the hospital operational kept him from laughing at their jokes. He was preparing to defend himself when Daily interceded on his behalf.

"Say what you will. How many of you could do what John is doing and also be the secretary of the National Hospital Association, a member of this executive board, the medical director and chief surgeon of the hospital, and the editor of the *Journal*?"

"And the painter, the janitor, the fireman, the laundry man, and who knows what else," teased Perry.

"I think that you men need to leave well enough alone," Daily admonished. "I admire his fortitude, and I know I couldn't handle all of those jobs. I think we need to give John a round of applause before he asks *us* to help!"

John took their teasing in stride, knowing that any of them would do the same things he had done and would be there if he asked for their help. Even he had to confess that he led a many-sided life. Too often he felt almost like a Dr. Jekyll and Mr. Hyde. His crazy schedule would often have him performing surgeries at three or four o'clock in the morning. While the nurses and interns were not happy about this, there was often no other alternative. As compensation, John always had a pot of hot coffee ready to help everyone wake up and stay alert for these early morning sessions.

One winter morning at four o'clock, one of the interns came into the operating room rubbing his red eyes and looking half asleep.

"Here, have some coffee, Doctor," John told him. "You need to be more awake than that to operate. Drink this and let's start scrubbing."

Soon, several other interns and nurses straggled in looking for coffee and, after a few minutes, they began to set up and take care of the patient. By the time they finished the procedure, everyone was excited at the outcome, and the formerly somnambulant group was on high alert. As they took off their surgical garb, one of the interns asked John if he thought what they were doing was worth all the extra effort.

"Think about this," John responded. "We are serving a community with little or no hope for survival without adequate medical care. In this ward we have the highest rates of tuberculosis, meningitis, and influenza in the city, and we are treating that. The mortality rate for colored babies in this area is beginning to improve, and our hygiene classes are elevating the standard of living for our people. The whole community is benefiting."

"That's all well and good; Dr. Kenney, but we can barely keep the doors open. With this Depression, people don't have the money to pay, and we can only cut back so much. If we keep going like this, no one will be able to get paid. I'm not convinced it's worth it."

"This is a business. In business you have to consider your assets and liabilities. We just talked about our liabilities; now let's look at the assets. We have a physical property that has met the needs and demands placed upon it. We have a facility for thirty-four patients. We have an outpatient clinic and room for expansion according to our needs. When the economy improves, we will be ready to meet the challenge of an improved way of life."

"*If* the economy improves," one of the nurses murmured, her voice trailing off and leaving the thought hanging heavily in the air.

"Listen, all of you," John urged, "don't dismiss this opportunity. This is the one opportunity in the entire state of New Jersey where our physicians and surgeons can come together, meet professionally, and practice medicine for the good of our patients. There is no other hospital in the State of New Jersey that will give you interns the year's training required by the medical examiner's board for your certificate. This is it!"

He looked at the nurses with dismay. "There are no hospitals in this state that will train you Negro nurses! If you don't like it here, you will have to go down South for your opportunity. There are some white hospitals down there that have made provisions for Negro nurses and interns, like Grady Hospital in Atlanta and the City Hospital in Knoxville, Tennessee. There are a few more such institutions scattered in various Southern states, but you will definitely have to leave this area."

"I think I'll go down to Atlanta," the senior intern said with a smug look. "It looks like they are more advanced down there than we are up here anyway."

"Do what you want, but I believe we have reason to be grateful for the opportunities that are afforded us right here." John slammed down his scalpel in frustration. "All of our physicians can practice either general medicine or their own specialties. We are blessed with a large consulting staff that stands ready to give us and our patients their considerable skill and expertise. There is not another situation like this one anywhere. Don't take it for granted."

"I'm not taking it for granted," the intern protested. "I just want to be wherever the greatest opportunity is. I plan to make a good living. And I intend to live in an area where people can pay me well for my services. I'm never going to be the 'cleaning man' either," he said sarcastically.

John's jaw muscles tensed and his eyes blazed. "This isn't about you, son! This is about the survival of the race. The greatest privilege is to be able to render needed service to our own people. This effort demonstrates our rightful claim to citizenship by contributing something worthwhile to the community. This is something you have to earn – by hard work and commitment. We are also showing the country what our doctors can do professionally, and that will ensure their right to claim membership in the grand profession of medicine. If you are only out for yourself, then Atlanta may indeed be the best place for you, and sooner rather than later."

John turned aside, clenching his fists and grinding his teeth. This new thinking was anathema to him. He had never made the quest for money his master, and he vowed he never would. Certainly it was all right to accumulate wealth, but to his mind the method one used to acquire it had better be based on the right motives, and be of benefit to someone other than just oneself. Any way you looked at it, becoming wealthy was going to require hard work.

John had inherited these views from his childhood, and he had always honored his beloved father and mother for teaching him the value of work and expecting him to do his share. Now, at this point in his career, he also felt fortunate that he had been inspired by his teachers at Hampton to aspire to the right motives, to value the dignity of work, and to learn the virtue of thoroughness. It was at Hampton that he had, for the first time, learned the term "stick-to-it-iveness." Had he not possessed some of that quality, he believed, he would have given up on the medical profession long ago, in the face of the rebuffs and discouragement he confronted during his life. Being taught to have faith in God and in his fellow man had enabled him to stay at the task, despite the difficulties.

Now, in these times, he could only pray that his faith would again carry him through this financial crisis. He didn't have much else to offer – or to hope for.

A Call to Duty

John could no longer ignore the truth. The very existence of the hospital was in jeopardy. He knew that the probability of continued operation was dubious, unless there was an influx of money from some outside source. Trying not to expose his worry to his family, he needed some time alone.

Pacing the floor in his favorite room, his library, John found comfort in the books that were his literary "friends." Ever since he had been a student at Hampton, he had collected volumes on a myriad of subjects, and he often pulled one randomly from the shelf for inspiration, distraction, or just to reminisce whenever he was troubled. Restlessly, he fingered his Shakespeare volumes and straightened his set of *Encyclopedia Britannica*, a gift from his first wife shortly before she died. Next to these books stood his beloved medical school books, and every issue of the *Journal* that had ever been published. John believed the answers to life's problems could be found in this room, in these books, and he frequently sought counsel here.

Now he picked up a book he had just finished reading, one called *Banting's Miracle.* John had been impressed with Dr. Banting's bull-dog tenacity and his refusal to take no for an answer in his quest to find a cure for diabetes. Banting had discovered insulin, which enabled medicine to bring comfort and long life to many thousands. John had promised himself that he would be just as tenacious in finding a solution to the hospital predicament and, at last, he had an idea. He could turn Kenney Memorial Hospital into a community hospital, owned and operated by the people.

He decided that this was a good time to test the spirit of cooperation among his colleagues and the public, and their willingness to embrace his idea. He wanted to expand and improve on the existing hospital and believed that, with community contributions and involvement, the race could support one of the best medical facilities in the East. To test this notion, he called a meeting at his home to determine if the ministers who had supported the building of the hospital and who continued to serve on the board of trustees would support his new proposition.

John opened the door to welcome his loyal stalwarts: the Reverends Borders, Hayes, and Nelson. They greeted him affectionately and took their seats, waiting to hear what he had to say.

"We are all aware of the financial problems of the hospital," John began, handing out a financial report, "and my proposition is that we turn the private Kenney Memorial Hospital into a hospital run and financed by the community."

"A community hospital?" asked Borders. "How would that solve our problem?"

"The community would purchase the hospital from me at fair market value, allowing me to get out what I put into it, and then we could finance the operations with donations from the community, which would own it. I would continue to operate as medical director on a salary, and it would be a joint venture."

"I think it's an interesting idea. I'm just not sure the community is ready to be so visionary. You know the trouble we had getting doctors to consider building the hospital in the first place," Hayes said, shaking his head in doubt.

"I can't think of any other alternative, my friends," John replied. "Look, carrying the existing institution has been quite a burden, especially since I am only one individual. The Kenneys have given to the limit of our means and resources, and we have never asked for a penny.

Our only income is from our patients, with the exception of our Women's Auxiliary, which supports the two charity beds."

"We are all grateful for your generosity, don't misunderstand us," Hayes said, "but I think we need to scout out some straight-thinking, visionary men and women of both races who will lend their influence and finances to support this idea."

"If we close this hospital," John argued, "there is no other hospital where the local doctors may go with freedom to look after their patients. Right now we have fifty-three physicians, mostly colored, but some white, who service the hospital. This may be taken as an encouraging index of what there will be for a larger, or community, proposition."

"I like the idea," Nelson decided. "We could appeal directly to churches, fraternal organizations, clubs, and the like for support. We could have membership drives, pageants, and similar activities to raise money. I think the Negro community would be proud to have an institution like this to call their own. In fact, why don't we plan to give a kick-off speech at my church and let the community know what this would mean for them?"

"Just let me know when, Reverend Nelson, and I will be there!" John said, more hopeful than he had been in a long time.

The four men spent some time planning the program for the meeting, and then John ushered his guests out. He was sitting at the kitchen table, lost in thought about the message his speech needed to deliver, when he heard Freida coming up the back steps. He opened the door to see her and Oscar loaded down with groceries, and he rushed to help them. He had not yet mentioned his idea to Freida, for he wanted to first see if he could get support from his board. Now that there was hope, he was ready to reveal his plan.

"I had a meeting with some members of the board this afternoon," he said in a confident tone, hoping to impress her with his positive demeanor.

"Oh, John, I was able to get some brisket for dinner," Freida said, with a pleased look on her face, busily putting away the groceries.

"Freida, I have something important to tell you," John uttered, his tone more insistent and with no acknowledgement of her comment.

She raised her eyebrows, knowing that it would take something very important to make John ignore the mention of his favorite meal. "What is it, dear?" she asked.

"I'm going to propose to the community that they take over the hospital and own it as a joint enterprise. I talked with Reverend Nelson and Reverend Hayes, and they agreed to let me have a meeting at the church. Reverend Borders also came to our meeting. We thought that I should give a speech, and tell our people what this would mean for Newark and for the future of our race's health."

"It's a fine idea, but...." Freida paused, bringing her brows together in thought. "Considering the trouble you had trying to get people to help you with the building of the hospital, I think you need to be careful about how you present this."

"That's what the pastors thought. How do you feel about it?" John asked.

"Don't make a speech. Try to appeal to people's emotions instead. State your case in ways they can relate to. Do you need me to help you with that?"

"I would like it very much, and thank you."

"You're welcome, dear. We'll sit down after dinner and work on some ideas," Freida said, as she put the brisket in the oven.

After dinner, Freida and John sat in the study going over his notes.

"I wanted to involve the religious community because the church is the Negro social center," John said. "When you take away our religion, you have robbed us of our richest earthly possession."

"That's true. Regardless of its faults and weaknesses, the church is the mainstay of our race."

"I know how much the minister influences the congregation. That's why I talked with the leaders of the church. The minister has the power to sway the congregation in any direction he wants. It really is quite a responsibility. Sometimes the power is used for selfish purposes, but more often than not it is used to uplift the masses."

"What is it that your colleague Dr. Roman used to say about religion?"

"He said that 'religion is an effort to interpret life – to satisfy the human intellect by resting it upon a certitude of knowledge.'"

"He really is a scholar and a gentleman," Freida mused, nodding in appreciation. She looked at John with a sly smile and added, "With a certitude of knowledge, I believe that if your speech is short and sweet and to the point, we all will be satisfied."

John had to laugh at his clever wife, who was right – most of the time.

The more John thought about Freida's advice, the more his excitement grew. Appeal to people's emotions? Well, he knew how to do that. The emotional heart of his people wasn't hard to find, and his mind filled with a rush of ideas for ways he could touch that heart and awaken it to achieve something grand. He could hardly wait to begin.

John and his supporters held their first public meeting at the Clinton A.M.E. Zion Church. Reverend James Nelson, pastor of the church, Reverend John Burke of the Mount Zion Baptist Church, John, and other dignitaries from the community sat together on a low stage. The church was impressive with its Gothic architecture, belfry tower, and ornate brass hood above its double mahogany doors. Inside, the parishioners enjoyed hand-painted murals of the crucifixion, the ascension, and the resurrection. Behind the altar were beautiful stained glass windows, the magnificence of which were illuminated every day when the sun's rays shone through.

Both ministers had combined their congregations for the meeting, and along with interested members of the community, the church was full. To get people in the right mood, the choir gave a beautiful concert, culminating with the singing of the spiritual "There Is a Balm in Gilead," which left the audience in the appropriate emotional mood.

Reverend Nelson gave a rousing address that promoted the idea of a community hospital. Then Reverend Burke rose and commanded the audience's attention. He spoke with sincerity, and also a sense of urgency.

"I want to welcome all of you citizens of New Jersey to this important meeting tonight. God bless you for coming. I want to impress upon you the importance and the significance of this occasion."

Amen's were heard all around. Then, Reverend Burke broke into song – singing the first few lines of the spiritual everyone had just sung, with the organ playing along.

"There is a balm in Gilead to make the wounded whole…there is a balm in Gilead to heal the sin-sick soul," he sang as the audience hummed along.

The feelings generated among the listeners during a church service often created a revival-like atmosphere, and many worshippers didn't think a minister had done his job if the congregation didn't get its "rousement" on. Tonight, Burke seemed to fill the stage, rousing his listeners with the strength of his voice and the power of his belief.

"Our business here tonight," he preached, waving his arms in emphasis, "happens to be connected with a hospital, the first and only hospital of, for, and by our group in the state of New Jersey. This is the balm in Gilead for all of our sick people of Newark. We need to take responsibility, and make this hospital a community hospital that will belong to us all! I wish to impress upon you, my friends, that you will make history if this endeavor succeeds. You will be placing the race to which you belong just one notch higher on the scale of civilization. Surely this is what we need. Let me hear you say Amen!"

The organ played, and several listeners hopped up and down to the music. One woman began to shout in a strange language, speaking in "tongues" and waving her white handkerchief in the air. The reverend gave her his blessing.

Another round of "Amen" and "Praise the Lord" resounded.

"You are showing the public your ability to conceive of and to do something constructive for yourselves," Reverend Burke continued. "The significance of this movement is far in advance of an ordinary mercantile enterprise. In the latter, you would be looking for individual profit. In this you are doing a piece of constructive work for the benefit of the public at large, particularly for the sick, the wounded, the helpless, the poor, and the infirm."

At this juncture, the organ piped in with an encore and the group rose and applauded the minister. The louder the music got, the more aroused the congregation became, so much so that several nurses dressed in white came forward to restrain those who were overly inspired. A few even had to be carried out to the vestibule. Under a spell that at times reached a veritable frenzy, the congregation stood ready to do almost anything the minister directed.

Those who were seated on the stage approved of, endorsed, and supported Burke's impassioned rhetoric, for they knew the intent was worthwhile and the result would benefit the entire community. Surely, John thought, this is one instance when the church can lift up the masses beyond a religion of emotionalism to embrace a cause based on reason and principle.

"Thank you, thank you, and please be seated," the minister responded, quieting the audience. "I want to tell you why we need to support this hospital. Ushers, please pass out those flyers. These will give you some information about the existing facility."

The ushers passed out the flyers, which recorded the number of patients who had been treated successfully and the number of lives that had been saved. Many of the patients had been indigent, and their care assumed by the hospital.

"You are looking out for the comfort and welfare of the man and woman farthest down, for those who are either outcasts of society, forgotten in their sufferings, or charges upon the public. In this act, you are showing the very highest type of citizenship in that you are willing to acknowledge your own individual responsibility to your race and to the public at large, and thereby to do your share in mitigating the sufferings of others less fortunate than you."

"Yes, Lord," one woman called out.

"You are making the greatest claim that you could possibly make for recognition of your civil and political rights, not by vociferously proclaiming 'I demand my rights,' but by quietly and unostentatiously showing that you are worthy. My friends, I congratulate you. You have come a long way. I hope that you realize just what you are doing, and that your chests swell with pride at your achievements."

The audience clapped and waved and fanned as the room warmed up even more. "There is no turning back – forward is our watchword! Forward is our cry! The only question is how fast can we go? Some of us are a little impatient because, like Moses, we have viewed the Promised Land, but unlike Moses, we want to go in and participate with those who will inherit it," he announced. "By making this hospital a community venture, we are building up good will. We are gaining friends in every section of our territory. Interest is growing in the hospital's work, and it is our duty and privilege to support it. Let this no longer be a private hospital. Let us buy it and take ownership, and let this hospital belong to the Negro people of New Jersey!"

The organ played, the audience cheered and clapped, and people waved their white handkerchiefs in the air. It took Burke about five minutes to settle them down so that he could make the next introduction.

"Ladies and gentlemen, let me introduce to you the man who built the Kenney Memorial Hospital single-handedly for the Negro people of New Jersey, Dr. John A. Kenney."

John rose and approached the rostrum to resounding applause. He held up his hand to quiet the audience.

"Thank you, thank you," he began. "I built Kenney Memorial Hospital because of the obvious inequities between the races with regard to health care in this great country. The Negro race furnishes one-tenth of the population of the United States, but its people have provided to them only one-thirtieth of the hospital space. For whites, there is one physician for every three hundred of the population; for Negroes, there is one physician for every three thousand."

John looked up from his notes. People gazed up at him with blank faces. Could this be the same group that had been dancing and testifying with excitement just a few moments ago? As he proceeded with his speech, he began to feel uneasy.

"There is one hospital bed for every one hundred and thirty-seven of the entire population, but only one bed for every one thousand, nine hundred and forty-one of the Negro population. There are five times as many white doctors for the white population as there are Negro doctors for the Negro population. Is it not then quite natural to expect that with our hospital facilities so sadly neglected, we should have a disproportionately high sickness and death rate as compared with the whites?"

The audience grew quiet, expressions giving way to scowls and frowns as the litany of serious statistics flooded over them. The mood had suddenly become somber. John saw looks of concentration begin to fall away, and many church members began staring into space. Others even opened their prayer books and seemed to be reading. He was losing them. Reverend Burke gave him a worried glance, and he knew he had to do something to regain people's attention.

He put down his notes, and walked to the edge of the stage. He held his hands out the way he had seen the minister do many times to command attention.

"Brothers and sisters, let me put this another way. The life span of the white man is fifty-five years; the life span of the Negro will bring you to tears. Forty-one years is all we've got – and that is the truth, like it or not."

"Amen, doctor," one man shouted. John could see people coming to attention as he tried to get into the spirit set by Reverend Burke. He saw Freida nodding encouragement.

"In God's infinite wisdom He gave us a test, a job to do before our final rest, to love one another and come together in Jesus' name, or suffer in silence and die in shame."

The organist began to play "What a Friend I Have in Jesus," and the "rousement" was back on.

"My friends help me keep our little hospital alive. We have nowhere else to go. If you get sick, where will you go to be treated? Where will you take your sick children, and where will you have your babies?"

"At the Kenney Hospital," someone shouted.

The church erupted in laughter, and the organ chimed in like an exclamation point.

"I want to take it one step further for my people. I want a hospital for ourselves, and by ourselves. And I want it to belong to you!"

Cheers drowned out John's words, and he had to wait to make his next point.

"There are some members of our own race who, ostrich-like, hide their heads in the sand and still say that we do not need our own hospitals. Some of them argue that we are citizens and taxpayers, that we contribute to the public institutions, and that we should demand recognition from these institutions. That position is all right, but there is one vital weakness in it. It reminds me of the story of the little Ford runabout and the huge freight truck. The little Ford started into the intersection, and the big freight truck practically mowed it down, plowing through first. When the driver emerged from what was left of his car, he called to a farmer who had seen the near tragedy: 'Say, didn't I have the right of way?' The farmer adroitly answered, 'Yeah! Maybe you did, stranger, but he had a five-ton truck!'"

Once more, the room erupted in laughter. John looked over at Freida, and saw she was laughing too. John's audience was back in the mood again.

"My platform is definite and concise. I recommend that we develop a community hospital supported by all of the people. While the basic idea of such a hospital will be for our group, it should serve any and all peoples. It should have a mixed board of white and colored citizens, and a mixed staff of white and colored physicians. Like Jesus, we will welcome all of God's sheep into the fold."

"Amen, brother Kenney!" the reverend shouted. "Amen."

"If we continue to sit on the stool of do-nothing like the deluded hen on the nest of china eggs, we will accomplish nothing. Demands without the power of endorsement will get very little. I believe that an earnest vote on this project by us will enlist the support of the white community to the extent that our idea will go over. This appeal is to both races. In every community, North, South, East, and West, there are some straight-thinking, clear-minded men and women of both races who are willing to face interracial injustice, and give of their influence and means to help us. I have faith that Newark is no exception to the rule, and I appeal to this group to relieve the situation here and establish the Kenney Memorial Hospital as the new Community Hospital of Newark!"

John had no desire to create or stir up racial hatred or animosities, or to appeal to racial prejudices. Rather, he was sure that the facts as they existed would be enough to impress people with the absolute necessity of taking action. He held up his hands and added, "If you have any iron in your blood, any sand in your crown, any steel in your nerves, any spine in your back, or any guts in your bellies – then act!"

The audience jumped up and began chanting "our own hospital, our own hospital" over and over until Burke had to ask for order.

"Everyone, be seated. It's time for us to take a vote on this project. The junior ministers will tally the count. Please sit down so that we can proceed!"

People hustled back to their seats, wanting to be a part of the historic moment.

"How many of you would support making the Kenney Memorial Hospital a community-owned hospital?" asked Burke, quickly holding up his hand to be the first vote.

Hands began to go up all over the room as the ministers started to count. In just a few moments, everyone in the audience had raised their hands, and some were even standing to emphasize their support.

The congregation voted unanimously in favor of the project. Excitement was in the air, and the optimism at having accomplished their task had everyone on the dais smiling. Reverend Burke hurriedly ordered the collection plates to be passed while the mood was so favorable. He asked the congregation for contributions to assist in the operation of the hospital at present. He also asked to set up a citizens committee to explore getting assistance from the white community – and to make sure that the colored community remained active. A group of citizens and several church members volunteered for the steering committee that night, resolute in their determination to make the community hospital a reality.

The committee met for the first time in the basement of Bethany Baptist Church, after having first sent a questionnaire to many in the community, asking if they would support the project. One of the committee members, a Dr. Mae McCarroll, who had heard that the initiative was being favorably received, agreed to tabulate the number of questionnaires. As the committee's first order of business, she counted the stack and reported on the results.

"My initial count is a total of more than four hundred questionnaires received to support the effort," she said, handing the papers to another member to validate her count. "That is very encouraging."

"I have the additional support of seventeen local physicians with whom I talked," said another member. "I think we have the support we need to proceed."

The committee's next move was to send a questionnaire to the white hospitals, seeking support. The members were curious to see what the sentiment was in that quarter. One survey question asked, "What would you recommend to improve hospital facilities for Negroes in this area?" One hospital executive responded laconically, "Go and build one for yourselves." In an editorial in the *Journal*, John reported this response and replied, "Bravo! You have done us more good than you would have done by saying that the latch string to yours is on the outside; come on in."

In some of the white press, articles appeared criticizing the supporters of the hospital movement. Freida showed John one such article that she'd just read in the morning newspaper.

"Look at this, John. It says here that we are trying to foster segregation of the races by wanting our own hospital." She shook the paper to express her disgust. "This reminds me of all the ridiculous complaints we got around the Tuskegee V.A. Hospital situation."

"And at the same time, white medical facilities aren't granting Negroes access to their services," John said. "You're damned if you do and damned if you don't. How can we stomach the humiliating and revolting hospital conditions available to us and then call a respectable, cultured and refined civic movement for our own betterment *segregation?*"

John continued to hear about such reactions, and each one made him even more determined to keep the hospital movement going. One day as he was leaving the hospital, he ran into George Williams, one of the city's leading undertakers.

"I just want you to know I am with you on this hospital thing," Williams said. "I am sick and tired of the way we are treated in those other hospitals."

"What do you mean?" John asked.

"I went over to that big white hospital the other day," Williams began. "You know the one I'm talking about. I went to pick up a deceased patient, and they told me he was up in the ward. I was told what floor, and when I got on the elevator, it took me all the way up to the attic.

"There was nothing but Negro patients up there," Williams went on, his voice rising and his face getting red. "I didn't understand why this dead patient was still up there with the living patients, so I asked the nurse. She told me that the hospital only had two boxes set aside for dead colored patients. If they were full and another Negro died, the body had to just stay put until the undertaker got there and emptied one of the boxes to make room for the most recently deceased."

"We won't have to deal with that much longer," John said, patting Williams' arm to calm as well as reassure him. "Thanks for motivating me to continue my quest."

When the *Newark Herald* newspaper, a Negro publication, featured an article voicing the opposition of a Mr. Hughes Robinson, who was a Negro, John was not surprised. Robinson was quoted as objecting to the community hospital, not only because he thought it would promote segregation, but also because he also felt it would lead to separate schools in Newark. He said he didn't think the doctors would be able to raise the funds to support the hospital, but he would oppose it even if they did.

John immediately published an editorial in the same paper defending the movement's position. He wanted the supporters' position to be clear – that they were the defenders of racial rights, and they *did* believe in equality of the races. "Being white is no badge of superiority," John wrote, "and the color of a man's skin or the texture of his hair is no index to the depth of his cerebral convolutions or the amount of gray matter therein contained." While he reiterated that Negroes had to recognize the status quo – the fact that segregation existed – he countered that they had to face it and fight it, not blindly, but scientifically and practically.

"It is widely admitted that the hospital experience is the *sine qua non* for proper development in medical science," he maintained. "This is so generally accepted to be true that the number of states requiring internships in an accredited hospital is at an all-time high." John did not at all agree with those who held that racial hospitals were not necessary in the North because Negro patients could be cared for in white institutions. "Even if that were true," he wrote, "what about the Negro intern or nurse who is well qualified but needs hospital training?" He went on to emphatically deny that, by organizing their own medical associations and establishing their own hospitals, Negroes were segregating themselves. "As little as we like to place emphasis on these things," he said, "we have to admit that the color line has already been drawn and that we are simply adapting ourselves to our environment. And if we do not meet the exigencies forced upon us by taking action along these lines, we will not be meeting the existing demands of our people."

John's plea was for better and stronger organizations for Negro physicians in their own medical societies – national, state, and local – and for the establishment of more hospitals by and for the Negro people, and for the support of those already in existence. Regardless of the conditions that made these hospitals a necessity, he asked, "Is it not a privilege for us to bring into existence something of our own that is worthwhile? We have to stimulate and nourish the quality known as race pride and, in its name and for its sake alone, exert ourselves to greater endeavor. We have to put greater stress upon the tremendous opportunities and, while not overlooking racial discriminations, emphasize them less."

One Sunday morning after John got home from church; he found the latest edition of the *Newark Herald* on the porch and began reading his article to Frieda. She was surprised that under the circumstances there would be any opposition among Negroes to the community hospital idea.

"D, I think that your article is quite good," she said. "I think more people should examine their consciences and ask God for direction. When one is forced to take ego out of the equation, the common denominator becomes what is good for all of the people. I think it is a matter of faith, and we need to encourage the ministers to continue to address this from the pulpit."

"Our people cause me great concern sometimes. It's quite a conundrum," John said, shaking his head in disbelief.

"We need to continue to pray over this," Freida stated. "We had a discussion at my church about the integrity of the soul, and when we stray away from those principles, we compromise our spirituality. It really is a matter of each one of us examining our thoughts, our motives, and our actions – and just doing what is right anyway."

"Darling, in some ways that makes sense but...." Just then the doorbell rang, and John went to answer it. Much to his surprise, it was Reverend Borders, whom John had just seen at church. Freida looked up as John brought the minister into the parlor.

"Good morning, Reverend Borders," she said.

"And the same to you, Mrs. Kenney," he answered with a nod. "I just came by to show you this article I have written for the newspaper in response to that Mr. Hughes Robinson. After a few inquiries, I have found that his opposition is inconsistent with his own actions."

"Sit down, Reverend; let's hear more," John urged.

"Well," he began, "according to my information, this gentleman has no experience in the public life of the colored citizens of North Jersey and has only lived in this section for a few months. He came from a Southern state where there are certainly no desegregated public or semi-private institutions. And when we learned that he is employed as an assistant manager of a group of apartment houses catering only to colored tenants and operated by a colored staff, we were doubly surprised that he is such an enemy of segregation. This apartment enterprise is owned by a large, white financial institution that refuses to write business for colored people and, aside from the employees in its housing project, has refused for years to even employ a colored janitor or messenger. It would seem more practical for this gentleman to protest against the exclusion of colored people from the great insurance company that employs him to manage a purely segregated housing project. Or maybe he should demand that white people be permitted to rent apartments in the building in which he is assistant superintendent."

"Well, well, well," John remarked, "the pot can't call the kettle black! I feel sorry for people who will adopt any stance just to further their own agenda."

"Yes, sad but true," the minister replied. "But we have work to do. Let's get our project under way!"

Soon, the steering committee for the hospital arrived to investigate the property and its management, and to verify the facility's value as an investment. After a laborious and exhaustive survey of all hospital operations, the hospital was certified and deemed a proper investment.

Based on the inspection and certification, the steering committee recommended taking over the hospital, and made plans to hold a formal public meeting of interested citizens in order to take a vote on the proposal. The meeting was held on July 23, 1934, at the Hopewell Baptist Church, with over seven hundred citizens in attendance. Excitement was in the air, and John had gotten word from some in the audience that the mood of the crowd was optimistic. He had picked up some backing from an ad-hoc citizens committee, and also from the Baptist Ministerial Union.

Once again he made his plea for the community project, ending by stressing the improved health and living conditions that would result:

"The hospital is like the hub of a wheel. It is the center of health activities, and from it, like the spokes of a wheel scintillating and radiating in every direction, these health influences are spread throughout the community. Such an institution will increase our self-respect, elevate our racial status, and bring us greater recognition in the entire territory."

As he finished his remarks, the ushers began to pass out the ballots. Reverend Hayes leaned over to John and whispered in his ear.

"If we win this one, we are going out to Tyler's Chicken Shack for dinner."

"If we win this one, I'm paying!" added John, laughing with his friend.

The ballots were marked, handed back to the ushers for collection, and then turned over to the citizens committee to be counted. The gospel choir from the church sang during the interim, but John could barely concentrate on the musical selections as he waited for the verdict. His heart was beating wildly, and he could feel a blush on his face as he tried to calm his breathing.

Hayes met quietly with members of the committee, who handed him a paper with the results. With no readable expression on his face, he took to the stage. "Ladies and gentlemen, may I have your attention?" The room grew deathly quiet. "I have the results of the vote on the community hospital project. There are seven hundred people in attendance, and the committee has counted seven hundred ballots. The results are as follows: the number of ballots cast in favor of the project is six hundred and ninety-nine! Opposed is one!"

John couldn't believe his ears. His mind overcome amid the cheers and standing applause, he simply sat, stunned and motionless, in his chair. Only when Reverend Nelson came over to get him, pulling him up, did he stand to salute the crowd. He couldn't believe that the people had finally come together to support something of their own. This was one of the most rewarding days of his life, and he was truly humbled.

After the cheering had died down, a member of the citizens committee, Grace Fenderson made an announcement. "Approximately seven hundred citizens have endorsed by almost unanimous vote the Community Hospital Project." She also stated that the citizens committee hereafter would be called the Northern New Jersey Hospital Association, and would become a permanent committee. Elected to work on the proceedings were Reverend Hayes, Dr. W. G. Alexander, Dr. Buckner, Mr. Thomas Smith, and some others. An attorney, Mr. Oliver Randolph, was selected to represent the committee. John selected a friend, Mr. W. P. Allen, to represent him as his attorney.

It was encouraging to John to discover that the Baptist Ministerial Union, in its regular session, had endorsed the movement and appointed a committee of forty of its regular members to cooperate in any way they might be needed. In addition, a Ways and Means Committee was selected to work out the details of transforming the Kenney Memorial Hospital into the Community Hospital. Members of the Committee were to tour the facility, review the hospital records, and be prepared to report at their next scheduled meeting, which was to be August 3, 1934.

The Ways and Means Committee met on the appointed date to tour the hospital and to review data submitted by John and his attorney, which included the sales price of seventy-seven thousand six hundred dollars. Reverend Hayes had been elected chairman of the Committee, and he introduced John to the others.

"As you can see from the information in front of you, this hospital is still solvent after seven years of operation, and that includes the past four years of operation under economic depression."

"That's quite an accomplishment," Mrs. Fenderson commented. "Looking at this financial report, I'd like to know how you arrived at your asking price."

"Look on page two," Attorney Allen said. "The total original outlay for Dr. Kenney was ninety-two thousand dollars. The real estate today is appraised at sixty thousand-six hundred dollars and the equipment is valued at seventeen thousand dollars, giving us a total asking price of seventy-seven thousand and six hundred dollars. The figure represents a discount of fourteen thousand-four hundred dollars. You should also note that it's usual to include in the sale of a medical practice a monetary amount for the value of 'good will' associated with a practice, but Dr. Kenney wants to forgo that."

"That's more than generous," Dr. Alexander said, nodding his head.

"The breakdown for the transfer of this privately-owned hospital to a community venture is listed on page three. There is also an estimate of the income possibilities for the next few years, based on the past incomes," Allen said.

"Thank you both for that thorough report," Hayes said. "We will study this in more detail, and report to you at the meeting on Monday night at Bethany Baptist Church."

John left the meeting with a strange, uncomfortable feeling that he couldn't explain. He knew that the financial reports were straightforward and concise, and for the first time there was an awareness of just how much money John had himself invested in the hospital. He also knew that the prospect of being reimbursed for his efforts, even at a discount - and of the community being charged with the obligation - threatened to awaken that sleeping green-eyed monster, envy, once again. What he really wanted was to get the hospital into the hands of the community while it was still viable and fiscally solvent.

The meeting on Monday, August sixth, went as John had expected. The committee offered to pay him seventy-thousand dollars, and said they would assist him with the original mortgage loan. John was disappointed with their offer but decided to have Allen present a caveat which would facilitate a quick closing. He wrote an idea on paper and handed it to Allen, who read it and nodded in agreement as the others chatted.

"I think," Reverend Borders commented, "that we should increase the hospital patronage by recruiting more physicians on the staff. That would entice more revenue."

"And we can start hospital auxiliary chapters in churches, clubs, fraternities, and sororities," Mrs. Fenderson suggested. "This will ensure cooperation and additional financial support."

"I believe," Dr. Burke mused, "that any feeling directed at one individual who maintains a private institution would be minimized by community ownership, and this will secure more cooperation, don't you think so, Dr. Kenney?"

"Yes, I do. It has been on my mind that some people might think that my owning it privately is suspect, but they have to remember the history. Now we as a community are afforded an unusual opportunity to take over a growing concern, one already equipped and in good community graces."

"Dr. Kenney will accept the offer," Allen interrupted, silencing the chatter. "He explained to me that he would like to give title to this property by the end of the month. To accomplish this, we propose to sell it to the community for one dollar as a technicality to effect an immediate sale. At the same time I will present papers detailing a payment schedule to pay Dr. Kenney. The amount will be – minus the one dollar – sixty nine thousand-nine hundred and ninety nine dollars."

"One dollar for the hospital? That's incredible!" Mrs. Fenderson exclaimed. "Since we've settled on an asking price, I'm sure we will be able to pay the doctor back. I'm sure we will be able to pay the doctor back as soon as we can take over and start making a profit." The other committee members nodded in agreement.

"Dr. Kenney will still be bound by the twenty-five thousand dollar mortgage with the building and loan company," Allen continued, "and he would still retain his interest in the institution by virtue of the amount he has at stake. Accordingly, he believes that he should be retained in a managerial or supervisory capacity to enable him to protect his financial interests and be paid accordingly." Allen paused. When no one protested, he went on.

"Dr. Kenney would like this finalized by September first. That way the community can begin to take over immediately, and the new staff can be assembled. Dr. Kenney, for sentimental reasons, would like the hospital takeover to be in September, since the hospital opened in September of 1927."

"We shall begin the incorporation process and meet to transfer the title on September first," Hayes declared. "All in favor say *aye*."

All the Committee members responded affirmatively, and John breathed a sigh of relief. Finally, there was an agreement between him and the committee, and at last his dream of a community hospital would be realized. He asked Attorney Allen to pencil in the date for the closure and to have all of the paperwork ready.

When John received a notice from the Committee that the meeting had been postponed until the next month, his old frustration returned and anxious thoughts troubled his sleep. The postponement had awakened old worries, and when another date was set for October first and then also passed without any formal action, John's frustration turned into alarm. While he waited, he was forced to put more and more of his own money into the hospital to keep it afloat, a financial drain that now seriously threatened the security and future of his family. He needed to make something happen, and he needed to do it now, but he had no idea what that *something* was.

Chapter 27

The Mind of Oppression

John sat at his desk at the hospital, trying to write an editorial for the *Journal*. Over and over, he balled up each sheet of paper and threw it across the room into the trash. A paper mountain overflowed the wastebasket, a measure of his growing frustration. It was already October, and there was no resolution to the hospital crisis - and no consensus in sight.

He turned at the sound of a faint knock on the door and, in one quick motion, slid his writing underneath the blotter. "Come in," he called, trying to keep the annoyance out of his voice.

Grace Fenderson slipped quietly into his office. "I'm glad that you're here, Dr. Kenney," she said in a whisper, closing the door, "but I hesitate to tell you what has just transpired."

"What is it?" John asked, offering her a chair. "Things can't have gotten much worse."

"You'd be surprised. The original Ways and Means Committee couldn't come to an agreement on anything and some of them formed a sub-committee to make their own offer."

Livid, John stood up abruptly, sending his chair flying backward and crashing to the floor. "What?" he shouted loud enough for those in his outer office to hear. "For how much this time?" He felt blood rushing to his head, pounding at his temples.

"Please be calm," Grace Fenderson pleaded. "I don't know what they will propose. Your lawyer will tell you, but please, no one must know I am here. I still want to retain my influence on the Committee."

John began to pace back and forth in front of his desk, trying to decide what he ought to do. "This is unacceptable," he said, banging his fist down on the desk. "These delays have been going on for months. I'm dealing with Negroes who have no foresight. They know that the community voted to move forward with this project. What's the use of taking months of valuable time to do what could have been done in a couple of weeks?"

"I know, but you should be getting a letter in a few days making you another offer. Attorney Oliver and Reverend Borders are working on papers for the first offer, which still stands, and both committees are meeting next month at the Baptist Ministerial Union in Newark. I'm sure the two committees can come to some agreement by then." Grace got up to leave.

"Thank you for coming," John said. "And please excuse my outburst, but this situation is becoming unbearable. I'll call Attorney Allen and fill him in," he added, reaching for the telephone as Grace quietly left his office.

Before John could make the call, his secretary notified him that Attorney Allen was on the phone.

"Welcome back, Doctor," Allen said, managing to sound both upbeat and puzzled. "I wanted to let you know that I have just received a letter from a sub-committee of the Ways and Means Committee. Wonders never cease, do they?"

"Not when you're dealing with our people..."

"They say they are making you an offer of...hold onto your seat...forty thousand dollars and an immediate closure if you agree." Allen paused a moment, waiting for John's response.

"Don't they know that seventy thousand dollars was the lowest possible bid I would consider?" John asked, anger forcing his voice to rise.

"They are apparently ignoring that," Allen said, "and all parties would like you to come to a meeting next month."

Stunned into silence, John stood quietly with the receiver against his ear. He could not, he decided, dignify such an offer with a rebuttal. After a moment, he simply said, "Send them a letter refusing the offer, and let them know that I will be at the meeting next month."

Over the next few days, John struggled with his frustration. He had never been so disgusted. Here was a group of professional businessmen and women who had come together to study a serious problem. They had reached a conclusion, come to an agreement, gone through the regular parliamentary practices governing such affairs, sealed it with a vote, carried it to the parent body with an unqualified recommendation in its favor – and it had been almost unanimously accepted. Then the committee itself, whose members were delegated to carry out the will of the people, blocked it. Why? Because some were dissatisfied, and others had criticisms.

What movement could ever progress without criticism? The wonder was that the hospital decision had gone over in as splendid a manner as it did. The aftermath only proved John's belief that the only way to escape criticism was to say nothing, do nothing, be nothing, and go stick yourself into some out-of-the-way hole and die! Anyone could blow with the wind or drift with the current, but it took friction to develop power. If there was no friction between the rail and the wheel of the great locomotive streaking along at ninety or a hundred miles an hour, the train would never move. John resolved to be the friction that would move the hospital train.

When the day came for the meeting, John arrived at the Baptist Union building at the appointed time. The discussion was already in progress, and he waited in the atrium to be called. He had already been advised by two members of the Committee not to press for action. He disagreed. No blacksmith waited for his iron to cool before striking – he struck while the iron was hot!

Seated near the meeting room door, he could hear the choir in the antechamber rehearsing for the Sunday service. He closed his eyes and followed along: "Listen to the lambs, all a-cryin', listen to the lambs, all a-cryin'…." He was lost in the spirit of the song when he heard his name.

"Dr. Kenney, we're ready for you."

As John rose, he realized how tired he was. It was an effort to drum up the stamina to plead his case. His mouth was dry, his legs weak, and his feet dragging. Before he entered the room, he straightened his tie, along with his back. Determined to at least give the appearance of a commanding presence, he walked in and took the only vacant seat at the table. There were about twenty members present, enough for a quorum. All eyes were on him.

He cleared his throat, took a deep breath, and began. "Ladies and gentlemen, thank you for affording me the opportunity to plead my case before you, again. This has been an arduous journey, and I'd like to reach the final destination. Lately I've heard many rumors and misstatements. Someone on the Committee supposedly said, 'Now that he has built that hospital by himself, let him run it by himself.' Someone else told me that it was 'professional jealousy' that was keeping my dream from become a reality. Right now I'm not sure what to believe."

John looked around the room at the faces of each Committee member. The fate of the hospital would be decided at this table. This was, he believed, his last hope.

"I can only say to this Committee that my motives are pure. I want to see my people survive, and have the good health to continue to make the progress we are entitled to by our very existence. Without our health, we have no hope of survival, and right now this hospital is the only thing we have in Newark to save us. There is nowhere else for us to go."

"All of us want a hospital for the community, Dr. Kenney; we just have to agree on how to make that happen for all involved," the Reverend Hayes said.

"Let me assure you one last time: my dream is for a hospital for all of us – there is no personal gain to be had. I have laid open the books, I have passed an inspection, and I have personally apprised you of my motives. I am just a poor man with altruistic motives, and I have allowed nothing, not even my family, to deter me from my objective. My heart is in this work, and I implore you to take a vote tonight that will bring the community back together so that we can all move forward. Make this project your own, remove the obstacles that are holding it up, and let us set ourselves to the task before us, happy in the fact that this is God's work and that there is glory enough in it for all."

"Thank you, Dr. Kenney." The chairman's tone was formal and dismissive. "We have reviewed all of the material and will make a decision tonight. We will inform you by written notice what our decision is."

"Thank you," John replied, rising from his chair. Whatever happened, he had done his best. He managed a weak smile and left the room, the door closing soundly behind him.

John returned home with no confidence in the outcome. His gut feeling turned out to be reliable, for the next evening he received a telegram from the group. Things had gone from bad to worse. Some members of the original committee had joined with the sub-committee, repudiating the vote taken at the approval meeting. The other members of the original Ways and Means Committee wanted to distance themselves from this new group, and decided to name themselves the Booker T. Washington Community Hospital Association. This group still insisted that a fair offer for the hospital was sixty-eight thousand dollars, while the sub-committee felt forty thousand was fair, based upon the present economy. Now a real price contention existed, not between John and the original committee, but between the two committees. And John understood far too clearly that the old "slave mentality mindset" still enveloped the psyche of too many of his race. This latest turn of events was ample evidence.

John felt betrayed. What could he possibly do now? He needed guidance, religious guidance. Although his medical duties prevented him from being a regular churchgoer, he still held grand rounds with the Lord on a daily basis, sometimes many times a day. For him, the profession required it. Now, at this juncture, he desperately needed a spiritual uplift. Confused, distraught, and thoroughly undone by the mental anguish to which he was being subjected, he went out into the night and walked for hours. He didn't feel the rain beginning to fall, and wasn't aware of where he was going until he found himself in front of the church.

He walked into the sanctuary, lit a candle, and knelt to pray. After some time, he felt a hand on his shoulder.

"John, what can I help you with?"

Reverend Nelson lifted John and, leading him to a pew, took a seat beside him. John tried to speak, but no words came. His brain was numb and his body weary, spent from the battle of repudiation.

"Take your time, it's going to be all right," the minister said with assurance. "Right where we are, God is."

"I just need to pray, Reverend. I'm trying to understand our race, and what has always kept us from working together. Is it a mental, physical, or emotional anomaly? As a physician I know that there are these connections in our brains, neurotransmitters actually, and they must be misfiring. We're not thinking clearly, and we surely aren't acting rationally. We are so fractured as a race that sometimes I don't see how we will ever survive."

"What you are saying is true, John, but whites have trouble working together too. As a man of the cloth, I would say that this is the struggle that God has given us to overcome. It is deep and has a lot to do with who we are in our souls. When our thoughts and actions deviate from what God has decreed, we get into trouble. When man leads from the ego, he will always have a lesson to learn."

"Yes, perhaps that's it. Or maybe it's a combination of things - a disease of the mind, the body, and the soul," John rambled on, not really paying attention to what the reverend had said. "From a medical standpoint, we doctors approach a disease by first finding out what it is. Then we study what tissues it attacks, decide what the effect is, and finally treat it accordingly. The process is methodical and scientific. But what afflicts us now will require divine intervention."

"I think the problem is really about faith, John, and about understanding the historical perspective of our people in this country. We have come a long way since we were captured and brought to these shores."

"I'm sure you're right. I'm sure that in our native countries the Negro was robust, virile, stalwart, healthy, and prolific. Then we were brought forcefully to an entirely different part of the world, and even under the galling yoke of bondage, we still maintained our physical and mental characteristics. We remained proud, intelligent, fearless, and elegant in our royal lineage. We somehow managed to maintain a strong sense of who we were."

Nelson put his hand on John's shoulder. "Faith will be our salvation, son. We must have faith in God's plan for us, and it will be revealed unto us. This doesn't mean that we won't have more difficult times ahead of us. It just means we have to be strong and persevere. Remember, 'They that trust in the Lord shall be as Mount Zion, which cannot be removed, but abideth forever.' Unto everything there is a purpose."

"It's still difficult to understand the purpose of our current discord. I liken slavery to cancer. It has somehow altered our cellular pathology on a genetic level, subjecting us to its myriad mutations through the continued procreation of the race," John said, offering a clinical explanation.

"A probable diagnosis, Doctor," Reverend Nelson agreed, "and one that can only be mitigated by each one of us doing the kind of introspection that you and I are doing now, and then having faith in that process. Until we do that, we will never be free."

"I'd take that point further," John responded. "When freedom for the Negro finally came, this thing that we had prayed for, had yearned for, had traveled for in the spirit and the flesh was now upon us, but we didn't know what to do with it."

"It was hallelujah time, sure 'nough," the reverend agreed.

"What was more natural than to put on our freedom like a brand new Sunday dress and parade it a little?" John continued. "It was easy to go into excesses – excesses of the mind, body, and spirit. No one but a physician can have the faintest conception of the far-reaching consequences of this kind of behavior; it ends up on my doorstep."

"And on mine too, Dr. Kenney," Nelson said, reminding John of a minister's responsibilities.

"I know you're right. I'm sorry, I wasn't thinking. So now we have our new freedom, coupled with our old slave mentality and our lack of preparation for this new existence; and this has become the breeding ground for physical, moral, and spiritual disease. And so the cancer spreads."

"I'm afraid so, but God willing, it won't be this way always." Reverend Nelson bowed his head and said a silent prayer

John found no comfort in his words. Instead, the entire conversation had left him feeling both hopeless and helpless. What could he do? He was only one man – and a very weary one at that – and this problem transcended generations. Leaning back in the pew, he closed his eyes, lost in thought. Nelson sat beside him without speaking, letting John reflect silently and come to his own conclusions.

After a few minutes, John opened his eyes and looked at the minister with intensity, as if he had reached a major realization. "This chaos will continue throughout future generations if we don't change our core beliefs and come to an understanding and appreciation of who we really are. The wounds of the past have got to be healed."

"Praise the Lord," Nelson said. "And the only way to do that is to mirror the soul virtues that we are all born with; love, compassion, kindness, honesty, and all the positive attributes that we bring with us into the world. If we believe that a part of God is in each one of us – His creations – then we'll have to honor that in others as well as ourselves. But first we have to learn to love ourselves exactly where we are and as we are. That requires a quantum shift in the way we *think* about ourselves. It's tantamount to undoing generational thinking and replacing the old negative thoughts with positive ones. But above all, we must always live in integrity with our souls."

Yes, that was it, John thought. The integrity of the soul – that was the missing link. "I think I have a better understanding of what ails us. It's *what* we think, not *how* we think. If we believe the lies that have been told to us about us, we are destined to become the lie. If we remember who we are, *who we all are deep in our soul*, therein lays our salvation. Thank you, Reverend, for your time and your inspiration."

"Don't thank me; your intuition was divinely inspired," Nelson admitted, walking John to the door. "God bless you."

Strangely relieved, John shook the minister's hand and left the church. He still had no an answer as to how to solve his dilemma, but for some reason he felt less troubled. At last, he had a logical explanation for the racial inertia, and knew he could go back and face his crisis anew. t was ironic that Freida's beliefs and thoughts had been making so much more sense to him lately. He knew that he would have to pray over the hospital situation and rely on his faith for a resolution. There was nothing else he could do. But right now he was tired and needed to go home.

When he reached the house, John went into his study to write down all that he and Nelson had discussed. It was cathartic, and he felt a sense of peace, something that had eluded him lately. After he was finished, he began to work on some manuscripts but was interrupted by chatter and laughter from the dining room. Jack was home from Bates College in Maine, regaling his mother and brothers with tales of what it was like to be in a predominately white college.

Because Freida had home-schooled the children rather than subject them to the inequities of the Newark school system, Jack had never been taught in the same classroom with white students. Although John regretted this on one level, he was incredibly proud of Freida for her selfless dedication to her family. He finally had to give grudging respect to the Christian Science religion she had embraced, if only because it seemed to have helped her physically as well as spiritually. And while she understood John's angst about the hospital situation, she never put any pressure on him to resolve it.

When she saw John staring toward the dining room, she came into the study with an impish smile lifting the corners of her mouth.

"How are you doing, Dr. Kenney?" she teased. "Will you be able to help with the year-end financial statement later?"

"I have to get these papers edited for the *Journal* by tomorrow, but if you get stumped, I can give you a few minutes. I was also thinking I would go and see Reverend Borders in the morning to find out if the Committee has made any progress. This indecision is still troubling to me."

"At times like these you must step back from the problem," Freida said with an expression of calm reassurance in her eyes. "There is a universal power in all of us, and it seeks an outlet through us. You have to get in tune with that power, which is actually the God within each of us.

Your answers will be revealed to you through Him – it is a wondrous thing. Look at me, John." She reached out and took his hand, and John noticed that she had tears in her eyes. "I have not told you this, but I know that the doctors did not think I would live as long as I have. I heard Dr. Miller discussing my case with his colleague when I was in recovery from one of the surgeries. He thought I was still under the anesthesia, but the conversation came back to me clearly once I fully woke up. I wasn't frightened, because I have been taught that the mind is the only healer. What matters is what *I* think. I took my mind off the prognosis and focused positive thoughts on the outcome I wanted. That's all I did – consistently. Obviously it works, for I am healthy now. Am I not proof?"

John nodded and smiled. He didn't completely understand the belief behind his wife's words, but what she said soothed him nonetheless.

"John," she declared, taking him by the shoulders and looking squarely into his eyes, "I am proof."

He felt the strength of her belief and embraced her. Surely, he had no choice but to carry on.

With his spirit restored anew, John continued to speak publicly on behalf of the hospital. Yet, with two hospital factions now making claims upon a Depression-ridden public, he didn't hold much hope for the success of either. Certainly his original purpose had been lost and defeated in the dissension. It was quite possible that each group could go forward and establish some kind of hospital, but it would not be the Community Hospital that was at the center of everyone's efforts, and the source of everyone's pride. Despite the fact that one group appeared to have the advantage because it already represented the hospital, needing only to change the name and proceed, John was convinced that doing this without the community's support and involvement was not the correct thing to do. He certainly had no desire for competition with a Community Hospital project. He preferred to continue the Kenney Memorial Hospital as a private institution rather than witness such divisiveness.

As fall gave way to winter, John was invited to speak at more and more churches and organizations to let the public know the fight was still ongoing. On a frosty November night, Reverend Ponder invited his parishioners to come to an evening service to hear John speak. Discussing community funding, John offered a novel approach that he hoped would generate more financial support and renewed enthusiasm.

"I want to talk about the dollar-dime movement," John said, hoping to communicate a feeling of optimism. "That involves each one of you here. I am not expecting a large sum of money from any source, but if we want this hospital, I expect the people of this community to put your dollars and your dimes together and, by doing so, show the white citizens of the world that we have decided to stop sitting idly by, begging others to do for us while we do nothing for ourselves."

Reverend Ponder stepped up to speak, putting his arm around John and interjecting his own story.

"Let me tell you about my experience at the Kenney Memorial Hospital. When I was gravely sick, I went there; and I was snatched from death by Dr. Kenney and his excellent staff. I am one hundred percent behind this hospital for the community, and I am passing the plate for you to show your support."

That evening, several thousand dollars was collected as evidence that the community supported the hospital.

The press also questioned John about his version of events, and asked for information on the progress of the transaction. When, the reporters from the *New Jersey Herald* wanted to know, would the contract be finalized?

"Your guess is as good as mine, gentlemen. But I have been grossly misrepresented by some opponents as a Shylock, have been accused of trying to gouge the community of their last dime, and have even been charged with placing a valuation on the property that does not exist. My offer is fair and reasonable, and both committees know that."

"How long are you willing to let this go on?" one reporter asked.

"If I read the spirit and sentiment of this community right, this discord will not continue very much longer, for already there are murmurings and rumblings in high places as well as low, and this shows me that the people have nearly lost their restraint, and may demand action. It is quite evident that the popular sentiment in this section is for the hospital project and the 'voice of the people is the voice of God.'"

Through it all, John kept pressing the committees for answers. In return, one committee member accused him of "driving us too hard." John took this as a compliment. He had been driving hard all of his life. His motto in business had been, "Drive your business; do not let your business drive you." To his way of thinking, the committees, by taking so much time to accomplish the objective, were impugning the judgment of the entire community, which had told them to purchase the hospital. Certainly that outcome would never happen if the current confusion were to continue. But the confusion did continue, and John moved resignedly from one obstacle to the next.

As hard as it was for John to accept that everything was unfolding the way it was, watching the desired outcome recede further and further away from closure was even more painful. With the calendar already on the verge of Thanksgiving and no substantial business to be done during the holidays, he didn't see how the hospital could financially exist much longer.

He remembered how Booker T. Washington had looked when the "game was lost." Would that be his fate too? If the game were truly lost, that meant there was nothing he could do. He would just have to accept whatever God had in store for him, and wait.

But time was not on John's side, and soon he would have to make a decision that no one in his family would like, least of all John.

Reopening the Wounds

The bank had confirmed John's worst fears. His account was scraping bottom. The mortgage was due, the children's tuition was late, and the hospital needed to order more supplies. John had exhausted his options. Whatever he did next would not be easy.

When he had first built the hospital, he had wanted it to be a legacy for his wife and children. He had hoped that it would afford them a comfortable living, unencumbered, and that if something happened to him, the money would both support his family and keep the hospital solvent. To ensure this, he had taken out a one hundred thousand dollar life insurance policy on his life, with his wife as beneficiary. Later, to protect his family even further, he secured another hundred thousand dollar policy with a different company. When times were good, he applied for yet another policy, but at that point, the insurance company balked. It was unusual for an insurance company to put even a hundred thousand dollars on any colored man's life, John was told, and never two hundred thousand.

Later, when John successfully obtained another policy, he was informed confidentially that the president of the company had said, "Dr. Kenney is a white man with a colored skin." Another official of the company revealed that they had investigated John from his beginning up to the present time, and as a result, they were granting him the largest amount that the company individually granted on the life of any person.

For sums larger than that, they called on other companies to share the risk. Encouraged, John had continued to pile on policies until he had in excess of a half-million dollars on his life. But now, where had all of that money gone? It had evaporated in the effort to survive the Depression, and to establish and hold on to the hospital for his people.

One of the saddest days of his life was upon him. He dreaded having to make his next decision, but he was left with no choice. He called his sons into his office and asked them to sit down. They could tell from his demeanor that something serious was about to happen.

"Boys, we need to have a serious discussion," John began, his voice cracking at the end of the sentence. His hands were trembling, and he tried to compose himself before continuing. "I know we are working very hard as a family to keep this hospital open. I want to thank each of you for doing your part. You have helped to save money that otherwise we would have had to pay to outside labor. The problem is – we are still not making ends meet. We are barely getting by, even with me putting whatever I can of my own money into the hospital. The end result is..."

"That we have to sell the hospital?" Howard interrupted before John could get the words out.

"No, son, the end result is that I can only afford to send Jack to college next year."

None of the boys moved or made a sound. They simply sat there, looking at John incredulously. Finally, Jack got up and walked over to his father's desk. Howard and Oscar stared with questioning eyes, knowing how important their education was to their father.

"It's not possible to sell the hospital privately in this depressed economy," John said hurriedly, "and I wouldn't do it anyway, not as long as there's a chance to make it a community hospital. I...we have worked too long and too hard to give up that goal now. Our hospital has saved so many lives and eased the suffering of so many others. We have to remember that our motive is to uplift our race in whatever way we can, and we are doing that. What would happen to the people in this ward if our hospital closed?"

"Dad!" Jack exploded - his face red and contorted with fury, "what will happen to us?"

John got up from his desk and faced his boys. "I am not saying that you won't all be able to finish college at some point. I just cannot afford to send two of you at once. I only have enough money saved for one college tuition next year. Perhaps things will be better next year and Howard can go too."

Seeing his father's pain, Jack relented. "I'll stay out next year and let Howard go," he offered, his hands shaking at the idea. John thought he saw a tear slide down his son's cheek, but Jack turned his head away before John could be sure.

A palpable feeling of disappointment turned the atmosphere oppressive. John felt the shroud of failure dropping over him, a garment that had become all too familiar in the last few months. To disguise it, he feigned a different emotion.

"Jack!" he said, forcing anger into his tone, "you will not miss college next year. You have already completed a year. Staying out would serve no purpose except to put you behind. You will go back to Bates College, and Oscar and Howard will follow you when I can arrange it."

"That's just great," Howard added with disgust and sarcasm. "It would have to be me."

"But, Dad..." Jack pleaded; now ready to make the case for his brother.

"No *buts,* son. There are times when a parent has to make unpopular decisions. You don't understand the difficult choices that we have to make. All sacrifices are not made on the field of battle, you know. This is very difficult for me and for your mother, and it is not the way we want things to be. But, it just can't be helped."

"I think it *can* be helped," Jack shot back, demonstrating an attitude of defiance that his father had never seen before. "You just won't change your mind. If Howard can't go, I'm not going either."

John shook his finger in Jack's face and ordered, "Not another word! What I've said is final. If you don't go back next year, you won't go at all – EVER."

Jack stormed out of the room, and Oscar and Howard followed. John couldn't remember ever feeling so alienated. He decided not to dwell on this tragedy any longer; he had to focus on how he was going to survive, and where he could get his hands on some money.

For some time now, John had put an average of three hundred and fifty dollars every month into the hospital, at the same time drawing no salary for his work there. He saw no way to stop now. He knew that this practice created the very conditions that would keep his sons out of college, but sometimes it was necessary to make personal sacrifices for the good of the community, for the good of the race. Right or wrong, he had dedicated himself to his work. He had to see it through. Giving up now would be tantamount to failure. His sons would survive. They were young. They had other options. But the hospital, his goals, his very dreams – without him, all would be lost.

John sat in his darkened library with the door closed and the shades drawn, pondering his situation. His mood was somber. He leaned back in his chair, closing his eyes. He had learned to sacrifice early in life, and he had benefited in the long run. His family might not respect his decision now, but he trusted they would later on. And if they didn't, well, that was the price he would have to pay.

Every day, the heavy atmosphere at home reminded John of his sons' disappointment, even resentment. During hospital rounds one evening, he met staff physicians Dr. Eagleton and Dr. Sprague on the floor. Both doctors were members of the Board of Directors of the hospital, and suddenly John found himself confiding his financial plight, and asking them for assistance.

"We all know that you have been personally making up the deficits of the hospital, Dr. Kenney," Eagleton said. "I noted on the last report that you have kept up every payment due to the Building and Loan Association. That's truly remarkable."

"I've maintained that record for eight years," John said, "and I want our credit to remain unimpaired. The only way to ensure that is for me to accept the responsibility."

"Let me share this with you, John. Some of your opposition comes from those who think the hospital is a 'hot potato' and you are trying to drop it on the community. We on the Board know that's not the case but, for many, the perception still exists."

"Then I'll have to prove that is not the case. Thanks for the advice."

Armed with this new information, John had the hospital accountant prepare updated financial reports to stem the tide of speculation. Despite budgetary verification that the entire hospital was being run for the paltry sum of two hundred twenty-four dollars a month, John's critics were not satisfied.

Now, after thirty-three years of successful practice, John found himself having to run out in answer to a call in the middle of the night, lugging his bag to some fourth or fifth floor apartment for as little as two or three dollars. Yet, he could not afford to spurn even that small payment. He had informed the public that he would continue to ensure the financial solvency of the hospital with his own money until the community could take it over. He didn't know how he was going to do that, but he vowed to do what was necessary to keep his promise. He was not about to let his life's work slip away on a technicality – that Negroes of the community could not come together in unity to do something for themselves.

Desperate for some way to convince others of what was at stake; John decided to publish a newsletter to speak on the community hospital issue. The publication was widely distributed and generated much heated discussion.

Kenney Memorial Hospital Newsletter

My fellow citizen, the Community Hospital is a self-help project. For all too long, we as a race have been willing, with outstretched arms, palms upward, to cry, "Give me, give me." The time has come when the only "give me" that is respectful is opportunity, and not in a suppliant manner, but in the spirit of a demand.

*I recently read an article in **Crisis Magazine** by Henry L. Mencken, who said that we consider ourselves romantics in believing that we have certain inalienable rights, both political and* *social, and that when we are deprived of them, we can get them back – by making an uproar. He reminds us that our rights under the Constitution, the Bill of Rights, the Thirteenth, Fourteenth and Fifteenth Amendments are worth nothing more or less than what the courts and legislatures from time to time make them. That means the consensus of opinion – not enlightened opinion, but general opinion, mass opinion, and mob opinion. After depicting that gloomy but true outlook, he says that much can be done about it; but it will take a long while. "If the Negro floats with the prevailing tide, such rights as he has now will follow those he has already lost, and he will end up with none at all. But if he throws himself wholeheartedly into the battle for the recovery of liberties in general, then he will be in a good place, sooner or later, to get back those rights he craves."*

The only rights we have are the rights granted by public opinion, and we know all too well the opinion is against us. Abstract demands mean nothing. We have been making them since 1865. They have gotten us nowhere. It is time to stop and make concrete demands, with capital, education, refinement, and good homes and living conditions for ourselves and our children. We need good associates, land, and, by no means least, proper cultivation of the good will of those in a position to grant our demands. Peremptory demands mean nothing unless backed up by the power from behind to enforce demands. An up-to-date, modern, well-run, and equipped community hospital would be the first and the most important step in our hospital demands, and the overwhelming support of the community will attest to this.

Another date was set for a meeting on the hospital issue. It, too, came and went without a resolution because some on the committee wanted to study the finances again. This postponement pushed John into a major depression and drove him, in desperation, to re-examine his intentions.

He had never intended to build a private hospital in Newark, but the lack of support from his colleagues and the community compelled him to take that route, rather than have no hospital at all. Now, with an NMA meeting on his schedule, he could not keep his mind from retracing old territory, questioning why the race didn't come together to offer financial support for a project so obviously needed by a community with inadequate health care and limited access to white facilities. To him, the decision was one of life or death for many in the community, and he found the willingness to turn away from this medical need perplexing, and even suicidal.

Of course, he told himself, he understood that the road traveled by the Negro physician was a rugged one. Chief among the Negro doctor's greatest handicaps had always been the prejudice of his own people. The near impossibility of convincing these people that colored physicians were capable and trustworthy only limited the care available. Where did this doubt and mistrust come from? How could it be overcome?

John was glad to be going to the NMA meeting in Nashville. He had never missed a meeting, and hoped he never would. Being around his colleagues on the editorial board of the *Journal* always gave him a fresh perspective and renewed energy. These men were physicians but, to a man, they offered varied opinions on a vast majority of influential issues and topics. Maybe they could help him understand the problem with the race.

*　　*　　*

The meeting was held again at Meharry Medical College, as it had been the first year that John became a member. When he walked into the executive meeting of the editorial board, he was buoyed by the sight of his old friends, Dr. C. V. Roman, Dr. Ulysses Grant Dailey, and Dr. A. W. Dumas, who welcomed him warmly.

"John, my friend, it's good to see you. How have you been?" Roman asked, giving John a bear hug before the start of the session.

"I'm doing well, under the circumstances," John said, smiling and returning the hug of a colleague whose philosophical insight and perceptive views he had always respected. "And how have you been?"

"I too am fine. I heard about your efforts to try to establish a community hospital. You have my admiration for that effort. I know the difficulty of dealing with our people," Roman said, sensing John's frustration.

At that moment the door opened and the current president of the NMA, a Dr. M. O. Bousfield, entered the room. "Welcome, gentlemen!" he said with sincerity. "Welcome to the fortieth annual session of the NMA. I'm going around and greeting all of the different committees, and I thank you for coming a day early to get your work done. Have a seat, everyone, and let's catch up on how you are all doing."

The men took their seats and had a roundtable discussion of the events that had transpired in their lives since the last meeting. Most of the topics centered around race as a mitigating factor: current civil rights legislation and proposed anti-lynching propositions, Negroes' lack of participation in electoral politics, and the shifting attitudes about race and class in America. The underlying theme was always the lack of racial cohesiveness and unity. What a perfect context for John to voice his frustrations.

"I am sorry to have to bring this up," he began, "but I was trying to fathom why our people have so much trouble supporting each other. Why can't we stick together when matters as important as our survival are staring us in the face?"

"I guess we are still in shock from being stolen from the mother country," teased Dailey. "No, seriously, we simply don't trust each other, and that is a tragedy."

"Perhaps that's true," John said. "But when I was a student at Hampton, I read a paper written in 1712 by William Lynch, a slaveholder, detailing his advice to other slaveholders. He preached that he had a method to keep the slaves under control for generations to come. He told them that they needed to give the Negro a 'common enemy' that would instill in them a slave mentality."

"What does that mean?" Bousfield asked, his face darkening. "What kind of common enemy?"

"The enemy of insecurity and fear. Lynch said that distrust was stronger than trust, and that envy was stronger than adulation, respect, or admiration. The point is, if you instill certain weaknesses in people, like those I just mentioned, the people will perpetuate the weaknesses themselves, eventually accepting them as a natural condition of their own existence. In other words, they become who they think they are."

The room grew quiet. John looked down at his hands and sighed.

"Go on, John," Dumas urged. "This is extremely interesting."

"Well, Lynch proposed using the differences among the slaves to cause division within the group, to pit them against each other. Pit the young against the old, the light-skinned against the dark-skinned, the straight hair against the kinky hair, the light eyes against the dark eyes, the men against the women, ad infinitum. That will go on and on until we're psychologically enslaved by our own thinking. 'I think therefore I am.' I call it 'Negro-auto-phobia,' fear or hatred of ourselves through auto-suggestion."

"That's brilliantly demonic," Dumas muttered. "We do the work for the white man without even realizing it."

"Lynch assured his listeners that if they practiced this 'mental method,' they could control our race into perpetuity. And lo and behold, here we are over two hundred years later, seeing how this method is still working. The more the race focuses on the negative beliefs about ourselves, the more we ensure negative outcomes. Negative outcomes perpetuate negative beliefs, and the blasphemy continues until the race is more alienated than ever. It's guaranteed. That mindset was responsible for my failure to get any help with the hospital initially, and it may be why turning it into a community hospital now will be more of a challenge than I realized."

"You know, given Lynch's treacherous technique, it's no wonder we have lost sight of our rich ancestry," Roman said. "We are descendants of royalty, you know."

"Yes, but *we* have forgotten that. In the face of our negative beliefs, we have no idea who we are. The question is, in our present state, are we an asset or a liability to this nation?" John asked the group.

"Can we turn the tide of self-flagellation and get the Negro to appreciate the positive accomplishments the race has contributed, or are we doomed to believe the lies we have told ourselves about ourselves?"

"Good question. As a race of people, are we progressing, or have we reached the stagnation point?" Dumas questioned. "The answers determine our right to be here – and our fitness to survive."

John leaned back in his chair, a dark frown on his face. "The late Booker T. Washington pointed out that we are the only people to have come to America against our will. Other races have flocked here in overwhelming numbers, and the great congress of the United States was forced to spend more time, thought, and money enacting laws to keep them out. People are deluded who can't appreciate what captivity did to our psyche and our soul, but now it is up to us to create our own destiny."

"Another one of the tragic delusions of our time is the white man's insistence that he knows the black man, and from that false premise, he is reaching conclusions inimical to us, to himself, and to our country. This is the true dementia in America," Roman pointed out.

All heads nodded in affirmation, and the mood was somber. Disillusionment and frustration intermingled in a cloud of hopelessness that hung in the air, permeating the atmosphere and creating a heavy silence.

After several minutes of quiet, John said, "Our great country was built on the democratic principles of freedom and independence. We have to inspire our people to these ideals, and we have to do it together, no matter what the obstacles are. It's time that the slave mentality is replaced with a 'can do' mentality. Otherwise, hundreds of years from now our people will still be blaming others for their lack of ability to get ahead and succeed. That would be a generational travesty."

"It already is," Roman added. "The problem is manifested by the fact that we don't even know our own ancestry. The graves of our heroes are unmarked, and the glory of our builders is unsung."

"Preach on," John urged, admiring his friend's wise words.

"To put it philosophically, we must tabulate the heroes of our guild and honor the exceptional men of our race. We may safely praise ability, honor age, and memorialize the dead without wounding our own egotism and minimizing our own importance."

"We're back to that Negro-auto-phobia disease again," John said with emphasis, "and with no cure in sight."

"Cure or not, our achievement rests as much in pride of ancestry as in hope of prosperity." Roman was energized now, passionate about this discussion and adamant in his opinion of how to solve the race problem. "Self-sufficiency is the road to respectability, and this will disarm prejudice. Races and people are never *lifted* up. They must *rise* up or remain down. This is what we must learn."

"Shakespeare said it best," John added, his voice tinged with sarcasm. "'The fault, dear Brutus, is not in our stars but in ourselves that we are dogs and underlings.' If we can admit our own culpability in the mess, then we can do something about it."

"You know," Roman said, leaning back in his chair, "for more than two score years I have been on the firing line of racial advance, and those of us who are so inclined have to do the work. Medicine is not only a noble art, but also an ancient brotherhood, and membership in such a fraternity is a rare privilege; a life sincerely and intelligently devoted to its principles is a passport to renown. Our group has led the way in progress, and we must continue to embrace that obligation. Agreed?"

"Agreed," Bousfield said. "For some unexplained reason, our group has been predestined to pick up the gauntlet and lead the way in medicine, and we're certainly trying to do that! Perhaps our efforts will inspire the rest."

"That's the only thing saving me right now," John said. "I feel that this is our God-given duty."

In spite of finding common ground among his colleagues, John drove home after the meeting still troubled by his earlier thoughts. The unusually gloomy mood among the members had not helped him shake his depression. Racial unity seemed an unconquerable goal; especially since the Negro race seemed so apathetic to the importance of its own history. Apathy begat callosity, which birthed cynicism and pessimism, the true precursors to the neutralization of racial pride.

How could a people move forward without understanding and appreciating the struggles, sacrifices and hardships suffered by those in the past?

John pulled his car up in front of his home and turned off the engine. He sat in the darkness and stared out of the window seeing nothing. The cold crept in, causing an involuntary shiver throughout his entire body. He gripped the steering wheel tighter and tighter until he felt pain, hoping it would distract him from his thoughts. He felt squeezed; caught in a vise between his dreams for the future and the dreadful reality of the present. Had his life's work meant anything at all? Or was he a pawn in one of life's inconstant and infinite cycles, a fool whose folly was a belief in the innate goodness of mankind?

John got out of the car quickly, more occupied with pondering the question than discovering the answer. Right now, that was too much to bear.

Heroes of Our Guild

John opened the front door and was surprised to see Freida and the ladies of the women's auxiliary finishing their monthly meeting in the living room. He quickly forced a smile and managed to seem happy to greet them. He owed a lot to this group who worked tirelessly on the hospital's behalf. In his opinion, these women had been an enormous asset to the hospital in good times and bad. Through outreach programs, bake sales, and hands-on teaching, they had become the social service workers who offered assistance in basic living to the less fortunate. At least this was one group that stuck together and accomplished something.

Freida turned to him with a smile. "We were just talking about all of the people we know back home, dear. Come and meet Mrs. Anderson. She and her husband have just moved here from Boston."

Mrs. Anderson reminded John of some of the society mavens he had seen at his wedding. She was very prim and proper, with her veiled hat and her white gloves in hand. John extended his hand and shook hers firmly, a gesture that she returned.

"It is a pleasure to meet you, Dr. Kenney. I have heard of your work here in Newark, and I knew that I wanted to be a part of it. My husband and I are educators. I teach History and he teaches English at the high school, and we want to help in the community as much as we can." Her eyes met his squarely, and John sensed her sincerity.

Surprised, John managed a sheepish smile. Looks really could be deceiving, he admitted to himself. He certainly hadn't expected an offer of assistance from newcomers to the neighborhood, but he welcomed the offer.

"How refreshing, Mrs. Anderson. I appreciate your help. I just returned from our medical journal's board meeting and we were just talking about the need for our people to live and breathe our history. This is where racial pride is born; in the knowledge of who we are. You are an example of exactly what we need – citizens willing to help and teach each other."

"If you don't mind, Doctor, I would like for you to come to the school and talk to my history class during career week. You can speak about how you accomplished all that you have. It's very inspirational to know that you are the son of ex-slaves but yet managed to build and run your own hospital. They need to know your story. We will have another other guest that day who will also speak of his accomplishments."

"I'll be happy to come. What grade level are your students Mrs. Anderson?"

"They are twelfth graders."

"Excellent. Please call the hospital to give my secretary a few dates, and we'll find a mutually convenient time." Here was a chance for John to motivate students and provide them with a perspective on their history, just as his friend Roman had argued.

The next day, Mildred came into the clinic to tell John that Mrs. Anderson was on the phone with several possible dates for his visit. They settled on one, and that very day John prepared a paper on his life and work. He was looking forward to sharing his ideas with those who were the future of the race. Given the depressive and troubling times, hope was in short supply and John knew that without hope the race was doomed. His job would be to let these students know that their forefathers lived and died in the hope that their example would inspire and encourage each successive generation to greater and greater heights. He also knew that his work was cut out for him.

Upon arriving at the Harriet Tubman School a few weeks later, John was escorted to Mrs. Anderson's classroom. He looked around and was surprised to see about fifty students, the girls on one side and the boys on the other. In an instant he was reminded of the little freckle-faced boy he had been, standing in the dusty church yard looking up at his new teachers, Mr. and Mrs. Jackson. He remembered how he had been very impressed but also somewhat uneasy in the presence of such educated Negroes. He smiled to put the students at ease, to let them know he was one of them.

The students were dressed in all manner of ill-fitting clothes, just as John had been when he attended school in rural Virginia. Although clean, the clothes were obviously well-worn hand-me-downs. Two students each shared a tattered book, and to accommodate such a large number, some students at the back of the class had wooden crates instead of desks.

John also noticed two other men, one black and one white, sitting in front of the class facing the students. Mrs. Anderson motioned for John to take a seat by the other guests. She turned to the students to make the introductions.

"Class, please welcome our speakers for the day. We have Mr. William Brown, an attorney for the NAACP, Dr. John Kenney, Director of the Kenney Memorial Hospital and...uh... a surprise guest, Mr. Mitchell Fergus, our current school superintendent."

The students clapped politely and Mrs. Anderson asked Mr. Brown to begin. Brown spoke of his humble upbringing in rural Georgia and his struggle to work his way through an integrated college and law school in the North. As he explained the involvement of his organization in the current "right to work' campaign aimed at African-Americans, he seemed to weigh his words carefully. He explained terms like "mass demonstrations", "labor movements" and "political allegiances" with caution; fully aware of his entire audience. Brown also took note of the expressions on Fergus' face during Brown's talk. His facial expressions changed from pleasant, to an obvious pout, to highly indignant as Brown's story unfolded. By the end of the speech,

Fergus was red in the face and he visibly shook his head in disagreement at the opinions Mr. Brown was presenting.

Before Fergus began the story of his rise to school superintendent, he prefaced his remarks with assurances that all Americans can achieve whatever they want to in the United States because this country was "America the Beautiful", and the Constitution entitled all of its citizens to certain inalienable rights, race not withstanding.

John clenched his teeth at this remark, and only Mrs. Anderson noticed the tightening of his jaw.

Fergus went on to stress that it was just a matter of hard work and perseverance for anyone, white or Negro, or even Indian to achieve success. Fergus then extolled his upbringing in Washington, D.C., his father having been a representative in the federal government and his mother a teacher in a private Catholic school. His life of privilege was interesting, if only for the obvious disparities it represented to this audience who could not envision the existence Fergus seemed to take for granted, or understand its relevance to their own lives. As he concluded his remarks, Mrs. Anderson indicated to John that it was his turn.

"This *is* a great country that we live in class, but sometimes we have to fight for those inalienable rights that the constitution granted to all of us. Let me explain."

Mr. Brown nodded affirmatively at John and smiled; clearly impressed with John's boldness.

Fergus crossed his arms over his chest and stared boldly in John's direction. John's determination to make an impression on his young charges helped him dismiss the image of the brooding superintendent from his mind. He stood and faced the students, turning his back to Fergus; the gesture did not go unnoticed. Fergus practically fumed.

All eyes fastened on John as he told his story. Their eyes widened as he related the poverty of his childhood and the death threats he faced at the hands of the KKK as a young man. Many of the students had received medical care at the Kenney Memorial Hospital, but had no idea of the struggle that John had encountered trying to get it built. Their undivided attention let John know that he was making an impression, and when he finished he asked if there were any questions. At least half of the students waved their hands in the air to get John's attention. He called on a young man in the first row.

"What do you think is the most important thing for us to know Dr. Kenney?

"Negro history," John said without hesitation. "We have to know the greatness that we come from before we can know the greatness that we are. We need to demand such study in our system of education. Unfortunately, this history is not generally taught in the public systems. In the Northern community, where schools are often a mix of Negroes and whites, there is seldom any reference to it. And unless some special means are taken to acquaint the colored boy and girl with the history of our race, they get no knowledge of it and grow up with no appreciation of it. So we must teach it to ourselves."

Fergus interrupted John before he could finish his answer. "The history books that the school board approves of have an excellent version of how this great country came to be and the principles which it was founded upon. George Washington, Abraham Lincoln and all of our founding fathers are represented there and that history goes back to 1776! What more do you need to know? "

John gazed intently at the faces turned toward him and, with unexpected emotions rising from his core, reiterated more strongly, "We have to know and teach our history! We cannot expect you to have the proper racial perspective or the proper respect for Negro achievement unless we pay homage to our past. We have to thank a leader like G. Carter Woodson, the 'Father of Black History,' for insisting that we know this subject. From this knowledge comes our pride in our culture. Nothing is more important." The students applauded tentatively; not sure how to react to the obvious conflict between the two guests.

Fergus started to speak, but then remained silent, staring straight ahead. John had had enough. He was frustrated with the hospital situation. He was tired of having to fight for rights which should have been granted to him at birth. He was an American, a man just like Fergus, and given all that John had overcome to survive he knew he was a stronger man. His mind flashed back to Tuskegee and the meeting with the white citizens' council. He had something to say and he would not be stopped.

Another hand went up. "What did you learn from your parents who were slaves?"

"I learned that I was supposed to *justify my existence.* I was expected to do something for someone other than myself and to make a contribution to society. What a concept; right Mr. Fergus?"

"Just let me say something…," interrupted Fergus jumping up.

"I'm not finished Mr. Fergus…," John shot back. Fergus flopped back into his chair in disbelief. How dare this Negro talk to him in such a manner. John continued.

"And what's just as important class, I learned that I needed to continue to make the kinds of sacrifices that my ancestors made – *to help to ensure the future of the race.*" John paused to let that notion sink in.

"For over two hundred and fifty years after we were brought to this country, the Negro slaves bore America's burdens. Never in history had there been a more patient, long-suffering, faithful, uncomplaining, and easily satisfied group of people than the American slaves. Any doubt of this was dispelled by the Civil War, because, while the subjugating master was at the front fighting to preserve slavery, the subjugated slave was back home praying for 'massa,' tending his flocks, protecting his helpless women and children, and raising the foodstuffs that kept the rebel army fighting! Can you imagine that?"

"The law at that time supported slavery and from what I have been told most everybody was happy to do their part for the country back then," mumbled Fergus in a whispered voice. John did not acknowledge his remark.

"Why would we do that if they wanted to keep us in slavery? Why didn't we just run away?" asked another.

Fergus looked as if he was going to interrupt again but remained silent; his manner more haughty and arrogant than before. He shrugged his shoulders and feigned disinterest but his hands were trembling as John kept speaking.

"It wasn't that simple, son," answered John. "We still had overseers on the plantations. We were still enslaved. In many instances, rebel officers had their body-servant slaves with them on the firing line. And many a heroic act recorded the bravery the slave exhibited when his master's safety or life was imperiled. The history of the world knows no parallel to this kind of devotion and fidelity. If for no other reason than for this pathetic, child-like devotion to duty, the American manumitted Negro and his offspring should be encouraged to attain good citizenship."

"What do you mean when you say that the slave bore America's burdens?" another student asked.

"Think about it. The Negro helped to clear the forests, till the soil, raise nearly all of the cotton, and build many of the railroads. We have gone into the bowels of the earth and brought out the coal, iron, copper, and tin. We have eased the white man's burdens all along the line."

"The women also worked the fields," Mrs. Anderson explained. "And they milked the cows, they did the cooking, washing and nursing, and they took care of the general home. Many of yesterdays - and some of today's - Southern statesmen boast of having been nursed by colored mammies. I guess I am glad that I was born and raised in Massachusetts and not in the South."

"With all due respect, Mrs. Anderson, lest modern Yankees point the finger of scorn at Dixie, remember that slaves were first introduced into the New England colonies."

"What?" several of the students asked in unison. A few giggled at hearing their teacher corrected, and others whispered as they watched her expression.

"And it would be many years before some Americans found the conscience to right the cruel injustices against the Negro; some are still looking." John glanced back at the superintendent.

Fergus stood up abruptly. He could hardly contain his anger. Spittle formed in the corners of his mouth and his arms flailed awkwardly in the air. "I thought this talk was about opportunities and jobs. We are way off the subject. I only came because I heard you people were discussing what kind of work you were cut out for, but all you want to do is reinvent history. I think I'm done here." Fergus grabbed his hat and hurried out the door almost knocking Mrs. Anderson over in his rush to get out. The surprised students began to discuss the rude exit among themselves.

"Forgive him children," Brown urged, more sardonic than serious, "for he knows not what he does!"

Mrs. Anderson blushed and regained her composure. She asked the students for quiet and took the seat vacated by Fergus. "Dr. Kenney's right," she conceded. "More people need to know about this aspect of our history. The knowledge will motivate us to do our part and more." She motioned for John to continue.

"In those times, the Negro was one of the greatest and most dependable assets that America had," John said. "In every war in which he engaged the Negro played his part. Crispus Attacks, a Negro, was the first to spill his blood in the fight to gain American freedom from the yoke of British bondage. Special mention for bravery also must go to the Negro troops in the War of 1812. In the Civil War, they rendered distinguished service on both sides. In the Spanish American War, they won honors for their famous charge up San Juan Hill; and in the great World War from 1914 to 1918, they left their impress upon history."

"You see, students," Mrs. Anderson added, challenging her charges, "there are many ways that you can follow in the footsteps of these great people. What do you think you could do to leave a legacy like this?"

Hands went up all around the room. John was delighted to see and hear such enthusiasm and aspiration among these young people. Perhaps all was not lost.

"Let me say one last thing to you," he added. His tone was quiet, measured, and thoughtful. "You ask what the Negro has contributed to American civilization. The answer is all that we have just talked about. In 1875, four million Negro slaves were emancipated. At that time, we had practically nothing, not even the proverbial forty acres and a mule. By the 1930s, we have amassed businesses, medical schools and colleges, insurance companies, hospitals, churches, beauty parlors, newspapers, and various other enterprises worth millions of dollars; and we helped to build this country!"

"Class," Mrs. Anderson said, "let me add one more thing to Dr. Kenney's excellent talk. We now have various socio-literary and athletic organizations in the Negro community where young people can develop their talents in poetry, music, prose, debating, and other athletic pursuits that help to make you well-rounded men and women. We will learn more about them next week."

"Remember that all of these endeavors make us an invaluable part of the American landscape," John concluded. "All I am asking is that you do your part. You are the future."

The students stood and applauded at John's last remark. He was humbled by the appreciation. He and Brown shook hands.

"Thank you, Dr. Kenney and Mr. Brown for coming to our school and giving us such an enlightening lecture. And thank you for setting such a fine example for our youth to follow."

"You're welcome," responded Brown.

"My pleasure, Mrs. Anderson," John said, reaching for his coat. "I'm sorry your other guest left in a huff, but I wasn't going to let him sugar coat the truth."

"No problem Dr. Kenney," Mrs. Anderson whispered to John. "He wasn't interested in us anyway, just how he could use us."

John found his way out of the school, feeling pleased that the students had responded so well to the discussion. Now if he could have the same effect on his peers his problems would be solved.

John realized that the country's current financial depression had started a leveling process, and on several fronts he could see incipient change and more cooperation. Thanks to the Depression, a new social order was developing. At the same time, the financial plight of Negroes was becoming even more insufferable, because their communities nationwide did not benefit from the few relief programs promised by the federal government. Perhaps that bleak situation would prompt the race into action – there was nowhere to go but up.

Soon after he reached home, John got a call from a man who introduced himself as Dr. James Smith, president of the North Jersey Medical Society. Smith, John remembered, had previously objected to the idea of a hospital for colored people, likening it to segregation.

"I am calling to offer you help with this hospital issue," Smith said. "Some of our colleagues are rethinking the community hospital idea, and we want to write a letter to both committees and encourage them to accept your offer in full. We would like to consider becoming a part of your effort. Things have changed in the past few years that make it necessary for us to find some common ground on which we can all work together and survive. Do you think that will help?"

"Of course it will, and I need all the help I can get."

Did this signal the beginning of the change John had hoped for? Could Negroes work together to stabilize the community and create jobs and revenue? What would it take for the race to come together, to cooperate? If it took the Depression to bring his colleagues together, John decided, then let the Depression continue. With a little help it just might purge his people of self-conceit, racial antipathy, auto-Negro-phobia, petty racial jealousies, and non-cooperation. In these times, the man most admired was the one who held a job, and there was no difference between the low-level toilers and the "white collars." How ironic that the worsening financial climate might create a security crisis that resulted in the community wanting something of its own to ground its future.

As a realist, John had a clear understanding that the old "slave mentality" mindset that Lynch had described in 1712 continued to envelop the psyche of too many of his race. It constituted a veil of ignorance that blurred their vision and blunted their reasoning. It still worked far too well.

Epiphany

John had received word that the committees were close to some kind of agreement, but he refused to think about what kind of offer might be forthcoming. He just hoped he wouldn't have to wait too long to find out what was in store for him. The hospital issue had dragged on way too long, and he was emotionally spent. With the Christmas season in full swing, he felt guilty that the holiday didn't seem to matter this year. He was in his office at the hospital one morning, trying to find the energy to focus on his work, when Mildred startled him by bursting excitedly through the door.

"Dr. Kenney, look what we just received! It's a public endorsement for the community hospital project from the mayor of Newark, Meyer C. Ellenstein!"

"Well, help is coming from some unexpected sources," John replied with a trace of the old enthusiasm he had not felt in some time.

"And this is even better," Mildred added. "This is another endorsement from the president of Beth Israel Hospital, Dr. F. I. Liveright. He says he knows you personally and that the endeavor deserves community support."

"How strange," John muttered. "You know, when I first came to Newark, I was denied permanent privileges there. How ironic to now have their support. That is some progress, I suppose".

In spite of these new supporters, however, no news was forthcoming from either of the two committees. With more and more of his time dedicated to trying to keep the hospital afloat, John was hard pressed to keep thinking positive thoughts as Freida had urged him to. True, the boys' feelings regarding their schooling had calmed, and the family was once again unified at home and getting ready for Christmas, but there was still no resolution in sight. His resolve was being fueled by a burning fire in the pit of his stomach. More than likely it was an ulcer; a sycophant feeding off of John's gastric juices. The pain was almost welcomed; not only because it was a distraction, it was his Red Badge of Courage, an internal symbol of his own tenacity and persistence.

One evening after dinner, to take his mind off his dilemma, John walked over to the hospital to do his rounds. He unconsciously massaged his stomach, a habit he had acquired lately after each meal. Freida had noticed this but she remained quiet not wanting to add to his worries.

John stood before the hospital entrance. He took comfort in seeing the dedication plaque mounted on the front door and paused to polish it a little with his handkerchief. Then he toured the grounds, reminding himself of all that had been accomplished in just a few short years. He smiled to himself as he remembered the two vacant lots and his wife trying to justify their purchase.

Once inside, his thoughts turned to what the hospital's future might be. He stepped out on the fire escape, trying to picture what the new addition might look like once the new Community Hospital was under construction. He could almost hear Freida advising him as he focused his mind on what he wanted to see, picturing the new addition with four operating rooms and a multi-bed convalescence center. He thought of the poor fellow now confined downstairs in a closed room on the ward and pictured a new wing with bright spacious rooms opening to a common area for patients and visitors. A beautiful garden, lush with plants and flowers, would surround a sunny solarium.

He imagined the new laboratory and an up-to-date mortuary with all the equipment every modern hospital should have. In his mind he saw elevators where there were now stairs, elevators that moved between floors, carrying patients on gurneys and allowing doctors to tend to them in transit, eliminating the inconvenience of porters physically carrying people up and down. In the chapel, there would be beautiful stained-glass windows depicting scenes from the Bible. These would be stunning in their reality, giving comfort and solace to those who were grief-stricken or needed to pray. Picturing that chapel, John said a silent prayer over his dream and went back inside.

Bereft of hope after all the factionalism and bickering of the past few months, he wandered into the hospital foyer, where a cross rested on a makeshift altar with a candle on the mantel behind it. A few chairs provided seating, and a tattered Bible on the altar had seen good use.

John slumped down into a chair and picked up the Bible, holding it close. He had always prayed to God to assist him during his life, and he had always laid out his plans and counted on the Lord and his own faith for the right outcome. But that winter day, something strange happened. He closed his eyes and actually saw the hospital with a sign over the front door that read "Community Hospital." He imagined what it would *feel* like to be relieved of the burden of running the hospital by himself, and a new serenity warmed him. As he felt his body relax, he experienced a floating sensation, a strange out-of-body experience. He was physically in the chair, but some part of him, his soul perhaps, hovered overhead, observing the scene. From above, he watched himself open his eyes and set the Bible on his lap. He opened it randomly, turning pages, not even sure why he was reading or what he was seeking. When he looked down, a passage from II Corinthians 9:7 caught his eye:

"Each man should give what he has decided in his heart to give, not reluctantly or under compulsion, for God loves a cheerful giver."

Jolted suddenly back to full consciousness, John almost fell out of the chair. He grabbed the Bible just before it hit the floor, and in that instant his full attention locked on the page. He reread the passage several times. "What in the world does this mean?" he thought. "Surely I have given all that I have to give."

Without warning, Freida's words came back to him, replaying in slow motion in his mind. "The answer is within, John. You just have to be still, and the truth shall be revealed. And you must trust that the answer is right."

His heart beating wildly, John clutched the book tightly against his chest. He was in shock, yet for some reason he was not afraid. A slight breeze brushed across his face, and he turned to see who had entered the foyer. The door was closed tight; he was quite alone in the room. A shiver traveled up his spine, and he closed his eyes once more. Something special was happening, something beyond the realm of his medical training. In his mind's eye, an order came like a flash of light: "GIVE IT TO THEM!" What kind of exhortation was this that had taken over his thoughts? Again the message seemed to flash before his now wide-open eyes: "GIVE IT TO THEM!"

And then it hit him.

John sat in stunned silence, dumbfounded, awestruck. With these feelings came relief, elation, and awe. Of course! *Give it to them.* Give the hospital to the community – as a Christmas present! This revelation, one that John was sure he had divined from above, was wrapped in the spirit of all that he had dedicated his life to – love of and service to his people. All of a sudden he felt weightless, as if the heaviness of the past months was floating off of him. He felt free and purposeful, a condition he needed to thrive.

John's body came alive as if he had received an injection of adrenaline. He could feel the blood coursing through his veins and every sinew strained to contain the power with which this command had instantly infused his brain and body. He was alert and electrified with the significance of this idea.

Such a gift would end the bickering and division within the community. It would allow the public to begin immediately focusing on funding the campaign instead of arguing about how to finance the sale. This would be an olive branch under which all factions could unite and go forth to give the people the hospital they sorely needed. This gift would show his people that sometimes great personal sacrifices had to be made in order to benefit the race as a whole.

John walked home as quickly as possible through the falling snow. The night was more beautiful than any he could ever remember. The bright light of a full moon made the snow glisten like crystal, and the stars twinkling in the sky seemed to wink at John as if sharing the good news. The crisp, clean air opened his nostrils, and he breathed deeply, feeling happy, peaceful, and incredibly alive. His excitement was almost palpable.

The minute he opened the door to the house, he called to his family.

"Everyone, come here quickly." Impassioned, he bellowed, "I have had an epiphany!"

The whole family rushed into the room, surprised and happy to see such energy from their father, whose mood had been far different for the past few months.

"A what?" Libby asked, wrapping her arms tightly around her father's waist.

"An epiphany, honey – a revelation! I have found the answer to this hospital problem." His heart was racing, and he could hardly contain himself.

Freida and the children gathered around him with expectant, hopeful eyes, waiting for the good news. "Tell us, Daddy," Oscar said with wide, expectant eyes.

"I was praying in the hospital alcove, and I took your advice, Freida. I listened with my heart and asked God to help me. I asked Him to show me the way. The answer came to me in a flash. I actually saw and heard the words at the same time. Something said, 'GIVE IT TO THEM!' I didn't know what that meant at first, but then I heard it again. Suddenly a realization came over me. I have been commanded to give the hospital to the community – as a Christmas gift."

"What?" the children asked in unison, aghast at the suggestion. Their expressions ranged from horrified to disbelieving to skeptical – and, in Jack's eyes, to downright fear.

"John," Freida said, "what are you saying? This is your life's work, our fortune, our legacy for our children and our children's children.

I don't understand. What are you saying?" Freida put her hands on her hips and pursed her lips, a sign that John knew often meant trouble.

"Father," Jack said in a tone that conveyed his seriousness, "you really need to think about what you are saying. First, you tell us that you can afford to send only one of us to college. Then you tell us that the hospital is our legacy for the future. And now you're telling us that you are giving our legacy away? How are we supposed to take that?"

"Yes," Oscar piped up, displaying anger uncharacteristic of him, "what about us?"

"We have all worked so hard to keep the hospital open," Howard said, his expression incredulous. "You were supposed to get your money out and let the community run it. Now we will have nothing. I don't understand."

"Poor as church mice, that's us," Libby added without emotion, seemingly unaware of the extent of what her father was saying.

Freida sat down in a chair and rocked back and forth. Humming to herself, she said nothing more about the announcement her husband had just made. She seemed lost in her own thoughts.

"Listen," John urged, "if we give the hospital to the community, it will be with the stipulation that I remain as medical director and be given a salary. In the long run, I may not make as much, but at least the hospital will remain open."

"No, I don't like it," Howard said with a frown. "It doesn't make sense. It's like going backward instead of forward." He crossed his arms disapprovingly and gave his father a defiant stare.

"I expect that no matter what my decision is, you children will live your lives as I have and justify your existence no matter what road you choose," John replied. "God gave you the gift, and you can become anything you believe you can. We will just have to continue to work hard at whatever we do, and we will survive as we always have. This is an opportunity to be an example for our people, to stand up for love and generosity and selflessness. We are a family of principle, not selfishness. Our first duty is to be of service, as I have preached to you over the years.

We can make a huge difference in our community by giving them an institution that will sustain life. What greater service could we offer?"

Rising suddenly from her chair, Freida interrupted. "Children, please go into the library; I need to talk to your father." She stood up and walked over to John with an agonized look on her face. She was almost in tears.

Howard took Libby's hand and joined his siblings in the library. Freida pulled John into the kitchen and shut the door.

"John, I can't go along with this suggestion. This is almost too much for me to comprehend or bear. After all that we have been through, all that we have sacrificed. We have been of great service to this community and continue to be so, but there has to be another way that doesn't threaten our children's future." Freida's eyes brimmed with tears.

"There isn't another way," John said, trying to control his mounting frustration. "The committees can go on bickering forever, and we can go on struggling to keep this hospital open like we are doing now, but very soon the hospital will have to be closed. There is no more money. Or we can do something really magnanimous, something that will not only resolve the problem, but will be a gesture of good will and solidarity for our people. This will show them that we can come up with new ways to solve problems, solutions that can benefit everyone. We have to change how we think and act. We cannot accept the status quo any longer, and somebody has to set an example. I accept the responsibility to be that somebody, and I am asking my family for their support."

"I'm sorry, John, I can't do this." Freida turned and left the room.

John, now furious at his family's unanticipated reaction, grabbed his hat and coat and headed for his car, slamming the front door behind him. In minutes he was driving down High Street, venting his anger. How could they behave like that? He was the head of the family, and without him there would be no Kenney Memorial Hospital. He had worked tirelessly for years to do something meaningful for his race, and this was his grandest gesture. How dare his family be so selfish!

In the house, Freida stood at the window, staring out at the dark sky and listening to the sound of the quickly departing car. After a time, she went into the library and joined her children, who were sitting together in silence. Her demeanor told them that something had changed, and they looked at her with curiosity and expectation.

Freida raised her chin slightly and, speaking softly, said, "Children, we need to talk. I want to know what you're thinking."

"I think that Father has lost his perspective," Jack said, both hands knotted into fists. "He expects us to follow in his footsteps, and then he takes the path away. What are we supposed to do?" he demanded, his voice rising in frustration.

"Calm down, Jack, or I'll have to ask you to leave the room. Howard, what do you think?" Freida asked.

"I agree with Jack, Mother," Howard said, sounding more hurt than angry. "We work hard to do what he asks, and he never says thanks. It seems like we are just expected to do it. Some times a little gratitude would be nice. Now he has gone too far!"

"Oscar?"

"I'm for finding a way to keep the hospital open. I don't think we should give away our hospital," Oscar said, siding with his brothers. "I don't understand what he's thinking!" he added with a trace of stubbornness.

"Libby, what about you, how do you feel?"

"I'm afraid of being poor, and that's what we'll be if he goes through with this," she answered with a fearful look. "Where did Daddy go anyway?"

"He went out, Libby," Freida said, somewhat worried by the late hour. "Children, I have given this idea some serious thought and soul-searching. Your father and I have been through a lot to get us to where we are today, and for both of us the focus has been on making a difference for our people. I'm not sure why things are happening like they are, but there is a reason for everything. My initial reaction was for selfish reasons, and I regret that. Our goal as a family has always been service; perhaps this is the ultimate gesture to represent that. I'm not sure I can do this, but let's all rethink it."

Freida's children looked at her in disbelief. They all began to speak at once.

"What are we going to do?" Jack asked in alarm.

"You've got to change his mind, Mother!" Howard insisted, slamming his fist into his hand.

"I'm not going to be a part of this," Oscar said, getting up to leave.

"Mother, I …," Libby began.

Freida held up her hand to ask for quiet. "Hush, everybody. Sit down and listen to me." They sat down and looked sullenly at their mother. Freida closed her eyes for a moment, appearing to be in prayer. When she had their undivided attention, she looked up and spoke in a soft voice.

"I was remembering the time when I first went to Tuskegee to teach," she said. "Dr. Washington was thanking me for coming all the way from Massachusetts to teach at his little rural school. We had a great conversation about why he started Tuskegee Institute and what his purpose was. I remember he said, 'Everyone's life is measured by the power that the individual has to make the world better – that is all life is.' I think, children, that this is a time that *we* could make the world better. Now, I don't want to discuss the issue anymore tonight. It requires the serious consideration of calmer minds."

Freida stood up to leave. "Everybody sleep on it and see how you feel in the morning. We'll talk at breakfast. Now go to bed. I'm sure your father will be home soon." No one spoke, and Freida left her children sitting in the room in stunned silence.

*　*　*

John drove for hours through the streets of Newark. Gradually, he began to calm down. As he thought back on his life, his family, and his blessings, his mood softened. He remembered with regret all of the health problems Freida had weathered, mostly alone and without complaint, to allow him to continue his work. He thought about what a wonderful wife and mother she was, and how lucky he was to have married her. And his children, they had done everything that had been asked of them to support their father, including wanting to be doctors and carry on the tradition. He had asked a lot of his family, and they had given their all to him. Suddenly he was ashamed at having asked so much for his cause. Just who was being selfish? Whose ego was calling the tune here? Feeling chastised and chagrined, he turned the car around and headed home.

As John entered his house, the quiet enveloped him. His family was probably in bed, he realized, and he peeked into each room to confirm that everyone was still there. He undressed and got in bed beside Freida, cuddling up beside her warmth. In a few moments he was asleep.

He awoke much later than usual, and the aroma of breakfast coming from the kitchen beckoned him. Downstairs, he found his family sitting at the kitchen table, eating. Not knowing what to expect, he stopped at the door.

"Good morning…," he said hesitantly, looking at each one.

"Good morning, dear," Freida replied, her tone giving nothing away. "Have a seat and I'll fix your eggs." She got up and put some butter into a frying pan. John took his usual seat at the head of the table, and Freida poured his coffee.

"Morning, Dad," the children said in unison.

Still unsure what everyone's mood was, John began, "I did some thinking when I was out last night and I just want to say…"

"John," said Freida, "please let us say something. We had a meeting this morning while you were asleep, and we have come to some conclusions. We would like to share them with you."

John took a sip of his coffee and cautiously waited for her to continue.

"We thought about your proposition of giving the hospital to the community and… after careful thought and consideration, we have decided to join you in offering that gift."

John couldn't believe his ears. His heart filled with pride. "I…" John opened his mouth to speak but no words came out. His family looked at him and then at each other and began to laugh. It was the first time in their lives that they could remember John being speechless.

"We're with you, Dad," Jack said. Howard and Oscar nodded their approval, and Libby got up from her chair to give her father a big hug and a kiss.

"We just feel that this is something the Kenneys should do," Freida said with a warm smile.

John's gaze moved from one to another, his heart nearly bursting with pride and love. "I was going to tell you that I've realized how selfish I've been," he said, his voice close to breaking, "and I'm sorry. I truly am. I should have known that everything would work out the way I prayed it would. I should have had more faith in all of you."

Tears welled in John's eyes, and he couldn't keep them from overflowing. He turned away for a moment, trying to regain control. His heart was so full that he felt too weak to stand. For a moment he was once again that little red-headed boy standing in the field, listening to his father. Once again he heard his father's words: "There will come a time when duty calls that you must take a stand for what you truly believe in as a man – no matter what the cost!"

"Thank you, thank you, all of you. Just give me a moment." John took out a handkerchief and wiped his face. Then he went to his desk and picked up the Bible he had been given by Mrs. Margaret Washington, the one that had belonged to Booker T. himself. "Let's go out by the mantle and light the holiday candles," he said. "We have a lot to celebrate."

With the candles lit, he turned to the passage in Corinthians and read it aloud. "'Each man should give what he has decided in his heart to give, not reluctantly or under compulsion, for God loves a cheerful giver.' This, truly, will be a gift from our hearts," he said and added, "and this will be the most special of Christmas Eves for the Kenney family."

A Christmas Gift to the City

John's hands shook with excitement as he phoned his attorney late that morning. "How soon can you get over here, William?" he asked. "I need you to bring an affidavit showing the hospital is financially solvent."

"I can be over there in a few hours. What's the urgency?" William asked, curious about John's enthusiasm.

"I'll tell you when you get here."

Less than three hours later, Attorney Allen walked into John's office at the hospital and handed him the documents. "All right, let me in on what's going on."

"My family and I have decided to give the Kenney Memorial Hospital to the community as a Christmas gift," John began as soon as Allen had taken a seat, "and I would like to do it tomorrow, on Christmas Eve."

Allen's mouth dropped open, and he gave John a look of utter incredulity. After a moment, he cleared his throat and said, "I'm taken aback. As your attorney, John, I don't feel this is in your best interest. You have financed much of the operation yourself over the years, and you certainly will not get a return on your investment if you give it away."

"I *will* get a return on my investment, William," John replied. "It just won't be monetary. But I'll have the satisfaction of knowing that the colored people of Newark will have an institution of their own that they can be proud of – one that will save lives. They can staff it, operate it, and see that the community supports it financially. Succeeding with this enterprise will give them the confidence to venture into other business enterprises, and before you know it, the community can be self-supporting and viable unto itself."

"I respect your philanthropy, John, but I'm sure that there are other ways to accomplish these things without giving away your most valuable asset."

John shook his head, and looked directly at Allen. "There isn't much time for discussion. My family and I have decided to do this. I need you to write up a document of assurance testifying that the hospital is indeed an asset. I want the people to know that the hospital has maintained a satisfactory credit rating that, to date, is unimpaired," John said, checking a hand-written list on his desk. "I want it known that we have never defaulted on any past note or mortgage and loan payment. I want you to state that there is no pending note or mortgage payment, and that we have never been denied credit. I don't mind if it is known that when I decided to build this hospital, I secured a personal loan from the New Jersey National Bank and Trust Company for fifteen thousand dollars. I paid that back with interest and principal, eighteen months ahead of maturity."

"What else?" Allen asked with a resigned sigh, writing John's requests on a pad.

"I want it made emphatically clear that the total financial investments in the institution were ninety-three thousand dollars: sixty-nine thousand in real estate, and twenty-four thousand in equipment. I want it made clear that the largest hospital supply firm in the country will accept an order for any amount of goods that we desire. That is the good will that derives from the stellar reputation that we have maintained in the business community. Suppliers do not even bother us with duns in the event that our payments are not made promptly. They know they will be paid."

"All right, John, I'll proceed right away. I'll be back tonight for your signature on the document." Allen put on his jacket, shook John's hand, and left, wondering what had prompted his client to make such a fiscally inane decision.

John immediately began implementing his plan. He called Attorney Oliver, who still represented the Booker T. Washington Hospital Association.

"Oliver, I am calling an emergency meeting of all parties at the hospital at seven o'clock on Christmas Eve. I have some urgent information that will affect the hospital sale."

"I need more information than that, Dr. Kenney," Oliver said. "I need to be prepared for any legal eventuality. And it's short notice, being on Christmas Eve and all."

"That's all I can tell you now," John said, "but anyone who is interested in the future of the hospital needs to be at the meeting. I would appreciate it if you would notify the sub-committee also, some of whom you originally represented. Given all of the machinations of the past few months, I am not sure who is who anymore."

Attorney Oliver was obviously annoyed at being kept in the dark, but he knew that he and his clients needed to be present at the meeting. He hung up and began making calls to inform the members of the committees; all of them said they expected to attend.

John's next call was to alert Reverend Nelson.

"Can you come to the hospital at seven o'clock on Christmas Eve, Reverend? I may need your prayers. I have made a decision regarding the hospital."

"I'll be there right after the five o'clock Christmas rehearsal, and I'll bring my Bible," the minister said.

"That's all right," John said, smiling into the telephone. "I'll be bringing a special one of my own."

John then called his secretary into the office. His excitement at the secret was growing stronger with each minute.

"Mildred, please put in a call to the North Jersey Medical Society, to all of the churches who supported me, and to all of the physicians on staff, saying that there will be an emergency meeting here on Christmas Eve regarding the hospital sale. And notify the press too."

"What's going on?" Mildred asked suspiciously, noticing John's exuberant mood.

"It's all about Christmas," John said, leaving the office – and leaving Mildred as confused as before.

That evening, Attorney Allen dropped off the legal papers for John's approval and signature. "This is still against my legal advice," he admonished, as John signed the papers.

"I know that," John replied, blotting the ink on the last document.

At last, John could leave for home to be with his family. They spent the evening doing what they always did at Christmastime: decorating the tree, wrapping gifts, and watching Freida and Libby make pound cakes and sugar cookies, while everyone sipped Freida's delicious homemade eggnog. He couldn't remember ever being happier.

On Christmas Eve, the Kenneys dressed in their church clothes, and then gathered in the living room before going over to the hospital to make the public announcement. As the time of the meeting neared, John glanced out of the window to see people arriving at the hospital next door. Stunned, he watched the crowd at the entrance grow larger and larger, as more and more people tried to get inside. Because it was Christmas Eve, he had expected a modest turnout, but curiosity clearly outweighed the traditional holiday obligations. Several hundred people had arrived already.

"It's time to go," he told his family, looking at them with pride. It still amazed him that each one had been willing, in the end, to do something so wonderful. "I'm so proud of all of you," he said with a full heart.

Hand-in-hand, the Kenneys walked over to the hospital and wound their way through the waiting crowd. As they moved slowly toward the entrance, John listened to the comments of the people he passed.

"I'll bet the place is bankrupt," said one bystander.

"No, that's not it," another whispered, loud enough for John to hear. "He wants to play on our holiday sympathies by asking us to give money at Christmastime."

"This could be a Charles Dickens story," someone else said, and laughed.

Finally, the Kenneys climbed the stairs and entered the room where the committee members were seated. Reverend Nelson and Attorneys Allen and Oliver were there, along with reporters, doctors, some city officials, and others from the community. Except for the chairs reserved for John's family, every seat was taken, and spectators lined the walls around the room. Murmured conversations gave way to utter quiet, as everyone waited for John to reach the podium. For a moment, he stood there, perusing the room. Then he began to speak.

"Thank you all for coming on such an important holy night, and with short notice. I know this is a busy time for all of you. My family and I have had a meeting, and we have come to a decision regarding the hospital situation. I would like to read a statement we have prepared to commemorate this occasion:

"In the spirit of this Christmas season," John read, "and of the Christ-like peace and harmony that should pervade the world at this time, Mrs. Kenney, our children, and I consider it one of the highest privileges of our lives to offer to our people of the North Jersey area this property, the Kenney Memorial Hospital, as a Christmas gift."

Expressions of disbelief and shock emanated from the crowd. Those forced to stand in the hallway tried to press their way into the room. Word quickly filtered outside to those who had been unable to get inside the building.

"By this means," John continued, reading in a voice that was clear and controlled, "we hope to make a lasting contribution to our race, to our city, to our country, and to our God. With this offer to the entire North Jersey community, we hold out the olive branch with an invitation to all factions, groups, and individuals to unite under it. Together, let us, in the interests of the health and the betterment of our people, give this neighborhood a hospital equal to its needs, and second to none."

As he finished, people stared as if they hadn't understood what he had said. Then, hesitantly, one spectator began to clap. Another and another joined in, until the entire room burst into applause. Cheers could be heard in the hall, and then at the hospital entrance and, finally, out in the street as the word spread. John had to hold up his hand for silence so he could finish reading his statement.

"I hold in my hand the Bible once used by the great Booker T. Washington, a Bible autographed by him. Many a time in my professional ministrations to him, I found him with this Bible in his hands. From it, he got inspiration and strength, and the courage to do the great work that he left behind. From this Bible, I now read and commend to you the immortal words of the Apostle Paul to the Philippians, chapter three, verses thirteen and fourteen. 'Brethren, I count not myself to have apprehended; but this one thing I do, forgetting those things which are behind, and reaching forth unto those things which are before, I press toward the mark for the prize of the high calling of God in Christ Jesus.' Particularly, I emphasize to you the words, 'forgetting those things which are behind.'

"And now, may the spirit of peace, which has directed me in reaching this conclusion and has guided me and mine through sacrifices, privations, and hardships unknown to most of you, guide you in reaching your conclusions as to your acceptance or rejection of this offer, whichever seems best. Thank you."

The crowd erupted into sustained cheers and applause. Several people began to chant "our hospital, our hospital!" over and over. Taken by surprise and overcome by the Kenney's' act of benevolence, people responded with a rush of emotion. Some women began to cry, and even a few men had to wipe their eyes. The crowd pressed in to pat John and Freida on the back, to hug their children, and to shake every family member's hand. Tears streamed down Freida's face as she accepted one hug after another from the grateful crowd, and John strained to hold back his own tears, overcome by the tumultuous reaction from his people. For the first time in a long time he felt hope.

The next morning, headlines in many papers, both locally and nationally, proclaimed, "Dr. Kenney Gives Hospital to Community." The local paper reported: "Although the public has become accustomed to sensational moves in Dr. Kenney's long and hard fight for a hospital for his people, they were not prepared for the climax that was reached on Christmas Eve. With a carefully laid plan that he kept secret, he called a meeting of the two opposing hospital committees and offered the hospital as a gift to the community. In the annals of charitable giving – this is a first."

THE CHICAGO
DEFENDER
DONATES HOSPITAL
AS XMAS GIFT

NEWARK, NJ., -One of the most sensational Christmas gifts ever given to a community was that presented by Dr. John A. Kenney when, before a called meeting of the two opposing hospital committees at the hospital on Christmas Eve, he offered his hospital to his people as a Christmas gift...

A Christmas gift to a city.

The offer to accept the hospital as a gift was unanimously approved by the people of North Jersey. Thus, on January 1, 1935, the Kenney Memorial Hospital became the Community Hospital of Newark, New Jersey. A provision in the contract insured, however, that so long as the hospital stood, the bronze plaque with its inscription would remain in place on the wall at the entrance: "Dedicated to my father, John A. Kenney, Sr., and my mother, Caroline Kenney, by their son John A. Kenney, M.D."

In addition to his parents and his family, John also credited his colleagues in the National Medical Association; those who had gone before him and paved the way, and those who were now doing that work for the future.

Near the close of an emotional Christmas day, Freida was cleaning up the dinner dishes when the newspaper article about the gift of the hospital, still lying on the kitchen table, caught her eye. Setting the dishes near the sink, she turned and put her arms around her husband. "You have truly lived up to the promises you made to yourself, John," she said. "You have dedicated your life to our race in service and by example, and that is the legacy for our children."

"I couldn't have done it without you and my family, and I know that," John said, holding his wife tightly in his arms. "We are a team."

"My hope is that our people will finally come together in unity and understanding," Freida said, looking up into John's eyes, "and that we'll learn to love ourselves so that we can love each other. That is my prayer to God."

"And that is all we can do now, Freida – just pray."

Dr. Kenney and The Community Hospital Staff

Epilogue

The Kenney Memorial Hospital served the people of Newark, New Jersey, as a private hospital for more than seven years. It cared for 4,543 hospital patients, treated 594 free clinic patients, conducted 1,109 surgical operations, and experienced only 19 deaths. This was remarkable, given the fact that white hospitals often shipped critically ill patients to the Kenney Memorial hospital so that those patients' deaths would not factor into their morbidity rates.

Kenney Memorial was served by seventy-six physicians, both white and black. Employment there from 1927 to 1934 included four graduate resident physicians, nine secretary-stenographers, forty-seven graduate nurses, and seventy-eight non-professional aides.

The Hospital, which now is the home of New Salem Baptist Church, was nominated by the Newark Preservation and Landmarks Committee for official landmark recognition. The building was entered on the New Jersey Register of Historic Places on January 1, 2004, and on the National Register on March 22, 2004. At the dedication ceremony, Pastor John White remarked that the building "used to be a place where the body was healed, and now it is a place where the soul is healed."

John A. Kenney, M.D., served as the medical director for the Community Hospital from 1934 until 1939, when he returned to Tuskegee to assume his previous position as medical director of the John A. Andrew Hospital. He returned to New Jersey in 1944 to resume his medical practice. On January 8, 1950, he suffered a stroke and died at his home in Montclair, New Jersey. In the previous year, on May 1, 1949, Freida Armstrong Kenney became ill while attending the Founder's Day exercises at Tuskegee Institute, and died at the John A. Andrew Memorial Hospital.

The Kenney children continued the family legacy of service. John Andrew Kenney, Jr., became an internationally renowned dermatologist, who founded the Department of Dermatology at Howard University Hospital, where he was known as the "Dean of Black Dermatology." In 1995, he was named Master of Dermatology by the American Academy of Dermatology, its highest honor. Oscar Armstrong Kenney became a pilot with the famed Tuskegee Airmen during World War II, and was killed in a training accident in 1943. Howard Washington Kenney became an internist, and served as medical director of both the John A. Andrew Hospital and the Veteran's Administration Hospital in Tuskegee. He later became the first African American medical director of the VA Hospital in East Orange, New Jersey; and was subsequently appointed Eastern Regional Medical Director and Associate Deputy Chief for Policy, Planning and Operations for the VA Central Headquarters in Washington, D.C., again, the first African American to hold this position. Harriett Elizabeth Kenney became a highly decorated medical social worker in Chicago, Illinois.

*   *   *

When I first started reading my grandfather's papers, I noted that he referred to his white colleagues as Dr. F. Johnston and Dr. L. Johnston. That had no particular significance for me. I was stunned, however, when later on he referred to them by their first names, Frank and Ludie. I realized that I had uncles named Frank and Ludie. I had met both early in my life, and they are now deceased. "My" Ludie and Frank had been very handsome, light-skinned *black* men who had left Tuskegee and moved up North to pass for white, because they could not find employment as black men. It was as hard to be black in white America as it was to be light-skinned in black America. At that time, they felt that their only hope for survival was anonymity. Ultimately, they moved to the Midwest, married, and had families of their own. My mother confirmed that they were the offspring of one of the Johnston brothers (my grandfather's white colleagues) by her mother's sister. All of these years had passed, and I would never have uncovered this "secret" if I had not read my grandfather's memoirs.

Writing this book brought me full circle: I learned more about my unique family history, and more about many of the contributions that African American physicians have made to the medical progress of our country. I discovered that my life was directly related to the events, places and people who had been important in my grandfather's lifetime, and I found my purpose in life: telling John A. Kenney's story and preserving his legacy. In his later years, he wrote in his journal; "Every generation should make and leave some contribution. It is only by that means that we grow. That means each individual has an obligation."

It is my hope that *Beacon on The Hill* illustrates that each generation faces myriad similar issues and challenges over time, and it is only in knowing, revering and honoring our rich history that we find the direction, motivation, and fortitude to carry on.

Acknowledgements

Eternal gratitude goes to the early pioneers in the National Medical Association whose words and quotations are documented in the earliest minutes and *Journals* of that organization. Without these records, a crucial part of our history would have faded into oblivion; and their valiant efforts to further the race would not have received the honor that they so justifiably earned.

To my friend and "soul sister", Dr. Jill Kahn, author of *The Gift of Taking*, thank you for your counsel, inspiration and encouragement. To my literary manager, Mardeene B. Mitchell, and my editor, Jan Stiles, your expertise and insight taught me so much about writing. To my sister and "final read" editor, Diane Kenney, your patience and advice were invaluable.

Thanks to my family, friends, and many others who helped and encouraged me in ways they may or may not be aware of: Lisa, Shelby, Mom, Phyllis, Pat Hoover, Phala, Myla, Teddy, T.J., Randy, Frances, Anne, Buddy, Reese Stone, Cheryl R. Cooper, Dr. Eleanor Traylor, Robert White, M.D., Edward A. Rankin, M.D., Margaret Washington Clifford, Winston Price, M.D., Willie Canady, Cassandra Collins, Muriel Aikens, Asa Yancey, M.D., Dr. James H.M Henderson, Dr. Mildred Dixon, Carole Darden-Lloyd, and Gloria Guerrero.

Special thanks to my husband Dennis, whose continued support and faith in this project never wavered over the years.

And to my family members, who have made their transition, your example inspired me and your unconditional love completed me:

Grandpa, Frieda, Uncle Oscar, Daddy, Howard Jr., Parshie, Granny, Angie-Lou, Aunt Libby, Uncle Quis, Aunt Marie, Gladys, Edwina, Uncle Jack, and Aunt Fern.